P9-BYS-735

THE FOOTPRINTS WERE AT LEAST TWO HUNDRED FEET LONG...

They were deep enough that they were clear, despite their size. They looked humanoid, but the toes were armed with claws.

Ahead, there were three carcasses, ripped apart and chewed and mangled.

Nearby were big trees that had been uprooted, probably by a kick, and others that had been broken off, as if the thing had stepped on them. The breathing and the sound like a mountain being torn apart were much louder now.

"I think we've come close enough," Vana whispered.

"Too close," Deyv said.

They ran. From behind them came a bellow, so loud that it was as though the sky had split. Then they saw the dim, gigantic hulk advancing toward them.

It was an unimaginably huge skeleton.

"FARMER LOVES GRAND LANDSCAPES. THIS TIME HE HAS RESTRICTED HIMSELF 'MERELY' TO THE WHOLE EARTH OF THE FAR FUTURE, WHEN THE UNIVERSE IS COLLAPSING—A SETTING WHICH ALLOWS HIM TO WRITE SF WITH A FANTASY FEEL."
—*Publishers Weekly*

"A BIG EPISODIC QUEST-NOVEL, FEATURING ONE OF THOSE END-OF-THE-UNIVERSE SCRIPTS . . . WITH ENOUGH PIZAZZ TO CARRY ONE AND ALL ALONG."
—*Kirkus Reviews*

Also by Philip José Farmer
Published by Ballantine Books:

THE LOVERS

TRAITOR TO THE LIVING

DARK IS
THE SUN

Philip José Farmer

A Del Rey Book

BALLANTINE BOOKS • NEW YORK

A Del Rey Book
Published by Ballantine Books

Copyright © 1979 by Philip José Farmer

All rights reserved under International and Pan-American
Copyright Conventions. Published in the United States by
Ballantine Books, a division of Random House, Inc., New
York, and simultaneously in Canada by Random House of
Canada, Limited, Toronto, Canada.

Library of Congress Catalog Card Number: 79-2279

ISBN 0-345-28950-1

Manufactured in the United States of America

First Edition: September 1979

Paperback format
First Edition: July 1980

Cover art by Darrell K. Sweet

DEDICATION

In alphabetical order, to my granddaughters
Andrea Josephsohn and Kimberley Ladd;
my daughter, Kristen; my grandson Mat-
thew Josephsohn; my son, Philip Laird; my
granddaughter Stephanie Josephsohn; my
grandson Torin Paul Farmer. And to any
descendants of my wife, Bette Virginia
Andre, and of myself fifteen billion years
from now, when this story takes place.

B LACK was the sun; bright, the sky.

Under the arc packed with dead and living stars, dark or blazing gas clouds and galaxies, on an Earth in which lay the bones or over which blew the dust of seven hundred fifty-four million or so generations, Deyv walked toward his destiny.

"Look for a mate and find a dragon" was a proverb of the tribe.

If you were a pessimist, it sounded ominous. If you were an optimist, it sounded rewarding. There were good dragons and there were evil. Or so Deyv understood. He'd never seen one.

Like most people, Deyv's attitude depended upon the circumstances. At the moment, he was scared and so pessimistic.

Deyv of the Red Egg walked away from the Turtle Tribe of the Upside-Down House. Towering behind him was the House, a cylinder three hundred feet in diameter, made of indestructible metal. Its red, green, and white checked walls slanted slightly so that the round base, ten stories above the ground, afforded an unimpeded view of the earth directly below. The conical tip was buried ten stories deep. Once, according to what the old women said, the House had been entirely under the ground. But erosion and numerous earthquakes had pushed it up ten generations ago.

To Deyv's left, in the center of the clearing, stood the soul-egg tree. Its gnarly trunk was bare of branches for twenty feet, and then the branches began that formed a cone standing on its apex. The bark gleamed red, white, green, blue, and purple, so heavily impregnated with quartz that it was hard as rock. From the branches dangled the fruit, the soul eggs, each as

1

big as Deyv's fist. Around the tree was a circle of dry, pale dirt a hundred feet in diameter, and outside the circle marched four bowmen. Up in the tower, near the base of the tree, were four watchers, each ready to beat on a drum if an enemy human or a predator beast was sighted.

Behind Deyv came the rest of the tribe—men, women, children, dogs, and cats. All the people were shouting the ritual encouragement, except for the appointed insulter.

"Yaaa, Deyv of the Red Egg! See how he has to be driven forth into the jungle! Does he go bravely like our heroic foreparents or like his own great-souled father? Naaah! He goes trembling, legs shaking, his bowels ready to loose themselves with fear, and that red egg . . . ! Ha! That red egg! It betrays the color of his soul! It's green, green with fear! Rabbit! Mouse! March like a man, like a warrior of the Turtles. Don't slink like a coyote!"

Gurni, the insulter, was having fun. He was also getting revenge for what Deyv had once cried at him when he had gone out to get a mate.

Deyv looked down at the soul egg hanging from a leather cord around his neck. His face felt warm, and he could see his body, except where the breechclout covered it, turning red. It was true. The translucent stone, a pale scarlet when he was in a good mood, had become streaked with green. The green pulsed swiftly as if it were connected with his hammering heart. Which, in a sense, it was.

How humiliating! How embarrassing!

"Don't pay any attention to that big-mouthed blow-wind!" his mother shouted almost in his ear. "No man or woman has ever gone out on a mate-hunt without showing some green. Except the hero Keelrow, and that was five generations ago, and maybe it's all a lie about him, anyway!"

The shaman, Agorw, danced up alongside Deyv. He wore a bonnet of tall feathers; the cheeks of his face and buttocks were marked with three vertical stripes, red, white, and blue; his breechclout was painted with the crooked cross; his knees were bound in leather, from which dangled seven coils of human hair; one hand was inserted inside a skull of a giant turtle and the other shook a staff from which hung three empty turtle shells. His own soul egg was a deep blue shot with pulsating aquamarine streaks.

"Shame on you, woman!" he cried. "The ghost of Keelrow will come to you in your dreams and put horns on your husband's head. And the child will drink you dry!"

"See these!" Deyv's mother yelled. "Do you think any baby, even if he were as big and fat as you, could empty these?"

The tribe howled with merriment, and the shaman, his face red, stomped off out of Deyv's sight.

For a moment, Deyv forgot his fear and embarrassment. He chuckled. His mother was afraid of nothing. He wished he were. But she was like him in that she had a quick temper and sometimes had to pay for it. The shaman would get back at her somehow. However, she would not regret her words. She was willing to take the consequences. Especially in this situation, where her pride in her baby overrode anything else.

Deyv, her baby, was six feet two inches high, the tallest of the tribe. His shoulders were broad, but he had the long legs and wiry build of a long-distance runner. His skin was a dark copper; his hair, black as a fly and as wavy as a wind-rippled brook. The forehead was high and wide; the brows, beetling; the nose, a hawk's; the lips, thick; the chin, round and clefted. By his features alone, any of the other people for sixty miles around would have known he was a Turtle.

He wore a shell of the checkered turtle on his head, a scarlet breechclout, and calf-high leather boots. A leather belt held a leather scabbard containing a slim sword with two cutting edges. Also held by the belt was a stone tomahawk. Over one shoulder was a case holding a blowgun, a compression cylinder, and in its pocket, twelve darts, the tips of which were coated with poison. A coiled rope was slung over the other shoulder.

This was what every well-dressed man or woman wore when seeking a mate.

After entering the jungle, Deyv stepped behind a delta-shaped feathery bush and parted its fronds. The tribe had turned away except for his mother and father and his dog, Jum. About twenty yards behind them, lying down sphinxlike, was his cat, Aejip.

Deyv waited until his parents had at last walked back toward the House. Then he whistled, and Jum, who'd been waiting for this signal, bounded up to him. He was a large wolflike beast with big pointed upstanding ears, a crimson coat, a tail edged in black, and slanting green eyes. He licked Deyv's calf until he was told to quit, and then he sat down, his tongue hanging out. His forehead was as high as a chimpanzee's and so was his intelligence.

Aejip was taking her time with all the nonchalance of any cat that had ever lived. When she stood, she was two and a half feet high at the shoulder. Her glossy coat was tawny and rosetted in black. Above the great yellow eyes were two vertical black markings. Her forehead was as developed as Jum's.

Deyv thought of whistling for her, but the cat had made it evident that she wasn't going to accompany her partner—no cat acknowledged a master—on his journey. Though she couldn't talk, she had put across the idea that she considered Deyv to be out of his mind. Besides, she was jealous because Deyv had been paying so much attention to Jum these past two weeks.

So Deyv shrugged and turned, with Jum a few feet ahead of him, and proceeded down the jungle path. Every step that took him away from the tribe was a pace deeper into loneliness and insecurity. If he'd been accompanied by anyone on a hunt for food, one which he knew would see him back with the tribe after a sleep or even seven sleeps, he would have been happy. But to go forth by himself for only The Great Mother knew how long was to be shivering with fear, sick with aloneness.

Nevertheless, he was not numb. His eyes, ears, and nose were alert. Behind every bush or tree could be a poisonous snake, a corps of the great ruddy cockroaches, the thing-with-a-nose-like-a-snake, a ghost-with-venomous-urine, the toe fancier, or an enemy tribesman eager to remove his head and his soul egg. There might even be an enemy woman out to catch a mate, though these were very few.

The wind was coming from ahead of him. Though it waved the upper leaves and caps of the tall trees, it pushed gently along the path. Still, it should carry the scent of anything ahead to Jum's nose. Anything except a ghost, and dogs were supposed to be psychically sensitive to those horrible things.

To expect to hear anything soft but sinister nearby was to be stupid. The jungle rang, shrilled, cawed, cackled, hooted, tooted, chortled, drummed, whistled, and screeched. Most of the noisemakers were hidden, but occasionally Deyv saw a bird, a gliding mammal, a fingered bear, a creature like a four-legged blowgun, a troop of scowl-monkeys, or a live-alone cockroach; and once he halted while a diamond-backed tortoise heaved its monstrous shelled bulk across the path. Though it was not his totem, still it was a cousin to it, and so he addressed it politely and wished it well.

After it came a regiment of small yellow mouse-sized cockroaches, hoping to eat its dung or find a crevice between flesh and shell into which to burrow. Deyv picked up a dry stick and beat a dozen or so into paste. The survivors scampered off into the green while Deyv called after the diamond-back, "You owe me one, O mighty sister."

Jum ate the corpses and sniffed around for more. He'd had his single between-sleeps meal, but, doglike, he would eat until he burst if he got a chance. Though it was not distasteful to Deyv, he didn't share Jum's food. Instead, some easily plucked large round yellow fruit, only half-eaten by the birds, tempted Deyv. Holding two in one hand and eating a third in the other hand, he walked along. To *find* food was no problem in his world. To avoid *being* food was.

Only thirty sleeps before, Deyv had been with the tribe at the Place of the Trading Season. Every forty-nine circuits of The Dark Beast, the nine tribes in the area put aside war and gathered peacefully at the Place. This was by a House occupied only by animals, birds, and insects, and possibly a nonmalignant ghost, a House centrally located. At this time, by custom immemorial and unstained by truce breaking, the tribes went down the paths and gathered at the Place. It was near a broad river in an overgrown area that was cleared every Trading Season. Here the artifacts that one tribe had and the others didn't were traded. It was a long leisurely business, with much pleasant haggling interspersed with feasts, drinking, smoking, eating of drugs, telling of erotic and sterculian jokes, athletic matches among the young men and women, exchanging of hunting information, warnings of ghosts, and boasting contests.

Deyv's tribe traded turtle and tortoise shells, the harps made from them, a large gourd which grew only in their area, a drug made from a plant and other ingredients which could evoke ancestors for brief conversations but was, unfortunately, accompanied by devastating winds from the bowels, and an insect whose bite assured the female bitee of a very pleasurable sensation. For some reason the bite caused only an itching in the male bitee. The effects in both sexes lasted about one-fourth of the time between sleeps.

For their trade items, the Turtle people got smoked meat of the checkered turtle, which they were forbidden to kill and which could be eaten only at certain required times; a liquor which the Coyote Tribe made from water seeping through a limestone cliff and a plant, the identity of which the Coyotes had kept secret for ten generations; bone noseflutes made by the Holecat Tribe, the minute carved decorations of which were beyond the artistic ability of any other tribe; a jungle pepper from the Whistling Squirrel Tribe; a perfume jelly from the Crawling Tree Tribe; smoked bladders guaranteed to bring good luck from the Nameless God Tribe; gourds filled with an exceedingly tasty paste from the Ruddy Cockroach Tribe; from the Tree-Lion Tribe birds and monkeys which could mimic speech; and soul eggs from the Red Skunk Tribe. The latter had found a burial ground of the ancients and had dared to dig up the soul eggs and barter them. These were rare and expensive items, only for the hardy shaman who was willing to take on additional ancestors and haggle for their power in his dreams.

Each Trading Season, a tribe was appointed to be the police. The men and the childless adult females walked around with clubs and kept the peace. The unmated men and women of the tribes walked around looking each other over. Only about 5 percent were serious, since most matings took place within the tribe. But there were always those whose soul eggs did not match any eligible person of the other sex within the tribe. These, like it or not, had to get their mates from one of the other tribes.

When a man or a woman did find a match in another tribe, a marriage was arranged. There was then the problem of which partner would have to leave his or her tribe and go with the new mate. To give up one's own people and live with foreigners was hard. But it had to be done if there was no other way out.

The decision of which person must go to the strange tribe was quickly made. A shaman from a third tribe spun a stick with a spear point on each end into the air. If the prospective groom's point stuck in the earth when the stick landed, then he took the bride to his own tribe. If the other point plunged in, that meant that he had to go to her House.

Deyv had wandered through the Place of the Trading Season. And, as was the age-old custom, when he saw an unmated woman, he introduced himself and then sat down to talk to her. It did not matter whether or not he found her attractive or vice versa. He must talk to her in the trading language until their soul eggs began to flash matching colors in synchronization. Or until it was evident that there would be no phasing-in.

Deyv had been relieved when he had not matched up with any of the eligibles. There were some pretty women among the candidates, but otherwise he hadn't been attracted to them. Among the girls who would be old enough next season he'd spotted two rather likable good-lookers. All he had to do was to wait another forty-nine circuits of The Dark Beast. Then, if his egg matched one of theirs, he could marry. There would still be the agony of not knowing whether or not he'd have to go to a strange tribe. But that would be over quickly.

In the meantime, he wouldn't be sexually frustrated. The Turtles, like the other tribes, had plenty of volunteers from older women, widows usually, who would like to satisfy the unmarried youths. One of these was chosen by the shaman's wife or husband and given a ritual name. Thereafter, the woman lived in a hut in which she entertained the young men. Her prestige was high, and she was always given a place of honor during the feast days.

Those young women who'd not yet found a match were similarly entertained by an older man chosen in the same manner. If any pregnancy resulted, the child was the woman's, and when she got married her husband formally and gladly adopted the child.

Deyv had grown fond of the woman who was taking care of him and was looking forward to spending more time with her. But a few days after he'd returned to the House, his father had called him aside. He hadn't looked happy.

"The men's councils of the nine tribes met during the Trading Season. They decided that it was time for new blood to be brought into our land. So, each tribe must send out those young men or women who found no soul-egg mates during the Season. You are the only one of the Turtles who failed. That means, my son, that you must go, and very soon, to the lands beyond our land. You can't come back unless you bring with you a woman whose egg matches yours."

Deyv had been so shocked he hadn't been able to say anything.

"The same thing happened in your grandfather's time," his father had said. "It was decided that the tribe needed new blood. So his friend Atoori was sent outside the area to get a woman. He never returned; no one knows what happened to him. Another young man, Shamoom, was then sent out, and he returned with a woman from a tribe far in that direction."

His father had gestured with his left hand. "She was much lighter skinned than we, and she had yellow kinky hair and blue eyes. She gave birth to two babies, Tsagi, who died before you were born, slain by a warrior of the Coyotes, and Korri, the shaman's wife."

Deyv had gulped and had said, "I've heard the story, Father, but I didn't think much about it."

"You'd better think about it now." Tears had rolled down his father's cheeks.

"It is hard to see your son go into the unknown dangers of the land beyond the nine tribes. The known dangers are bad enough."

"Is that why Mother has looked so sad the last few days?"

"Yes."

His father had begun weeping and sobbing, and Deyv had had to hold him for a few minutes until he had recovered. Then Deyv had stumbled off weeping to be consoled by his mother, only to end up consoling her. That evening he'd gone to Pabashum, the young unmarried-men's woman, only to have to console her.

His dog, Jum, couldn't talk, though he did whimper a lot, but Deyv had wet him with his tears, and when Jum licked his face Deyv felt that he was finally being consoled. It hadn't been as satisfying as he had wished, however. His egg had been filled with roiling black clouds and dark-green streaks for days afterward.

2

S O here he was in the jungle, with no idea of where he would go or just how he would do what he had to do when he got there. First, though, he had to get out of the land of the nine tribes. It was now a bad time to be alone in the jungle. After fourteen sleeps of the honeymoon, the bridegrooms had to sally forth to kill a dangerous beast or an enemy tribesman and bring the head back and lay it at the feet of their women. This period would start just when he had to set out on his quest. The tribe might at least have considered this and allowed him to wait until the headhunters had gone home.

Thinking this, but not so deeply that he wasn't alert, Deyv walked on. After a while, he emerged into a wide open area on the hillside. Here the path led downward through plants that were only waist-high. These had slender stalks topped by flowers with a black center, a blue iris, and twelve tawny sword-shaped petals. Those near him turned their flower tops toward him as he passed.

Deyv urged Jum to run. The plants, detecting a possible victim, released a perfume that signaled to swarms of a large stinging insect. If they stung him to death, they would burrow into his corpse and lay eggs in it. The plants would put forth roots, which would eat his flesh.

Suddenly a heavy, heady odor rose about him. But he and the dog had reached the jungle before he heard the clicking sound. He kept on running for a while, since the insects were known to occasionally chase their prey a little way into the trees. As soon as he was beyond pursuit, he slowed down. It was dangerous to

run in the jungle. The noise warned predators or
enemies that someone was coming.

Presently he emerged into another open space on
a hillside which had once been overgrown by the
vevshmikl plant. A score of gigantic beasts were moving slowly down the hill, devouring the plants. Their
legs were black columns. Their bodies were massive
yellow pods. Their necks were thick but long, and at
the ends were heads with long drooping lips and a pair
of twin horns above each eye. Their big blue fan-
shaped ears flapped slowly, and their blue tails flipped
back and forth.

Deyv and Jum moved down the hill, giving the
beasts a wide berth. If you didn't bother them, they
didn't bother you.

Almost three-quarters of the plants were gone. In
the stands still left, their heads were turned toward
their oncoming doom, though it was doubtful that they
could "see." From the bases of the stalks came a loud
clicking, the insects striking their horny antennae in
unison. They, too, were doomed. They would rush out
when their floral partners disappeared into the gaping
mouths of the *atadeym*, and they would try to sting
through the thick hides. But the great feet of the
beasts would crush them, and after a while, there would
be neither plant nor insect symbiont.

Grass would move in and flourish for many sleeps.
Then, slowly, the seeds of the *vevshmikl* would sprout,
and in time the open area would be filled with them.
The *fookooki* insect eggs would burst, and the space
would again be dangerous. Then the *atadeym* would
saunter out from a jungle trail and begin eating once
again.

The sky was still white, so bright that Deyv could go
blind if he stared directly into it for several minutes.
The wind swooped down over the trees and across the
hillside, cooling his sweating body somewhat. Behind
him, black clouds were beginning to build up. Before
the next sleep, heavy rains would come.

In the opposite direction the first of the strange forms drifted. It was high in the sky and approaching against the wind. Ever since he was a baby, Deyv had seen such colossal black things over the tribal area. They came every twelve sleeps without fail, though they couldn't be seen if there was an overcast sky, of course.

Soon the first figure was close enough so that Deyv could make it out. It floated parallel to the earth, a form that had to be longer and wider than the clearing in which he stood. Much larger. It was composed of two parallel lines crossed by two more: #.

Then the second figure came into view, and when it was close enough it was revealed as: S.

The third was: O.

The fourth: X.

The fifth: H.

On they came, but Deyv went under the trees and could not see the forms, the ceiling of the jungle was so thick.

The shaman had said that these were the words of The Great Mother, and the person who could understand them would become as one of her divine children and would have great power.

However, a woman from the Avadeym Tribe who had married a Turtle had a different explanation. She had said that they were boats sent out by The Mother. When the time came that the sky grew too hot and bright for life to endure here, the boats would come down so that the people could board them. Then they would carry their passengers to a far-off place where it would never be too hot and where no dangerous beasts existed and people would live forever and always be happy.

Deyv believed the shaman. What would an Avadeym know about such matters? And why should the Avadeym be allowed to live in such a place? What had they done to deserve it? Weren't they enemies of the Turtles? The Turtles would go there, if there were such a place. But the Avadeym? Never!

Deyv and Jum came to a small river. Jum drank thirstily; Deyv swallowed one mouthful. At this point the bank sloped down to a thin sandy beach. On the sand there had been some tall white big-beaked birds and a huge long-tailed pale-blue riverbeast with long jaws and big teeth. When Jum came out of the foliage ahead of his master, the birds had trumpeted and then flown off. The riverbeast, which looked big enough to handle a dozen men, had croaked and then slid off into the water.

Deyv knew that the *athaksum* wasn't scared of them. It was in the river now, the eyes on top of its head looking at them, hoping they'd try to cross the stream. It would eat humans, but it craved dog. Jum knew this, which was why he was whimpering.

The waters were fairly clear, since it hadn't rained for about thirty sleeps. A swirl showed where the *athaksum* had dived. It would be somewhere near the bottom now, waiting for them to enter its domain, its eyes sharp and its flesh-buried ears receptive to any disturbance in the water. Then it would slide incredibly fast through the liquid, its tail waving side to side, its webbed paws digging into the water, its jaws closed but ready to open just before it sank its many sharp teeth into flesh.

Jum was looking at Deyv, and he was still whimpering.

Deyv patted him on the head. "Don't worry, we'll get by it."

Jum quit making sounds of distress, but he looked as worried as his lack of facial muscles would allow him to look.

There was a lot of driftwood on the beach and the bank, detritus of floods. Deyv dragged two trunks down to the river's edge, and then he cut lianas from the trees with his sword. It took him some time to bind the logs together. Meanwhile, the tall birds returned to the beach but stayed about ninety feet from him. Once, the knobs holding the eyes of the riverbeast appeared, looked coldly at its intended victims, and then sank again. Some time later, Deyv glimpsed the *athaksum* a few feet below the surface. But it was quickly gone from sight.

When he was ready, Deyv told Jum to get on the forepart of the logs. The dog walked out cautiously and sat down. Deyv pushed the two-log raft, if it could be called such, out from the sand into the water. He'd intended to launch it, and then to jump onto its aft end and sit down. Immediately thereafter, he would draw the blowgun from its case and fit a dart into it.

But just before he slopped through the shallow water and seated himself on the logs, he felt a faint trembling of the sand under his feet, followed by a violent upthrust of sand. Something cracked like a whip. By this time he was in the river. The sand was replaced by mud, which lifted and sank, lifted and sank. The river suddenly rose, churned, and swept in a small wave toward him.

He thought, Earthquake!

It was too late to return to shore. Besides, if he was anxious and uncertain, the *athaksum* would be too. On the beach opposite, about nine hundred feet away, the trees dipped and waved, and the sand swelled as if it were the skin of a heavily breathing animal.

Deyv gave a yell, which was half-fright and half-bravado. He shoved the logs out, hopped up on them, and then straddled them. Jum was too scared to whimper; he was standing up, poised, his hairs bristling. The raft slid outward, rose as a wave lifted it, then dipped.

"Hang on!" Deyv shouted. Later, he was to think that this had been nonsense advice, since the dog had no hands. But he had to say something; that was the essence of a human being. Say something, even if it means nothing, because as long as one is talking, one is alive.

Though he was shocked, he still had enough sense to pull the blowgun out of its case. A moment later, he had the dart in the barrel.

The riverbeast always rose to the surface just before

it plunged again to seize its prey from under the water. Or so Deyv had been told by the hunters of his tribe.

He planned to point the gun in the direction from which the beast would come. Just as it raised its eyes clear of the surface, he would blow the dart into the nearest eye. Then the mighty creature would be blinded in it; and the venom of the snorting snake, the quickest-acting and most painful his tribe knew, would race through the blood and send the beast into spasms and death.

Now only The Mother knew what would happen. The earth was quivering like jelly. The water was lifting in waves higher than his head, all going in his direction. At the same time that he had to watch for the brief emergence of the *athaksum*'s eyes, he had to dip his left hand into the water to drive the raft toward the other shore, while his feet were moving to help propel the logs, and he had to hold the blowgun in his right hand, ready to use it on the beast.

Jum was barking crazily, which meant that the sound would course through the waters and reach the ears of the hungry *athaksum*. With the sound as a target, the beast would drive toward them, and then the wide jaws . . .

Halfway across, while Deyv was paddling desperately and at the same time trying to watch where the beast might pop up, a wave reared before him. The quake must have intensified at that second to create such a wave. The crest rose above his head by the height of two men, the largest so far, and fell on the front of the logs. He cried out as he saw Jum swept off. Then the irresistible heaviness of water struck him, and he too was torn off the raft.

Still, Deyv had enough self-control to hold the blowgun above his head while he moved his feet and his left hand. He was numb but not so much that he was helpless. There was no thought that he might drown. The only thing that concerned him was the riverbeast.

As he was turned about despite his struggles, he saw the two half-arcs appear. They were not, as he had expected, on his right. They rose boiling from his left. Either the beast had adopted a course which Deyv's elders said it never took, or the turmoil had swept the thing beyond its intended path. Whatever had happened, there it was, and he wasn't able to cope with the change of events. His blowgun was in his right hand, the thing was on the left. No matter how swiftly he turned, it would have dived before he could do anything about it. And then, below the heavy element, where his dart could not penetrate, it would have come up and gripped his leg with teeth not to be denied.

For a second or two Deyv looked into the pale-blue eyes of death. The eyes began to sink. Deyv tried to twist himself around in the water as it broke over him. It was too late. He knew that. Once those long sharp teeth sank into his leg, he could struggle and struggle, but it would make no difference. His strength would be no match for its.

His sword was in his hand without his thinking about it, and he leaned over. The monster's near eye was only a few inches below the surface when the point drove into it.

The water boiled; the blood spread out. A thick tail came up into the air and crashed down against the water.

Deyv almost dropped the sword while trying to pull himself back onto the raft. His fingers slipped on the wet wood, caught a knob, clung, and soon he was sitting upright again. Immediately, he pulled his legs up and put his feet flat on the logs.

The leaves of the trees on the opposite bank were still fluttering, but the trunks had stopped swaying. The quake was—for the moment, at least—over. The waves were beginning to subside.

Deyv rose to his feet. Crouching, he put one hand on the top of the raft to steady himself while he looked around him. Jum was also crouched, and if his coat hadn't been so heavy with water, the hairs would have been bristling. He was facing Deyv's right now. Hoping that the dog had detected the *athaksum*, Deyv looked at where he was pointing. There it was. A large shadow at first, then a clearly visible body, then a huge head. Its good eye was turned toward Deyv, then the body was turned toward him, and it was coming as swiftly as if it were sliding down a mudbank.

Deyv stood, balancing as the raft rocked in the swells. Just as the thing shot out of the water, its mouth open to seize him and carry him on out onto the other side of the logs, Deyv leaped to one side. At the same time, he brought his sword down across the neck. But as the creature soared over the raft, its tail whipped around and knocked Deyv off.

He came up out of the river sputtering water. His arm felt as if it had been struck with a heavy club. He couldn't move it. Too numb even to know whether or not he still gripped the sword, thinking that by now it must be on the bottom, he treaded water. Barking, Jum crouched near Deyv as if he intended to spring off the logs after him.

Deyv's foot touched mud. He kicked backward, and both feet were on the river's bottom. He whirled as swiftly as he could in the cloying element and pushed toward the shore. The water receded, was up to his waist. He drove forward, fearful that at any second those big sharp teeth would close on a leg and drag him back.

Now the water was up to his ankles, and he was on the sand. Stumbling, panting, he ran toward the jungle. A bellow sounded from behind him, but he did not look back. His feet kicked up sand and then were on soft earth. Another bellow, so close that he thought a hot breath was on his legs.

He dived between two frondy bushes, rolled, and was up on his feet and making for a tree with low branches. A bush cracked behind him as a huge body crushed it. Deyv leaped to grab a branch, but his foot slipped, and he fell heavily on his back. It seemed to be just about all over then. Still, he tried to get up, but he made the mistake of using his right arm. It caved under him, and he fell again.

Then he heard a low growling, a thrashing, and he saw that Jum had come ashore after him. The dog was leaping toward and away from the *athaksum*, snapping at its good eye. The riverbeast was being distracted, but its counterlunges would bring those teeth down on Jum's head at any second. Blood, however, was still flowing from the pierced eye, coating blue fur with red, soaking the dirt and making a pale-red mud.

It was no use for Deyv to try to climb into the tree. He could grab a limb with his left hand, but the useless right would keep him from pulling himself up onto it. He could run on into the woods and leave Jum to be sacrificed. Or perhaps Jum, knowing his master was safe, would also run.

No, Jum was too busy even to see him. He'd keep tormenting the *athaksum* until it got him.

Deyv reached around his front with the left arm and plucked a stone tomahawk from the belt. Yelling, he ran up to the beast and brought the heavy stone head down between its eyes. The creature turned, reared up, and swallowed the tomahawk just as Deyv awkwardly brought it down again in his left hand. He was lucky he didn't also lose his hand. Hard lips brushed his fist.

Then he and the dog leaped away to escape the monster's agony. With the tip of the weapon sticking out just beyond its lips, the riverbeast rolled and thrashed, crushing and splintering some bushes. Its good eye bulged; the blood from the wounded eye ran even faster; a deep gargling sound issued from its throat; its legs waved frantically. Finally, lying on its back, its spine curved, the top of its head digging into the ground, the monster died.

Deyv heard a screech behind him and whirled to face another danger, though he didn't feel up to dealing adequately with it. There was a large cat, tawny, with black rosettes, golden eyes, and wet fangs, crouching to spring.

"*Now* you show up!" Deyv, between pants, said.

For a long time, Deyv and Jum searched in the mud for the sword. Deyv dived many times groping for it, but the dog, after only three attempts, surfaced and barked to indicate its location. By then Deyv's arm was beginning to regain some mobility. Aejip had taken no part in the search. Though she could swim easily enough, she didn't like the water. Besides, she was hungry and totally occupied in tearing meat from the carcass's flank.

Using the sword, Deyv hacked off some portions and threw them to the dog. Then he dragged the tomahawk from the monster's throat and cut out the tongue. Some time later, he got a fire going with the bowdrill stored in a pocket of the gun case. The cooked tongue was delicious.

Meanwhile, birds, a troop of small meat-eating monkeylike creatures, and several hoglike beasts sat around at a respectful distance. When Deyv and his pets moved on, they heard the squawks, whistles, grunts, and squeals of the scavengers as they closed in on the feast.

3

By the time the three had crossed to the other bank, the clouds almost covered half of the skies. A wind preceding them was shaking the upper parts of the trees and rippling the water. The last of the shapes floated over Deyv and then was swallowed up in the black mists overhead. A few minutes later, rain fell upon the forest, battered at the upper levels, crashed through the heavy foliage, and spilled thickly to the ground.

Deyv, Jum, and Aejip, shivering, took shelter under a gigantic toadstool, but the water flowed over their feet and paws. Aejip looked as if she were cursing. Jum looked miserable. Deyv huddled between the two,

trying to get some warmth from their bodies. Thunder
and lightning were by then ripping the air apart. From
a distance came a crashing as a jungle patriarch fell,
tearing off many of the lianas that grew around it but
restrained by the rest from striking the ground.

"Aren't you sorry you changed your mind and
decided to follow us?" Deyv said to Aejip.

The cat snarled.

After the lightning ceased, Deyv somehow managed
to sleep. He awoke with the skies still dark but rainless.
Stiff and cold, he set off down the path with Jum and
Aejip ahead of him.

Sometime later the cat went hunting. She returned
with a large rodent with almost square ears. They
sought out a *shwikl* tree and ran its batlike inhabitants
out from the cavity halfway up the trunk. There was
just enough room for all three to cuddle inside. Nice
and warm. First, though, Deyv found some leaves and
dead wood that weren't too wet for a fire, and he
cooked his part of the rodent. Then he climbed up
beside the hole and drew the dog up with the rope.
They slept well, though they were occasionally
awakened by especially vicious bites from the parasites
the previous owners had left behind.

Their journey was delayed in the morning. Deyv
went hunting with the blowgun and brought down an
ushuthikl, an animal which looked much like an ape
but whose ancestors had probably been coyotes. The
three companions ate well before proceeding. Deyv
carried the uneaten portion for a time in its own skin.
However, it attracted so many stinging flies that
eventually the three stuffed themselves and then left
the rest for the insects.

Two more sleep-times passed without special incident. The clouds had dissipated; the air had become
much warmer. But a blackness was building up again.

Shortly before the trio reached their immediate goal,
Jum stopped and growled. Deyv hurried into the
bushes and called the animals to him. Presently three
young men of the Red Skunk Tribe trotted up. They

wore their glossy black hair in coils atop faces painted scarlet; big wooden rings hung from their ears; and wooden plugs tufted with feathers at each end stuck out from their septums. Their legs were painted with vertical bands of green, red, and black. The men carried blowgun cases on their backs, long spears tipped with chert in their hands, and stone tomahawks in their belts. Obviously they formed a war party.

Deyv was tempted. He could shoot the rearmost with a dart after they'd passed. Then he'd loose his animals on them, and before they could recover from their surprise, he'd shoot at least one more. However, it would be a great bother to carry their heads and soul eggs along. Far too much so. Still, it would be possible to cache heads and eggs in a tree hollow and pick them up on the way back.

But what if these were only the scouts of a larger party? Then he'd be in a bad situation. Best to play it safe. Nevertheless, he sighed as he watched them disappear around the bend. He'd never killed a man, never had a trophy.

After waiting a long time to make sure the three weren't a vanguard, Deyv returned to the trail. Jum again preceded him. Aejip followed the dog at a distance of seventy feet in case the three men had somehow seen Deyv and were sneaking back. The cat's nose wasn't nearly as sensitive as the dog's, but her hearing was almost as good.

On the way, Deyv spotted a meatfruit tree off the trail and collected what little the birds and beasts had missed. All three ate the conical protein-rich but evil-smelling fruit. By the time they'd finished, they came to an *ujushmikl*. A highway of the ancients.

Fifty-two feet wide at this point, it was made of a somewhat resilient orange substance and was marked with three white lines which formed four lanes. Deyv had no idea why the ancients had made the road or what the markings meant. Nor did he know which ancients had laid it here. According to his grandmother's stories, there had once been a series of ancient peoples, some unimaginably old. The ones responsible for this road may even have been those who'd made the Houses. And had also made the swords, rustless and self-sharpening, and the other wonderful artifacts which the earth now and then yielded.

The ancients had had great powers, though not enough to keep them from dying out. This highway, for instance, had existed long before Deyv's great-great-great-great-grandfather was born, and probably many generations before that. But it was not overgrown with plants, nor had trees been able to tear it apart. The green life, except for a short grass, encroached but withered when within sixty feet of the road. Floods sometimes washed out the earth beneath it here and there. By some magical means, earth sifted back under it and packed down. Earthquakes twisted it, but as time went on, it straightened out.

However, there were vast movements of the ground that even this wonderful substance couldn't resist. Deyv had heard that far down the road, a mountain had grown up under it, and the road ran straight up the elevation and over it. The substance should have snapped apart in many places, but it had merely lengthened.

After looking up and down the road from behind a bush, Deyv stepped out. He kept to the exact middle so that if anybody blew a dart or threw a spear from the foliage, they'd have a long distance to cover. Two years ago he'd come to this spot with a small hunting party, and he'd walked on the smooth rubbery surface for a few miles in the opposite direction. When he had turned back, he'd gone as far from home as he'd ever been.

The miles trudged by. Aejip walked on one edge of the road and Jum on the other. It was pleasant for Deyv to walk unimpeded and with a good view of at least two miles behind and ahead. On the other hand, he felt very exposed and vulnerable. If something came from one wall of the jungle, he could run toward the other. What would he do, though, if enemies came from both sides?

The thought was troubling. Still, he stayed on the road. He knew no other path. Besides, he could really make good time on it. If what his father had said was true, a few more miles would put him outside the land of the nine tribes. However, there would be other hostile beings beyond that. And only The Brooding Mother knew what beasts, familiar or unfamiliar, also dwelt there.

After a long time, he came to a place where the earth had sunk an unknown depth from an old quake. Here the road disappeared under water that had collected from the recent rain. Halting, Deyv speculated about walking on the highway or skirting the edges of the water. The latter course would take him into the jungle. Who knew what humans or beasts lay near in wait, understanding that any passer-by would probably detour around the lake and so come within easy reach?

He decided to walk straight ahead until the water was too deep for that. Then he would walk on the shallower ground near the forest. The sword and the tomahawk were too heavy for him to attempt to swim very far. However, maybe he wouldn't have to swim at all.

The water rose to his ankles and then to his waist. The two animals were swimming along behind him, with Aejip making sounds of unhappiness. Deyv turned toward the right to wade where the water was shallower. Suddenly he screamed with agony and thrashed around. By the time he reached the edge of the lake, he was limping badly. He held his teeth firmly together to keep from yelling again. He hoped nobody heard his cry.

He sat down in the mud and looked at the network of thin red welts on the side of his left thigh. The pain was slowly easing, but the muscles of his thigh were still knotted. After he'd rubbed his thigh for a while, the muscles began to relax. He then rose and walked slowly through the water by the jungle. After walking a few miles at this pace, he could feel only a slight itch. He saw something round and pale rise briefly from the lake. It could have been the creature that had stung him with its poisonous tentacles.

When the road was no longer flooded, he returned to it. Far off the tip of a mountain showed, the one which his father had told him about. It didn't seem to get any nearer even after he had walked for many miles. Deyv decided he'd go to the territory at its base and work around there—unless he found a tribe along the way. At that moment, Aejip gave a soft warning cry. Deyv turned and saw a large whitish object floating about three hundred feet in the air a mile away and approaching at the speed of the wind, which was rather slow then. Deyv ran for the jungle, with the two animals close behind him. As the thing passed over he could see the boat-shaped bottom and the round holes in it. He expected to see dark objects drop from it, but he did not. It was no disappointment.

When the *tharakorm* was out of sight, Deyv went back to the road. He looked back often, however, since others could be coming along. After another mile Deyv came to a junction of two roads. For a few minutes he sat down at some distance from it, wondering if he should take the other road, which was at right angles to the one he'd been on.

He also looked at, but did not go close to, the strange objects at the junction. There were four tall metallic posts, each bearing a round box with four round eyes. Deyv had never heard of these. Though they seemed to be inanimate, he did not care to investigate an unknown work of the ancients. If the posts were their totem poles, it was dangerous to get too close to them. As everybody knew, totem poles were charged with magic: good magic for those who came under their protection, bad magic for their enemies.

When Deyv was about a hundred yards from the junction, the poles clanged, and the top eyes of the two poles facing him gleamed bright with a green light. Startled, Deyv gave a little leap and gasped. Jum barked once and was silent. Aejip growled. For a long time, Deyv stood still, his eyes on the glowing green lights. Then, slowly, he backed away. Suddenly, the eyes went dead, and three clangs came from the two poles.

Deyv froze again. The cat and the dog pressed against him.

After a while, Deyv whispered to Jum to go ahead on the road. The dog didn't want to do so, but he obeyed. Again, the poles clanged and the green lights came on. Jum turned to look at his master. Deyv called him back. When the dog reached a certain point, three clangs sounded, and the green lights went out.

A minute later a large rainbow-colored bird swooped down toward the road near the poles. Before it landed, the poles clanged and the green lights glowed. Startled by the noise, the bird veered away. More clanging and extinguishing of the green followed.

Deyv didn't know what was going on. He did know he didn't like it. He led his two companions off the road and out across the angle between the two roads. When he stepped upon the second road, the poles facing his way clanged and their eyes shone greenly. He went across the rubbery substance quickly, and the moment he and his pets were on the earth, the poles clanged again and the lights went out.

When he returned to the first road, he was a long way from the poles. They remained silent and unlit.

Deyv said, "Whew!" and wiped the sweat from his brow.

A few minutes later he had to run into the jungle again to hide from another *tharakorm*. This time he saw some heads, very tiny at this distance, stick out of the holes at the bottom.

Another sleep passed and then another. Deyv and his companions came across two other junctions guarded by poles that spoke with metal tongues and cast green with their eyes. Deyv skirted these and kept on. Not once did he see human beings, for which he was thankful. On the other hand, their absence also made him uneasy. Were the locals so scarce because there just weren't any? Or did they avoid the road for a good reason which he ought to know?

By then more of the mountain was visible. Its top was still covered with something white, but lower down it was black. Rain came again, and there were more lakes to go around. He came to a place which had suffered some catastrophe long ago. A lot of rotting trees lay along the edge of the jungle, but full-grown new trees reared above them. The road was raised from the ground and twisted like a piece of leather. Deyv, Jum, and Aejip passed by it, regaining it when it became flat enough to walk on, even though it was rippled. About two hundred yards beyond this point was another junction. The poles there were leaning at crazy angles, and a bulge showed in the area between the two sets.

By then Deyv had realized that the poles did not react until he was about one hundred and twenty yards away. But now, just before he was about to leave the road, the poles clanged, and the eyes directly above the lowest turned a baleful red.

Deyv jumped, though not so much from the unexpected reaction of the poles. The animals went into the air, also, Jum barking and Aejip yowling. When he came down, Deyv howled. Something was sending a shock through him, something from the road itself. It was painful, and it made him leap about like a mouse on a hot stone. He tried to run off the road, but the repeated shocks caused him to fall. Then he felt the horrible sensations most strongly on the side on which he'd fallen.

Yelling, he managed to roll off the road and lie panting in the dirt. Aejip landed on her stomach, which drove the air from her in a great whoof. Jum, howling, tumbled head over paws onto his master's legs.

Finally, his breath regained, his muscles having ceased to quiver, Deyv sat up. The poles were still clanging and flashing a red light. He rose unsteadily and looked around to make sure that no person or beast had been attracted by their screams of agony. No one was in sight.

Yes, there was.

Drifting slowly at an angle across the road, about two hundred feet up and half a mile away, was a *tharakorm*. Its sides and upper works were visible now: the whitish hull, short masts, yardarms, and unfurled sails. The thing could only drift with the wind, but the creatures aboard could fly against it.

Even as Deyv caught sight of the vessel, dark objects dropped out of the holes in the bottom and other objects leaped off the sides. They were only tiny beings at this distance. Deyv, however, knew what they looked like. He also knew why they were leaving the *tharakorm*.

4 ᴗ§

THERE were perhaps a hundred of them. They flew swiftly, cutting across the wind, their leathery wings flapping. Deyv staggered across the short grass. His legs felt weak, and his head swam. He drove on, aware that Jum and Aejip were not running in their best form by any means. Nonetheless, they were faster than he. A glance showed him that the *khratikl* had veered to cut him off. He tried to increase his pace, and he did. But not by much. Whatever had shocked him had taken a great deal out of him.

Before he reached the edge of the trees, he looked back at his pursuers. They were close enough so that he could see the ratlike heads, the flat rudderlike tails, the furry black bodies with long legs trailing, and the black wings. These were formed of thin skin stretched between body and back legs and a long bony finger extending from the wrist. He could also hear their chittering.

One *khratikl*, the speediest, and also the bravest or most foolhardy, swooped ahead of the pack. Aejip whirled, snarling, leaped up, and hooked her claws into a wing. She came down with the thing fluttering and squeaking at the end of her paw, and she bit off its head. Then she spun and dived under a frondy bush, with Deyv close behind her. Jum was ahead of them, streaking through the sparse undergrowth.

The things were at a disadvantage now, though it wasn't much of one. They had to descend to the ground to get through the barrier of bushes and vines lining the edge of the forest. Once inside the barrier, they needed at least twenty feet of bare ground for their runway before taking to the air again. They just didn't have the room here, so they'd have to run on their long, comparatively weak legs. If it hadn't been for the shock he'd suffered, Deyv could have outdistanced them.

Furthermore, the *khratikl* had a limited amount of time to catch their prey. If the *tharakorm* kept on drifting, it would soon be out of range of its guests. On the other hand, a *tharakorm* sometimes released its gas and landed. Usually, this occurred when hunting had not been good, and the host lacked food from which it made the lifting gas.

At least, this was what Deyv's father had told him. Actually, it was only a guess on his father's part, though he had once inspected a dead *tharakorm*. The creature hadn't really been dead, though, just inactive. Later, when his father had passed the place where it had been, the thing was gone. Apparently, a *tharakorm* could come to life again. Or maybe a big wind had blown it away.

In any event, there was no telling what the hungry *khratikl* were going to do. Deyv could only run and hope to find a good place for defense or hiding. As he ran, he drew his sword. He spared a look behind him. The things were still after him, a hundred at least, their wings flapping to help them with their running, their mouths open, and the big incisors visible despite the pale light under the massive branches. The nearest was a hundred and fifty feet behind him.

Ahead of him, Jum stopped and began barking. A few seconds later, Deyv saw what had attracted his attention. Through the dimness a great bulk loomed. It was high and round, and fallen jungle giants and growths of liana half-covered it.

It was a House of the Ancients, lying on its side.

He hoped that it was deserted. It should be, from its vegetation-littered appearance. However, it was possible that a tribe lived in it and used the vegetation as camouflage.

When Deyv came closer he looked quickly around. No soul-egg tree was in sight, but this did not mean that no humans dwelt in the House. Some tribes had their trees at a distance, in a hidden place.

By then Aejip had climbed up a mighty tree leaning against the House. Jum followed her a moment later. His claws slipped a few times, but he made it. He turned and faced Deyv, his tongue hanging out, his sides heaving.

Deyv ran up the trunk. A thin screech came from behind him. Aejip, roaring, leaped over Deyv's head. Gaining Jum's side, Deyv turned around. Below him the cat was engaged with four *khratikl*. One, two, three! The fourth broke off and ran for the main body of his fellows. Aejip picked up a carcass in her fangs and leaped up the trunk.

Deyv put the sword into its scabbard. He let himself down off the side of the trunk, clinging to knots and the rough bark. When his feet were on the smooth cold surface of the House, he worked his way up its rounded side, still clinging to the tree. Ahead of him, Jum landed on the surface and slid backward into Deyv's legs, his claws unable to get any purchase.

Hanging on with both hands, Deyv shoved the heavy dog up the slick curve with a foot. In the meantime, Aejip had worked her way farther up the trunk. Now she leaped outward onto the House, landed some distance above Deyv, slid, yowling, and abruptly disappeared.

Deyv shoved the dog ahead of him until they were opposite the place where the cat had dropped out of sight. He could see then that she had fallen into an opening. From his position, Deyv could move on all fours, cautiously, and perhaps reach the opening. Jum would never make it on his own.

Deyv bent his neck far back to look above. A dozen rattish faces looked down on him from the tree. If their owners had any guts—and they weren't noted for lacking courage—they would glide down toward him. The sheer weight of their bodies would send him scooting on down the curve and onto the ground.

Desperate, Deyv did the only thing he could do. Bracing his back against the trunk, he shoved the dog with all the strength in his legs. Yelping, Jum shot out, then dropped into the round hole.

Deyv leaped outward, his arms stretched out, slammed into the cold surface, slid, and suddenly was falling. He yelled and then crashed into a floor. He wasn't hurt, though he was shaken up. Fortunately, the floor, which was really a wall of the House, was that of a small room. If it had been as large as some in his tribe's House, he would have had a bad fall.

The animals were standing but shaking themselves as if they were trying to locate loose parts. Aejip had dropped the dead *khratikl*. Deyv stood and looked upward. The window opened from the inside; the round port hung down. A snarling head appeared in it. Deyv yelled, and the thing disappeared. It would be back soon with much company.

At one end of the floor was a door. Deyv climbed over the piles of dirt and leaves and skirted a nest some creature had abandoned. He scraped the accumulated mud off most of the door and used an ornamental projection to heave up on it. It rose soundlessly. The room below was much darker than that in which he stood. Without a light he couldn't tell how big it was and hence how deep was the next floor—or rather, wall. Still, he couldn't stay where he was.

Jum protested, whining, but through the opening he went, pushed by Deyv. A moment later he was barking. He didn't sound hurt, so Deyv told the cat to follow him. She didn't like it, but after looking down with her eyes wide-open, she leaped down.

Deyv dropped, his knees bent.

Another small room.

A flurry of chittering and squeaking came from above. Outlined in the dim light were a dozen heads.

There was some dirt on the floor. Deyv felt along it until he found another door. This, too, gave him a grip with its projections. He got that up, and the frightening process was repeated.

Apparently, the *khratikl* had given up. That showed good sense on their part. Only a desperate being would enter a House from the top side. The three continued. Each time Deyv prayed that the room below would not be a big one. Each time The Great Mother heard him. It didn't get any darker, since it was possible to get only so dark. The air got mustier with every level. He also began to get thirsty. At last, they reached the lowest floor, what would have been a window in the wall on the opposite side if the House had been standing upright. Deyv pulled it up and found mud below it.

Unless the room contained more doors than the one through which they had dropped, they were done for. There was no furniture to stack up and try to climb back up on. Nor did he have a hook on the end of his rope to throw back up with the hope that it would catch onto something. Even if it had had a grapnel, there would have been nothing for it to snag on to.

The House of Deyv's tribe, according to tradition, had contained some furniture when it was found generations ago. But this building had been looted.

Fortunately, the walls of the rooms were as rounded as the outside of the building. Deyv managed to run up the curve in the dark until his hand felt a door.

After sliding back down, he sat down to get his wind back, and then he ran up again. Groping, he felt a projection but slid back before he could seize it. The next try, he hung on. The door swung down, and he rolled back to the floor—that is, the wall.

On the third attempt, he grasped the edge of the door and hauled himself over. Before going up, he'd tied one end of the rope to his waist and the other around Jum's body. The dog howled with protest, but he went up kicking and was scraped against the edge of the door. Deyv untied Jum. Aejip, no matter how much Deyv coaxed, wouldn't leap up through the doorway. Deyv couldn't blame her, since even her light-sensitive eyes could not see.

If she did try to jump, she'd probably slam her head into the edge of the door. He climbed back down, tied the rope to the cat and to himself, and got over the door and through the doorway. Dragging her up, however, was even more laborious and exasperating. But he did it.

And then there was the next door. And the next. By the time they had reached the last room, all three were hot, very tired, and very thirsty. Since Deyv had done most of the work, he was in the worst condition.

Here, though, the window in the wall gave light. Deyv was glad that they had not dropped through the doors on this side. The room was huge, big enough to hold his entire tribe comfortably.

Not only was there light, but the window was open. Apparently, it had not been closed for a very long time. Only a small amount of dirt had gotten in, though. The window was far enough above the ground to keep splashes of mud out except during the most driving rains. It was not high enough to keep animals out, yet there was no evidence that any had ever been there.

This was strange, since the cavernous room was festooned and carpeted with a thick growth. There was enough light to see that it was a sort of fungus. Deyv laid down on it to rest and found it a very soft bed. After a while, he had to get up and climb out through the round window. Thirst drove him and his companions to seek water. They found a pool in a hollow and drank deeply. Then he searched around until he found a gourd tree. He picked four of the fruit, cut them open, and shared the sweet meat with Jum and Aejip. Having hollowed out the thin hard shells, he filled them with water and returned to the room.

Deyv removed his compression cylinder from a pocket of his blowgun case after making a torch of twisted dried leaves that had blown into the room. He ignited some punk in the cylinder and used this to ignite the torch. Its flame showed that the fungus, so dull in the dim light, was actually a purple-and-red-striped glory. Stalactites of it pointed down from the ceiling, and here and there on the floor were stalagmites. Spider-weblike strands of the plant filled the corners from ceiling to floor. Many small hard nodules were visible just below the surface of the growth on the walls and ceiling.

Before the blaze went out, he saw he'd been mistaken in thinking that no beast had ever laired there. In one corner was a protuberance which looked like a bone. He picked it up, brushing off the sticky growth, and examined it. It looked like the thigh bone of an animal the size of Jum. It must have been there a long time, though. It was badly decayed.

He poked around under the surface and found pieces of rotted, deeply pitted bones, including the fragment of a skull. Deeper he found a long curved canine tooth, also pitted. Some large cat had once made this room its den or else it had crawled in here to die.

By then Aejip had returned from a short hunt. She dropped a dead bird in front of Deyv and sat back on her haunches. Deyv took it outside and skinned the fuzzy, almost wingless creature, gutted it, and cut off portions for all three. The cat and dog devoured their share, including the bones, before he had gathered together enough dry wood for a small fire.

Soon the odor of flesh had attracted a horde of black

beetles spotted with green fleur-de-lys. Deyv caught a dozen of them and ate them as appetizers. The things were utterly without caution when swarming over dead meat, so he called the two pets and they lapped the insects up, crunching them between their teeth and swallowing them half-alive. A number fell in the fire, so Deyv picked them out and ate these. They were even better half-roasted.

When it was sleep-time, Deyv closed the window, and they bedded down. But the air got too stuffy. After a while he opened the window. Though this allowed access to predators, the window could be guarded. He stationed the two animals just under it and then half-closed it, propping it up with a stick. His sword was by his right hand and his tomahawk was by the other. Both animals would instantly awake if they heard strange noises nearby or smelled a dangerous creature.

Then he got an idea, and he rose again. He tied one end of the rope to the stick so that he could pull on the other end and yank the prop out. The window would then bang down, frustrating anything that intended to get in.

Thus assured of safety, or as much as was possible in this place, he went to sleep.

5 ·ᵉᔓ

IN his dream Deyv had just leaped from behind a bush and grabbed a woman of an enemy tribe. He'd been watching her as she came up the path from the river. She was tall and had a beautiful figure, and the soul egg between her breasts was glowing with streaks of color that matched those of his egg in color and waveform. She was just what he wanted as a wife, and if he could subdue her before she screamed and warned her people, he would take her away to his tribe.

While grappling with her, he smelled a faint perfume, very pleasant. Her body was covered with some oil, which made it difficult for him to keep hold of her. It was this oil that exuded the perfume, which, the longer he wrestled with her, made him the more excited. Unfortunately, the oil also made her slippery.

Eventually, she got loose and ran away. Then, just as he rounded a bend in the path, he was seized by her relatives. They tied him up with leather ropes and stuck the ends of sharpened bamboos all over his body until he bristled with them. Then the shaman danced in front of him and waved a sword. Deyv cried out with fear, though he didn't want to. The shaman grinned, and the woman Deyv had grabbed came close to him and dumped a gourd full of the perfume all over him.

The shaman's sword lashed out, and its tip raked Deyv's chest. He cried out with pain.

His eyes opened, and he knew that he'd been dreaming. But he still smelled the heavy perfume. His body felt as if it had been penetrated by a hundred bamboo ends. And his chest felt as if it had indeed been sliced across with a sword tip.

Aejip's snarling face was above him. Her paw raised and flashed down, and it struck him on the stomach.

Deyv thought that the cat had gone insane. He tried to call out for Jum to help him, but his voice was only a croak. His mouth and lips were very dry; his tongue seemed to be swollen.

Aejip struck him again, this time on the leg. Deyv tried to reach for his sword, but his arm seemed heavy. The perfume clogged his nostrils, and its heaviness suggested to him that he should go back to sleep.

The cat, still snarling, bit down on Deyv's foot. It wasn't a hard enough bite to wound his foot, but it was certainly not the love bite Aejip often gave him. It hurt, and it made him sit up.

His legs and belly were covered with things. They were about the size of his fist, if the long thin legs were included. They had small heads with long beaks, and these were inserted into his skin. A number of their dead bodies lay around on the fungus; their smashed bodies had squirted blood.

Jum lay beneath the window, at least twenty of the things, like huge wingless mosquitoes, feeding off him.

Deyv, still somewhat stupefied, looked down. His chest was bleeding where the cat had raked it. But she had done it to awaken him before he had been sucked dry of blood.

One of the things raced up his arm and leaped, landing on his cheek. Its beak stung him, and he slapped it. Its body spread out under the slap, and when Deyv removed his hand, the thing fell off. Meanwhile, Aejip was rolling over and over, crushing the frail creatures attached to her body.

After that Deyv got to his feet and began striking the things on his body. Some of them were so swollen with his blood that they popped when their shells broke. Having gotten rid of them, though not those which were swarming on the floor and dropping from the ceiling, he ran to the window. He opened it all the way to help dilute the perfume. Then he pounded on Jum's body until his attackers were dead and the dog had been roused. Jum stood there, swaying and blinking for some time, watching Aejip and his master striking or stomping on the insects. Finally, he became fully conscious and joined in the battle. He didn't help much; the things were agile and darted out of the way of his snapping teeth.

Eventually, the battle was over. Deyv stood panting, looking at the smashed bodies of at least a hundred of the things. There might have been more at the beginning, but these had gone out the window or into the next room. The perfume seemed to be fading away. His body was covered with itching swellings. Though their fur hid them, the two animals must also have been thickly spotted with welts.

Deyv went out the window and covered himself with mud to relieve the itching. Jum scratched vigorously until ordered to stop. Then Deyv came back and poked around the thick woolly stuff of the fungus with his sword until he uncovered more fragments of bone. These lay deep under the growth, though he suspected that they had once lain on top. They looked as if some kind of weak acid had eaten them away.

All the nodules just under the surface of the growth had burst open. It was obvious to Deyv that these had contained the insects. They had been curled up within them, waiting for whatever signal the growth sent out to awaken them. They would descend upon the unlucky victim, sleeping heavily with the aid of the perfume emitted by the fungus. Then the things, their bodies expanded with blood, would return to the nodules. The growth would dissolve the flesh of the dead victim with some sort of acid. It would open its body to allow the bones to drift downward, where they too would finally be dissolved. Deyv didn't know for certain that this was the way events went. It did seem a likely explanation, however.

When he saw a half-eaten rodent in a corner near the window, he knew why Aejip had not been overcome by the perfume. Some time during the sleep-time, before the plant had emitted its perfume, the cat had gotten hungry. She'd gone ahunting, and she had returned with the remnant of the carcass to devour it at leisure. She'd arrived just as the insects were starting to feed.

Deyv patted the cat's head. "Good girl. You saved us."

Jum was too miserable from his bites to growl with jealousy.

There was no sense in staying even if all the symbionts of the plant had been killed. It would be impossible to sleep. He picked up his weapons and ordered the animals to jump out of the window. The cat picked the rodent up by her teeth and obeyed. But Jum acted strangely. He trotted over to Deyv and looked up, whining.

"What's the matter, boy?"

Jum fixed his eyes at a point below Deyv's.

Deyv looked down. Was he bleeding through the mud he'd plastered over his chest? Suddenly he knew why the dog was so disturbed.

His soul egg was gone!

6 ◄§

LATER, Deyv figured out that the thief had come in after he and the dog had fallen into a semidrugged sleep and before the cat had returned. Jum hadn't smelled the thief because of the perfume's overpowering odor. It had taken excellent timing and great daring, but the deed had been done.

At the moment, and for a long time after, Deyv was too distressed to reconstruct the situation. Nor did he wonder then *why* the soul egg had been stolen.

Since he'd been a baby, he'd only removed the egg a few times, when a new cord had to be strung through the carved opening at one end. No person ever willingly let his egg out of his sight. When he was buried, the egg still lay on his chest.

To be without an egg was to be without a soul.

Deyv was a living ghost unless he somehow got his soul egg back. His own tribe would drive him back into the jungle if he appeared without his egg. He'd be doomed to wander alone, shunned by all, friend or enemy, until he died. A foe wouldn't even boast about killing Deyv or hang his head up as a trophy, since the head of a man without a soul was worthless. His killer would bury the body so that Deyv's ghost wouldn't haunt him.

Deyv had heard some horror tales about people whose eggs had been stolen by fellow tribesmen or women who hated them. This hadn't happened very often, and only a great hatred would bring a person to do such an evil deed. If the culprit was found out, he'd suffer a terrible death, and he'd be buried without his egg. According to the stories, the persons from whom the egg had been stolen left the House. And they sat down in the jungle and grieved themselves to death within a few sleeps.

Stunned, Deyv squatted within a corner of the room and moaned. Jum whimpered and nuzzled him. Aejip had returned to the room after eating the rodent, and she too was puzzled and distressed.

For a long, long time, Deyv sat, staring ahead, ignoring the animals, sinking deeper into paralysis and blackness. All was lost forever. He'd never again see his parents, brothers, sisters, or friends. He would never know the joys of a wife or children. He was in a state of living death, and when the true death came, he wouldn't be any better off. He'd be a ghost forever wandering the Earth, denied that pleasant place which The Great Mother provided for those with eggs. The place where it was never too hot or too cold, food was easy to find, and he would have lived in a great House with his family and all his ancestors.

The dog refused for a long time to leave Deyv's side. Finally, hunger and thirst drove him out. When these had been satisfied, he came back to sit and look at his master with questioning eyes or to sleep. Aejip also went out, and when she came back she offered Deyv part of a carcass. Once, Jum tried to eat it, but she snarled and drove him away. When she was finally convinced that Deyv wouldn't touch it—by this time the carcass was stinking—she permitted the dog to eat it.

The stench of rotten flesh, dog urine, and dung filled the room. Flies and other insects crawled over Deyv, over his ears and eyes, and tried to go up his nostrils. At first the mud on his body gave him some protection. Then it dried and flaked off, and they had more skin to bite or sting. His belly swelled with gas, and the stench of that was added to the others. His thirst increased; his dry lips cracked. Still, he sat motionless, ever withdrawing into himself.

He was scarcely aware of anything by then, though he dimly heard the great storm outside the House. Thunder boomed; lightning hissed; trees toppled under the wind; rain blew through the window.

These sounds meant nothing to him, though Jum whimpered and quivered, and Aejip lost her cool nonchalance. Deyv might have died during the storm had not a lightning bolt sent a feeler on the breeze through the window.

Much of its force was spent, but the shock was enough to knock him backward against the wall. Shaking his head, he crawled on all fours to the center of the room. The cat and the dog lay paralyzed and shivering, their eyes upon him. He got shakily to his feet and staggered to the window. Ignoring the flashes that seemed to hit very nearby, he stuck his head out the window.

"Thank you, O Shrekmikl, Great Son of The Great Mother!" he croaked. "You sent your sky-fire to wake me up, to drag me back from death! You showed me that I was wrong to just sit there and die! You showed me that I must be angry at the evil wretch who stole my soul egg! And you showed me that you favor me!"

It was possible that without the lightning, he might have sunk just so far in his despondency and then hit the core of anger that was deep inside him. Whatever might have been, the bolt had struck, and it had roused him.

He waited until the storm was over, then climbed out of the window, dropped onto the ground, rose, and walked weakly to the nearest pool. After slaking his thirst, he searched for and found some fruit which the wind had knocked off a tree. It was, however, two sleep-times before he felt strong enough to continue.

By then the thief's trail, if there had been one, had been washed away. Deyv had no idea where to look. The thief had the whole world to hide in. Yet Deyv set out with an optimism unjustified by the facts. He felt that Shrekmikl had taken an interest in him, and he would surely set his worshipper upon the right path.

He went back on the road he'd left when the *tharakorm*'s tenants had chased him. He continued in the same direction. After many sleeps, he was at the foot of the mountain. The road ran up it, but was twisted and sometimes went straight up a precipice. There was no use trying to travel on it. Despite this, Deyv decided to see the other side of the mountain. Though he had seen evidence that a tribe was in the neighborhood, he felt that he could do better elsewhere. There was no rational basis for this; he just felt it.

Instead of climbing the mountain, he went around it. This involved much struggling through a sometimes dense forest and through many swamps. He kept on and finally had rounded the peak. The country on the other side looked much like that he'd left behind. Nevertheless, he felt that he had accomplished something worthwhile. Just what, he would have found hard to define.

Here the ancients' highway, coming down off the peak, curved toward his left. Some time later it split into two, and he took the left. That was an unlucky direction, just as the left hand was the unlucky hand and a wind from the left was unlucky. However, Shrekmikl was left-handed, and he was the favorite son of The Mother.

Deyv observed a herd of huge pink bipedal beasts with long tails walk calmly through the next junction. They paid no heed to the clanging or the flashing green lights. If they could do it, why couldn't he? Though somewhat apprehensive, he followed their example, and nothing happened. After that, he saved time by not detouring around the crossroads.

Once, while looking in the forest for a good place to sleep, he came across the remains of a fire in a thorn bower. It had been made by a single person who'd left some footprints in the mud. They looked human, but the big toes were exceptionally long. Deyv wondered if the prints had been made by a Yawtl. Though he'd never seen one, his grandmother had described this legendary creature. One of its features was a very long big toe.

Another characteristic of this creature was its addiction to stealing. Deyv brightened when he remembered this.

Perhaps he was on the right trail.

Unfortunately, the Yawtl was not going to leave any tracks while he was on the highway. Also, he could take another road any time he came to a junction. Despite this, Deyv always took the highway to the left. He also stepped up his pace. The animals complained in their way about this, but he ignored them.

Then one day after breakfasting, Aejip decided that she'd had more than enough for the time being. She curled up in the cave they'd found and refused to get up. It was evident that she intended to sleep for a long time before she would go on.

Deyv was frantic. The delay might enable the Yawtl—if that's what it was—to get another sleep-time ahead of them. It was no use, however, trying to change Aejip's mind. If stubbornness was a characteristic of a cat, and if cats admired it, she was a cat's cat. Leaving her behind was unthinkable. He needed her as a sentinel and also as a food provider. Besides, he was very fond of her, no matter how often he got angry at her.

He finally decided to take a rest himself. He could use it, and Jum's feet seemed to be getting sore. First, though, they had to hunt. A few minutes later, the two left Aejip snoozing and went down a little-used path.

When they came to the deep tracks of a giant turtle that had crossed the path, they followed them. Sometime later they came back out on the trail with two huge eggs. Fortunately, these had not been laid by a checkered turtle; Deyv could eat them.

Just as they stepped out, Jum froze, growling softly. Deyv laid his ear to the ground. Faintly, the thud of running feet came to him. He and Jum stepped back into the cover and waited. The path at this point was rather straight, enabling Deyv to see the intruder at least a minute before she came past him.

This was a woman who would make a good mate, if physical appearance meant anything. She was tall and had an excellent figure. Her skin was pale; her kinky hair was yellow; her eyes were blue. A bone whistle hung from a cord around her neck. She wore a short kilt of some green material supported by a broad leather belt. A stone tomahawk was tucked into it, and she held a stone-tipped spear in her right hand. A blowgun case rested on her shoulder. Her expression was one of strain, possibly of desperation. Sweat coated her lovely skin.

Deyv had thought to step out behind her as she went by and stun her with a blow from the flat of his tomahawk. But her haste could mean that she was being pursued. It would be better to wait until he was sure no one followed close behind her. That meant that he would lose his chance for complete surprise, but it was smarter to lose her than to lose his life.

She came closer. And he suddenly knew what had made him vaguely uneasy about her without quite knowing why.

She had no soul egg.

7 ◂᪥

JUM was ready to go silently into action the moment he received the signal, but Deyv cautioned him not to move. The woman ran by, her panting deep and sawing. She did not look behind or ahead but down. It struck him then that she might not be fleeing. She might be trailing someone. Or hoping she'd find some tracks, since there were none in this part of the path. However, when she got a few yards on, she would see the imprints his boots and the dog's paws had made.

She did. She halted suddenly and bent down to look

at them. She straightened up, looked around, and darted into the foliage. Deyv could see a small patch of light skin through some leaves. She was waiting there, hoping that whoever had made the tracks had gone off the trail for some reason other than ambushing her.

Deyv kneeled down on the ground and laid his ear to it again. If anyone was coming around the bend, he—or they—wasn't running. He decided to move farther along the path. Should warriors notice the prints going off into the jungle, they might look for him. As for the woman, he was no longer interested. She had no egg and thus was not for him. She was a pariah, an outcast, a soulless contemptible being.

Besides, now that he considered it, he must have been crazy to think he could catch her for his mate. He had to track down the person who'd stolen his own egg. How could he do that and also drag her along even if she had had an egg?

He looked back down the trail. The patch of skin was gone. For a moment he considered sending the dog to sniff her out. It was possible that she had glimpsed him as she passed and was now prowling through the bush, looking for him. He didn't think so. But there was no sense taking chances. He'd just move on, keep ahead of her. No. He couldn't do that. He had to return to the cave to get Aejip.

If the woman was aggressive, if she wasn't just running away from him, and if she thought him a danger, she'd have to go along the edge of the jungle until she was past a turn. Then she could cross to his side and sneak back.

On the other hand, she was probably as eager to avoid conflict as he, which meant she'd get out of his sight and then run as fast as she could down the trail away from him.

Maybe she hadn't seen him. More likely, it had only been his tracks going off into the brush that had spooked her.

He gave the word to Jum, and the two moved slowly through the foliage. They kept an eye on the path, pausing now and then to search it out through the vegetation and so keep from going too far away from it.

He wondered if she came from the same tribe that Shamoom had stolen his woman from. She certainly fit the description. She looked strange to him but at the same time attractive. Those blue eyes had caused him a pang of repulsion for a second. They were so pale, so washed out, so much like the eyes of ghosts were said to be.

Her nose was too small and straight, and her lips were not the splendid thickness of his. But, in their way, they had a certain appeal.

Her breasts were not the large ones he admired. Yet, though small, they weren't too much so, and they certainly were well shaped. They seemed to defy gravity, those upright cones, not at all like the melon-shaped breasts of his tribeswomen.

There was something to be said for the exotic. But she was eggless. That made all the difference . . .

He stopped. What was he talking about? He was eggless, too! It was then that it struck him that he might have a very good reason to meet her. Could her egg have been stolen, and by the same one who'd lifted his?

When he was opposite the place where he'd seen her, or had thought he had, he stopped. After carefully watching and listening, Deyv sent Jum across the path. The dog bounded out of the foliage and dived into that across the trail. A minute later, he emerged. Jum's actions indicated that the woman had gone along the edge in the direction from which they had come. Deyv took a chance. Instead of having Jum sniff her tracks in the bush, he had the dog follow him down the trail. As he had expected, he found her prints where she had come out onto the trail. He didn't need Jum to follow her scent.

Presently, he caught a glimpse of the woman ahead

as she rounded a turn. A little later he caught up with her. She turned when she heard him running, and she waited, spear ready.

Deyv stopped and asked her what her name was and what she was doing there. She replied in her speech, of which he did not understand a word.

He pointed to his chest, bare of an egg. Then he pointed to hers. Her eyes widened, and she said something. It didn't sound threatening. Nevertheless, he approached slowly, speaking in a soft tone. Jum stayed at his side until Deyv thought it might make her less uneasy if the dog remained behind.

Though it took some time, Deyv got his ideas across. If he understood her rightly, her egg had also been stolen. She had been looking for the thief ever since, which was not too long a time ago. The signs and gestures she made seemed to indicate that the egg had been taken during her last sleep.

If he understood her further, the thief had left some tracks. They had gone in this direction. Then she'd lost them, but she had continued in this direction hoping to pick them up again. Deyv indicated that if this was so, the thief had slipped around him undetected.

He said, "Yawtl?"

She didn't know what that meant. Perhaps she had another name for Yawtl.

Deyv stepped closer to her. She didn't flinch. He reached out slowly, touched her smooth shoulder, then touched between her breasts. He touched his own shoulder, then his chest. He pointed down the trail and waggled two fingers.

She shook her head. Did this mean no? Or did it mean that she didn't nod for yes but for no?

Suddenly, she smiled. It was strained, but its meaning was obvious.

He walked past her, not looking at her, and started on down the path. In a moment Jum had caught up with him. After twenty or so steps, he looked back. She was following him. In a short while, she was walking by his side.

Now and then Deyv talked to her in the low tones that ever-possible danger made necessary. Before they turned off the path to go after Aejip, he knew her name. Vana.

Aejip seemed to be sleeping, but her ears flicked when the three were close to her. Then, catching the scent of the stranger, she shot to her paws, half snarling. Deyv quieted her down. The cat sniffed the woman's feet and legs and crotch, which Jum had also done. Vana reached out a hand carefully. Deyv was both surprised and jealous when Aejip submitted to a scratching behind the ears and a stroking of the forehead. She even purred.

A few minutes later, they left for the trail. This led them back to the ancients' highway. Jum cast about, sniffing, and started to the left. Not wanting to waste any time, Deyv at once started language lessons with Vana. He pointed out parts of his body, named them, then indicated objects along the road. Vana had no trouble remembering the names. Her pronunciation left something to be desired, however. Two of the sounds seemed to be entirely unfamiliar to her, and she was not quite accurate in reproducing five others.

A perfectionist, Deyv insisted that she master these. When sleep-time came, she could utter most of them to his satisfaction. They ate fruit, the leaves of a root plant, and a 10-pound hoofed rodent which Aejip had killed. They bedded down high up in a tree in an abandoned nest. Deyv made no moves to lie with her although he felt passionate. It had been a long time since he'd been with the woman of the young bachelors. But Vana was forbidden to him for several reasons. One, the law of his tribe was that a bachelor could lie with only one woman until he got married. Two, even if he had felt like breaking that law, he wouldn't lie with a woman who had no soul egg. Three, the presence of his pets inhibited him. Four, if she had rejected him, he would have been humiliated.

He slept with Jum and Aejip between him and Vana.

Just as they were about to emerge from the jungle, they saw twenty warriors walking along the highway. These looked as if they could have been of Vana's tribe. Deyv quickly drew his sword and put its edge across the woman's jugular vein. She nodded, indicating in her strange way that she wasn't going to call out. Later, he would find out that the warriors were enemies of her people. In any event, she wouldn't have tried to get their attention. Eggless, she no longer had a tribe.

While they sat behind a bush, they continued the language lesson. By the time the war party was out of sight, she had learned ten more words.

They set out at a leisurely pace so the swift-walking warriors could get even farther ahead of them. While they were eating some freshly picked fruit, they saw the nose of The Dark Beast rise ahead on their right. Within seven sleep-times it would be fully exposed, a black object that would fill most of the sky. A pale darkness would fall over the land, and the air would become cooler. More rain would fall, and the winds would grow stronger. It would be a bad time to travel then. Visibility would be much less; they wouldn't even be able to see down the road. Nevertheless, they had to keep going. The thief might not be daunted by the darkness.

A heavy rain came and washed out the faint traces of the thief. Two slight earthquakes momentarily rippled the road. Near sleep-time they came to another junction. Deyv started to detour around the poles, fearing a recurrence of the shocking incident, but he stopped when he saw Vana's curious behavior.

She had boldly walked up to the poles. Before reaching the intersection, however, she sank to her knees. After bowing deeply three times and chanting at the same time, she rose and walked between the poles.

Deyv was amazed. He had thought that these clanging, light-flashing things were strange animals. It had not occurred to him they might be gods of some sort. They'd accepted her prayers and let her through.

Would they do the same for him? Or, since he didn't belong to their totem, would they blast him? Best not to tempt them. After he'd taught her enough to ask her about the poles, he'd get the truth. Meanwhile, he'd just detour.

She stood with a puzzled, half-amused expression until he and the animals joined her. She asked him something in her barbarous speech, but he ignored her. He felt that he'd somehow made a fool of himself, and she was laughing at him.

A little later, during another driving rain, he glimpsed something ahead. They retired quickly into the jungle. Along came the warriors with the kinky yellow hair, this time trotting. As far as Deyv could determine, they hadn't succeeded in acquiring any heads. The war party quickly disappeared into the rain, but Deyv restrained his companions from returning to the road. There had been something of haste about the group, something that suggested they were being pursued. A little while afterward, his caution was vindicated. Another war party, of about forty men, dogtrotted by them.

Deyv waited a while longer to make sure that they wouldn't run into a rearguard. Then they moved out. They were so miserable from the cold, drenching downpour that they didn't talk much. Aejip went off to hunt their next meal. Shortly before sleep-time, she caught up with them. No carcass dangled from her mouth. Hungry, shivering, they sought out a dry, safe place. Unable to find either, they took refuge under a tree and tried to sleep. It was a grouchy bunch that took the road after they'd given up getting anything but a few very short naps.

Then the skies cleared. Though The Beast still cast its cold shadow, they felt somewhat better. Aejip slid into the jungle and came back rather quickly with a fawn she'd killed. Since it was impossible to find dry wood, Deyv and Vana ate the meat raw. Shortly thereafter, Vana relieved herself. Deyv was disgusted. His tribe always went into the bush when they had to obey the call of nature. So did all the nine tribes of his area. They might have some customs which he found repulsive, but at least they were modest.

Their campsite was about two hundred yards into the jungle. They had started for the highway when they heard to their left loud buzzings and whistlings. Unable to resist their curiosity, they walked cautiously toward the noise.

Deyv pushed on stealthily through the foliage until he could dimly see something through the leaves. He stopped so he could distinguish whatever it was that was moving out there. Unable to see anything more clearly, he started to move closer to the objects. At that moment, something touched his shoulder from behind. He was in such a state of nervous concentration that the unexpected touch startled him. He whirled, ready to fight or run away from whatever was behind him. But it was only Vana grinning at him. She held up her bone whistle and gestured that he should let her precede him. He didn't like this. After all, he was the leader. However, this was her territory. She would know more than he what to do there. In certain situations, anyway.

He waved her ahead. They went through some dense bush which suddenly gave way to a large open area. In its center was a cylinder about forty feet high with a diameter of thirty feet. Its walls were of some rough grayish substance. From its base the same substance spread out, paving the area and preventing the growth of any plants. Round holes perforated the walls of the cylinder, and to and from these holes large insects darted, whistling. These were honey beetles, greenish winged things that had built the edifice with a quick-hardening saliva which resisted the heaviest stone axe. The bite of one was painful but not fatal. The bites of a dozen could kill a man.

Deyv had seen honey-beetle buildings before. He'd assisted at attempts to smoke out the beetles, attempts he would just as soon forget. A wealth of delicious honey was stored in that structure, but very few men or beasts could get at it.

What was not familiar was the creature that had disturbed the beetles. The thing was huge, its head three feet higher than Deyv's. It had four massive legs ending in broad round pads. The body was shaped like a bean pod. That is, the main body was. From its front a trunk reared at a right angle. This was shaped like the torso of a man and had shoulders, two arms, a neck, and a head. The hands had a thumb and four fingers.

Vana turned and said, "Archkerri."

The word meant nothing to Deyv. He had never even heard of such a centaurial being.

Its body was enough to startle and frighten him. But it was not an animal. At least, it was not a thing which he could define as such. Instead of hair or fur or smooth naked skin, it was covered with leaves. These were green, about the size of Deyv's hands, triangular and overlapping, the points downward. They were all over the body and limbs, though the red hands lacked them. The head looked more like a cabbage than anything else. From its center protruded a long thin whitish tube from which the buzzing was coming. When the thing turned its head, it revealed two huge eyes with a black pupil and leaf-green iris and cornea.

If left to himself, Deyv would have departed with all possible haste. Vana, however, stepped out into the clearing and raised her bone whistle to her lips.

Deyv said, "Don't!"

He was too late.

A series of long and short whistles in groups of from two to five came from her bone. The thing immediately stopped trying to beat the honey beetles off with its red hands. It turned around slowly, its eyes fixed on Vana. Then its tube emitted buzzes, some longer than others and also arranged in groups.

8

THE beetles swarmed about the centauroid as it moved ponderously toward Vana. Their efforts to bite it were futile, the leaves apparently being tough and thick. Dozens of the insects fell off it, striking the pavement and kicking their legs feebly. Deyv assumed that its leaves contained a poison.

He didn't have any such protection, so he retreated as the creature entered the jungle. Jum and Aejip left even faster than he. Vana was following Deyv, the thing about twelve feet behind her. By the time Vana called a halt, all the beetles had dropped off. The others quit pursuing it as soon as it left the paved area.

Vana then resumed her peculiar conversation with it. After a minute of this, she turned and led all of them to the road. Deyv's back felt cold, and he was nervous. He assured himself, however, that Vana wouldn't be dealing with the thing if it was dangerous. Or maybe she felt secure, since it was friendly to her. That didn't mean that it was not a peril to him.

When they reached the highway, the woman and the Archkerri whistled some more at each other. Finally Vana stopped, and she tried to explain to Deyv what was going on. He spread his hands out and hunched his shoulders in the age-old gesture of incomprehension. She shrugged and then started down the road. The thing slowly followed her. Aejip and Jum were even more nervous than Deyv, but they were willing to go wherever he wished.

When he could stand the suspense no longer, he stopped Vana. He made signs asking her why the thing was going with them. At first she didn't understand. When she caught on, she went up to the Archkerri and pointed at its chest. Or at what might be a chest under the foliage. Then she pointed at her chest and Deyv's.

"You mean," he said, "that its soul egg has been stolen, too?"

She must have understood his tone if not his words. She shook her head. Yes.

His attitude changed somewhat. The thing was no longer a monster. Not entirely, anyway. If it had had a soul egg, then it had to be a human, even if it didn't exactly resemble one.

Deyv also got it across to her that he would like to know the creature's name.

Vana blew a series of groups of long and short whistles. By then his ear was becoming sensitive. There were five sounds of unequal length. If the shortest was 1, the next longest, 2, and so on, then its name was . . . what? It was too hard to figure out at the moment. Besides, it wouldn't mean anything.

Vana appeared to be thinking hard on the problem. After some brow-wrinkling and lip-chewing, she said, "Sloosh."

He didn't ask her how she arrived at that. She couldn't have told him, anyway. But she had made some correlation between the sounds of her speech and of the thing's.

Deyv felt he was getting somewhere, though not very far. The time he'd spent teaching her his language was wasted. Now he had to learn hers so he could translate the buzzes of the Archkerri. It irked him to have to do this. Since he was the leader, he should teach them his speech.

They went on after Deyv had signed to Vana that she should speak to the plant-man as little as possible. It was safe to converse in a low tone. Loud whistles were out. They carried too far. She shook her head and whistled at the thing. It came close to them and buzzed a series of groups in a very low tone. They could talk under these conditions.

Deyv set himself to the task of speaking her language. Sleeps went by, and he learned swiftly even if its structure wasn't at all like any of those of the nine tribes. After a while he understood that the Archkerri wasn't using his own language. It was the Trade Language of the tribes in Vana's area. The Archkerri had arbitrarily matched certain groups of buzzes with the sounds of the trading language. This enabled the Archkerri to carry on a fluent if simple conversation with the humans.

Deyv carved a whistle for himself from the leg bone of a dead bird. While he was learning Vana's tongue, he learned how to transpose it into the whistling. Later, he started learning Archkerri.

Meanwhile, they found no more footprints or campsites of the Yawtl. Deyv would have been worried except for one thing. The Archkerri had its—his, rather—infallible means for tracking the thief.

Vana said, "He is following its ghostly prints."

"What do you mean by that?" Deyv asked, turning pale. "It's a *ghost*?"

"No," she said scornfully. "Can a ghost carry a soul egg? Of course it can't. The egg would burn it, send it screaming."

"I never heard of that."

"Everybody knows that. At least, I thought they did until I met you. What I'm talking about is the ability of Sloosh, of all his people, to see what we humans can't. He says that every living thing leaves in its path the impress of its form. To him it is a reddish color which looks, vaguely, like the thing which left it behind."

After some more questioning, Deyv understood that the "tracks" were psychic impressions. When he could converse with Sloosh, he asked for more details.

"Yes. What Vana said is true. I feel sorry for you humans. Your world must be very pale and comparatively uninteresting. I not only see what you see—and, I don't mind saying, much more understandingly—but I see many more things.

"My world is filled with the forms not only of what is but of what has been. It glows with the designs made by these trails, designs of breath-taking beauty and complexity. Of course, that is redundant. I mean, complexity *is* beauty. Beauty is complexity."

Sloosh paused, then said, "Vana is mistaken when she tells you that these forms are reddish. I told her that the thief's prints are reddish. But every form of life leaves its own color. I see hundreds of hues and shades of every color. The thief's impressions are not, as Vana said, tracks like footprints. They are one continuous impression, linked, like a thousand Yawtl standing in line, each one pressing closely against the next. A thousand Yawtl that are yet one. Shimmering with a pale-red fire. Transparent yet clearly visible.

"You and Vana, though, are pale red shot with threads of twisting green, scarlet, and black, each a generic design yet recognizably individual. Your forms trail behind you like giant caterpillars, getting paler near the end. Which, of course, I can't see because they drop below the horizon. But if I were to trace you back, I could go for many sleep-times before your impressions faded out.

"It is too bad that you can't see them. But that is the way things work out. Some forms of life have this ability. Some don't."

Deyv was a little irked by Sloosh's complacency, his sense of superiority. He didn't allow his irritation to show, however. He needed the Archkerri.

"Then we'll have no trouble catching up with the thief?"

"I didn't say that. I said we'd be able to follow his impressions. But he may go someplace where we can't follow him. Or we may be killed by some beast. Or we may be . . ."

Deyv walked away. The Archkerri was so pickish about things that humans took for granted or didn't say because it wasn't necessary.

Nor was Sloosh as superior as he liked to think. For one thing, he was very slow. He either couldn't or wouldn't walk as fast as his companions. He went at his own pace, a majestic elephantine amble. He ignored the requests of the others to speed up. This had made Deyv nervous for a while because at every sleep the Yawtl was gaining distance on them. However, after some thought, he had calmed himself. Though it would take longer to run the thief down, the Archkerri made its capture inevitable. His presence assured them that they couldn't lose the trail.

Still, the time Sloosh took in finding and eating food continued to be a trial to Deyv. The Archkerri's mouth was concealed beneath the leaves on the "chest" of the upper body. Finding that out had been a shock to Deyv. It had seemed grotesque and also a little frightening. His grandmother had told him about a monster which was human-shaped, unlike Sloosh, but which had its mouth on its breast, and its diet was confined to human children. As a child, Deyv had been threatened with it when he didn't behave.

Sloosh would eat meat, including the rottenest carrion, when it was available. But mostly he ate fruit and vegetables, and he required great amounts of these. To speed up the search for food, the two humans would forage the edge of the jungle. They'd woven some large baskets from reeds, and they used them to store the fruit. Thus, they could walk faster, feeding Sloosh from the baskets. But collecting the food took much time, too.

"You are quite wrong about the Yawtl stealing my soul egg," Sloosh said. "We Archkerri don't have such things. Eggs are for humans only. Indeed, they're an ancient human invention. I don't know why the ancients made the soul-egg trees, but they must have had what seemed to them good reasons. My people wear a crystal which Vana's people call *caqghwoonma.* It is as large as your head but much better shaped. It's a prism included within six equal rhombic faces. It can be mined, since it grows underground, unlike the soul-egg trees, which grow mostly above the surface. These crystals are rare, which is one of fifteen reasons I was in the area of Vana's tribe area looking for them."

"Wait a minute," Deyv said. "Your tribe doesn't live in the same area as her people?"

"I don't have a tribe. That's a primitive social unit we Archkerri grew out of long ago. No, I was there to investigate. After a long time—"

"How long a time?"

Vana said, "He appeared when I was a child, shortly after I was weaned. But he left shortly before I did. He couldn't find any *caqghwoonma,* and he'd found out everything else he wanted to know. Whatever that was. What I think is—"

"Impatience is the mark of a retarded mind," Sloosh said. "And interrupting a person is a mark of impatience and of a great ego. Let me continue. The crystal rhombohedron is an invention of my people. It shows moving pictures. These are the electrical constructs of the thoughts of the vegetable world. You see —I hope you see—all plants contain ancestral impressions. And all the units of the vegetable world together constitute one body. One mind, I should say to be exact. Though so far the distinction between body and mind has not been satisfactorily made.

"But I must not give you the wrong idea. We Archkerri are not part of this mind. We're sentients, therefore individuals, though not in the same sense you are such. That is because, though of vegetable origin, we Archkerri are half-protein. If we weren't, we'd be as immobile as that tree there and dependent upon the radiation from the sky and—but I digress.

"The rhombohedra are our means for communicating, or, rather, I should say, for receiving the 'thoughts' or impressions of the vegetable world. If we communicated, they, it, would also have to be sentient. Communication is a two-way gate."

What Sloosh said, in essence, was that the crystals could tap and then process the ancestral impressions in the cells of vegetable life. The crystals showed visual interpretations of past and present events.

Deyv was staggered by this revelation. "You mean,

if you had your crystal now, you could tell us exactly where the thief is?"

"Not exactly. But the general area, yes."

"Well," Deyv said, "if this crystal can show you such events, why didn't you know the Yawtl was going to steal your crystal?"

"An excellent question. But one characteristic of us Archkerri is that we tend to get wrapped up in certain problems. When that happens, we often don't notice what's going on around us. I did see the Yawtl in my crystal, but I didn't pay him much attention. After all, the crystal doesn't read the minds of flesh people.

"Furthermore, I have to sleep, unfortunately, and the Yawtl crept up on me and removed the neck-cord, which was attached to my crystal. Of course, when I woke up, I knew everything about the theft. A lot of good that did me then."

"You have no idea why the Yawtl took our eggs and your crystal?" Deyv asked.

"I could find out if I backtracked the thief and if the backtrack didn't fade out too soon. That would be silly. It will be much faster to run him down and then ask him. I could also contact my vegetable brothers and find out. But that process would take a very long time. Besides, I don't have the crystal to do this."

The Archkerri then fell into a reverie from which he didn't want to be roused. Some part of his mind must have been conscious of the outside world, though. He didn't wander off the road. And when he was offered fruit, his hand came out and stuffed it into his mouth.

Deyv asked Vana why the tribes in her land hadn't attacked Sloosh when he first appeared.

"We thought he was a demon or perhaps a god or goddess in a strange form," she said. "By the time we found out he wasn't, we knew he wasn't dangerous. Besides, he told us a lot of things which we found interesting." She paused, then said, "Some of them were frightening. For instance, the world will soon end."

9

SHE said this so calmly that Deyv wasn't sure he'd heard her correctly.

"What do you mean? The world will end? How? When?"

"Ask Sloosh. He knows about it. I don't really understand it."

The Archkerri was quite willing to enlighten him. It took, however, a number of conversations before Deyv could visualize what he described. Even then, he wasn't sure that the pictures in his mind corresponded to reality.

He told Sloosh this, and Sloosh replied, "No one, not even I, can see reality. Our senses filter it out to make sense of it. We make constructs with which we can deal. To see the genuine reality, that is, the totality of it, requires the mind of one who made it. If any Person did make it."

Deyv didn't understand this, and he wasn't sure that Sloosh did either. No matter. He was convinced that what Sloosh told him, the section of reality he described, was true. He had the good sense not to tell Sloosh that, since the Archkerri would then have gone into a long disquisition on the nature of truth.

According to Sloosh, the world had started out as an unimaginably large ball of fire and an equally unimaginable amount of empty space. Really empty, with nothing, absolutely nothing, not even a speck of dust, in it. Or perhaps, Sloosh said, there was only the ball of fire, containing all the matter there was. Which meant that there was only a tiny bit of empty space around it—if any. Then, when the ball exploded, its matter created space as it expanded outward. Or perhaps it expanded inward. Where there was no space, there was no "direction" out or in.

Whether the space was created as the ball blew out or in, or there was already a vast empty nothing for it to explode in, made no difference. Except to Sloosh and his kind. What did matter was that the ball of matter tore itself apart when it blew up.

"What was the ball before it was on fire?" Deyv asked.

"I'll get to that in due time. Please be patient."

The material ejected by the explosion thinned out as it flew through space. It cooled, and it became dust. Some pieces of dust were larger than others. These attracted smaller pieces, and many of them began to form larger bodies. These drew to them still more pieces. Eventually, dust pieces spread throughout the space and among these the bigger ones kept on collecting more matter until the space around them was emptied of most matter.

Some of these formed new balls of fire, much smaller than the original one but still quite respectable in size. The balls of fire attracted other, smaller collections, some of which fell into the larger. But others escaped destruction by going into orbit around the larger, which were the stars. Many stars formed aggregations which circled around a common center, and these were the galaxies. And some galaxies had a supercenter around which they circled.

At the same time, while the galaxies were circling a center, they were traveling outward and the space between them increased. However, the process of forming new stars with their planets went on, so that in the spaces between the stars and the galaxies, new stars and planets were born.

This took an incredibly long time. While some stars were being born, others died. Their fires went out, and they sped black and cold through the universe.

"Toward what?" Deyv asked. "Wasn't there a wall they would eventually crash against?"

"Perhaps. But that wouldn't be a tangible wall. It

would be a wall composed of limitations. Of principles."

Eventually, the big and small pieces of dust in space were so far apart from each other that they had no aggregate effect on space itself. They couldn't create more space. So, their force lost, they started falling back. And space itself began to shrink, following the retreating matter.

Meanwhile, during this process, one of the stars had gathered to its round bosom some children. The planets. One of these was Earth, the planet on which Deyv and Sloosh were now talking. At this time, Sloosh didn't want to go into how air and water had been formed on Earth and how life had originated. But he would say a few words now on how life had developed from a simple one-celled creature to a complex creature with a nervous system capable of self-consciousness.

Deyv later thought that these few words must have been twenty thousand or so.

"Then mankind was the first sapient creature?" Deyv observed.

"Yes. Your kind is much more ancient than mine. And, like the even more ancient rat and cockroach, it's survived in an essentially unchanged form. Though those two have given rise to new forms which survive along with the ancestral forms."

Man had come up from an apelike creature to his present form. He had gone through savagery to a state in which he had had great power. Sloosh described some of this power, which to Deyv seemed like magic. But, time and again, man had reverted to savagery, only to begin the slow painful climb toward power again. Power was the ability to change one's environment and to make the tools, social or physical, with which to do this.

During man's long stay here, he had visitors from other stars and he had ventured to other stars. He had also made new forms of life or altered those pre-existing forms.

"Three times the Earth would have been utterly destroyed," Sloosh said. "But, fortunately, during those times man had the power to save himself and his planet."

Deyv grasped only a fraction of the explanations of moons, red giants, and black dwarfs. He could visualize somewhat, though, how the blazing yellow star that was the sun had expanded into a red giant. Before that occurred, man had moved Earth far out into space. To provide heat and light, man had turned Earth's moon into a small artificial star. Thus Earth had escaped the vaporization of the sun's inner planets.

"When the sun went into its helium-burning stage," Sloosh said, "Earth was moved back into an orbit closer to it. And it was moved out again, this time with another planet as its little sun, when the sun went into its second red-giant stage. Now the Earth was a moon around the planet-become-a-sun. When this burned out, another planet was used, and then another.

"During all this time, man's civilizations crumbled a number of times. But he was lucky enough to have risen to great power each time his planet had to be saved.

"Long, long before this, matter had reached its limits and was falling back toward the center of all things. Stars died; stars were born. Finally, Earth's sun became a black dwarf. You can see it as a tiny dark speck against the blaze of the jam-packed stars and gas sheets when The Beast is not up. The Beast, by the way, is a gigantic cloud of burned-out galaxies. It shows up during Earth's very slow rotation on its axis."

Deyv looked toward the horizon. A band of bright light existed along it. When The Beast had dipped out of sight, all the sky would blaze, mottled here and there by single black dots or larger black shapes. These were sometimes referred to as The Beast's Children, the largest of which had names.

Deyv choked a little before he could speak again.

"The time will come, you say, when the stars will be so close together that their heat or other radiation'll kill all life on Earth?"

"If the earthquakes don't destroy it first. The in-

fluence of so many celestial bodies so close to Earth is
responsible for the quakes. There won't be any volcanic
eruptions—I explained those to you—because the center
of the Earth has cooled off. One of the sources of
power the ancients used was the molten nickel-steel
core of this planet. They tapped it, and now the core
is cold, or perhaps I should say lukewarm. Also, they
mined a certain amount of the core for its nickel and
iron. There wouldn't be any iron of any significant
amount in the upper levels of the Earth's strata if the
metals hadn't been brought up from the core."

"How long do we have?" Deyv asked.

"Perhaps a hundred generations as you humans
figure generations. That estimate is based on the death
from heat. I can't predict what effect the earthquakes
will have. It may be that long before the jam-packed
stars blind all eyed-life and then cook it. Or this land
may be torn up soon and life swallowed by the
cataclysms. Or this land may sink into the ocean."

Sloosh had explained that all land was now one
mass. Once, there had been a single land mass, long
before man evolved, and then this had broken up into
land masses. These wandered over the face of the
planet, came together again, split, wandered, and
coalesced again. Parts of the land masses had sunk and
become seas and then risen again. And so on and so on.

"This land stretches along the equator around the
planet, but its two ends do not meet. All the rest is
water. Not salt water but fresh. The last ancient people
removed the salt from the ocean, perhaps two thousand
generations ago. It wasn't the first time."

At the moment, the ground felt solid, and Deyv had
no sensation of moving. Yet, if what Sloosh said was
right, he was falling toward the fiery doom. He
wouldn't see it, but his descendants would. Or, if he
didn't have any progeny, his brothers' and sisters'
would.

Vana had heard all this from the Archkerri when he
had resided in her tribe's area. "Sloosh is very wise, and
he knows much," she said to Deyv. "But he can be

wrong. He is no god or goddess. My shaman said that if Sloosh was right, then our religion would be wrong. Therefore, Sloosh must be wrong."

"But he knows all about the past," Deyv said. "So how could he be wrong about the future?"

"He doesn't know all about the past. What he says about it is a pack of lies."

"Sloosh doesn't know how to lie."

"*He* says! Would you take the word of a liar? But perhaps I'm being too harsh. Let's say that he isn't a liar but is badly mistaken. That is what our shaman said about him."

Sloosh's account didn't agree with Deyv's religion either. But he felt that perhaps the Archkerri had access to a greater power than did the Turtles' shaman. Wasn't Sloosh a brother to the trees and the grass? And weren't the trees and the grass the hair of Mother Earth herself? Weren't they, according to his tribe's religion, also Her earliest children? He told Vana this.

She said, "Maybe Sloosh is right. I don't like to say that. But perhaps, just perhaps, and may my ancestors forgive me if I speak against the shaman, Sloosh knows what he's talking about. If so, so what? You and I will live out our lives and our children theirs and their children theirs. I can't imagine a hundred generations. It's too far off for me to worry about it.

"We'll have children and grandchildren, if we're lucky. And we'll eat and drink and have fun. And then we'll all die. And the fate of the world will be no concern of ours.

"Meanwhile, we have to find that thief and get our soul eggs back and then get back to our families. And some day I'll be an old woman, and then I'll die. And my tribe will eat me, and—"

"What? Your tribe will eat you?" Deyv asked.

"Of course."

That she was a cannibal shocked him much more than the impending end of the world.

10 ⋖§

THE Yawtl had made the mistake of trespassing into a village instead of robbing isolated individuals. His ghostly red trail led his pursuers to the edge of the village. These people had no House but lived in wooden thatch-roofed houses inside a tall log stockade. There seemed to be many women and children in the village and a shortage of men. A dead man lay in the center of the village, and a shaman and the women danced mourning around him.

Deyv, looking down from a tree, noted that the corpse's soul egg was missing. When he descended, he and Sloosh put together what they had observed. Sloosh concluded that the Yawtl had been surprised while lifting the egg. During the struggle, the man was slain. The tribe, aroused, had chased the Yawtl, and then most of the warriors had taken off after him.

The Archkerri followed the trails to the highway. Evidently the thief had fled down this road, continuing the same course. Unless he had a big lead on the would-be avengers, he would not, however, stay on it long.

While they were traveling at a faster-than-usual pace on the road, Deyv questioned Sloosh.

"Why do you think the Yawtl went so far afield to get the eggs? Why didn't he just pick tribes near his area and then waylay individuals in the jungle? Wherever he lives, it's a long way from my land."

The huge eyes in the cabbage-head closed. After a while, they opened.

"I'd say that he was looking for eggs of a special kind. Not just anybody's would do. Don't ask me what kind. I don't know."

The wind had shifted toward them right before sleep-time. Just as they were talking about retiring into the jungle, Jum bristled and growled. They couldn't see anything ahead on the road, but Deyv knew that someone was coming.

From behind the foliage they saw the returning warriors. They were tall, long-legged wiry men with almost-black skins, very thin lips, large hooked noses, long straight black hair, and dark-brown eyes. They were barefoot and wore fringed blue kilts, orange belts, and human skulls on top of their heads. These were secured by straps under their chins.

Their weapons were blowguns, stone axes, spears, and swords made of wooden blades with the tips of sharp stones set along the edges.

This was of passing interest. What riveted the hidden watchers was the person in the middle of the band. He was shorter than the others, of stocky build, and his body was covered with a fox-red fur. The face was near-human, though the jaws protruded considerably and the eyes slanted like a coyote's. His ears were like a wolf's. The pale-red face itself was hairless except for a broad black furry band across the reddish eyes. His nose was as round and black as Jum's. He wore a black breechclout, and if he had had any weapons, they'd been taken from him.

His hands were tied in front of him.

One of the warriors was carrying a leather bag. This had to contain the soul eggs.

Deyv groaned, "What do we do now?"

There was only one course. Or so Deyv and Vana thought. Sloosh was of another mind.

"I was willing to pursue the Yawtl as long as he continued in the same direction I was going. I would even have gone out of my way, if it wasn't too far, to help you. I find you very interesting, if a trifle pathetic. Also, there was the somewhat fascinating mystery of why he would want the eggs. These are useful only to their owners. Or so I'd assumed until now.

"But to try to get the eggs from this tribe, when the

odds are so high against us, is to be irrational. Not to mention stupid. The two are not necessarily the same, you know.

"I don't place a high value on my life. Even so, if I lose it, I'd like it to be for something of high value. So, I'll just continue on my way. I wish you good fortune, though I doubt very much you'll have it."

The Archkerri stopped talking until the slight temblors of the latest quake ceased.

"But your crystal?!" Deyv said.

"I'll be handicapped without it. However, I have enough confidence in my own intelligence to believe that I can make my way back to my land. I'll get another one there. And then I'll resume my interrupted quest.

"By the way, have you ever contemplated life without your soul eggs? Are they really vital?"

"You're crazy," Vana said.

There was a silence for a while. Finally, Sloosh opened his eyes. He said, "I've traced my line of thought. It's rational and analytic. No. I'm not crazy."

"What did you mean by 'quest'?" Deyv asked.

"Two, actually. My first concern was to locate a certain artifact reported to be in the area of Vana's tribe during my grandfather's youth. Since I'm a specialist in that kind of artifact, I went to that area. But shortly after I got there, a particularly big quake buried it. I couldn't get the locals interested in assisting me to dig it up. So I stayed a little while to study the natives."

A little while, Deyv thought. Long enough for Vana to grow up.

"Then I set out for the second and more important phase of my quest, during which the thief stole my crystal."

He pointed upward. Deyv looked but could see nothing except the blackness of The Beast and a few birds.

"Those mysterious figures which float over the sky from that direction," Sloosh said. "For countless generations my people have tried to interpret them."

"Why do you care about them?" It was difficult expressing anger with a whistle, but Vana managed. "You know your people'll be dead within one hundred generations. So why bother?"

"Knowledge is a joy and a beauty. I would seek it if I knew I would perish a second after I'd gained it. Or a second before, too. The quest for knowledge is as thrilling as the thing itself."

"Go on your own way!" Deyv said. "We don't need you! In fact, you'd be a great hindrance!"

"Why is that?" the Archkerri asked calmly.

"You're too slow. If we have to run, and we will, you couldn't keep up with us!"

"Undeniably so."

"You're a pain in my ass," Vana whistled.

"Very poetic," Sloosh said. "I must use that some time."

Deyv threw his hands up. What could you do with such a creature?

The Archkerri ambled away without another word. Deyv turned to the woman. "It's up to us. Maybe we can think of something to do on our way back to the village."

Between them, they worked out a plan. It was not one to lift up their spirits. So much depended on exact timing and on the circumstances being such that they could carry out the plan.

They proceeded cautiously down the path leading to the village. Long before they reached it, they could hear, faintly, the beating of drums and the shrilling of flutes. Some time later, they could also hear the high-pitched chanting of the tribe.

Just before the clearing outside the stockade, they stopped. Vana and Deyv went up a tree to look the place over. But a horde of stink-roaches poured out of a hole and attacked them. The two slid and jumped back down as swiftly as they could. They landed on the ground bruised, bark-torn, and covered with a vile spray. It stank so badly they could scarcely endure themselves. The dog and the cat sped away and cowered behind some bushes. The humans could do nothing else but go to the nearest stream and hope they could wash off the retch-making stink.

Deyv had managed to glimpse inside the stockade just before the attack. When they had slid into a muddy stream, he said, "Those people have tied the Yawtl to the man he killed and hoisted both from the arm of a pole. I didn't see the bag with the eggs."

"Then it could be anywhere."

"It might be in the shaman's hut. That's the biggest one, and it's in the center of the village."

"Perhaps we could get over the wall and sneak around to it while the black people are busy with the Yawtl."

"That's no good," Deyv said. "The villagers have dogs. They'd smell us if we were anywhere near. In fact, I'm surprised they didn't smell us when we were on the tree."

"The tree is so close to the village they must be used to the stink."

They left the creek. About the only effect the bathing had was to clear the immediate area of fish, amphibians, and snakes. No, there was another. The flies were no longer crawling over them.

"If they would go to sleep, we could do something," Vana said. "But we'd have to do it quickly. The dogs might be used to roach odor coming from the tree, but they'd notice at once if we got within the stockade."

Deyv said, "You know, we really don't have to do anything now. All we have to do is wait. After they've tortured and killed the Yawtl, they'll go back to normal living. We can hang around and watch them. When our chance comes, we'll strike."

"That might not be so easy. The longer we're here, the more chance we give them to discover us. I think we ought to hit now. They'll be very excited and preoccupied with the Yawtl, so they won't be as alert as usual."

Deyv thought about this. Then Vana said, "Besides, I'm afraid that I might lose my courage. I'm keyed up now. But hiding in the jungle and watching them could cool me off. I'd see so many reasons not to take a chance that I'd get too cautious."

"You could be right. Anyway, if we don't succeed this time, and we escape, we can always come back later."

"I don't know how long I can endure it without my soul egg. I don't know about you, but the emptiness and the meaninglessness increase all the time. There are times when I think I'll just sit down and die. Get the horror over with."

For the first time, Deyv looked at Vana with genuine sympathy. It was so powerful that it came close to empathy.

He rose and said, "In any event, we have to watch them. So let's go." He took her hand and pulled her up. At the same time, despite his surge of feeling for her a moment ago, he thought, She's an eater of human corpses.

He could never marry her or even lie with her. But that didn't mean that he couldn't like her—to some extent, anyway. If she were a male cannibal, she could be his friend. So why should her being a woman make a difference?

For some undefinable reason, it did.

Some time later, they were on a branch high up in a tree. This was roachless, though it did have some tiny pesky ants. They could see everything within the stockade. It looked as if almost the entire population was getting drunk. The exceptions were the dogs, chickens, pigs, the four guards, and the Yawtl. Even the children, babies at the breast, were being plied with alcohol. In addition, a bonfire in front of the shaman's house was covered from time to time with some kind of plant. This burned, emitting a greenish smoke through which the people walked slowly from time to time. Evidently, they were breathing it in. And they found it even more exhilarating than the liquor.

Neither Deyv nor Vana knew what the plant was. It certainly wasn't anything like the drugs their tribes used.

At each corner of the square stockade wall was a roofed platform holding a guard. Ladders led from each guard post to the grounds inside the stockade. The guards were, aside from the prisoner, the only unhappy ones in the village. They didn't like it at all that they couldn't join in the celebration. Deyv wished that they could. It would make it easier for him and Vana to get over the walls.

In the middle of the open square was a tall vertical post, across the top of which was a shorter post. From one arm of the T, two ropes had been attached. The other ends of the ropes held the dead man by his waist and the Yawtl by his. The latter was face to face with the corpse, his wrists bound to its. His toes were just touching the ground.

So far, only the children were allowed to touch the Yawtl. Encouraged by their laughing elders, they beat on his legs and buttocks with light sticks or threw mud and pig dung at him. Once, a toddler drenched him with the liquor, but he was reprimanded for wasting it.

As time went by, the drummers and flutists fell into rhythms of their own, each wrapped up in his small tight world, ignoring or unaware that he was out of beat with the others. The shaman's dance became a series of staggers, and the bullroarer he'd been whirling above his head sometimes struck the ground. A woman fell into the fire and had to be dragged out. She was lucky that anyone noticed her.

"I'm glad that smoke isn't blowing our way," Deyv said. "If it was, we'd probably fall out of the tree."

They munched fruit and brushed off the ants. Jum and Aejip waited patiently at the foot of the tree. One by one, sometimes by twos, the tribespeople dropped off. The children were first. Then the men and women. The shaman kept up the travesty of a dance, stumbling over bodies, laughing, striking the fallen with the bullroarer. Perhaps it was the exercise that kept him going after everybody else was out. But the time came when he could go no longer. He toppled while breathing in the greenish smoke.

Deyv, coming down the tree, saw this just before the top of the stockade cut off his line of sight.

When they got to the edge of the open area, Deyv ordered Jum and Aejip to wait. He planned to return to this spot, where the animals could ambush any pursuers.

The guard nearest them had been looking outward. It seemed a futile duty. If he did see attackers and gave a warning, he'd be able to alert only the other sentinels. Ten warriors could have taken the village easily and butchered the sleepers at leisure. Deyv left Vana and circled the open area, keeping behind the foliage, until he was opposite her. Then, summoning up his courage, he stepped out. Vana came out of the bush a second later.

He had expected to be seen at once, but just as he emerged he saw the two guards on his end of the stockade turn away. They were shouting and gesturing with their spears at something inside the walls. The dogs were barking as if they'd cornered a tree-lion.

11

DEYV didn't know what was causing the agitation. He didn't care. This was a lucky break which he was going to take advantage of. Holding his blowgun in one hand, he sped toward the stockade. Through the dim light he could see Vana's white body, her legs moving, a long blowgun in one hand. They'd planned to dash up and shoot the nearest guards with the poison darts. If they missed, they'd have to dodge some thrown spears. But they might be able to entice the two guards to pursue them.

If that happened, which really wasn't likely, Deyv would lead them to Aejip and Jum. Or if one took off after Vana, he would have to follow her into the jungle, if he was foolish enough to do so. Vana could get him with her dart then.

The plan had a lot of *if's*, all fueled by desperation. It wasn't hopeless, though, because there were only four men to deal with. And now the gods favored him. For a little while, anyway. He didn't ask for any more time than that.

The guard nearest him disappeared, going down the ladder inside. The others, however, stayed at their posts. They didn't see Deyv or Vana. Their attention was fixed on whatever was going on below. Deyv shifted his blowgun to his left hand and removed the coil of rope from his shoulder. When he got to the corner of the stockade, he threw its loop up. It caught on the pointed end of a log, and he tightened it.

Vana got to her corner about thirty seconds later. She had a little more distance to cover than he did and was not as swift a runner. She placed the dart in her pipe but did not shoot at once. She had to get her wind back first.

The guard above her still hadn't seen her.

Deyv thrust the blowgun into its case and hauled himself up hand over hand, his feet braced against the rough bark. The guards were still yelling. The dogs seemed to have gone crazy.

Halfway up, he saw Vana drop the dart into her gun. When he reached the top of the stockade, he saw her lift the gun to her lips. Something whitish sped out from the pipe. He was too busy then to watch the aftermath.

His hands gripped the conical top of the log, and he pulled himself up and over. He rolled onto the platform but did not get up. The guards at the other corners might see him. Here, in the half-light under the roof, he might be unnoticed as long as he didn't silhouette himself.

He looked to his right. The guard there was visible only as a dim motionless bulk on the floor behind the railing. Vana had got him with her first shot. The

poison of the striped hole-beetle had taken almost
instant effect. The guard would have felt the sting of
the sharpened point and would have whirled, startled.
Before he could cry out a warning, his muscles would
have been locked. A second or two later, he would
have fallen. And now he would be close to death, his
heart convulsing.

Deyv would have liked to raise his head to look over
the wall. Vana, however, would be running toward his
corner now. He'd been lucky enough that he wasn't
seen when he'd come over the top.

The guard who'd left his post was in the middle of
the village now. He was doing something with the
Yawtl. Ah! The prisoner had somehow gotten one arm
loose; it flailed out for a moment. Now the guard had
grabbed it again and was trying to tie it back to the
dead man's wrist. The Yawtl had twisted his head
around, and he'd bitten the guard on the nose.

Screaming, holding his nose, the guard backed away
and fell backward over one of the dogs. The other two
guards were coming down the ladders now to help.

Another lucky break. Deyv rose, crouching, and went
quickly down the ladder. On the ground, he ran alongside the wall until he came opposite the shaman's hut.
Then he dashed down the lane between two rows of
huts to the back side of his goal. It had no rear doorway,
and the windows were too small for him to crawl
through. Like it or not, he had to use the front
entrance.

He spared a second to look up over the conical roofs.
There was Vana, outlined vaguely against the light.
Suddenly she was gone. She had come up the rope like
a squirrel and was on her way. Wherever and whatever
it was.

He raced around the shaman's house. He glimpsed
the guard whose nose had been bitten. On his feet now,
the man was surrounded by barking and snarling dogs.
His spear was raised, butt first, ready to come down on
the back of Yawtl's head. The other guards were almost
to him.

The interior of the shaman's hut was dark, its only light feeble, coming from the two back windows and the doorway. He blundered around, feeling with his hands, tripped over something, and swore. He rose and began groping along the walls, thinking that if the bag of eggs was here it would be on a shelf. And then he almost cried out with exultation. His hand had closed on leather and within it were at least ten round objects which had to be the soul eggs. But he had to make sure.

He took the bag to the doorway, untied the leather thong, and brought out what he'd hoped for. Since he didn't want to take the time to search for and put on his own egg, though the temptation was almost overpowering, he put the egg back in the bag. Before running out, he paused to look the situation over.

It had changed unbelievably fast. The guard about to hit the Yawtl over the head was down among the dogs. Deyv guessed that the prisoner had kicked backward into the man's stomach or crotch.

There went the Yawtl, somehow freed from his bonds. The fellow must be double-jointed or as slippery as a wet rock. Behind him came the two guards and close at their heels a pack of dogs. One man hurled a spear. Deyv couldn't see if it struck its target, but he didn't think so. The guards weren't shouting triumph, though it would have been hard to hear them over the uproar of the dogs.

Now those dogs that had been concerned with the fallen guard were chasing after the others. They left an open space in which Deyv could see the man. He was on his knees and holding his belly with both hands.

From the direction in which the Yawtl had run, Deyv guessed that he would make for the ladder of the sentinel Vana had shot. That was good. Their entrance route was open for an exit. But where was the woman?

No sooner thought of than she appeared. Panting, she stepped around the corner. Deyv came out of the doorway, grinning, holding up the bag. She squealed with delight and threw her arms around him. He turned his head so that she kissed him on the cheek, not the mouth. He couldn't help thinking, even in this triumph, that those lips had eaten human flesh.

She drew back and said, "Give me my egg!"

"As soon as we get out of here and away from the guards," he said. "We can't spare the time."

She looked hungrily at the bag, but she nodded. "Let's go, then!"

Without asking him which way they should take, she ran around the hut and back down the lane. He would have preferred going to the wall in which the gates were set and then along it back to the guard post. That way there would be less chance of encountering the guards or the dogs. It angered him a little that she hadn't waited for his decision, but there was nothing he could do about it. He went after her, his sword in hand. She still gripped her blowgun.

Before she reached the end of the lane, the Yawtl dashed in front of it. A moment later, some of the big yellow dogs raced barking after him. Then the two guards, and behind them more dogs.

Vana dodged into a house. But one or more of the canines at the rear must have caught her scent. A big brute stopped, whined, then dashed back, barking at the house she'd entered. Five dogs followed him; the others kept on the original chase.

Silently, Deyv sped up to the now-snarling beasts. Two were in the doorway, then one suddenly yelped and fell down. Vana must have shot it or struck it with her tomahawk. By then he was slashing at the three still outside. One died, its spine severed. Another staggered under a slash alongside its neck. The third whirled and bounced away, snarling, its teeth white, dripping saliva.

Deyv glanced sideways. The other dog in the doorway was also crumpled, and Vana was stepping out over the two bodies. Deyv charged the dog, which ran away, then stopped to face him again.

Something small shot over and past him and ended

in the dog's side. Its legs gave way under it, its eyes rolled up, and it was dying.

Deyv waited for Vana. He said, "Good shooting. But you've got only six darts left. Save two for the guards."

Vana said, pointing, "There they go again."

The Yawtl flashed by. Somewhere in his run he'd picked up a spear. Dogs bounded after him, then the two tribesmen. But one of them looked aside and saw the two strangers. His alarmed yell trailed after him down the lane.

From a house nearby a man, head hanging, crawled out.

"Some of them will be waking up," Deyv said. "Follow me!"

He ran between the houses to the right of the broad lane. Vana's feet thudded behind him. They broke out from the cluster and angled toward the corner guardhouse where Deyv had tied his rope. But the Yawtl came around the corner of a house, the dogs snapping at his heels. Some of them were wounded. The Yawtl whirled and plunged his spear into the neck of his nearest pursuer. The others dodged around him, trying to hamstring him. And then some of them saw Deyv and Vana.

That helped the Yawtl for a few seconds, but the two guards, their chests heaving, sweat-covered, appeared.

Deyv ran at the dogs, his sword raised.

The Yawtl hurled his spear, and its stone head drove into a guard's shoulder. He spun then as Deyv sped by him.

A reddish hand reached out and yanked the bag from Deyv's grasp. The Yawtl's howl of triumph faded as he ran down a narrow lane between the houses.

Deyv was shocked. And he couldn't pursue the thief because he was surrounded by dogs. His blade slashed out as he turned to keep them from his legs.

During one of his swift circles, he saw the remaining guard clutch his chest and fall on his face.

Four dogs lay dead from his sword, and two had

limped off howling. One fell from Vana's dart. Another.
The four survivors fled his charge.

"Did you see that?" he gasped.

She shook her head. Her face was pale.

"Go after him! I'm out of breath!"

The man who'd awakened staggered out from between two houses. He held a spear, but he didn't seem
to know what to do with it. Deyv chopped its head off
with his blade, and he half-cut the man's arm off with
another stroke. Breathing heavily, his legs feeling a
little tired, he ran after Vana. He found her lying on
the ground, face up. A bruise across her forehead
showed where the Yawtl had struck her with the butt
of his spear.

Her unconsciousness lasted only a minute. Still, she
didn't know where she was or who Deyv was until he
had helped her halfway to the sentinel platform. He
told her what had happened.

"Our eggs! They're gone!" She began sobbing.

He didn't say anything. He felt a burning anger. At
the same time, he felt humiliated. The Yawtl had
made a fool of him.

She had to be supported to the ladder. When he saw
she couldn't get up without falling, he hoisted her on
his back and carried her up the ladder. She sat on the
platform a minute or two, then said, "I can get down
the rope by myself."

Deyv blew on his bone whistle. Jum and Aejip burst
out of the foliage and came running. Vana stood up
unsteadily, but she successfully slid down the rope to
the ground. In the village, a few people were beginning
to stir. He thought of setting some houses on fire.
That would keep them busy for a while and delay any
pursuit. However, he didn't want to spend the time on
arson. Besides, they really weren't in any condition to
chase him. By the next sleep-time, maybe, and he'd be
long gone before then.

He untied the rope and dropped it, his weapons, and
the blowgun case. He climbed over the pointed ends of
the log, hung from his hands, and dropped. The soft

mud eased the impact to his feet. He rolled over, and just as he stood up, the animals arrived.

Deyv set Jum and Aejip on the Yawtl's tracks. They sped off silently. He and Vana followed at a leisurely pace until she was fully recovered. They found the animals on the bank of a creek. Jum was running up and down it trying to pick up the scent. Aejip was sitting on her haunches and looking disgusted. Deyv took Jum across the broad shallow stream, but the dog could find no traces anywhere. For a long time, all four went up and down both banks before giving up.

Deyv was sick with the pain of his loss. Yet he could not help admiring the wily, slippery-slick thief.

12

SLOOSH was walking in the middle of the ancients' highway as if he owned it. Hearing Vana's whistle, he stopped and turned slowly. If he was surprised, he had no way of showing it. It was impossible to see any expression on that cabbage-head face—if there was a face under the leaves. For all Deyv knew, the head contained no bones.

"So, you got out alive," the Archkerri buzzed.

"But without our eggs," Vana whistled.

"I knew some time ago that you didn't get them," Sloosh said.

Deyv and Vana stared open-mouthed. Deyv asked, "How could you know that?"

"I saw the Yawtl just before the last sleep-time. He was carrying the leather bag with the eggs."

The thief had come up softly behind him and then run swiftly past him.

"He had the effrontery to slap me on my rear as he went by," Sloosh said. He added a modulated buzz, an abrupt rising and then slow falling to express his indignation. "What's more, he laughed at me."

Deyv ignored that remark. He had just thought of something that worried him. "What about your prism? If he finds out how to work that, he'll always be able to keep ahead of us. We won't be able to sneak up on him because he could see us in it."

Sloosh replied calmly, "He might find out how to operate it. But he won't be able to interpret what he sees in it. However, he might just throw it away if he thinks it's of no value to him. Still, the Yawtl are not only thieves, they're magpies. They find it difficult to abandon anything that looks interesting, even if it is not utilitarian for them. On the other hand, the crystal is heavy, and he might feel that it weighs him down too much. It would then be a battle between his desire for survival and his cupidity. Still . . ."

Deyv waited, impatiently, until the Sloosh had considered all possibilities. Then he asked, "Aren't you interested in what happened to us?"

"Keenly. But there is plenty of time to hear every detail of your adventure. If you have more urgent matters to tell, do so."

Deyv sighed, and he related how the Yawtl had managed to snatch the bag from him. "And don't tell me," he said, "that we should have taken the time to hang the eggs around our necks. We're painfully aware of that."

"Then I won't. But I'll point out that you should also have removed my crystal so you could have brought it to me."

Vana said angrily, "You walked out on us, left us on our own. Why should we bother to chase you down just to give you the crystal when you wouldn't bother to go after it yourself?"

"I mistakenly thought you didn't have a chance of getting the eggs. I supposed that you'd be killed in the attempt or, seeing the futility of it, would give it up. In a sense, I wasn't mistaken. I lacked the data to form a proper conclusion. I didn't know that you two had such determination and vigor. Nothing in your behavior and attitudes had evidenced such strong characteristics.

"As for your returning my prism to me, well, that would have expressed your gratitude. You humans are always talking about gratitude, you know. Maybe it's just talk; maybe you lack it to any great degree but feel that you should exhibit it. A moral trait which is satisfied by being discussed but not practiced. However, since you could not have tracked the Yawtl without me, just as you can't in the future, you could have thanked me by bringing my crystal to me."

"We might have," Deyv said. He didn't believe it, though.

"Does the Yawtl know that you can see his ghostly tracks?" Vana asked.

"I don't know. That would depend upon whether or not he's had extensive contact with my people."

They came to another junction of the highway. Vana got down on her knees and bowed three times. Deyv followed her example. The Archkerri, however, just walked through. Deyv, watching him, was amazed that nothing happened to him. There was no lightning nor any terrible pain transmitted through the surface of the road. He arose and hurried after Sloosh.

"Do you have a pact with the gods?" he said. "Or are you yourself a demigod?"

Sloosh didn't have to ask him what he meant. That brain in the cabbage-head had figured it all out. That is, if his brain was in his head. Since his mouth was in his chest, his brain could be there, too, or perhaps in the lower body.

"Why should I make obeisance to light signals for traffic that ended twenty thousand or so generations ago?"

Deyv was so flabbergasted he couldn't whistle for a moment.

"You mean that the ancients made these signals that long ago?"

"Yes."

"But they're still operating?"

"Why do you insist on commenting on the obvious?"

Vana had overheard most of the conversation. She said, "Then the poles are not gods and their flashing eyes are not really eyes?"

"In a sense, they are eyes. They detect traffic, and when there is a chance of collision they emit the red lights to stop traffic on one road so that traffic on the other may go through unimpeded! But the poles have other means of detection than visual ones."

"What kind of traffic did the ancients have?" Deyv asked. "Why should the ancients worry about people on foot? Or did they ride animals, as the legends say?"

"They rode in great metal vehicles which were suspended above the road by a power which you wouldn't understand without a great deal of explanation. Though I'll be happy to explain. They went at speeds unmatched even by the swiftest of birds. As fast as the greatest of winds."

"By Tirsh!" Vana swore. "Why didn't you tell me what they were instead of letting me make obeisance to them?"

"You didn't ask me about them."

Vana threw her hands up in disgust.

Deyv, using his own language, said, "You *are* a cabbage-head!"

If Sloosh was affected by their gestures and inflections of disgust, he didn't show it. He merely ambled ahead, leaving them standing, looking at each other.

Two sleep-times passed. Except for a pride of spotted lions, they came across nothing disturbing. The lions, however, had just eaten a large animal, and so they only roared at the travelers to keep their distance.

After the third sleep-time, they came to another junction. The Archkerri and Deyv walked through the signals as if they didn't exist. Deyv was amused, though, when he saw Vana start to get down on her knees, then, with a shamefaced look at him, resume walking. Old habits were hard to break.

By then Sloosh had described, in general terms, the

kind of power the ancients' vehicles had used to float and to propel themselves. Sloosh also gave as his opinion that the power source for the signals came from the core of the Earth. There was still enough heat there to supply the power.

"But sometime in the future the heat will be gone, and the lights will cease operating. Or the highway will break someplace, and the circuit through which the power flows, that is, the highway itself, will be severed."

Deyv asked why he had gotten a shock from the highway near the flashing lights.

"I suspect that the quake caused a malfunction. Or perhaps something else did. Whatever caused it, a shock, something like that which a lightning bolt gives, was transmitted for a certain distance along the road. Or perhaps . . ."

Sloosh listed ten other possibilities, none of which Deyv wholly listened to. It was the shock itself, not its reasons, that concerned him.

Slowly, The Dark Beast passed over them and then dipped beyond the horizon. They were thrown to the ground four times by quakes. They came to an intersection where the road had been so violently twisted that the lights were parallel to the ground.

"Amazing stuff the ancients used to make these highways," Sloosh said. "Its stretching capabilities are incredible. Moreover, it has a built-in self-straightening quality. Within thirty sleep-times, this junction will have righted itself, and the signals will be in their normal position. That is, they will be if they're not further disturbed. Which isn't likely."

Deyv asked if the ancients who'd made the roads were the same as those who'd made the Houses.

"No. The House-Makers preceded them. By the time the most recent ancients started to ascend from savagery to civilization, the Houses were deeply buried. Most of them, that is. But the Earth's upheavals and the effects of erosion have exposed many."

Deyv wondered which ancients had made the sword his father had given him.

"I could tell you if I had my crystal."

The rains ceased, and the clouds ceased to drift over. The blazing jampack above made every sleep-time hotter. Their eyes began to suffer from brightness, so they made wooden protectors with narrow slits for their eyes. Now the leaves of the plants stayed curled up longer, the tough thick undersides reflecting the heat and preserving the moisture inside.

"This is the longest time without rain that I can remember," Vana said.

"Not I," Sloosh said.

"How old are you?"

"About six of your generations. If nothing happens to me, I should live about ten more."

The two humans were awed. In his eyes they could be only children. Perhaps he couldn't be blamed for his attitude of superiority. It would be nice, however, if he would not be so frank about it. But then a plant-man couldn't be expected to understand human feelings.

Meanwhile, the Yawtl's pace had slowed. Though he left no tracks on the highway, the color of his linked impressions was getting deeper. According to Sloosh, he could not be more than a sleep-time and a half ahead of them.

"Either he thinks we have given up, which is doubtful," the Archkerri said, "or the heat is fatiguing him. Unfortunately, it is also weakening us. We're pushing harder, but I don't know how long you two can keep this pace up. Your animals are suffering even more than you. And, to tell the truth, I'm not as energetic as I'd like to be."

Finally, the snout of The Beast poked over the horizon behind them. A cooling wind raced ahead of it, and several light showers wet them. As this happened, the leaves and petals of the plants unfolded.

"We're only three-quarters of a sleep-time behind the Yawtl now," Sloosh said. "If only he would decide to take a long rest, we might catch up with him."

"I could stand a long, long rest, too," Vana said.

They were walking toward another junction then. They had to stop for a while because a herd of strange animals was passing through it. These stood about twelve feet high at the shoulders, had four massive legs, and long thick tails. Their necks were very long, terminating in relatively small sleepy-eyed heads about twenty feet from the ground. Their hairless skins were pale gray.

"They look like some of the herbivorous monsters that lived when the Earth was young," the Archkerri said. "Those were warm-blooded, too, but, unlike these, they were not mammals."

The herd passed, and the party resumed their walk, glad for the enforced rest. However, when they got to the junction, Sloosh turned onto the road to the left. The humans didn't ask him why. Evidently, the Yawtl had also taken this direction.

After half a sleep-time, the Archkerri left the road and headed for the jungle on the right.

"His impressions don't come back out," he said. "So he didn't go in there just to sleep. Perhaps he is getting close to his home."

There were high mountains straight ahead. If the thief was headed for them, he had about three sleep-times before getting to the foothills. Traveling in the jungle was not so swift as on the open roads.

Before they had gone a few steps into the foliage, Deyv said, "Sloosh, we'll have to quit using the whistles so much. Their sound carries farther than voices. Even though you can buzz softly, you should do so only when it's absolutely necessary."

"In that case," Sloosh said, "why don't you quit using your whistles? I can understand you when you speak Vana's language, you know."

Deyv gritted his teeth, and Vana's face and body grew red.

"Do you mean that we've been blowing these whistles all this time and we didn't have to?"

"Yes," the Archkerri said. "I had thought that was obvious until you made that remark a moment ago. I didn't know you were so stupid."

"By Tirsh and her nameless sister!" Vana said. "Sometimes, sometimes—"

"I see you're angry again, and as usual I have no idea why. How could I have correlated my buzzes to the sounds of your language unless I could understand them? I thought you knew but just wanted to practice with the whistles so you could be fluent with them. So . . . that's why Vana's tribe never spoke to me but always used their whistles."

Deyv suddenly broke into laughter. "He's right, Vana. We have been stupid."

Sloosh said, "I suggest, though, that when we get to a place where the whistling won't be so dangerous, that you resume it. You could get out of practice, and that might cause trouble in certain situations."

The three sleep-times passed with only one incident of note occurring. Going down the winding path which the Yawtl had taken, they came around a bend. And there, only forty feet away, was a thing-with-a-nose-like-a-snake. Deyv, who was in the lead, froze. Jum and Aejip came up close alongside him, but they made no move to continue. Nor were they growling. Vana gasped, but she made no noise after that. Sloosh stopped. His buzzer was silent, but under its leaves his chest-mouth smacked its lips.

All of them had known for some time that something unusually perilous was in the vicinity. The uproar of birds and beasts had suddenly died down, and a tense, heavy silence prevailed. The party had gone on ahead, though they moved slower than usual. Here was the cause of the breathlessness.

The huge purple-skinned biped stood for a minute as fixed as they, except for its waving yellowish nose. Its purple eyes were upon them. The strangely human hands were held out in front of it, the fingers bent, the yellowish claws glinting in a beam of light falling through a hole in the dark ceiling of the forest.

Then it snuffled, turned, and disappeared into the foliage. Though it stood twice as high as Deyv and must have weighed three times as much, it made no sound.

Deyv held up a hand to indicate that the others should keep on being statues. Slowly, he turned to look behind him. The thing might not be hungry. Its gorillalike belly looked as if it were stuffed. But it might be planning to leap upon them from the jungle.

Time passed, and then suddenly the clangor of animal life burst out. Deyv sighed with relief. It had passed on, and he hoped that it never came back this way again. At least not while he was in the area.

It took Deyv some time to get over his shakes, and Vana didn't get control of herself any sooner. Sloosh seemed unaffected, which meant nothing. Who could tell what was going on behind those leaves?

The tail-end of The Beast had a quarter of the sky to go before it disappeared. They came to the foothills. The long dryness had been overcompensated for by especially long hard rains. These had slowed down the Yawtl. But they had also made the going difficult for his pursuers. Nevertheless, they were keeping up with him until they came to the open end of what looked like a tunnel under the mountains.

13⋘

THEY stood before the entrance in a driving rain that made all of them miserable. Aejip, as was the wont of cats, suffered the most. Somehow, she identified being drenched with humiliation, and it hadn't done any good for her temper. Deyv, long familiar with the cat, knew better than to get near her during these times. So did Jum. Sloosh and Vana, however, had to learn the hard way. The woman still had a wound on her leg, not deep, which she'd gotten earlier when she had tried to console the cat. It had taken her some time to heal it. She'd sat down, and she'd closed her eyes and mentally explored her body, finding the exact healing agents, sending them to the location of the wound, urging them to fight the bacteria and to build up the flesh that would close the scratches.

Deyv tried to urge her to go on, to ignore the wound, letting the normal processes heal it. Vana had said, with a validity against which he couldn't argue, that if she allowed the wound to go untreated, it might get to a point where she couldn't control it. The jungle swarmed with invisible evil agents, and they drifted near or brushed against every opening, looking for a way in.

Sloosh didn't object to the interruption in their chase. The Yawtl couldn't get away. His red trail would lead them to him; there was no way he could cover it up.

But now they stood before a pipe which was large enough for all but the plant-man to traverse. The humans could go through it at a slight crouch. He, however, would find it very hard to travel through. He'd have to bend his upper trunk parallel to it, and his lower torso would have to bend its legs considerably.

"I can stand it for some time," the Archkerri said. "If the pipe extends a great distance, though, I'll become immobilized. My strength is much more than yours, but I am not capable of matching your suppleness. Sometimes, a big size is a disadvantage. This seems to be one of those situations."

"What is the pipe?" Deyv said.

"This pipe is *a* pipe," the Archkerri said. "I don't know what *a* pipe *is*. I can describe a pipe for you. You would understand a pipe, then, as an ideal, though the description might not fit what others would consider a pipe. *The* pipe *is*—what? Verbal equivalence—"

"Please, let me rephrase my question," Deyv said. "What is this metallic tunnel for? Who built it? And why?"

"I don't know. If I had my crystal . . . Sometimes, I wonder if my brothers, the trees and the grass, are giving me the correct data. Or they might be giving the data correctly, but then they have their own ways of recording, and during the passing of data to them to me, something is distorted, lost, translated incorrectly."

"She who knows all knows nothing," Vana said.

"Is that a proverb of your tribe?" Sloosh asked.

"Who cares?" Deyv said angrily. "Evidently, you haven't the slightest idea where this pipe comes from, who built it, or why it was made. Really, it doesn't matter. What does is that you're as ignorant as we are."

"No," Sloosh said. "What matters is that we don't know where the other end comes out. Or if there are perhaps many branchings of it. What matters even more is that I can't go into the pipe. Rather, I should say, I can go into it. But will I be able to get out the other end? I know I won't be able to back out if I go too far into it."

Deyv felt good because the huge, very strong, very knowledgeable creature was inferior in some respects to him.

"What I see here," Deyv said, "is that we can go through this pipe. I mean, all of us except you. This pipe may have junctions, like the roads. But which path do we follow if it does? We won't know which to take, since you won't be present to follow the Yawtl's impressions."

"Excellently put," the Archkerri said. "So, you four enter this while I go over the mountains by myself and hope that I come to an area where I can pick up the Yawtl's impressions. But if the pipe has many branchings, you might come out in a place I won't be near. We might lose touch with each other. You might accidentally follow his trail, but I might not be where I could see it. After all, my psychic ability to see the impressions has, coincidentally or not, the same distance limits as my visual perception."

Vana said, "I think it's better for all of us to go over the mountains together. Then we can see the whole situation, see where the trail comes out. Nothing will be lost doing that. But if we go into the pipe alone, we may get lost. And we don't even know if it *does* come out the other side. And if there are branches, we could get lost. Who knows where they go? They might lead us out of the mountain area, maybe back into a branch that comes out on this side of the mountain."

Deyv said, "What you're saying is that Sloosh might go to the other side and see nothing. He needs to be on both sides but he can't."

What a wily person the Yawtl was! He must have known the dilemma he posed when he went into the pipe. Or did he? That depended on whether or not he knew the tracking abilities of the Archkerri. And also if he knew this pipe. If he was familiar with it, then he would know where its branchings—if any—were.

"You can see the Yawtl's impressions whether or not they're in the dark?" Vana asked.

"Yes," Sloosh said. "But I can't see any farther than I can with my eyes in full light."

"It can't be more than a mile through this mountain," she said. "Do you think you could endure that distance?"

"I don't know. The question is, is it worth it to me to attempt that distance? Another question, even more pertinent, is, will it be only a mile? If the trail leads into branchings, and it could, what then?"

"We'll go over the mountain instead of through it," Deyv said. "If Sloosh doesn't see the tracks from there, then we can backtrack and see if they come out this side."

"But," Vana said, "they might not come out on the other side. What if the pipe has a branch that comes out where Sloosh can't see? And what if it doesn't come out of the mountain at all?"

This was a valid suggestion. But Deyv felt that they must come to a quick decision. The possibilities were so many that they could argue for a long time. Meanwhile, the Yawtl was traveling through the pipe. More likely, he had already done so.

Sloosh said, "In any group, there should be one leader. So far, we've not been able to determine that. I would assume the position, since I'm more intelligent, that is, in my definition, more knowledgeable than you two. But you humans have something which we Archkerri don't have. That is, a fierce drive toward leadership. That is, some of you have it and some don't. But there is among you always the feeling in a group that one person should be the leader. The idea of committeeship—"

"I don't want to discuss that idea now," Deyv said. "One of us should be the chief. We need quick decisions, not one arrived at after many long discussions, sometimes so late that the problem has been succeeded by another and the first is dead."

"All right," Vana said, looking angry. "You can be the leader. Now. But if you don't make the right decision, then you're out. And I'm in. I think I'm as quick and accurate as you are. But—"

"That is good thinking, Vana," Sloosh said. "So, we'll go over the mountain. And we'll see what we'll see."

"Good," Deyv said. "Only I'm sending Jum through the pipe. This is a situation where his sense of smell should be right on the nose—if you'll pardon my pun."

"Ah," the Archkerri said. "I forgot about that. In certain circumstances, the dog's abilities in tracking can be as good or even better than mine."

Jum didn't like Deyv's commands, but he entered the pipe. The others started climbing the slopes.

It took two and a half sleep-times. Deyv worried about the dog. What if Jum got lost and couldn't find his way out? It was possible that the Yawtl would pass through water, in which case Jum would lose his scent. Moreover, there might be predators in the pipe which could quickly dispose of Jum.

They came around the shoulder of the peak, half of which towered almost vertically above them. Below, at the foot, was an immense valley. It was covered with forest except in the middle, where a river ran. Far to their left, the valley was blocked by something gigantic and shiny green. From this distance it was impossible to tell what it was. Water flowed around its sides, forming two cataracts.

Directly opposite them was a mountain even more precipitous. Beyond that, more peaks.

"If the pipe has one or more terminations on this side," Sloosh said, "we're too far away to see them. Even if they weren't covered by the jungle."

Deyv wondered if he'd ever see Jum again. He felt pangs of guilt about having sent the dog into the pipe alone. Sighing, he started the descent.

Within a sleep-time and a half, they were by the river. This was about half a mile across and, judging by its smooth green surface, at least as deep.

The Archkerri studied the river for a moment and said, "We're in luck. I can see the impressions of the Yawtl out there. He went that way."

He pointed through the thick brush and giant trees along the bank. Aejip disappeared to hunt. There was plenty of fruit here, so the three had no trouble stuffing themselves. Just as they were about to look for a good sleeping place, they made a discovery. It was the site where the Yawtl had recently fashioned a dugout. Chips of wood, the trunk of a small tree, branches, and severed liana made this obvious.

"He used an *iyvrat* tree," Deyv said. "Its wood is very soft; he could hack the tree down and chop out its interior in half a sleep-time if he worked hard. There are plenty of *iyvrat* here. We can make our own dugout."

He looked at the Archkerri's great bulk.

"Dugouts, I mean. Do you think you could paddle, Sloosh?"

Sloosh buzzed, "Yes. Your dog has been here, too."

"I know," Vana said. "I just stepped in his mess."

She went to the river to wash her foot. A little later, Jum bounced from the jungle and leaped all over Deyv, his tail wagging, his rear wiggling, his tongue licking. Deyv grabbed him and hugged him and scratched him behind the ears.

"It's evident now that we should have gone through the pipe," Sloosh said. "We might have caught up with the thief while he was making the boat. I'm surprised that Jum didn't—"

"He may have lost his trail for a while in the jungle. The Yawtl could have taken to the trees, you know. Besides, the Yawtl was far ahead of us. Maybe he had time to build the boat and get away before Jum caught up with him. Anyway, I'm happy that he's still well and alive."

"More probably Jum went hunting and so wasted time," Sloosh said. "He can't be blamed for that, though."

They set to work chopping down two trees. Sloosh had no weapons or tools, so he was of no help. He did watch the humans' techniques carefully, though. By the time Deyv and Vana were into the hollowing-out of the trunks, the cat showed up. She was panting and worn out, having dragged a large bird some distance by the neck. When alive it must have stood about six feet high. Its wings were rudimentary; its head was huge and armed with a sharp curving beak. Its three toes bore large sharp talons. Evidently, Aejip had managed to surprise it from above and killed it almost at once. Given a chance, it would have been dangerous prey for Aejip.

Vana and Deyv peeled the skin off with the feathers still on, cut the bird up, and cooked it. All five ate until their bellies bulged, and then they went off to find a good sleeping place. By then carrion birds, insects, and several crocodilian mammals, the *athaksum*, had gathered nearby to clean up. The travelers could hear the furious squabble as they went through the bush.

After the party had slept awhile, though not nearly long enough, they returned to the half-made boats. Aejip went off hunting again. By the time she'd returned, empty-jawed this time, the craft were done.

Paddles were fashioned then, during which time Sloosh fished with a pole, line, and hook Deyv had made. The Archkerri didn't catch anything.

The smaller boat was for Vana and Aejip. The larger was an outrigger, since Deyv figured that Sloosh would tip the boat over easily unless provisions were made to prevent this. They launched the craft, and soon they were heading upriver along the bank, where the current was weakest. Sloosh sat in the rear on his haunches, his front legs folded, an enormous paddle in his hands. Deyv was in the middle, the dog in front of him.

Shortly before it was time to sleep again, Sloosh said, "The Yawtl went over to the other bank. He didn't go ashore there, though. His impressions continue upriver."

They were very tired by then, even though they'd rested often, beaching the boats. Deyv insisted that they might as well make an effort to cross the river. They did so, and they slept ashore. When they awakened, Deyv started to fish, but Sloosh demanded that he be allowed to try it. His failure had disturbed him; he regarded it as a challenge. Deyv went out with Jum, and Aejip went by herself to hunt. Vana looked around for fruit and berries. All got what they wanted, so they set out with stuffed bellies. Most of Vana's pickings were in woven baskets in the boats. They ate these during the rests.

The strange gleaming green object at the end of the valley grew larger. By now they could make out its details. It seemed to be about half a mile wide and almost as high. It was set where the valley walls suddenly narrowed, forming a natural dam. However, when they saw that its surface was cut into facets, Sloosh said that it couldn't be natural.

"What it is," he said, "believe it or not, is a *trishmaging*."

Deyv called to Vana, whose boat was alongside his. "What's a *trishmaging*?"

"It's a beautiful, very rare semitransparent hard stone.

The ancients cut facets into it. My shaman has one like this, though it's very small. Small enough to be worn on a finger if it's set in a wooden ring. The shaman got it during the Trading Season. The warrior who traded it had found five of these stones, each different from the others. They were in the dirt of a hillside washed down by rains along with a few other things made by the ancients. One stone was set in a ring made of a yellow metal. Evidently, the ancients wore the beautiful cut stones in rings."

"But this stone! What sky-high giant wore it in a ring?"

Sloosh said, "Those stones were probably natural. But this one . . . it was manufactured by the ancients. For what reason, I do not know. Perhaps as a dam which the waters would never wash away. I doubt it, though."

Deyv looked at the colossal precious stone with awe. How mighty the ancients! Yet, they had perished, and all that remained of them were a few relics.

14 ✑

THE trail left the river near the foot of the Brobdingnagian stone, where the waters fell in roaring sheets. They followed it into the forest until they came to a very narrow, very deep canyon. This gave them rough access to the other side of the mountain. There they were confronted by another valley, but it was much wider than the one they'd left. Much of it was occupied by a large lake, the other side of which was too distant to be seen. Several miles from the shore was an island. It seemed to consist mostly of steep-sided hills centered around a peak perhaps three thousand feet high. Small black clouds circled around and over the island, settled down on it, or suddenly ascended from it.

"Flocks of birds," Sloosh said.

From the top of the peak something whitish and fluid flowed out, running down the sides in great streaks.

A tiny white object floated up from the foothills of the island and was swept with the wind from the end of the valley. It rose higher and higher, gleaming, then was lost. It was headed toward the other end of the valley, where it could exit between two peaks.

Near the travelers was the freshly cut stump of another *iyvrat* tree, severed branches, and chips.

"He went to that island," Sloosh said. "Whether or not he got there, I can't tell. But he did get near his goal."

Sloosh's doubt was caused by the monstrous fish that now and then surfaced or dived back into the water. They looked big enough to swallow a war canoe of twenty men without straining themselves.

"We could go around the lake and pick up his trail on the other side," Deyv said. "That would put us far, far behind him, though."

"We wouldn't find his trail there," the Archkerri said. "The crafty creature intends to get aboard a young *tharakorm* and sail off with it."

Deyv and Vana asked him what he meant.

"That island must be a breeding grounds for the *tharakorm*. 'Breeding' is not the correct term, though, since the *tharakorm* are not animals. You remember my description of the tiny invisible-to-the-eye creatures called bacteria and viri? Those white streams from the top of the peak are the overflow from a great mass of viri continually duplicating itself. The mass lies in a hollow within the top, and it draws those birds you see circling around within the peak and onto the sides. It does this by emitting a powerful perfume, clouds of molecules which entice the birds.

"As you know, I have no sense of smell, unlike you humans. That is one sense you're up on me, though of course I'm compensated by my greater intelligence, not to mention other senses.

"However, we can observe these molecular masses, which draw the birds as if they were tied to strings. The birds eat the boiling pulsing mass of viri, and they die shortly thereafter. They continue to flock in by the thousands, though they see their fellows die. The dead are used as food by the viri to duplicate themselves. Hence, the continual ferment and flow of the viri down the mountainside."

"I don't smell anything unusual," Vana said.

"That is because the wind carries it off at right angles to us. But when we get near enough, if we get near enough and are not swallowed by a great fish, then you'll smell it."

"Will we be enticed as the birds are?" Deyv asked.

"No. In fact, human beings find the odor most disagreeable."

"Where does all the stuff go?" Deyv asked.

"To the foothills of the island, where it collects in pools and then into hardening clumps. These eventually form into the young of *tharakorm*, those creatures which generate a levitating gas from dead flesh and plants and which sail the winds. That object in the sky you saw a little while ago was one of the young. Ah! See! There is another!"

Sloosh was silent for a moment as they watched the white thing rise and float toward the pass. Then he said, "The Yawtl is on that one. I can just make out the thin reddish line trailing from him."

Deyv was in despair. Even if they could get on a *tharakorm* and take off into the air, how could they ever trail the thief? The winds would change, and the Yawtl's ship-creature would go on a different path from theirs. Their situation was hopeless.

Vana looked pale, and her features were drawn. But she said, "Well, let's get busy."

They set to work and by sleep-time almost had their work done. This time, they were using a single large boat.

When they woke, they saw a great flock of birds flying upwind toward the island.

"More food for the pot," Sloosh said.

"I would think the valley would be cleaned out of birds in a short time," Deyv observed.

"The odor is strong and doesn't thin out entirely for hundreds of miles. And sometimes the supply of birds is low. When that happens, the viri become inactivated. There are long periods when there is no odor emitted. During that time, the birds breed and flourish. Moreover, for some reason, not all birds of each species are attracted, and those that are are usually males. There is a very complicated balance of nature in this, which I hope to study some time. Meanwhile, don't you think we should launch our craft?"

They paddled upwind along the bank for a long time. Then they set out directly toward the opposite bank. They knew that the current would be strong and that it would carry them at an angle downward. They hoped the angle would end on the island. According to Sloosh, the Yawtl had done the same thing as they. Its trail went along the shore and when it turned, they turned too.

Despite the group's fears, the giant fish didn't attack them. Once, one fish chasing a somewhat smaller one, though still large enough to engulf their boat, came up alongside them. An eye, as large as Deyv's head, looked coldly at them. Then it dived, causing a small whirlpool to rock the boat.

As the craft got closer to the island, its occupants could hear the screaming of the birds. A short time later, they smelled the odor. Deyv thought he was going to vomit. Vana looked as if she'd like to. Though they didn't seem sick, the animals were uneasy. Jum whined, and Aejip growled deep in her throat.

The Archkerri said, "From your reactions I'd say that lacking a sense of smell has advantages in certain situations. But then anything that has its advantages also has its disadvantages."

Some of the white stuff had failed to collect in the

hollows and was running off into the lake. Birds were swarming on the rocky beaches and diving into the water. Fish made the offshore water boil as they fought with each other and the birds for the stuff.

The group beached the boat and advanced through thousands of screaming, cawing, shrieking birds. These hopped or ran out of their way but immediately closed behind them. Carcasses lay around by the hundreds, many of them covered with birds tearing at their flesh. Now and then one of the feeders staggered around in circles, then fell, its wings flopping, its eyes glazing.

The stench of decaying flesh was horrible, but it wasn't as bad as the viri perfume. Feathers swirled and fell on or in front of the group. Now and then dung spattered on their hair or skin. Deyv and Vana were in terror that these droppings might infect them.

Sloosh, however, said, "As far as I know, the viri can't attack humans. Of course, I could be wrong."

"Thanks for your reassurance," Deyv said.

At last they got to the hills. Here they roamed around looking for the hollows. They saw some young *tharakorm* being formed in the pools, a fascinating sight. Apparently, first the keel was shaped by the uncountable number of viri. Then the hull was formed as the things lined up row upon row, each virus attached to its neighbors.

"I think the viri go into a sort of suspended animation when they're in place," Sloosh said. "It's a wonderful thing, this organization of mindless nerveless half-alive units. I believe that something that might be called a mind even forms deep in the hull. And lines of them form analogs of nerves. Of course, the brain, if it can be called such, is unconscious. But by the time the *tharakorm*, the ship-creature, is complete, it is ready to take on its symbionts, the *khratikl*."

Deyv looked around nervously. "Where are they?"

"Don't worry. Not yet anyway."

A number of the pools contained only the unformed sticky-looking liquid, in which lay many birds, dead and alive. Some pools had half-laid—half-formed, rather

—keels. Others held almost complete *tharakorm*, which now did not emit the stink. Not until they had gotten to the foot of the mountain, where the odor choked the two humans and brought tears to their eyes, did they find what they sought.

It stood at the bottom of a deep wide hollow supported by buttresses of the hard stuff. These, Sloosh said, would separate from the hull when it was time for flight. The creature had a long and rather wide hull. Its front was shaped like a ship's, but the back part was flared out to make a nearly square stern.

"So it'll give the wind plenty of area to push against," Sloosh said.

Deyv estimated that it was about one hundred and twenty feet long, thirty feet high, not counting the masts, and forty feet across, not counting the flared stern. It had three mastlike projections about ten feet high. On each side, at right angles, thin arms extended for about fifty feet. The sails, so thin that light shone through them, were furled on the bottom arm. Threads ran down the arms to the sails. The whole ship was composed of very thin material, which was semiopaque.

Going closer to look, because the birds swarming over it were obstructing his view, Deyv saw knoblike swellings on the masts and arms. These, Sloosh said, were mechanisms for hoisting or lowering the sails. They also allowed the arms to swing out to a limited degree.

"It can sail against the wind if it's not more than a gentle breeze."

"How can it do that?" Deyv said. "It doesn't have the resistance against the hull that a water boat does."

"It creates a magnetic field which operates with or against the currents of the Earth. But that requires some power, so I suppose the *tharakorm* seldom does anything but go where the wind pushes it. It does, however, have sensors which detect both the strength of the wind and the alignment of earth currents. In former times, I believe, it could tack against stronger winds. But now that the Earth has a more feeble magnetic field, it lacks the power."

There were also round openings on the sides. Deyv couldn't see those on the bottom, but he knew they would be there.

From the top of the hill, he could see that there were three larger openings on the deck.

"Observe," Sloosh said. "The birds are disappearing into the hull. They're being tempted by a perfume even stronger, hence, more enticing, than that emitted by the liquid."

It was true. The avians were fighting to get through the openings.

"They'll be trapped and eaten belowdecks. The *tharakorm* then uses their bodies to generate the gas."

They waited until sleep-time. Sloosh told them they must appoint watches.

"Notice that more birds are settling on it. But a time will come when the birds will suddenly avoid it. You'll smell another type of perfume then. This will drive the birds away. When this happens, the watch must wake everybody up. I can't smell that perfume, of course, but if I'm on watch then, I'll see that the birds are staying away from it."

Deyv didn't ask why this happened. He had figured out that the thing was repulsing the birds so that it could lift up. If it was covered by hundreds of them, it would never be able to get off the ground.

When all were awake, they saw that the time had not yet come for levitation. They sat under the bright hot sky or took short walks. The fruit and berries they'd brought in baskets were eaten. Jum and Aejip devoured some of the newly dead birds. When they wanted water, they went down to the shore and looked for relatively unpolluted water.

"What'll we do for food and water when we're aboard?" Deyv asked.

"We'll suffer until we can endure it no longer," the Archkerri said complacently. "Then we'll punch a hole in the gas containers of the *tharakorm*. It'll sink, and we'll get off when it grounds. That, I imagine, is what the Yawtl will do."

Another sleep-time came. The humans and the Archkerri were getting hungry. But they went to bed, such as it was, with Vana standing watch. It seemed to Deyv he had just shut his eyes when he was awakened. Vana was shaking his shoulder. A very fragrant odor hung in the air.

"It must be time. The birds are gone."

He got up. The others were all awake. At least, he supposed the Archkerri was. He slept standing up.

"Now's the time," Sloosh said.

They went down the hillside and onto the sticky white-streaked mud at the bottom of the hollow. Deyv felt repulsion and some fear. Despite what the Archkerri said, or maybe because of it, he wasn't sure that the stuff wasn't fatal to humans.

Approaching the *tharakorm*, Deyv looked up one of the supports. Then he climbed up its curve, gripping with his hands and walking on his feet like a monkey. While Vana was ascending, he lowered his rope. Sloosh tied the end around Jum, and Deyv hauled the dog up. He repeated the feat with Aejip, whose claws couldn't grip the smooth hard stuff.

Sloosh then tied the rope around the junction of his lower and upper torsos. He bent the latter until it was parallel to the ground, and he began inching up the support. His four thighs gripped the arch of the *tharakorm* and moved in coordination with his two hands. Meanwhile, the two humans pulled on the rope to relieve him of some of his weight. After much sweating and straining, they got the plant-man over the edge of the deck.

He stood up and said, "Now, we'll see if my weight added to yours is too much. I doubt it, since the pack of *khratikl* it carries must be more than our combined weights."

Deyv, Vana, and the cat went belowdecks to explore. Instead of ladders, the thing had grown ramps with corrugated surfaces. These allowed the claws of its symbionts enough purchase to ascend them. They were also good enough for the humans and the cat. But the dog and the Archkerri might have trouble.

There were four decks, each about seven and a half high. The *tharakorm* had a number of rooms and corridors, but most of the ship-creature was walled off. According to Sloosh, the space behind the walls contained the large cells for the gas, the gas-generating organs, the central nervous system, or what corresponded to such, and perhaps space for unknown "equipment" and ballast.

The illumination within was enough to see by. The portholes on the sides and bottom and the entrances on top admitted light. The very thin though hard walls leaked light. Only in the innermost rooms was it so dark that the humans could barely make out their way. The *khratikl*, however, had catlike eyes, so they would have no more trouble seeing than Aejip.

Deyv and Vana went back up and described what they'd found to Sloosh.

"It's like all the others. I've examined a dead, or, to be exact, a nonoperating, one."

They waited. Deyv and Vana became more and more nervous as time passed. Finally, just as it was about sleep-time, the *tharakorm* began lifting. Its ascent was so gentle that they would not have noticed it if their eyes had been closed and if the supports hadn't fallen in the mud with a soft sound. The area around them receded below.

Deyv was frightened. He felt that he was in an unreal situation, one which he'd never experienced before and which shouldn't have ever happened. But there he was. The birds and the island they were on began to shrink, and presently they were over the lake, the island below and behind.

One of the strange sensations was that he didn't feel the wind.

"That's because we're going at the same speed as the wind," Sloosh said.

He was walking around the deck, so Deyv decided

that he could get up. Evidently, the deck wasn't going to tilt if he went to one side of it.

The animals didn't seem to be bothered. Deyv felt somewhat ashamed of his near-panic. However, Vana's paleness and tight voice indicated that she shared his reactions.

The powerful pleasant perfume had faded.

"Soon will come the hard part," Sloosh said.

He estimated they were about five thousand feet high. A thousand feet ahead was the pass. Deyv became alarmed then because it looked as if the *tharakorm* would come very near one side of a mountain.

"I wouldn't worry about that," the Archkerri said. "The two we saw ascend also floated close to that projection of the mountain. There's a reason for it. The reason is what we have to worry about."

The trees along the edge of the outthrust were alive with *khratikl*. Their squeakings and chitterings reached Deyv before he saw them. Then, as the *tharakorm* drifted nearer, he saw the brownish shapes swarming everywhere along the lip. Now he understood what Sloosh had meant. The dangerous animals were waiting for the *tharakorm* as it came along. There would be a race, and those who got there first would be its crew. If you could call them a crew, since they'd have nothing to do with the sailing. All they did was to provide food for the generation of gas. But that was a vital service. In return, the ship-creature gave the crew a splendid chance to feed themselves, to observe from above potential victims, and to swoop down on them. Their feeding territory was constantly changing, and so they couldn't deplete it.

"The Yawtl's impressions go as far as I can see," the Archkerri said. "Evidently, he made it to that point, and he had nobody to help him. However, the tracks of the *khratikl* also go as far as I can see. So perhaps they overcame him. Well, we shall see what we can do."

Before the *tharakorm* got to the nearer edge of the projection, a cloud of *khratikl* dropped off the outer tips of the tree branches. They fell toward the lake, their wings flapping. Presently, long before they neared the surface, they ceased to fall, and their wings caught hold of the air. Then they were coming up toward their intended berth.

Deyv counted about fifty of them.

They came in a closely packed group from ahead and below and then were around their would-be host. Instead of attacking at once, as he had expected, they broke into a circle four deep. Around and around they flew, getting nearer as time went by. Then he could see the rattish faces, the wet dull-yellow incisors, the humanlike hands, the leathery wings, and the yellow eyes. Their cries came to him, and after a while he thought he could detect intonations and rhythms similar to human speech.

Whether they were actually using language or had a system of signals, they didn't sound angry or hostile. They seemed more puzzled than anything else.

The vessel passed beyond the mountain, and soon they were over a broad plain. Beyond that were other peaks, but these seemed less tall. Now the calls from the wheeling beasts were plaintive. No doubt about that. Then one, probably the leader, headed back for the pass, and the others followed.

"By Tirsh, what happened?" Vana asked. She looked as relieved, but as astounded, as Deyv felt.

"I don't know," Deyv said.

"It's a revelation to me," Sloosh said. "But you can't blame me for not knowing what would happen. The crystal never showed me anything like that. And apparently the crystals of my predecessors and contemporaries didn't either. I think, though, that I know why we, and the Yawtl, survived."

There was a long pause while Sloosh stood with his eyes closed. Finally, Deyv, irritated, asked, "Why?"

The Archkerri opened his green eyes. "That opened a path to relevant exploration. Yes. What happened was that the *khratikl* came against a novel experience. They seem to be fairly intelligent, though they are not sentient, that is, capable of self-consciousness. Still, it might be possible that there could be an intelligence equal even to mine which could, at the same time, be without self-consciousness."

Sloosh closed his eyes again.

After a short while, Deyv said loudly, "Sloosh! Where are you?"

"I'm here, where I've always been. I was here when you last addressed me. Oh! I see what you mean. These symbionts of the ship-creature, though they have a certain intelligence, are still primarily guided by instinct. They expect, guided by their evolutionarily programmed genes, to board an unoccupied *tharakorm*. So, when they encountered a *tharakorm* occupied by the Yawtl and one occupied by us, they were in a new situation. They didn't know how to handle it. Thus, instead of attacking us, as true sentients would have, they rejected the situation as outside their instinctual experience. And they returned to the ledge of the mountain to board the next *tharakorm* that comes along.

"However, their programs have been upset. What will happen to those who come back but who should have been comfortably situated? Will they then have to battle with those who expected that they would inhabit the third one? Is there a pecking order that determines who gets in the front of the line? Or is this determined entirely by the age of the *khratikl?* Or . . . ?"

Deyv sometimes found the Archkerri's speculations interesting. Just now he wanted to know how they were going to survive. Everybody aboard was suffering from hunger, and soon they'd all be thirsty.

WITHOUT symbionts to supply food for gas generation, the *tharakorm* would slowly settle. At least, that was Sloosh's theory. However, if the cell walls did seep gas, they were not doing so swiftly enough for the present crew. Its members would be dead long before it touched the ground. At Sloosh's direction, they punched one spot on a wall with the sword and beat it with the tomahawks. The wall, though thinner than Vana's fingernail, was amazingly tough. It took all the time between two sleeps to break through. However, lack of food and water made the job longer. The labor also made them hungrier and thirstier than if they'd been resting. At its end they were utterly exhausted.

A strong wind came up and sped them along for at least a hundred miles. The Archkerri lost the red trail of the Yawtl then.

"We may never find him now," he said. "For one thing, he's alone. He may not be able to make a hole in the cell of his *tharakorm*. Even if he does, he won't be able to do it as quickly as we did. Thus, his *tharakorm* will go much farther than ours. And it is undoubtedly traveling in a different direction from ours. The wind must have shifted and blown him off our path before this big wind came up."

"At the moment," Vana said in a dry, cracked voice, "I care only about getting water to drink. And then some food."

At last the ship-creature landed on the roof of the jungle in the midst of the tossing tops of the trees. The moment it struck, it tilted, and all its crew were rolled off the deck and into the trees. The second it was relieved of their weight, the *tharakorm* soared and was gone.

Deyv, the last to be shed, saw it rise even as he pitched sideways into the foliage. Yelling with fright, he clawed outward. His hands caught liana, which broke, and he fell deeper. Something, probably a branch, struck him, knocking him half-senseless. Somehow, he caught hold of a thin branch. It broke, and he fell flat on his back on a large branch.

The wind was knocked out of him. For a moment, he didn't know where he was. But once his wits were gathered, he knew that he was, for the time being, safe.

Miraculously, nobody was seriously hurt. Sloosh, by far the heaviest, had plunged deeper. A network of liana had finally held him. Jum had landed almost by the Archkerri's side a few seconds later. Unable to hold on to the branch above Sloosh, the dog had been precipitated, howling, onto the plant-man.

Vana was clinging to the end of a branch bending under her weight. She managed to crawl up it to a thicker part. Aejip was hanging on to the trunk, her claws digging in.

It took a long time for Deyv to work his way above the Archkerri and the dog. He tied one end of his rope to the junction of a smaller branch and to that on which he lay. Sloosh tied the other end of the rope to Jum, and Deyv lowered the dog to a big branch. Sloosh went down the rope then, his immensely strong hands and arms gripping it and supporting his six hundred pounds. Deyv expected the rope to break, but it held.

They rested on the branch a long time, eating fruit plucked from surrounding branches. Once his belly was filled and the juices had eased his thirst, Deyv slept for a while. On awakening, he and Vana began the work of getting the dog and the plant-man to earth. When the four of them had reached the ground, they found the cat devouring the decaying carcass of a 10-pound rodent. Deyv insisted that she share it with the dog. Though she snarled protest, she did as ordered.

Within two sleep-times, they'd healed their bruises,

scratches, and contusions. They came out of the jungle onto a wide plain. This was covered with grasses of various kinds, none higher than three feet. It was populated by herds of herbivores, attendant predators, and vast numbers of birds and flying mammals. And, of course, the ever-present insects and quasi-insects.

Halfway across the plain they came across a strange object lying against two small trees. Its cylindrical shape and the cone at one end made Deyv think at first that it was a House of the ancients. It was a hundred feet long, had a diameter of thirty-five feet, and was of some hard greenish material. On seeing that it had no windows and only one entrance, Deyv decided that it wasn't a House. How could anybody have entered it when it was upright? The doorway would be fifty feet above the ground.

"Very curious," Sloosh said. "I don't remember coming across anything like this in my studies."

The round door had no handle, but there was a plate that was slightly inset nearby. Deyv pushed the plate, and the door began to swing inward.

He and Vana jumped back, ready to run if anything dangerous-looking came out. But when the door stopped, it revealed a room empty except for some furniture.

Sloosh buzzed his equivalent of "Hmm!"

Jum growled, and Deyv looked at him. The dog was not facing the cylinder, as he'd expected. He was pointing back toward the direction from which they'd come.

"Oh, oh!" Deyv said. "Trouble. Maybe."

The others also looked. Trotting toward them was a pack of big ugly creatures larger than Jum. Their heads were somewhat doglike but they had two canines which extended at least a foot below the lower jaw. They were somewhat humpbacked, and their rears sloped downward. The bristly fur was gray and marked with small black crosses. Now and then one gave a peculiar high-pitched cry, half-snarl, half-laughter.

When they got about a hundred feet from the

travelers, they stopped and seemed to go into a conference. In the center of the ring they formed was the biggest and the ugliest one, and they seemed to be addressing their horrid cries at him. By now the strong wind carried their odor to Deyv's party, a stench like rotten flesh mixed with a light odor of skunk and garlic.

Vana said, "I don't like this at all. Are they actually talking?"

"I doubt it," Sloosh said. "Their foreheads aren't high enough for that kind of intelligence. It's just a behavior pattern. Which doesn't make them any less dangerous."

The plant-man went up to the doorway and looked inside. "The walls are even thinner than those of the *tharakorm*, but they're opaque. The furniture seems to be glued to the floor. Or perhaps it's just a formed extension of the material, a seamless extrusion design."

He bent his knees and leveled his upper torso with the ground. He thrust his huge hands under the cylinder where it met the ground.

Deyv gasped when the giant object lifted up above Sloosh's head.

"It's no cause for wonder," Sloosh said. "Come here. You can raise it easily."

Fearful but afraid to show that he was, Deyv put his hands by the Archkerri's. Sloosh stepped back, leaving him to support it. Deyv cried out because he expected the cylinder to drop. But he had only a little trouble keeping it propped up against the trees. It surely weighed no more than eighty pounds.

He let it down and said, "What is it? It's not a House."

"Not the kind you're used to, anyway."

Sloosh looked at the ugly beasts. "They're breaking up now. I think we should take refuge in this artifact."

The circle had become an extended line, with the leader in front of it. Instead of an immediate advance, as Deyv anticipated, the line spread out to the sides, then the ends began curving in. The predators were not only going to make a frontal attack but also intended to charge on the flanks as well.

Sloosh buzzed that Deyv and Vana should get at one end of the cylinder and he would take the other.

They obeyed, though they wondered what he was up to. Sloosh, having stationed himself below the conical end, shrilled, "Now, you two! Lift up on it and carry it my way!"

It would have been easy to do so if the wind hadn't pressed it so strongly against the trees. They had to lift it up and slide it along at the same time. The side of the cylinder was like a big sail.

Though occupied with his task, Deyv didn't forget the gray cross-marked beasts. Glances showed him that they had stopped. Their cries were puzzled. The leader had trotted closer to the cylinder, then stopped, his head cocked to one side.

When the one tree had been passed, and the other was halfway along the cylinder, Sloosh said, "Put it down! But hang on to it! Otherwise, one of the ends may swing around, and it could roll away!"

"I think I see what he means to do," Deyv muttered.

Vana asked, "What?"

Sloosh buzzed, "Now, Deyv! Tell your animals to get inside!"

Under other circumstances, Jum and Aejip might have been reluctant to enter the cylinder. The obvious intent of the ugly beasts made them eager to take shelter, however. They dived into the doorway.

Sloosh said, "Now, Vana, you get in! Hang on, Deyv!"

Deyv struggled to keep his end from swinging around under the wind. Vana darted alongside the cylinder and into its doorway.

"Now work your way toward the entrance! I'll be doing the same! If one end swings out, run as fast as you can and get inside!"

Synchronizing their progress step by step, they moved toward each other. Deyv's push against the cylinder wall would not have been as strong as Sloosh's, but the plant-man was trying to push with the same force as Deyv's. Before they were within twenty feet of each other, the cylinder began to swivel out at the end behind Sloosh.

By then the pack leader decided it was time to attack. Though no doubt hesitant because of the strangeness of the cylinder, he couldn't stand seeing his prey get away. He howled wolflike sounds and sped toward the doorway. Those behind him also charged, and the flanks broke into a run.

Deyv got inside first, then turned to pull Sloosh in. The Archkerri fell in just as the leader snapped at his hind legs. Vana stepped into the breach and slammed the edge of her tomahawk down across the top of the brute's head. The beast fell back, stunned. Some of those directly behind it leaped over its body and jammed themselves into the doorway. Others began tearing at the leader. The door started swinging inward. Sloosh reached up and pressed an inset plate inside the doorway.

All this action had taken place within a few seconds. Then the cylinder, still turning, also began rolling over. The door closed just in time. And they were off, the wind spinning the cylinder across the plain. Inside, all five were running to keep from being turned over. It didn't help any of them, since the room was square, and they missed their step when they tried to get off the floor to the wall, which became the floor for a few seconds. Then the ceiling became the floor, then the wall, then they were back to the floor again. That it was totally dark inside made the situation worse. Deyv fell through the door into the next room and slammed against a wall so hard that he was stunned.

A moment later, Jum, yelping, rammed into him.

Deyv was beaten, bruised, and shaken up worse than when he had been thrown off the *tharakorm*.

The nightmare finally ended, as all nightmares do. The cylinder stopped with a crash, and its occupants lay wherever they had fallen. There were groans and

moans and whimperings. Deyv got up and groped to
the doorway, the bottom of which was at chest-level.
He hoisted himself through it into the first room. At
least, he hoped it was the room with the door to the
outside. In his confusion, he might have gotten into
the room which led to the interior.

From the noise, though, he was sure he was in the
right place. He checked everybody out. Nobody was
incapable of responding, but all were complaining of
numerous pains.

His hands found the doorway, and a moment later
he pressed the inset plate. Light flooded in as the door
opened. It was at a 45-degree angle to the ground.
Righting the cylinder was easy, however, as soon as
they shifted their weight properly. Then all got out and
were glad to do so.

The cylinder had stopped by the trees at the edge of
the plain. Far off was the pack of gray cross-marked
brutes. They were heading after some horned animal.

"Something happened there while we were rolling
along," Sloosh said. "Did you press any other plates?"

Deyv looked inside. The furniture was gone.

Sloosh went back in but came back out in a few
minutes.

"Where the furniture was, there are now a few places
almost imperceptibly thicker than the floor," he said.
"The furniture just folded up. But what caused it to
do that?"

Deyv said he had no idea, which, of course, Sloosh
knew. He'd survived the ordeal and wanted nothing
more to do with the cause of it. Even if he was as
curious as the Archkerri, he didn't have the knowledge
to dare experiment.

Sloosh insisted they make a bunch of torches from
rushes, which they soaked with flammable sap. After
eating, they set out—in, rather—to explore the cylinder's
interior. It wasn't easy even to walk around in it.
Because of its extreme lightness, it tended to roll when
they started up the steps to the upper level. They

retreated, made some crude wooden shovels, and then piled dirt along the bottom. They also lugged in a big pile of heavy stones to place on the bottom floor. Since stones were scarce in the area, a long time was spent in search of them.

By then it was past sleep-time. Despite the plant-man's protests, they bedded down. Whatever else it was good for, the cylinder did make a perfect protection from the rain. The door couldn't be shut entirely because they would soon exhaust the oxygen supply. With the animals stationed just behind the opening, they could sleep in relative safety, especially after they erected a barricade of thorn bushes across it.

When they did begin their investigation, Vana and Deyv held the torches for Sloosh. It was tedious work for them and a little spooky. The lack of good air circulation drove them outside from time to time. Sloosh was hot on the scent, though, and he wasn't to be stopped by anything.

Most of the rooms were empty. The plant-man pointed out the very thin thickenings, which he said were collapsed furniture or devices. He ran his fingers along the walls and ceilings, tracing thin lines throughout the cylinder.

"These must be strips through which power was applied. So, let's track down the power supply."

They found it in the central portion. It was a cube about six inches wide. From one side of it protruded a long thin rod.

"I think it can be pushed in," Sloosh said. "But I won't do that. No telling what might happen. I wish I knew what fuel is used. There has to be some left, even after this long time. Otherwise, the door wouldn't have opened."

Finally, they entered the nose of the cylinder. This contained two chairs and a number of square very thin plates on a curve in front of the chairs.

Sloosh studied the room for a while.

"This has to be a vehicle. Probably to fly through the air. It's even possible it traveled through space.

Those plates would be viewscreens of some sort. They indicated flight data and who knows what else?"

Sloosh did some tracing of the strips. Finally, he stopped at a cluster of thumbprint-size plates. He reached out a finger to one, hesitated, then pressed. The humans jumped back, alarmed, as the chairs and the plates before them shrank, then folded up.

"Hmm! All this collapsing!" Sloosh said. "Could it be that . . ."

He stopped his buzzes and closed his eyes. Deyv looked at Vana and rolled his eyes. She coughed from the dark fumes of the torches.

Sloosh led them out of the room and back to the power cube. He looked at it for a while, then said, "Let's get all the rocks out of here."

"Why?" Deyv asked.

"No time to waste breath now. I'll tell you why later. If I'm right, it'll be obvious why I want the stones out. By the way, pick up all the torches you dropped and clean the sap off the floors. I don't want anything in here that wasn't here when we entered."

By sleep-time, the rocks were gone, and with them any trace of the travelers. Sloosh told Deyv and Vana to stand back from the cylinder, and he went inside. Deyv had expected, for some reason, that Sloosh would go to the upper deck where the cube was. How he was going to do that without tipping the "vehicle" over, Deyv didn't know. However, Sloosh went only just past the doorway, reached up above it to press something, and then came out, rather quickly for him.

"Maybe we should get even farther away," he said.

Except for the plant-man, no one knew what to expect. Deyv had some fantasies about it, but what happened wasn't one of them.

Slowly, the cylinder collapsed, then began to fold up. The two sides straightened up, forming a flat oval. Then a seam appeared along the middle, and it folded, folded, folded.

When this process had ceased, the cylinder had become a cube with a thin rod sticking out by an inch.

The rod was the same one Deyv had seen projecting from the power supply. The cube was almost three feet across.

Though Sloosh's face couldn't show expression, his delight was obvious. He danced around like a drunken elephant, his fingers snapping, his beak buzzing nonsense. When he regained his usual demeanor, he went to the cube and pulled on the rod. They cylinder started to unfold, but after a few seconds he pushed the rod in. It folded once more.

"Of all the ancients' inventions, this must have been the most wondrous!"

"It is indeed a great and awesome magic," Deyv said. "But what will we do with it?"

"For the time being, we'll make straps, a saddle, and a girth so I can carry it on my back," Sloosh said. "At sleep-time, we'll use it for protection. It's also useful as a refuge in times of danger. I shouldn't have to explain that to you."

Deyv reddened. "I know all that. I was just wondering if perhaps . . . well, maybe if it's supposed to fly, we could fly it. And then we could easily find the Yawtl."

"A good idea but most impracticable. Perhaps. In the meantime . . ."

16

"THERE it is," Sloosh said, pointing down. "The Yawtl's impression."

Deyv looked but of course didn't see the tracks. What he did see was a very wide valley through the center of which a river snaked. All five were standing high on the slope of a mountain. The plant-man had insisted that they climb over it so that he could get a view of a large expanse of territory. The labor had been hard but had paid off.

"The thief came around the foot of that mountain," Sloosh said. He indicated one to his left. "Then he made a dugout or a raft and went down the river to that point there." His finger jabbed toward a mountain across the valley to the right. "He abandoned his dugout or raft and went through that pass there."

Vana groaned and said, "I hope he's getting close to his home. Do you realize that we must have traveled over four hundred miles?"

"Five hundred and fifty-six to be exact," Sloosh said. "That is, if you include both horizontal and vertical travel."

Deyv didn't ask him how he could be so certain. Though the plant-man had little sense of time, he seemed to have a inborn sense of distance. Actually, Deyv's own idea of it was rather vague. A *vathakishmikl*, a mile, was a measure which depended upon psychical as well as physical factors. If a half-*vathakishmikl* tired you as much as a full *vathakishmikl* did, then one length was equal to the other.

Sloosh estimated that the travel from where they were to the place at which the Yawtl had left the river would take four sleep-times. That is, approximately forty miles. But if the terrain slowed them down, then it might be fifty miles. Or even more.

As it turned out, it took them sixty miles. What delayed them was the Athmau.

They went down the mountain, built a raft with a rudder, and floated down to where the thief's trail went ashore. The path he'd taken led them to a village on a tributary of the river. After sneaking around this, they traveled on another much less used path. Two sleep-times later, they came to an open area. Long before they reached it, they heard a hubbub which made them very cautious.

From the jungle they peered out at an interesting but possibly dangerous situation.

In the midst of the clearing was a low broad hill made

of a cementlike substance resembling that which the honey beetles excreted. It was dotted with numerous small holes. At the moment hordes of creatures were pouring out of them to defend themselves. These were a strange mixture, purple antlike things about a foot long and six inches high, covered all over with breathing pipes, ten- to twelve-foot-long snakes, and furry bipedal mammals. The latter were about two feet high and gray-colored except for their badgerlike faces, which were white. Their paws were wide and armed with short curving nails. Their teeth looked like the teeth of humans.

A hundred or so human warriors, all wearing wet bark-cloth filters over their noses and mouths, were battling the hill-things. They had the light skin, thin lips, and kinky yellow hair of Vana's tribe. Deyv thought they must be from three different tribes who had banded together for the onslaught. A third of them wore feathered headdresses; another, fur caps with horns; and the rest, tall conical hats of woven reeds. All carried shields with the different tribal markings, and they fought with spears, axes, and flails. Some carried nets, but these warriors hung behind the others until a furry biped had been seized. Then they dashed in and threw the net over the captive, tied it up, and dragged it off struggling to the edge of the clearing.

"The Athmau," Deyv said. "I've heard of them, though they live far away from my tribe. My grandfather, however, said he once brought one home."

He became aware of a musky reek and said, "That strange odor's from the Athmau. We'd better move on."

Sloosh was curious, as usual. "Why the face masks?"

"The Athmau exudes a perfume which makes those who breathe it very happy but also very indolent. That's why the tribes are raiding. They want to bring the Athmau to their villages. They'll put them in cages and then enjoy them. The trouble is, the Athmau don't breed in captivity, and they die too soon."

There were about ten of the little animals in nets, lying together, five warriors standing guard over them.

Their captors had paid for them, however. The poisonous snakes had felled four men; the long mandibles of the antoids had severely wounded six and killed three. And the Athmau's claws had dragged down and ripped apart five.

"Why don't they just stay in the hill?" Vana said.

"If they did, they'd be smoked out. They know that, so they come out and fight. At least, that's what my grandfather said."

By now the men were outnumbered six to one. Though the flails crushed the antoids and the spears stabbed the snakes, there weren't enough men to stop the hill-things. A tall warrior wearing an orange kilt, the only such color among the raiders, blew a piercing note on a bone whistle. Immediately, the warriors turned and ran for the jungle. The netted Athmau were picked up and carried away.

However, one of the furry bipeds was being pursued by two men. It ran directly toward the hiding place of the travelers.

Deyv said, "Run!"

It was too late. Before they could get back on the path, the Athmau had burst through the foliage and was among them. Behind it came the two warriors. One of them threw his axe, and its blunt side caught the animal on the back of his head. It was an excellent throw, doing just what it was intended to do. It stunned the Athmau, which fell by Deyv's feet.

Aejip leaped for the axe thrower's throat. Jum grabbed the leg of the other, whose spear was raised to drive into the dog's back. Vana forestalled him by hitting him on the head with the sharp edge of her axe. Then she slammed the tomahawk into the side of the other warrior's head. Aejip finished him off.

Meanwhile, Deyv had sat down with the Athmau in his arms. He cuddled it, rocking it back and forth, and looking pleased and dreamy.

Vana started toward him. Sloosh buzzed, "Stop! He's been caught by the perfume! Don't go near him! I'll do it!"

The Archkerri grabbed hold of the still half-senseless creature. Deyv tightened his embrace on it. Sloosh said, "Let loose!"

He lifted the Athmau up with Deyv clinging to it. At that moment another warrior, bleeding from a dozen wounds, staggered through the bush. Aejip leaped on him, and the man went down screaming.

Sloosh dropped Deyv and the Athmau, and he grabbed Deyv's hands and pulled them outward. The animal fell away, rolled over, then stood up unsteadily, chirruping. Sloosh seized it and threw it at least ten feet. It rolled away behind a bush.

Vana pulled Deyv to his feet. He stood smiling, seeming not to hear her cries to run. By then the cat had stopped the warrior's screams by tearing out his throat. The yells of men on the other side of the bushes showed that they were aware that something was wrong.

Vana took Deyv's hand and pulled him along, at the same time ordering Aejip and Jum to leave the trail. She dragged Deyv off it after them, and Sloosh joined them a few seconds later. By the time they'd pushed and shoved their way through the dense undergrowth, far enough so that the tribesmen's voices were faint, Deyv had begun to recover.

"What happened?" Deyv asked.

Vana told him. He looked ashamed, but he said, "I couldn't help it. And it was a wonderful experience. Better even than when I chew *thrathyumi*."

"Think about that when they find you and kill you," Vana said.

Deyv said angrily, "It wasn't my fault."

By then the warriors were beating the bush. Sloosh led his companions through the heavy thick vegetation, his great body crushing the growth. He made noise, but their hunters were yelling so loudly at each other and thrashing around so much that they wouldn't be able to hear the Archkerri. After a long struggle, the party came to a trail. Possibly, this was the one they'd left, but the tracks in the soft earth indicated that they had been made by some very large hoofed animals.

Presently, they came to another plain covered with yellow grass, dotted here and there with trees. Halfway across, they heard the yells of their pursuers. These warriors had come out of the same trail and now, twenty strong, were running after them, their spears held high.

Sloosh said that there was only one thing they could do. Which they did. They removed the cube from his back, and he pulled out its rod. By the time the warriors reached them, they found the cylinder fully expanded and their quarry inside. Fortunately, the wind wasn't strong enough to roll the cylinder with its occupants.

After a long while, during which they heard no sound, Sloosh opened the door. A cautious reconnoiter convinced him that the men had given up. Since there had been no beating on the walls, the warriors probably hadn't even come close to this strange and thus scary object.

Sloosh looked across the plain at its far end.

"There are the impressions of the Yawtl. We won't have to backtrack to pick them up."

Deyv awoke after the next sleep-time to find the rooms of the vehicle ablaze with light. He jumped up, his heart beating hard, and called, "Sloosh!"

The plant-man appeared from the next room a minute later. "I found the plate that activates the mechanisms that provide the illumination."

"Where does it come from?" Deyv said.

"From the entire material itself. Note that there are no shadows. I have also located the plates for the illumination of individual rooms. I'm progressing, progressing."

Deyv was pleased that they would no longer have to be in the dark. However, the Archkerri's investigations made him uneasy. One of these times he was going to make a mistake and press the wrong plate. Then, willy-nilly, they'd be flying through the air with no idea of how to pilot the vehicle.

They went on through a high pass, and they came

to another valley. This was far broader than the one behind them. Sloosh stood looking down the slope at the smaller mountains in the valley.

"The trail ends there."

A river twisted and turned from one end of the horizon to the other. In the middle it split to form around a large island. Something tiny hung above it, gleaming whitely.

"I hope it's where he lives and that he's not just resting," Vana said.

It took them two sleep-times to get to the foot of the mountain but a short time to reach the river. They made another raft with a rudder and floated down, using a sweep to give them more control. The river was about a mile across until they came to the roughly diamond-shaped island. Here the right branch was only half a mile across. It was unusually heavily populated with *athaksum*. These came close to the raft, regarding its passengers with cold blue eyes though making no attack. A swimmer would not have lasted long.

The object hanging above the island was larger. It was still so far away, however, that it could not be identified.

Evidently, the island had no paths through the jungle, which meant that there were few if any people here. Sloosh waded into a swamp, following the impressions visible only to him. The others followed, putting each foot down with dread. Snakes hissed at them and slid off branches or rocks into the stinking bubbling dark-green water. Swarms of insects attacked them. Froglike amphibians weighing perhaps fifty pounds leaped out from hummocks of mud and belly-crashed resoundingly. Then they dived, only to reappear close to the legs of the travelers. Their tongues flicked out and lacerated legs with tiny sharp barbs.

Sloosh said, "They may hurt, but they can't be fatal. If they were, the Yawtl wouldn't have passed this way."

The water got deeper. Aejip and Jum started swimming. Abruptly, the bottom sloped upward, and they were soon on higher land. Now they were beneath colossal trees under which little brush grew. They stopped to smear mud over their insect-bitten bodies and to rest. There was a strange silence under the branches, no buzz, hiss, caw, scream, chitter. A greenish-gray fungus clothed the lower trunks of the trees, a fluffy ill-smelling stuff two to three feet thick.

Nobody spoke. Sloosh held a finger to the end of his beak to indicate quiet. After a while he gestured, and he started walking. They rose wearily, since it was past bedtime, and followed. In a short time they'd passed through the forest and emerged on the rim of a shallow valley. Its surface seemed to be covered mostly with sand and gigantic dark-blue boulders. Here and there were some lone trees or small copses.

About a mile away, above the center of the valley, hovered the white object. It was restrained from floating away by a massive cable of some sort in its center and slimmer cables on its edges.

Deyv spoke softly. "Three *tharakorm*. Tied together side by side."

Sloosh's gaze circled the area. "The Yawtl has been up on them. But he came down without the benefit of a ladder."

"What do you mean?" Vana said.

"He either jumped or was thrown off." He pointed. "He's out there now, somewhere behind that extraordinarily large rock."

They went down the slope and onto the soft, very warm sand. They had not gone more than forty feet when Sloosh stopped, holding up a hand. They wondered why he'd done so, but his manner indicated that they keep silent.

Presently, the sand began boiling. A little pit appeared, and two long tentacles, bilious green with narrow yellow stripes, slid out. They snaked around as if feeling for something. Sloosh gestured that they should back up. After about twenty paces, he stopped. They waited while the tentacles slid out to a length of fifteen feet.

Then, so suddenly that it caused them to jump back,

a long curved barbed pole like a giant scorpion's sting shot out of the sand not ten feet ahead of them.

A minute passed. As swiftly as it had appeared, the sting-pole slid back beneath the sand.

"That's strange," Sloosh buzzed softly. "It shouldn't be there. It's right in the Yawtl's trail."

"What do you mean?" Deyv whispered.

"I can see the impressions of many creatures I've never encountered before. It's evident that they are under the ground. I suspected that they've been set there to catch the unwelcome. But the Yawtl's path curved here and there so much that it was evident he knew where they were. I followed his path so we, too, could avoid those sand-beasts.

"But then I perceived one directly under the trail over which the Yawtl had gone. I also see the impressions of three humans around here. They've moved around freely. And it looks to me as if they've led the sand-beasts to other places."

"Why didn't you tell us this?" Deyv asked fiercely.

"I would have. In time. It wasn't necessary as long as we were on the safe path."

Sloosh looked at the side-by-side *tharakorm*. "Let's hope that their sleep-times correspond to ours. And that they don't keep a watch then. Otherwise, they've seen us. We will proceed as if they haven't. There is nothing else to do."

He closed his eyes for a while. When he opened them, he said, "The Yawtl's impressions are still strong. I can't see their end, so I don't know if he's still living."

Deyv understood this. He'd been told that when a creature died, it emitted a large yellow ball. No matter what colors its living impressions made, its decease was marked with yellow. Sometime later, the yellow ball would fade and eventually disappear.

"A good thing, too," Sloosh had said. "If every impression didn't fade out, my vision would be so full of them, I'd never be able to untangle them. The world, to me, would be a nightmare of complexities."

Sloosh emitted a long rising and falling buzz, for

him a sigh. "As before, single file. Step softly. And don't stray from the path."

It took a long time. Sloosh zigzagged and even circled and once took them back only a hundred yards from their starting point. When they finally got close to the tremendous boulder, he stopped.

"Now be especially careful. There is a sand-beast on each side. If you panic and move too far to one side to avoid one, the other will get you."

Aejip was directly in front of Vana, and Jum was just ahead of Deyv. Though extremely nervous, the two animals did just as Deyv ordered. The cat slunk along, looking quickly to each side. The dog's hair was bristling, but his bushy tail was high in the air. Every now and then he growled softly.

Now the sand boiled at either hand, whirlpools formed, and tentacles shot out. They slid like snakes toward the ankles of the trespassers, stopping only a few inches from them. It was terrifying to walk between the two pairs of waving seeking tips, each ending in a long hooked claw. Deyv whispered soft encouragement to Jum, and Vana urged Aejip to stay immediately behind the Archkerri.

Deyv sweated more in a minute than he had in most hours.

Then they were out of danger.

Sloosh veered away from the boulder and approached it in a wide arc. When they got to its other side, they saw that a copse of trees was beyond it, about twenty yards away. Deyv thought that the Yawtl might be hiding in it. Sloosh, however, turned toward the base of the boulder. As Deyv neared it, he saw the rim of a large pit.

The Archkerri stopped short of the edge and pointed downward.

"There is the thief."

At first, Deyv thought that the Yawtl had been seized by a sand-beast and dragged into the pit. There was no evidence of a struggle, though. It was also doubtful that the Yawtl could have resisted for very long anything so monstrous. Whatever had happened, he was injured and in pain. Nevertheless, the reddish eyes glared challengingly at them. He tried to raise himself and to lift the rock gripped in one of his hands. He grimaced and fell back.

Though he was naked, his loincloth having somehow been lost, he had managed to retain the bone whistle. Sloosh pointed his beak down at him and said in Archkerri, "We are not here to kill you, Hoozisst. All we want is the recovery of the eggs and my crystal."

Once more, Sloosh had flabbergasted Deyv. Deyv said, "You *know* him?"

"Yes. I met him a long time ago when he visited us with some others of his kind. How else would he know our language?"

"You knew it was him all the time? Why didn't you say so?"

"It was his theft, not his identity, that concerned me."

Vana, her face twisted, said, "I swear, I swear, I'm going to kick you so hard all your leaves will fall off!"

"If it will help your infantile emotional state, go ahead. However, you'll only hurt your foot."

The Yawtl said, "If you don't mean to kill me or torture me, then quit standing there talking. Get down here and get me out. I have a broken arm, my pelvis feels as if it's fractured, I've bled a lot, and I'm very thirsty and hungry."

"Where are the eggs?" Deyv whistled.

"Tell me, or I'll tear your heart out!" Vana whistled.

The Yawtl's thin lips opened in a very malicious smile, revealing the teeth of a carnivore. Then he closed his mouth and put the whistle to it. "They're up there. On the ship-creatures. Feersh the Blind has them. Help me, and I'll help you. I want my own egg, and even more I want *revenge*."

The two humans went down into the pit and carried him back up between them. When he was let down on the edge, he said, "They're all sleeping now, or should be. Let's hope so; otherwise we're done for. Get me back to the forest, and I'll tell you my story. You can't do anything without knowing it."

"That seems sensible," Sloosh said. "Put him on my back."

They had to endure the ordeal of the tentacles again, but otherwise the return was much less frightening than the original venture. Once within the shelter of the trees, they gave Hoozisst what he wanted. They set his arm and put it in a splint. Vana brought water to bathe the bruises and lacerations. Deyv threw his spear up among the tree branches and knocked off many of the large purplish pear-shaped fruit. The Yawtl devoured a dozen of these with such pleasure that the others decided to eat some with him. Deyv thought they were the most delicious fruit he'd ever tasted.

When the Yawtl's needs had been fulfilled, he closed his eyes. No one bothered him until he opened them a long time later. They understood that he had to probe his body with his mind to locate every cell that needed repair. Having done this, he could then direct the healing substances to those parts. He could also fix the rate of speed at which the healing would be done. There was an upper limit to this, but the procedure was considerably faster than the natural process. However, the degree of speed depended upon the amount of food and water ingested. Which meant that since Hoozisst had to get well soon, he would require much sustenance. Which meant that his captors were going to be busy providing him with all his belly could hold.

The probing and directions would take about half an hour if he was as skillful in technique as the two humans, and he was. Then he would sleep for a while and wake up ravenous.

The animals curled up and went to sleep. Sloosh and the humans would have liked to join them, but they had to find fuel for the Yawtl's racing metabolism. Deyv and Vana speared two of the froggish beasts. The Archkerri tore out a young tree, trimmed it with Vana's tomahawk, and used its end to knock off more fruit. Then the vehicle was opened, and they carried Hoozisst into it.

Between eating and sleeping, the Yawtl talked.

"Feersh the Blind is a wicked old witch."

Sloosh, interrupting, said, "By 'witch' he doesn't mean one who practices magic. Such a being exists only in the minds of the ignorant and superstitious. He means one who has found artifacts of the ancients and has discovered how to use them."

Hoozisst looked annoyed. "Like most of her kind, she is tribeless. She lives with her family, some human slaves, and some *beezee* (or *khratikl*), whom she's raised from cubhood.

"My tribe has had some contact with her, since her sons and daughters occasionally visit our village. We give them smoked meat and other goods. In return, she doesn't use her powers to do us evil. This burns us, but we can do nothing about it. Anyway, when one of her sons, Skibroziy, came to our village, he drew me aside and ordered me to come with him to see his mother. I asked him why she wanted me. He replied, in that sneering imperious manner we Yawtl have to endure, that she would tell me why when she saw me.

"I was afraid. I've no shame admitting that. But I went. Besides, I thought there might be some profit in it for me. After all, I'd done nothing to offend Feersh. Skibroziy and I traveled through the jungle—our village is only three sleep-times away—and he guided me through the sand trap, and we climbed the ladder which hangs down from the central part of the three ship-creatures.

"Feersh sat me down and gave me the best food and drink. Then she said she'd picked me to run an errand for her. Some *errand*! She had heard that I was the bravest, most cunning, and stealthiest thief of all the six tribes of this area. Thus, I was the best candidate to do what she wanted.

"She demanded that I go out, no matter how far or how long it took me, and steal soul eggs. Not just anybody's. They had to indicate a certain type of character. She described the character of the owners, and she also described, in minute detail, how the eggs would indicate this.

"I didn't like leaving my tribe for a long time, nor did I care for the unknown dangers I might run into. On the other hand, I was flattered because she'd chosen me. I wasn't going to do it for nothing, though. So I asked her what reward I would get for my time and perilous labors. To my surprise, she replied that I could have whatever I wanted from a group of rare or unique treasures of the ancients. She took me to where they lay on the deck and asked me to pick one. I finally did so after some agonizing and chose the Emerald of Anticipation. I'll tell you what it is later.

"I was somewhat suspicious and didn't really believe her promise. But I thought that if she went back on it, I'd steal the Emerald from her. That shows you how valuable it was, that I would think of doing that when I was so scared of her powers. Though I must admit that there isn't a Yawtl around here who hasn't dreamed of stealing from Feersh. We all lacked the guts to try it, though.

"So I went out, and the first egg I stole was from the Riverpig Tribe. I wouldn't steal from my own tribe unless it was absolutely necessary. Anyway, mine had no eggs like those she wanted. Except for my own egg. Which, as you see, she now has. I found two more in other Yawtl tribes, and then I had to go to the human and Tsimmanbul villages and Houses."

Deyv asked, "What's a Tsimmanbul?"

"A sapient species descended from an animal that once lived in the ocean," Sloosh said. "They didn't evolve naturally from their flippered state into land-dwelling bipeds. The ancients used their powers to change them into these. But their intelligence was equal to that of humans."

"I think I must sleep now," Hoozisst said.

This irritated and frustrated his listeners, and he probably enjoyed their reactions.

When Deyv relieved Vana from guard duty, he stationed himself on the edge of the forest. Standing there facing the sand traps, he thought that if it hadn't been for his missing egg and the nearness of Feersh the Blind, he could enjoy being there. For some reason which the Yawtl didn't know, this thin circle of woods was free of insects. Moreover, the animals, safe or dangerous, avoided it. If this was because Feersh had cast a spell on it, the magic hadn't influenced Jum and Aejip. They seemed at ease. The hunting in the swamp and the fishing in the river beyond the forest were as good as could be asked for.

He fantasized the Earth as a place where such forests were interspersed among the jungles he knew. After the necessary hunting, a man could retreat to such a forest and enjoy life without the dangers of predators and the vexatious and sometimes painful or fatal insect and snake bites.

Deyv was, however, a realist. Into his thoughts of the paradise of such forests crawled visions of humans. There would be bachelors who'd sneak in and kill, or a raid by warriors fixed on wiping out Deyv and his tribe. And there would be bothersome and sometimes infuriating interferences by parents and other relatives, not to mention the shaman and his wife or friends. And there would be a wife who would too often want her own way. And . . .

But this was normal human life and, whatever its

vexations, it was overall enjoyable, rewarding, and fulfilling. This was the only way open to a man if he was to be a completely rounded human.

So, counting all the advantages and disadvantages, there would be no better place than a forest like this.

Deyv couldn't see the humans aboard the *tharakorm*. But at least fifty leathery-winged ratlike *khratikl* were out feeding the sand monsters. They flew in couples which carried between each member a large chunk of raw meat. When they came above the places where the beasts hid, they dropped the flesh and flapped off for the jungle beyond the ship-creatures. The Yawtl had said that there were corrals there where cattle were raised. These were tended by *khratikl* supervised by human slaves. They provided food for the sand things, the slaves, the *khratikl*, Feersh's family, and the captive *tharakorm*.

Deyv, watching the tentacles crawl out to seize the meat or giant stings readying to pierce it, thought that the feeding was a flaw in the idea of the sand traps. An observer in the forest could note the location of the *shishvenomi*, as Hoozisst called the sand-beasts, and then avoid the traps. But he'd have to have a good memory.

Hoozisst had also told them that the *shishvenomi* didn't need food very often. They went into a semi-hibernation until their sensors detected vibrations on the surface. Then they became fully awake, only to fall back into their sleep after eating or if their prey eluded them.

Deyv had asked why the slaves didn't try to escape.

"They have a fairly good life," Hoozisst had said. "And they're descendants of slaves. Feersh's great-great-grandmother captured their ancestors. In fact, they worship Feersh as a goddess. They also sacrifice to her. When the population gets too large, they reduce it by killing the useless old people and the babies who don't have matching soul eggs."

Deyv was indifferent to the babies' fate, since his own tribe had the same custom. But he was horrified by what happened to the old people. "Those slaves are beasts! They deserve to be slaves!"

The Yawtl had smiled but had not replied.

Now, watching the *khratikl*, Deyv didn't feel as repulsed or as indignant. It seemed to him that perhaps Feersh had done the right thing. After all, if the slaves got too numerous, they'd starve. And they couldn't just drive the old ones into the jungle to fend for themselves. It really was better, more humane, that they be spared that horror.

Perhaps he'd misjudged the witch. Could anyone who'd prepared a forest like this, such a delightful place, be wicked? It didn't seem likely. And if she wasn't a witch but was a good-magic person, then perhaps her motive in stealing the soul eggs was good. She may have intended, and probably did, some benefit for those who had been robbed. However, since they wouldn't have voluntarily come to her with their eggs because of her bad reputation—no doubt the result of lies by her enemies—she'd sent the Yawtl to steal the eggs. Thus, the robbed would have to track him down and follow him to Feersh. And she would then explain just why she'd done this thing that had seemed so terrible to them only because of their ignorance of her true motive.

Hadn't the Yawtl said that he took care that those pursuing him didn't lose the trail? If he'd not left much physical evidence of his passage for Deyv's party, it was because he knew Sloosh was in it. Contrary to what the plant-man had stated, Hoozisst was well aware of Sloosh's ability to see psychic tracks. Deyv couldn't actually define what connection this had with his growing belief that Feersh meant them no harm. But he was sure that it strengthened his reasoning about her.

He didn't understand why Feersh had placed the dangerous *shishvenomi* in ambush. That certainly wasn't friendly. But then she could have excellent reasons for it. Maybe she had to have some test to weed out unfit candidates for whatever benefits she would bestow. Deyv's party had proved itself worthy.

Since they'd come this far, and since the goal was in sight, why not just come out of hiding and show themselves?

So thought, so done. Almost, anyway. He had to talk to his colleagues and find out if they agreed or disagreed. If they should disagree, though it didn't seem likely, since Deyv's logic was irresistible, then he'd act on his own. But he owed it to them to discuss this with them first.

He was pleasantly surprised when the Yawtl said that he'd been thinking along the same lines. Hoozisst was up and about, his broken arm almost entirely knit, his bruises and contusions gone.

"Let's see what the plant-man thinks."

"Where's Vana?" Deyv asked. "We should talk to her at the same time and so save time."

"She went hunting with Aejip."

Deyv felt a little angry.

"Why should she want to do that? We don't need meat any more. The purple fruit is more than enough to eat. It's all we need."

Hoozisst nodded. "That's what I was thinking. Why go out into that swamp with all its stinging insects and poisonous snakes and only Khrukhrukhru knows what else? She was inclined to agree, but the cat was hungry and wanted Vana to go with her. She's very fond of Vana, isn't she?"

The Yawtl had needled Deyv before about this. Deyv, however, no longer felt pangs of jealousy.

"There's no reasoning with a cat. She'd bug Vana until she got her way, and Vana knows that. Well, we can talk to her when she gets back. There's no hurry."

Sloosh was stuffing the purplish fruit into the chest-mouth when they came up to him. His eyes were closed, his brain seemingly orbiting, or perhaps entangled with, some philosophical problem.

Deyv was mistaken. Sloosh had been engaged with the same subject as the others. His logic was similar, too.

"As soon as Vana gets back, we'll tell her what we're

going to do. I'm sure she'll agree with us. If she doesn't,
then we'll leave her here. After a while, she'll follow
us. What else can she do?"

They strapped the folded-up vessel onto the plant-
man's back and then ate some more of the fruit. It
didn't sate or cloy but seemed to get more delicious
with each bite. The time passed pleasantly as they
talked idly of many things. They noted that The Dark
Beast would soon be covering this part of the sky.
They'd planned to cross the sand traps when the semi-
darkness would make their passage much less visible
from the *tharakorm*. Now they wouldn't wait.

Presently, they heard Vana calling loudly, and they
walked slowly to the edge of the forest facing the
swamp. Here she came, splashing through the dark
stinking waters, blood upon her arm and the tip of her
spear. Behind her swam a dozen or so sleek greenish
creatures about two feet long. They had weasellike
heads with long thick whiskers and large blue eyes.

"Anything wrong?" Deyv called out.

" '*Anything wrong*?' " she screamed. "This is no time
for your twisted sense of humor!"

She left the swamp and ran up the gently sloping
bank and into the trees. There she sat down, panting.
The beasts followed her a minute later, clucking, their
sharp teeth exposed in wicked grins. But they stopped
when they came within a few feet of the edge of the
forest. Some sat up on their hind legs and waved
broad paws with webbed toes.

Having regained her breath, Vana stood up. The
blood on her arm was flowing heavily. Deyv suggested
that she stanch the wound with mud.

"What's the matter with you?" she cried. "You're
all acting as if you didn't care that I could've been
killed and that Aejip is treed by those beasts. I killed
six with my darts and two with my spear. They could
have caught me when I was in the water, but they were
so busy eating their own dead that they let me get
ahead of them. As it was—!"

"Well, you're safe now," Deyv said. "But I suppose we'll have to rescue Aejip."

" '*Suppose*'!" she cried. "What's the matter with you, Deyv? What's wrong with all of you?"

"Nothing at all," he said. "We feel really fine."

He proceeded to tell her what he and the others planned to do.

Vana heard them out with increasing incredulity. She didn't, however, say anything until after she'd smeared mud on her wound.

"Do you know, I'd been feeling somewhat the way you have. Not nearly to that degree, though. Still, I was wondering this morning if perhaps we weren't mistaken about Feersh. But when I went with Aejip I got too busy to think about anything but hunting."

She paused to look at them.

"You're all eating that fruit. Standing there munching away and looking blissful. You aren't bothered by what happened and yet you should all be excited, ready to drive those beasts away and save Aejip. For all you know, she could be dead by now. Those beasts can climb trees, you know."

Deyv began to feel just a little uneasy.

"What're you thinking?"

Narrow-eyed, Vana stared closely into his eyes. Then she looked into Hoozisst's and Sloosh's.

"Yes, they seem a little glazed. I'd be in the same drugged condition if I hadn't gone hunting and gotten rid of some of its effects. That has to be it."

"What do you mean?" Deyv asked.

"It's that fruit! It's making us think this crazy way! I'll bet that Feersh planted these trees here. She did it so that if people hid here to spy on her, they'd eat the purple stuff and it would affect their minds."

The three males looked at each other. Deyv and Hoozisst burst out laughing. The plant-man buzzed his equivalent of loud scornful mirth.

Her face flushed and angry, Vana said, "You lamebrains! You can't see I'm telling the truth because you're drugged!"

Sloosh buzzed his equivalent of "Tut, tut!" Then he said, "Even if we were, why should we decide that Feersh wasn't dangerous? You're surely not saying that the fruits contain mental suggestions implanted somehow by the witch? That'd be a scientific impossibility."

"No, but the fruit might affect you so that you'd want to take the easy way out, no matter how foolish it might be. Look at you now! You're not the least bit worried about my wound or the cat!"

Sloosh spoke even more slowly than usual. "I think you're quite mistaken. However, there is only one way to determine if you are. I'm loath to take that course, since it means giving up the eating of this superb fruit. It also entails a considerable output of energy, which, frankly, I don't feel up to just now. But if it's to be done, we should do it now."

Deyv and Hoozisst didn't want to venture out into the swamp. The plant-man said that he sympathized with their feelings, but logic demanded that they test Vana's theory. They armed themselves and went out to meet the greenish beasts. Sloosh carried a big dead branch, the first time Deyv had seen him bear a weapon. The Yawtl and Vana shot darts with their blowguns; Deyv slashed with his sword. Within a few minutes, the predators were dead or fleeing.

They sloshed through the water and the mud, Vana leading. When they arrived at the tree up which Aejip had fled, they found some dead or dying beasts at its foot. Aejip was also there, eating one. She was bleeding lightly where claws had raked her, but evidently she'd not been bitten.

When they returned to the forest, Vana said, "If I catch anybody eating that fruit, I'll knock his skull in."

"That would be a rather excessive measure," Sloosh said. "Or are you exaggerating again?"

"You should know by now."

Sloosh buzzed the equivalent of a sigh. "Ah, the hyperbole of humans. Why can't you be exact in your speech?"

18

TWO sleep-times passed. The Dark Beast dragged a heavy twilight behind it. The only light from the sky was a narrowing band around the horizon. The Yawtl's and Vana's wounds were entirely healed. In the meantime, they all stayed away from the purplish fruit, and their minds became clear.

"We owe the woman an apology," Sloosh said, "even though it was an accident that she didn't succumb, too."

Reluctantly, Deyv and Hoozisst thanked her.

"You two don't have any more gratitude than you have brains," she said. "As for you, plant-man, you might compliment me just once without making some reservation."

None of them replied; they wanted to forget all about the fruit and their foolishness.

"It's time to set out," the Archkerri said.

They strapped the cube to his back and rechecked their supply of poisoned darts. Then with Sloosh leading as before, they went single file across the sandy plain. Though they knew what to expect, they felt terror when the tips of the tentacles writhed within a few inches of their ankles or the sting-poles exploded from the sand. On leaving the trap area, they sighed with relief, though greater danger might be ahead.

Presently, they came to the three ship-creatures, which Hoozisst had told them were not tied but glued together. Also, what they had at first thought was a single cable attached to the central underside was actually three thick vines wound about each other. The Yawtl cautioned them again that the vines would send an alarm up to the *tharakorm* if they were touched.

"During sleep-time, each vine is sensitized. But only

137

to animal life. If a leaf or an uprooted plant should
blow against the cable, it won't register the contact. It
would be nice if Feersh's crew had forgotten to draw
up the rope-ladder, but they didn't. However, we're
very lucky in having Sloosh. He's a plant, so he won't
trigger off the alarm."

"Don't be so sure," Sloosh buzzed softly. "I'm half-
protein."

Hoozisst grimaced and said, "We'll know in a
minute."

Sloosh walked up to the triple cable. Without touching it, he looked up into the darkness. The *tharakorm*
was a vague whitish bulk. Hoozisst had assured him
that the hole from which the cable hung was large
enough to admit even his giant body. He had wanted
to check this out for himself, but he couldn't see in the
dim light and at this distance.

He put his hand out without hesitating and grabbed
the cable. Deyv expected to hear the alarm. He didn't
know what it would be, a loud scream or a roar. The
silence continued. His relief was short. Sloosh commented that possibly the alarm was audible only to
those sleeping above. If they were all sleeping, that is.
It was true they hadn't been visible from the *tharakorm*
when the party crossed the open area. But then a
sentinel might have missed them or perhaps have been
absent from his post when they passed.

The Archkerri took hold of the thick cable with both
huge hands. Deyv climbed onto his back and with his
rope tied his waist to Sloosh's upper torso. Sloosh
began pulling himself upward, his upper trunk extending straight out from the lower, his legs wrapped
around the vines. Up they went, slowly but unceas-
ingly. Deyv hung on to the rope, making sure that no
part of him touched the vines.

Halfway up, the Archkerri stopped to get his wind
back. Deyv looked down. The ground was a long way
off, though he could see it only dimly. The group below
wasn't even visible. That assured him that a sentinel
wouldn't have been able to see them on the plain.

Now, however, if the sentinel looked down the hole, he might be able to spot Sloosh and Deyv. On the other hand, why should he?

The cable did not rise straight from the surface but was at a slight angle because the wind was pushing the *tharakorm*. Now and then the wind lessened in strength, and then the cable swayed back and forth. Deyv had been in situations where he had felt more secure.

"I wonder," the Archkerri buzzed softly, "if it's possible, as the great Sindsindbat maintains, that the oscillation of matter in this universe is caused by psychical means rather than physical ones? Or perhaps I should say psychophysical."

"By Skreekmishgakl!" Deyv said. "What are you talking about?"

"Sindsindbat says that the matter expelled by the primal fireball explosion doesn't keep expanding outward to infinity but instead eventually falls back toward the center of the matter because of the angry, hence negative, charges radiated by the zillions of sapients on the quadrillions or perhaps quintillions of inhabited planets. These charges cause the stars and indeed all matter to stop when the influence of all this anger and hatred achieves a certain intensity. The negative energy slows the matter down, then causes a reversal in direction. A fall, as it were."

"It sounds interesting, though I don't have the faintest idea what it means," Deyv said. His voice was low but angry. "Do you think this is the place to tell me about Sindsindbat's theory, whoever he is?"

"My grandfather on my mother's side but my great-grandmother on my father's side," Sloosh said. "Undoubtedly one of the greatest, if perhaps somewhat unstable, minds of the Archkerri. It's his—"

"Shut up!" Deyv said. "Your own mind can't be too stable if you start propounding some irrelevant nonsense about stars falling because people are mad about something. Here we are—"

" 'Irrelevant nonsense' is a redundancy," Sloosh said. "All nonsense is irrelevant."

"That shows what little you know about humans," Deyv said. "Anyway, be quiet! Sound carries upward. What if somebody is awake up there?"

"True. But my comment was caused by my recently hearing you and Vana quarreling about whether or not women should be taboo, that is, ritually unclean, for a certain period after childbirth or menstruation. She claimed—"

"Shut up! Shut up! Do you want to get us killed?"

"Well, your argument led me to think about anger, and—"

Deyv managed to stretch himself far enough to place his hand over the plant-man's beak.

"Now, be quiet! Or I swear I'll lop off your buzzer with my sword!"

Sloosh said nothing after that. He resumed climbing; and after what seemed a long time, and may have been, they rose through the shaft in the center of the middle *tharakorm*. The cable was wound around a huge windlass suspended about ten feet above the top of the shaft. On the edge to their right was a smaller windlass, used to let down or draw up the rope-ladder.

Deyv looked around quickly. No one was in sight, though due to the dimness of light, that didn't mean that no one was on the decks of the two *tharakorm* attached to the central one.

However, that no one was around was good. But they were still in trouble. Sloosh couldn't go any higher than the point at which the cable came off the monstrously large drum of the windlass. There was nothing for him to grab on to. The cable was wound too tightly around the drum.

It might have been possible for Deyv to crawl up Sloosh's body and, standing on his shoulders, dig his fingers into the cable and draw himself on up. This was out. One touch from him, and the alarm would go off.

The rope ladder hadn't been drawn all the way

around its windlass. About ten feet hung down below the edge. Deyv explained what he had to do. The Archkerri didn't reply, but he must have been thinking of what would happen to Deyv if he failed. He may also have wished to tell Deyv not to cry out if he did fall. Or perhaps he was calculating how long it would take Deyv before he struck the ground. Who knew what went on in the mind behind the cabbage leaves?

Deyv wondered, fleetingly, what Vana would think if his body came through the darkness and splashed in front of her. That was a strange thought, he thought even more fleetingly. What did she care?

Or perhaps he might fall on the Yawtl. Though he hadn't killed Hoozisst, as he'd felt like doing, and though he'd treated him as a comrade, which he was, in a sense, he still was angry because the Yawtl had stolen his egg. At least, if he, Deyv, fell on Hoozisst, then the thief would die, too. There was some satisfaction, though not much, in that visualization.

Deyv would have liked to ask Sloosh if his grip was still strong. He needed reassurance. It didn't matter, however. He had to act now, whatever the situation was.

Gripping the Archkerri's lower body with his legs, Deyv untied the rope around his waist. Then he slowly slid down the rope, only a few inches from the triple cable, and when he was a few feet below Sloosh's legs, he began to swing on the rope. Back and forth he went until he could almost reach the dangling rope-ladder with the fingertips of his extended right arm.

Then, at the next swing inward, he released the grip of his left hand and fell outward. His right hand missed the first three rungs but closed on the next to last. And his left hand snapped around and seized the bottom rung, and his toes banged into the side of the shaft.

The ladder held firm.

He gasped with relief. Until then he couldn't be sure that the windlass around which the ladder was wrapped had been locked. If it hadn't been, the drum would have spun out, and he would have fallen clinging to the ladder, which would have smashed on the ground below.

He pulled himself up with arms and shoulders until he was up enough to get a foothold. Then he climbed quickly up the ladder and was over the edge.

Sloosh's leaf-covered head was turned toward him. Deyv signaled that he must return down the cable to the ground. There was no way of getting the plant-man onto the *tharakorm* except up the rope-ladder.

While Sloosh was letting himself down, much more quickly than he'd ascended, Deyv studied the windlass at close range. Though he'd never seen such a machine before, he figured out within a minute how to unlock it. Having done this, he began to unwind it slowly. The weight of the rope-ladder, over six hundred feet long, was immense. The windlass had a brake, however, which was operated by foot. And it must have been oiled recently, since it didn't squeak.

Looking down through the hole, he could not see the ground or the people on it. The Archkerri had disappeared into the darkness. Deyv wouldn't be able to see the ladder reach the earth, but when it could no longer be let down, he guessed it would be there. If there was a surplus, it wouldn't matter.

When the drum was almost bare, Deyv relocked the windlass. It would take some time before the first person came up, so he might as well look around. He would not go out of sight of the windlass, however. He didn't want any of Feersh's crew to find that the ladder had been lowered and to raise an alarm.

Having taken his blowgun out of its case and fitted a dart into it, he went to the center entrance of the ship-creature. A wooden cabin had been built over it. Its door was closed. He circled the cabin, noting that it had two windows on each side, both too small for him to wriggle through. At least one person was inside, snoring.

For a moment, he considered entering through the door and killing the sleeper. There might be others, however, and so more than he could handle. It was best to wait until all his party had boarded and rested after the arduous climb. He prowled the deck, looking through the windows of the other two wooden cabins. One seemed to be unoccupied, but that could be because it lacked snorers.

The *tharakorm* on each side of that on which he stood also had cabins. According to Yawtl, the center creature was the residence of Feersh the Blind and her brood. The one on his left, looking toward the bow, held the *khratikl*; the one on his right, the human slaves. The witch and her family numbered six.

The Yawtl had said that one of the major dangers was Feersh's Emerald of Anticipation. This was a large green translucent stone she always wore suspended from a leather cord around her neck. Its name came from its ability to predict events anywhere from a few minutes to a few hours before they happened.

"She told me that it was a stone of some sort which grows in the land of The Shemibob," Hoozisst had said. "There are uncountable numbers of these stones, but very few dare enter the glittering ever-growing land which is known to some as The Shining House of Countless Chambers. Others call it The Jeweled Wasteland or The Bright Abomination.

"Feersh, however, must have had the courage to trespass on its very edge. She would've chipped off a jewel and fled with it. It is said that she was stricken blind shortly thereafter. I don't know if there is any truth in that story. I doubt it. Not the story about The Shemibob. There is no doubt that the monster-witch exists. I mean Feersh's claim that she stole the Emerald herself. As is well known, witches seldom leave their homes, be they Houses of the ancients, castles, caves, or *tharakorm*."

Sloosh interrupted then. "That is because they have become too dependent on their ancients' artifacts, and they feel uneasy unless they are surrounded by them. They have no tribes, and they can't trust anyone except their families, and sometimes not even them. In fact, most witches suffer from a sickness of the mind that makes them unable to venture from their homes without great fear. They are prisoners of their own powers."

"Anyway," Hoozisst had continued, "the witch told me that she can 'speak' to the Emerald and give it information about situations that might occur. The precious stone then replies, telling her what is most likely to occur. I don't mean that the Emerald actually has a voice. It responds by showing within its interior certain designs. Only the witch can interpret these. Or so she said."

"If she's blind," Vana had asked, "how can she see the designs?"

"She is dependent upon her eldest daughter, Jowanarr, who describes the designs to her. Jowanarr will become the head of the family when Feersh dies. If she isn't too old to bear children then, she will have them by a slave picked for his intelligence, good looks, excellent physique, and virility. If she's barren, then her sister Seelgee will bear the children, but Jowanarr will still head the family.

"But that doesn't matter. What does matter is that Feersh promised that after I'd stolen thirty eggs, I'd get the Emerald. She would then teach me how to give the information to the stone and how to read the designs. I should have known that she was lying, the bitch!"

"You were very lucky you weren't killed," Deyv had said. "You should have been, even though a tree broke the fall."

"We Yawtl are tough," Hoozisst had said. "Besides, I'd grabbed a blanket from the shoulders of her son Jeydee, and by holding on to its four corners I slowed my fall somewhat. Still, it was luck more than anything else that kept me alive. The tree-gods saved me so that I could get my revenge."

Whatever the abilities of the Emerald, it wasn't warning Feersh now. But then she didn't know about his party, Deyv thought. Or, if she did, she wasn't worried about them. After all, the stone was dependent upon the data she gave it, and if that was insufficient, the stone didn't have what it needed to make the right prediction.

On the other hand, for all he knew, Feersh was well aware of what was going on. She'd set up a trap; she was watching them from the dark cabin. Those within were awake and pretending to snore.

He looked down through the shaft. Here came the first climber, Sloosh. He bore on his back the collapsed vessel and Aejip, tied to him. The cat was scared, but she wouldn't make any noise.

At that moment, he heard a cough. Down on his hands and knees, he turned around. He could see no one. That meant that either someone had coughed in the central cabin or that he or she had come out of its door. This faced the bow, and he was behind the cabin.

He rose with the blowgun in his hand. Softly, he walked to the cabin and along its side. The cough was not repeated. There was no one in front of the cabin, but its door was open. Someone was out on the deck. But where?

He quietly shut the door and went to the other side of the cabin. The cougher was walking toward the bow, which was pointed downwind. Deyv looked back toward the windlasses. He could see them from the cabin plainly enough. The man hadn't noticed that the rope-ladder windlass drum was almost bare. He couldn't escape noticing it on the way back, not if he was more fully awake.

There was only one thing to do. Deyv walked toward the man, who by now was standing near the bow, getting ready to relieve himself. He was very intent on his business when Deyv's tomahawk struck him in the back of the head. He went over the low railing of wood glued to the deck and disappeared without an outcry.

19

DEYV whirled, tense, hoping nobody had heard the crack of weapon against bone. Sometime later the faint splop of a body smashing into earth reached him.

Deyv went back to the hole quietly, pausing to listen at a cabin window. There wasn't a sound. Sloosh came up shortly after, breathing heavily through his chest-mouth. Deyv helped him up, unloaded the cube, and untied Aejip. The cat bounded onto the deck, grimacing soundlessly. Deyv patted and stroked her to soothe her and whispered that she should stay there until Vana came. It had been agreed beforehand that the woman would be Aejip's partner during the attack.

The Yawtl came next, toiling upward with Jum bound to his back. Deyv also petted and quieted him. Vana boarded close behind Hoozisst. Deyv told them what he'd observed and that he'd killed a man.

"I thought I saw something falling through the dark," the Yawtl said. "I was afraid it was you. But when I heard no alarm, I knew that it must have been one of them. If he came from that cabin, he was one of Feersh's sons. I hope it wasn't Skibroziy. I want him to suffer much before he dies."

Hoozisst had described in detail the layout of the rooms and corridors of the ship-creatures. Feersh slept in a chamber on the lower deck. Sometimes, she was alone; sometimes, with a male slave. Jowanarr spent her sleep-time in the aft cabin with two or three slaves, male and female. Seelgee was in the cabin nearest the bow. Kiyt was in a cabin near his mother's. Jeydee and Skibroziy were usually in the middle cabin, either by themselves or with a couple of male or female slaves. Hoozisst had also described the sons and daughters so that they wouldn't be confused with the slaves.

The only way to get belowdecks was to go through the cabins—unless you were a *khratikl*. The plan was to seize Feersh as a hostage. Hoozisst had said that he believed they would be safe as long as they had her in their power. The others would do what she said—he hoped. Of course, there was the possibility that Jowanarr, who no doubt was impatient to be the chief, might let her mother be killed.

The raiders went behind the central cabin, where Vana passed around torches she'd brought up on her back. Using the cabin and a fiber sheet, found on the deck, as protection from the wind, they lit the torches. First, they poured out from a gourd some fish-oil they'd prepared. Then the Yawtl used his iron and flint to rain sparks on the oil. After a few failures, it finally lit. He poured more oil on the blaze, and they took turns dipping the ends of their fish-oil-soaked torches in the fire.

Just as the third torch was set to burning, they heard a scream to their right. They spun toward the sound but could see nothing. A moment later, a furious shrieking *khratikl* swept at them from the darkness. Its leathery wings beat at Deyv, and its claws ripped into his face. Shouting with pain, he dropped his torch and grabbed the stinking loathsome thing and threw it on the deck. Before it could rise, it was tomahawked by the Yawtl.

It was too late to carry out their original plan. They'd intended to split up the party so all three cabins could be invaded at once. Now they had to get inside the central cabin at once. Somewhere something metallic was being struck, its deep bongs vibrating through the air. And from the *tharakorm* housing the *khratikl* came many screams of rage.

Hoozisst, holding his torch in one hand, opened the door to the central cabin with the other. He snatched his tomahawk from his belt and, yelling, charged inside. Vana followed, the now roaring cat close behind her. Deyv picked his torch up, felt the blood streaming down his face, grimaced at the pain, and, sword in hand, bounded after the others. The dog, growling, leaped after him. The plant-man, the slowest, had been chosen to form the rearguard.

The cabin was made of a heavy wood stained a brown-reddish color and painted with horizontal bands of yellow and green. Spears, blowguns, tomahawks, war clubs, and one of the ancient metal swords hung on the walls. Two corners held beds, wide, mattressed, and covered with some beautiful cloth Deyv had never seen before. There was a chest of drawers and two stands with washbowls, and soap, towels, and bottles of some dark-green substance.

In the middle of the room was a table of glossy hardwood which held a base on which was a large ball of quartz. It pulsed with a fierce orange glow that made the torches unnecessary. It struck Deyv with astonishment, since it had not been on fire until a moment before. Jowanarr must have summoned the light through witchery.

A man, a well-built slave with dark-brown skin and wavy hair dyed green and yellow, lay face down on the floor. Blood spread out from under him. On the bed by him sat a naked woman, Jowanarr. Her hands were clutching her chest and under her dark skin was a paleness. She was long-legged and slim but had huge breasts and a long narrow face, a long hooked nose, and dark eyes great with terror.

On the other bed sprawled another male slave, Vana's short spear sticking out of his throat.

Jowanarr, seeing Deyv's bloody face, started to stand up. Aejip and Jum snarled at her, and she sat back down.

Deyv went past the table with the glowing quartz sphere and removed a square trap door by its metal ring. The opening revealed a dark well from which descended a flight of wooden steps that had been placed over the steep ramp grown by the *tharakorm*.

He looked up. Vana was pulling on the spear caught in the slave's windpipe.

"Forget that!" he said. "Take that sword off the wall!"

The Yawtl beat her to it. Swinging the blade around over his head, he whooped.

Deyv had no time to be disgusted with Hoozisst's greediness. He could handle the sword better than Vana anyway, being the stronger. She shot out her tongue at him, an expression of contempt in her tribe, and turned around to withdraw the spear.

Sloosh had closed the door behind him. A good thing, too, for immediately thereafter paws pounded on it, claws scratched, and screeching filled the cabin. Ratlike faces looked through the windows, followed shortly by bodies. Aejip flew along the walls, raking the faces with her claws. Jum leaped up and bit down on others. Vana thrust her spear into a dripping mouth.

"Tell the witch's daughter to order them to stay out!" Deyv whistled at the Yawtl in Archkerri.

The Yawtl spat words at Jowanarr. She hesitated, but when Hoozisst, his sword raised, stepped toward her, she screamed out at the beasts. They ceased trying to get through the windows, though their din filled the cabin.

Deyv grabbed the woman's hand and yanked her off the bed. He pulled her to the opening in the floor and thrust her down ahead of him. She fell down the wooden stairs but would have been up on her feet and down a corridor if he hadn't leaped down on top of her. Her head hit the floor, and she passed out. He hoped he hadn't killed her, since he might need her later.

Vana came down swiftly, followed by the two animals. Hoozisst took the steps two at a time, surrounded by light. He'd abandoned his torch for the glowing quartz sphere.

"It makes a much better light," he said, grinning. "Besides, I want to make sure nobody else grabs it."

Deyv didn't wait for the Archkerri to make his ponderous way down the steps. He raced ahead toward where the Yawtl had said the witch slept. Open entrances, dark, silent, flashed past. The doorway to Feersh's room was about ten feet away when he slammed headlong into a wall that shot out of a recess. He fell back onto the floor, the sword and the torch fallen from his suddenly limp hands. For a moment he didn't know what had happened. Added to the flow of blood from the claw wounds was blood from his nose.

He rose shakily and picked up the torch. The wall had slid out or dropped down from hollows within the corridor walls. It had come out so swiftly he hadn't even been aware of it. Nor had he heard it thud into the floor.

He turned, automatically picking up the sword. Ten feet behind him another wall barred his passage. He was trapped.

Someone was hammering on that wall. He strode to it and shouted. Silence rolled through the chamber. He put his mouth as close as he could to the very tough but very thin material and yelled, "It's I, Deyv! Who's there?"

Putting his ear against the wall, he heard, "Quiet, Jum, Aejip!"

Now he could distinguish the low growlings of the animals.

"Vana! I'm caught between two walls. Where are the others?"

"Hoozisst has gone down another corridor. He'll then go down the one which runs alongside the hull and see if he can get to the witch's room from its other end."

"She wouldn't leave that side open—I think," Deyv yelled back. "Where's Sloosh?"

"He's holding off the *khratikl* in the room below the entrance."

Deyv managed to shove down the panic that was growing like yeast in a pot, pushing up the lid of his self-control. The air in this chamber would last only so long, and any energetic action would burn it up that much faster. He knew that Feersh wouldn't want to trap herself, so she must have an escape route. It wouldn't be through the bottom of the hull because she'd have to have a huge windlass to let herself down on a rope-ladder to the ground. Besides, she wouldn't abandon the *tharakorm* and so be at the mercy of enemies who might be below.

This was the lower deck. At this point the hull curved inward, like the hull of a canoe. This level had no direct contact with the hull of the neighboring *tharakorm*. But there probably was a window through which Feersh could put a plank so that she could then cross over to the adjacent ship-creature. She might already be in it. Or she might be waiting to see what happened.

Deyv told Vana his speculations. Then he said, "I'm going to cut through the hull—if I can—and find out if she's gone across. That'll give me air, too. I only hope that the hull isn't as tough as the walls guarding the gas cells."

"But even if you find that out," Vana called, "what good will it do? You won't be able to follow her."

"I told you I have to have air. And for all I know, there is more than one wall between her door and this wall."

Vana shouted, "Sloosh is having trouble. I have to go. I'll be back soon, if I'm able."

He listened but could hear nothing. He called to her and got no reply. Shrugging, he turned and began punching at the hull with the point of his sword. It was hard work, the stuff resisting over fifty punches before the tip of the blade went through. He would have liked to quench his torch because it was burning up the oxygen so swiftly. But he had to see so he could hit the same spot each time. Besides, there was nothing with which he could put the flame out. When it did go out, it would have used up all the air, and he'd be dead.

By the time he made a small slit, he was sweating heavily, his arms were getting numb, and his senses were fading. He lengthened the incision a trifle, then inserted his blade, and with a mighty effort—relatively mighty, anyway—bent the edges of the cut outward. He put his nose to the hole and breathed in. Fresh air greeted him. He managed to smile, he was so relieved. There could have been an inner wall to the hull, and if there had been, he soon would have been dead.

His strength regained, he worked until he'd made a hole big enough to put his head through. Above him was much noise, men and women screaming and yelling, *khratikl* screeching and chittering. To his right he could see a large opening in the hull. The witch could have gotten through that, but there was nothing bridging the gap. However, Feersh wouldn't have left the plank there so she could be followed.

He turned to batter at the wall through which he'd spoken to Vana. Suddenly it shot up into its slot, startling him and leaving him with a knocking heart.

Behind him the Yawtl said, "I thought you might be dead by now."

Hoozisst, holding the glowing sphere, was standing just beyond where the other wall had been. He was grinning as if he'd played a big joke on somebody. Sweat plastered his long reddish hairs to his body.

"I cut through the wall barring my way," he said, "and I got to the witch's quarters. She was gone from there, but I saw the edge of a board on the rim of the window of the *tharakorm* opposite. I looked around, and I found the control which operates the traps. It's a strange little animal which seems to be glued to the wall. It—"

"Never mind that," Deyv said. "Follow me!"

He ran down the corridor toward the uproar, holding the torch in his left hand. He found Sloosh standing near the bottom of the steps, gesturing at the small remnant of survivors with his torch. Bodies lay around him, *khratikl* battered with his club and burned with his brand. Vana and the two animals were not in sight.

Seeing the two newcomers, the *khratikl* fled back up the steps.

Deyv, panting, said, "Where's—?"

"Down the corridor," Sloosh buzzed. "She thinks

the slaves and Feersh's children are waiting above to get us when we come back up. They aren't capable of much action on their own. They depend upon the witch too much for orders. Which is a weakness we must take advantage of. I presume the witch escaped, otherwise you'd have told me differently."

Deyv nodded. Above them, ringing the opening, were the pointed faces and bright-yellow eyes of the *khratikl*. The steps were smeared with blood from the wounded who had fled up them. The Archkerri had lost some of his leaves and others were torn. His skin was pink but looked thick. No veins were visible.

Deyv said, "Feersh should be up there by now organizing the humans and *khratikl*. We must've killed half of their beasts, though, and I doubt that the slaves will fight well."

"That's right," Hoozisst said, great contempt in his voice. "Slaves don't make good warriors. Not unless they're fighting against their masters."

A high harsh voice reached them. They looked up to glimpse a narrow bony face with a gray topknot of hair. The Emerald, an egg-sized stone, dangled from a cord around her neck. The face shot away, and the *khratikl* by it also disappeared. A moment later, the trap door slid out to cover almost the entire opening. A thick dark fluid began flowing down the steps. It had an acrid odor.

The Yawtl said, "She's going to smoke us out!"

20

THEY raced down the corridor in the direction where Vana and the animals had gone. Just as they got to the steps leading up to the fore cabin, ten *khratikl* raced around the corner ahead of them. Evidently, these had flown down to and through the windows in the bottom and sides of the hull, hoping to surprise the invaders. The bodies of six *khratikl* lay at the foot of the steps, their wounds showing that the dog and the cat had disposed of most of them. The trap door was also almost closed, leaving a narrow space, and the same kind of fluid was being poured down the steps.

Deyv looked behind him. Shadowy figures were moving toward them. The *khratikl* were going to try to kill as many of their enemy as possible before the smoke drove them back out the way they'd come.

Deyv shouted a warning to the others, and he charged the beasts at the corner. They flung themselves at him, but his sword cut them or his torch, thrust into their faces, burned them. Screaming, leathery wings flapping, they ran off. He didn't pursue them; he didn't want to waste his time. The Yawtl had driven off the five behind them, but the things leaped around within the edge of the light from the sphere. When Hoozisst charged them, they retreated. When he back-stepped to the stairs, they followed him.

"Vana must have gotten out this way," Deyv said.

Had she broken through to the deck? Or was she dead? And Jum and Aejip, too?

Now the *khratikl* he'd chased away were back, looking around the corner.

Slooshi said, "I hope they don't set the fluid on fire while I'm on the steps."

He clumped up the stairs, turned around, lowered his upper torso until it extended straight out, and then began pushing upward with his rear. His legs slowly straightened; the trap door began to rise. From above came frightened yells. Deyv hastened to aid him, while the Yawtl remained below to keep the *khratikl* away.

Reaching through the widening gap with his sword, Deyv slashed or stabbed at the humans. They merely defended themselves, leaping back to avoid being wounded on their legs and making sure that they didn't come too close. They thrust spears at him from three sides. One man willing to take a chance could probably have run him through.

But the trap door started to open. Had the slaves been standing on it so their weight would keep it closed, they would have fallen off. Suddenly, the Archkerri raised his upper body, his massive arms reaching to each side and pushing up. The door fell over with a bang, and Sloosh reached down and picked up his club from the step where he'd put it.

The Yawtl turned from the *khratikl* and ran up the steps, dropping the sphere as he did so. He reached for his tomahawk in his belt with his left hand, and he threw it so that its edge sank in under the chin of a spear wielder. Deyv had a momentary thought that this fellow was indeed talented. Right hand or left, it made no difference to him. He was adept with both.

The three remaining male slaves fled screaming from the cabin, jumping over the bodies of two dead men near the doorway. They knocked over two females who'd been standing behind them, holding torches. If they'd had sense enough, the slaves would have set the fluid blazing while the invaders were standing on the steps. But then they were slaves and unaccustomed to doing things without orders from their masters.

The two women, abandoning their torches, got up and dashed out of the cabin. Deyv picked up a brand and threw it down the stairwell. The stuff caught fire quickly, effectually barring the *khratikl* from pursuing them. But they would go out of the hull openings and fly up to the deck.

The Yawtl shrieked, "The sphere! The sphere! You fool, you'll burn it up!"

"It's stone," Deyv said. "Forget your greed, Yawtl. Dead men don't have possessions."

Hoozisst gave him a nasty look. He picked up a tall ceramic vase filled with the fluid and heaved it down the steps. Deyv threw another after it. They broke on the steps, and suddenly the cabin was filled with smoke, flames leaping up through the opening, heating their skins.

The Yawtl heaved a vase through the open door onto

the deck, where it shattered about seven feet away. He cast a torch upon the spreading pool, and it flamed. Deyv ran out then, hoping that if any slaves were waiting beside the doorway to spear him, they'd be shaken by the fire. There were none; they weren't even in sight.

Sloosh followed him, bearing a vase in one arm. The Yawtl, coughing, came after him, also carrying a vase. In one hand he held the other torch.

By the light of the fire, Deyv saw Vana. She was hacking away with a sword at the central cables. Where had she gotten it, from one of the slaves she'd killed when she'd escaped from the cabin? But why was she severing the mooring cables? He ran toward her, shouting. She stopped; then, seeing it was he, she resumed her cutting. A moment later, both were busy defending themselves against a swarm of the winged beasts. Most of these, Deyv presumed, were those who'd attacked him belowdecks.

Jum and Aejip joined them, leaping out from somewhere and taking the *khratikl* from behind. The cat was like a spring, bouncing up and down, to and fro, raking the *khratikl*, biting down on their necks or breaking their backs with blows of her paws. Several times, in their efforts to avoid her, the beasts flew within range of the swords, and they were cut in half or run through.

The four or five *khratikl* left unscathed flew away and settled down for a moment on the railing, far from the immediate danger. Or so they thought. Jum and Aejip followed them, and they leaped screaming off the *tharakorm*. Deyv tried to whistle his pets back to him, but he was out of breath. They came trotting back anyway.

Vana, panting, said, "I sent Jum and Aejip ahead of me, and while they were keeping the slaves busy, I got out. I thought I'd cut the mooring lines to scare them and that they'd leave the cabin to stop me. But they didn't."

"The slaves had their orders, and they followed

them, regardless of changes in the situation." Deyv paused to draw in some much-needed air. At that moment, flames burst through the central cabin, and with much yelling and shrieking, people poured out of it. The blaze showed Sloosh standing by a window through which he'd thrown the vase and after which he'd cast a torch. In the van was the tall skinny figure of Feersh. She must have been standing in the doorway, ready to be the first to leave the *tharakorm* when the fluid poured down the steps was set afire. There she went, knocked down by the slaves and *khratikl* in their panic.

Now the aft cabin suddenly glowed, and flames were leaping out the windows. Revealed in their light was the Yawtl, standing by the window through which he had heaved his vase of fluid. Men and women, among whom must be the witch's children, tumbled out the doorway. The last to fall through was a man, burning.

Vana turned and brought the edge of her blade down against the cables. They parted with a loud snap, the ends whipping by her face with such force that they would have ripped it off if they'd struck it.

"There's no need to cut those now!" Deyv shouted.

She said, "Yes, there is. I saw some *khratikl* fly off toward the slave compound. They'll be bringing back more. Remember what the Yawtl said! There are at least a hundred *khratikl* there, maybe more. They may be flying toward us now. They can see this fire; they'll be alarmed!"

"Yes, but we'll be adrift!" Deyv cried.

"I don't like it, but how else can we avoid them?"

The wind had increased while they were belowdecks. Now the smoke from the fires in the cabins had covered the top deck. Deyv could see nothing through it. Yes, he could. Several figures had plunged through the roiling black clouds. One of them was the Yawtl's.

Deyv cursed and ran to the railing to start hacking at the cables on the sides. Vana had gotten there before him. He followed the railing around the bow, only to find that she had severed these. He went to a point where the hulls of the two *tharakorm* joined, and he leaped onto the deck of the next one. Furiously, he started cutting.

He thought, We only have to drift out of reach of the *khratikl*. Then we can punch holes in the gas cells and sink down slowly.

Sometime later, the Archkerri and Hoozisst joined him. In a short time, Vana was with them. Sloosh stopped cutting the cables and said, "One of you find the vases of fluid on this creature and empty them along the railing where this one joins the other. They haven't seen us yet. Perhaps the fluid can be set on fire to keep them from going over the railing and getting to us."

"I should've thought of that," Deyv said. He scabbarded his sword and ran to a cabin. The light from the fires was just enough for him to see torches in racks on a wall. A box on a shelf held several flints and irons.

He took one of each and groped his way down the steps of the opening. He didn't want to start the torch burning where its light would attract the attention of the enemy. At the bottom of the stairs, he knocked off sparks onto the oil-soaked tip of the torch until it finally caught. He went up and down the corridors, searching each room for the fluid. Though he knew that there was no one aboard to spring the trap of the sliding walls, he still felt uneasy.

The fourth chamber he looked into held jars of the fluid on wooden racks. He put one in each arm while holding the torch in one of his hands, and returned to the bottom of the steps. Here he dropped the brand and went up to the cabin. On the deck he saw the Yawtl, who'd found vases in the bow cabin. They broke the wax sealing in the fluid, and they ran, crouching down along the railing. When they met in the middle, they had poured the fluid from the bow to the stern. Deyv ran to get the torch. The Yawtl did the same; he had also been astute enough to conceal his below the cabin, where its flame wouldn't be seen.

As Deyv came out of the doorway, he heard a disconcerted cry from the next ship. The *khratikl* had seen the flames; they also must have seen his figure by the light. He dashed up near the railing and threw the torch against the bottom of the railing. Flames raced along it in both directions, going faster downwind. The Yawtl's torch set the trail ablaze near the bow, and the two streaks of fire met. Smoke billowed and was caught by the wind and hurried toward the stern.

The two men went to the aft cabin, where Deyv thought he could get vases quicker than by going belowdeck. They spread more oil a few inches away from the original trail. Then they set this afire and went back to get more vases. These they threw at a distance, breaking them. The fluid spread out and caught on fire. Now the slaves and children of Feersh would have to jump down into the burning oil if they wanted to get at them.

Deyv's grin of triumph faded. He said, "I forgot! The plank! She might have others hidden in other rooms. If she does, they can cross over these."

"Not likely," Hoozisst said.

Deyv understood what he meant. How could the enemy get below to a plank, if there was one, through the fires? Nevertheless, he wasn't going to leave anything to chance. Taking a torch, he went down and found the room in which the plank was located. He had to give Feersh credit for courage. Though blind, she had gone on the plank, crawling, no doubt, and had then found her way up to the deck and back onto the first *tharakorm*. She would be thoroughly familiar with her home.

Deyv returned to the top deck. He was startled to see the flames and the smoke going straight up. Nor was any wind blowing against his face.

"We won't drift now," he shouted at Vana, who had just leaped over the railing. "That's rotten luck! The *khratikl* from the compound will soon be upon us!"

She was sweating, and there was blood and soot on her. But she was grinning.

"No, the wind hasn't stopped. If anything, it's gotten stronger. I think it's going to storm. We're cut loose now, that's why you don't feel the wind. Sloosh said we're going the same speed as the wind."

Deyv looked toward the horizon where a thin band of light shone between it and the lower edge of The Beast. He picked out a silhouetted landmark, an especially tall tree. It was true, it was slowly moving past them. Rather, they were passing it.

Hearing cries above him, he looked up. The *khratikl* had flown from the other deck and were now sitting on the yardarms or clinging to the masts of the creature occupied by their enemy. Evidently, they were hesitant about attacking, and with good reason. They numbered only twelve. So, they would be waiting for their fellows from the compound. These would have no trouble finding the creature, since the fires would be a beacon.

Presently, he saw tiny black dots against the band of horizon light. They were coming at an angle, hoping to intercept their quarry. Time passed, and then it was evident that the *khratikl* would have to chase the *tharakorm* from directly behind. They'd be going faster than the wind, since it was behind them. Could they catch up?

Though all four were very tired, they got more vases and added fuel to the fire. At least they wouldn't have to worry about a flank attack from the humans. Then they used the last of the oil to set fires at the bases of the masts. The smoke rose up to drive the *khratikl* away. However, they merely flew over to the third *tharakorm* and settled on its masts.

The four found kegs of water and stores of dried meat and fruit, fresh vegetables, loaves of bread, and jars of butter. They ate eagerly and then rested by the stern. The wind had turned the *tharakorm* around, and this place was the nearest to the pursuing fliers. Deyv and Vana prepared their blowguns, which could be shot with good aim in such still air. The Yawtl brought a big double-headed metal war axe for the Archkerri. He'd found it in a cabin.

"It must have been made for a giant of the ancients," he said. "No slave or any of us for that matter can handle it." He dropped a bundle of spears. "We can throw these when we run out of darts."

By then they could see by the firelight the first of the fliers. These were evidently straining to catch up, their wings beating hard, their labor so great they had no breath for their cries. Though gaining, they were doing so very slowly.

"They might peter out before they get here," Deyv said. "And if they do catch us, they're going to be very tired."

The Yawtl handed Sloosh a spear. "Here, try your luck. They're too far away for us weaklings to hit them, but you might do it."

The Archkerri hefted the weapon and said, "I'll wait until they get a little closer."

His first cast missed the body of the leader, but it went through a wing. Shrieking, the *khratikl* dropped into the blackness below. The others did not slow down.

Jum barked loudly. They turned in the direction at which he pointed. The beasts that had taken refuge on the masts of the *tharakorm* were swooping silently down upon them. They meant to keep the four occupied while their fellows landed.

With a rush of beating wings, they dived, then pulled up and swung around just above the reach of spear or sword. They circled over the deck, rose, and prepared for another onslaught.

Deyv turned his back to them, uncoiled his rope, and tied one end around the hilt of his sword. Then he closed his hand on the middle of the rope. When the *khratikl* came down in close formation, they found the blade suddenly in their midst. The sword swung at the end of the rope, its edge scraping a beast across the front of its grotesquely outshelving chest, another across the front of its head, and a third through the leather of a wing. Two of the creatures flopped onto the deck and then got up to run. Vana speared one.

Hoozisst smashed the head of the other with his tomahawk.

Shrieking, the rest withdrew to the yardarms to confer.

Deyv turned around. Their chasers were within spear range of the humans now. The closest numbered twelve. The rest of the flock had fallen behind and would never catch up.

All of the spears were thrown. Three found their mark, but one went through the skin of a wing without hurting its owner. The hole, however, made it unable to keep up with the rest.

"Nine to go!" Deyv shouted.

Vana fitted a dart into her blowgun, took aim, and blew. Another shriek, another casualty. She hit two more, and then, amidst the cheering, buzzing, barking, and yowling of the defenders, the *khratikl* turned. They were quickly lost in the dark.

Those on the mast made one more dive. It was a half-hearted attempt. Deyv's sword sliced the rear leg off one. Hoozisst's tomahawk thudded into the breast of another. Crying, the survivors flew off for home.

21 ∽

VANA said that they should rest, perhaps sleep, while the fires kept Feersh from attacking. They could take turns on guard duty.

"No," Deyv said. "I realize we've been through an exhausting ordeal. I'm shaking, I'm so fatigued. But we can't allow them any breathing space. There's no telling what ancient devices she might have aboard but which she can't get to yet. Besides, she's vindictive enough to drop our soul eggs over the side. We'd never find them, and all this would have been in vain."

Sloosh started to buzz. Deyv kept on talking.

"Another thing. She may have more than one plank. She could send her slaves and children over it to take us by surprise. For all we know, she may be doing it now or may have already done it. But I'm hoping that if she does have one, she hasn't thought about using it. Or maybe she lacks the nerve to try it; though, from that one glimpse of her face, I'd bet she lacks fear, whatever else she lacks.

"So, I say we put our planks across and storm her *tharakorm*. Now! Before she gets over the shock of seeing her *khratikl* fail!"

"Excellent!" Sloosh buzzed.

Vana said, "You're right. But I'm so tired. I don't know if I can even lift my arm any more."

"You're as tough as the rest of us," Deyv said. "If we can do it, you can."

"Besides, we've eaten," the Yawtl said. "We'll begin feeling stronger shortly."

"There's a point at which food doesn't help," she said. "But I'm not letting you down. Or my tribe."

Deyv understood by this that she meant her tribe was the inferior of no other. She knew she was no longer a member of her people, but she still had hopes of rejoining them. She hadn't given up, though her body was warring with her will at that moment.

He was ashamed that he had thought only of dying when his egg had been stolen. She'd not even considered the idea. She'd set out at once on the trail of the thief. Her people didn't look at things the way his did. Was their attitude superior? Considering the way events had gone, they were. If he'd let himself perish in that terrible room in the House, he wouldn't be here now.

Suddenly, he was aware they were looking at him. He shook himself, like Jum just coming out of a river, and said, "Then here's what we'll do."

After igniting two torches, they went belowdecks and got the plank. They carried it to another room, the window of which was opposite another in the *tharakorm* occupied by Feersh and brood and slaves. She might be thinking by now of doing the same thing as they were. Just from habit, she might use the same window.

The board was just long enough to span the entrances with a few inches extra on each end. Feersh must have had some trouble finding the window across from her, and she must have had great confidence in her ability to estimate distances. But she had probably gone through drills many times. She wasn't one to ignore what might ensure her survival. Not if what Hoozisst said about her was true.

She also must have been very strong despite her scrawny physique. Deyv had trouble holding down his end of the plank against the edge of the window when it was almost fully extended. However, he told himself, he *was* almost exhausted.

Once the board was on the rim of the window opposite, he started across it. Below was an abyss, the bottom of which he couldn't see and was glad he couldn't. The Yawtl followed. Vana and the two animals were next. Deyv and Hoozisst held the board steady for the Archkerri. Before Sloosh was halfway across, his weight had bent it down so that the few inches within the edge of the window had become less than an inch. Deyv hissed at him and then told him, in a low voice, to go back.

Sloosh walked backward and gingerly eased himself, rear first, through the window. Deyv would have liked to call to him to ask what he intended to do next, but he was afraid that his voice would be heard above. The sides of the two *tharakorm* curved up and joined, forming a canopy. Those above couldn't see him, but there was a slight chance that they might detect a loud sound from the window.

"We need him," Deyv muttered, "but we don't have him. So . . ."

They left the torches in the room because their light might be seen by those on deck. The corridor was dark, the fires having burned out, though the stench of the fumes and of burned bodies was heavy. Deyv led the way, groping along, until he went up the stairs into the cabin. Light from torches outside the cabin enabled him to distinguish objects in it. The stink of the charred corpse of a slave made him feel like retching.

He walked softly through the door and looked around the corner. The fires and the torches revealed Feersh, her children, and the slaves behind the cabin. The witch was saying something to them in a low voice. When she'd finished, she put her hand on Jowanarr's shoulder. The daughter turned toward Deyv, who quickly ducked back around the corner.

"Get to the other side!" he whispered.

A moment later, they heard their enemies enter the cabin. Someone was climbing onto the roof. Deyv stepped back from the side of the cabin, where he'd been crouching, and he dared a quick look upward. A slave woman was standing on the roof, her back to him, trying to see through the fire and smoke along the railings.

He shot back to the cabin wall and said, "They've left a lookout up there. But where are the others going?"

The Yawtl said, "I think they're going to do what we just did. But in the other direction."

"Then they have other planks."

"Wouldn't doubt it." The Yawtl chuckled.

"Then they'll see the lights of the torches we left behind!"

If they ran to the fore cabin, they might be seen by the sentinel. A scream would alert the witch. There was, however, no time for much consideration of action.

Without telling the others what he was going to do, he leaped up, slapped his hands on the edge of the cabin roof, and pulled himself up and over. The woman whirled on hearing him, but he was on his feet and lashing out with his tomahawk. Its edge caught her above the ear, and she crumpled without a sound. He leaped off the roof and ran toward the fore cabin. Those below might hear his feet, but there was nothing he could do about it. Behind him Vana and Hoozisst's feet thudded and Jum's and Aejip's paws slapped the deck.

They were in luck. Coming into the corridor, he saw that Feersh and her party were all looking down the corridor that led straight out from the bottom of the stairs. It looked to him as if she'd sent people down it, and they were waiting for them to return. Ah! Some slaves had gone after a plank.

The doorway of the room through which he had entered this *tharakorm* shed light. It would be feeble if seen by the witch's party, but they must have noticed it. That no one had been sent to investigate, however, showed that they had given the light little thought. Why should they? There were plenty of burned-out torches lying around where the battlers of a short time ago had dropped them.

Still, Feersh would have been told of the light. She might decide to have someone investigate when she got near this room. He turned and pressed the others into a room on the other side of the corridor. He got down on all fours and stuck his head around the corner of the doorway. They'd been just in time. Here came a slave running ahead with a torch, two slaves carrying a long plank, and another slave behind them.

The man in the lead raced ahead of the others until he came to the room containing the torches. He looked through the doorway and then sped back to report. Deyv couldn't hear what he said, but evidently Feersh wasn't alarmed. She said something, and the two slaves maneuvered the plank through the door of a room about twenty feet beyond the hiders.

Deyv had to withdraw his head. When the light from the group had dimmed somewhat, he looked again. Nobody was in the corridor.

He waited, then sped silently down the corridor. Hoping that they would be intent on their business, he dared a glimpse into the room. All were watching the two slaves put the plank across the gap.

When he'd told the others what he'd seen, Vana said, "Sloosh will surely see them."

"I don't know. They didn't see him. Maybe he went back to the top deck. But he must've decided to pull the plank back through the window. Otherwise, they'd have seen it."

"In which case," Vana said, "he's still at the window. He'd have to stay there so we could get back if we had to run."

"Not so," Hoozisst said, and he groaned. "You never know what he's thinking. If he happened to recall some philosophical question he'd not solved, he might be digging through it."

After telling Vana to post herself by the doorway, Deyv went back to the room he'd first entered. He didn't think that anybody would come out from the other room. They had no reason to fear attack from behind.

When in the room, he cautiously looked out the window from a distance and at an angle. They couldn't see him, but he could see them. Two big male slaves in Indian file were carefully walking over the board, their hands out to balance themselves, the right hands grasping spears. They were spaced so that their weight didn't bend the plank too much at one point. One went through the window; in a few seconds the other was in. Then a female, carrying a torch, followed them.

Deyv watched more go across, including the witch's two surviving sons. Feersh was preceded by a female also carrying a torch. Feersh had her hand upon her shoulder. They went across more swiftly than the others had, the witch urging the obviously frightened woman ahead with low but fierce words.

Seven were left to cross. Deyv ran back to the room where Vana and Hoozisst were and told them what to do. They followed him, and when they got to the room only five were in it. Jowanarr and Seelgee, the daughters, were on the plank. Jowanarr seemed to be suffering yet from the blow to her head. Her sister was behind her, her hands on Jowanarr's shoulders to steady her.

A woman slave was standing by the window, a torch upheld to help light the two daughters' path. Another woman was in the window of the *tharakorm* opposite, also with a torch.

Deyv gave the word to attack. Aejip bounded in, yowling, and hurled herself at the nearest man. Jum launched himself at a man's throat. Deyv came next, and his sword cut into another slave's neck. The Yawtl stuck the point of his sword into the belly of the fourth man. The woman, screaming, dropped her torch and got onto the plank. Deyv kicked her hard, and she went off the side of the plank.

While the animals were still struggling, quite successfully, with their victims, Deyv and Hoozisst grabbed the end of the plank. They heaved up on it. Jowanarr fell through the window headfirst, but her sister, shrieking, toppled off it.

That left Feersh, her two sons, a daughter, and the slaves in the other ship-creature. Sloosh, if he was still in the room and not on the top deck, must have seen the situation. He'd be hurrying down now to bar their exit from the door. That is, unless he was putting the plank back so that Deyv's group could get over it and help him.

Deyv stuck his head out of the window. The plank was already bridging the gap. He turned and told the others they had to get going. By then the animals had finished off the two male slaves. Deyv ran down the corridor, dark by now, his fingers groping the wall to count the doorways. When he got to the fourth, he stopped and entered. Somebody bumped into him from behind. He stumbled forward under the impact, swore, grabbed the window edge, and halted himself. He made sure that the plank extended far enough into the room to be safe. He climbed onto the board and, his fear of being too late overcoming his fear of the abyss, ran across.

Sloosh was gone. Evidently he'd put the plank across

and then hurried toward the room where Feersh was. Or where she had been.

He rounded the corner. Down the corridor light shone from a doorway. Sloosh was illumined in it, one hand holding up the great war axe, the other holding his club. When he got to the doorway, Deyv found Feersh railing at her children and slaves. It was no use. They feared her, but they feared the invaders more.

22

GREEDY Hoozisst had taken the Emerald and hung it from his neck, and then the captives' hands and feet had been tied. All but one had been put in a room whose open exit was a window to the outside. Hoozisst had told Sloosh how to control those chambers which had sliding doors. They used the little animal on the wall of Feersh's quarters to close the room in which the bound prisoners were kept. To make sure that the witch couldn't kill herself by getting out through a window, they enclosed her in a room without one. Since she would soon have died of oxygen-starvation, Sloosh punched a hole in the hull.

All of Deyv's party except the Archkerri wanted to puncture the gas cells immediately. Sloosh, however, said that it would be too dangerous at this time. To convince them, he took them back up to the top deck.

"Look at that peak on the horizon," he said. "Notice how fast it's going by, yet it must be a long way off. We must be traveling at least a hundred miles an *ukhromikhthanshukh.*"

"What's that?" Deyv asked.

Sloosh had given the particular groups of buzzes corresponding to certain sounds in Vana's language. But the word was unknown to her.

The Archkerri explained that the Earth rotated on

its axis about once every 142.8 hours. An hour, that is, an *ukhromikhthanshukh*, was a unit of time. There were about thirteen of these between sleep-time and sleep-time, though that was not by any means exact. At one time the Earth had rotated on its axis once every twenty-four hours. At other times, it had not rotated at all, but this state had not lasted long, since the ancients of that time had set it back to spinning every twenty-four hours.

The others still didn't at all understand what the word meant.

"That is because you have a very feeble idea of time. You can't be blamed for that, since your technology and science are undeveloped."

Stung, Deyv said, "You have much less sense of time than we do!"

"Not true. What I have is a lesser sense of urgency. Though it's much more developed now because of my association with you people. My people would be appalled if they knew how strong it was. Perhaps it would be better if all the Archkerri had this, however. A lack of that sense may explain, in part, why we are so few and you other sapients are, in comparison, so many."

He closed his eyes, then opened them.

"Let me put it this way. You remember when we crash-landed in that other *tharakorm*? We were going only about fifty miles an hour. We're going twice as fast now. If we land now, we'll be killed. The *tharakorm* probably wouldn't be damaged, but we'd be smashed to pulp. So, landing now is out."

"But this storm might last a long time!" Vana said. "By the time we could land, we might be more than a thousand miles from our home!"

"More like three thousand miles," Sloosh said. "It could even be six thousand or ten thousand. Who knows?"

They were horrified. Tears ran down the cheeks of Vana and Deyv. The Yawtl didn't weep, but he looked as if he'd like to. Jum and Aejip didn't know what the cause of the grief was, but the dog whimpered, and the cat licked Vana's leg. Perhaps they thought that the approaching thunder and lightning were making their masters afraid.

After a while the roar and crash and dazzling whiteness drove them belowdecks. Deyv had thought that they might as well question Feersh now, but he decided that it would be well near impossible. It was far too noisy. Every time a lightning bolt exploded nearby, he jumped and then shook. He wouldn't have the concentration that the interrogation would require.

Even so, he regretted that he couldn't make her tell him where his soul egg was. It would be so soothing to hold it in his hand, to stroke it, to press it against his chest, to kiss it. It radiated comfort and courage, and by bending his thoughts around it, he could make the thunder and lightning seem remote, undangerous. At this time, he hated the witch more than he ever had. When the storm was over, he was going to make her reveal the hiding place of the eggs if he had to unravel her nerve by nerve.

He huddled in an inner room, where Sloosh said they would have less chance of being struck by the lightning. His arm was around the dog, who pressed closely against him. Vana was embracing the cat. Sloosh stood in a corner, his eyes closed. He might have been asleep or thinking about something remote from human affairs or even his own. The Yawtl was nervous, but he had no one to cling to, so he had gone into an embryonic position. His knees were against his chest, his arms around his knees, his head bent to touch them. When a bolt ripped the air close by, he started as if he had awakened in his mother's womb, hearing the call to be born.

Now and then Deyv managed to doze, only to be awakened trembling from sleep by a deafening and darkness-dispelling blast. He ate now and then, and when he had to relieve himself, he would go to the room where the witch was imprisoned. The others also did this to lower her morale. None of the captives were fed, though they were given water. If hunger weakened them, so much the better. They would have less resistance to the inquisition. And lying in their own excrement would make them more miserable.

After an almost intolerable length of time, the black thunder and his white sisters went away. Observation from the top deck showed that the wind was still as strong. Moreover, they were just over a particularly mountainous region, and now the *tharakorm* dropped sickeningly in downdrafts or cannoned upward so suddenly that they momentarily floated. They had to go back to their room and lie down again.

Sloosh, who should have known better by now, insisted on telling the others what might happen.

"The downdrafts could take us all the way to the ground. The updrafts could take us so high we'd pass out or even die from lack of oxygen. And we might be dashed against a mountainside."

He couldn't understand why they told him to shut up.

"Ignoring the facts or wishing to be ignorant of them is unrealistic. However, as you wish. So . . . I won't irritate you by telling you about these mountains."

"Good," Deyv said. After a while, though, he asked, "What about the mountains?"

"Ah, curiosity is stronger than fear. These mountains are part of a mighty range that extends from one ocean-shore to the other. It bisects this land mass. It'll make our return on foot very difficult. But we can bypass it by making a boat and traveling along the shore. Of course, that isn't without its perils. There are tsunamis and giant carnivorous fish and sea-mammals and hostile sapients. It might be better to take the land route. But if we do, we'll take much more time for passage. Also, the quakes make the range very perilous. Landslides, the earth opening under us, all sorts of unpleasant events."

"Shut up!" the others said in unison.

The mountains fell behind, and the flight became more comfortable. The wind slackened considerably, though Sloosh estimated by a little less than half. The band of light on the horizon widened a trifle, causing Sloosh to remark that he had seriously underestimated the wind velocity.

"It must have gotten up to one hundred fifty miles per hour at times, maybe even two hundred. In any event, we still can't take a chance on landing. However, the *tharakorm* haven't been fed since we took off, and eight sleep-times without food will result in some loss of the lifting gas. So, eventually, like it or not, we'll sink to the ground."

Deyv regretted that they'd thrown the corpses overboard instead of feeding them to the ship-creatures.

By then the stink of excrement and unwashed bodies was pervading the *tharakorm*. The captives were released, by couples, to clean up themselves and the floors. There was still enough drinking water to spare for washing the filthier parts of their bodies. Empty vases and bowls were set out to catch rainwater. So far, the food supply was sufficient. Even so, the captives were now fed only sparingly.

After the tenth sleep-time, the wind began dropping. In the meantime, the *tharakorm* were thoroughly searched. Even the yardarms were examined. They could find none of their soul eggs or the Archkerri's crystal. It was time for the questioning.

The slaves were tried first, though it was unlikely that they would know where the soul eggs were kept. Feersh and her children were present at the sessions so they could witness—in the witch's case, hear—what was in store for them. The slaves were not tortured, since it wasn't worthwhile, but Deyv and his companions made plenty of references to their plans to do so.

As expected, the slaves had no idea where Feersh had put the eggs. Even when they were threatened with being thrown out a window, they insisted on this. The Yawtl was all for heaving them out anyway, but Deyv and Vana felt that they might be useful later on. Sloosh said nothing about this. He either didn't care or had not yet considered the problem.

Next, the two surviving sons of Feersh, Kiyt and Jeydee, and the daughter, Jowanarr, were worked upon. All three normally wore floor-length robes, but they'd been naked when captured and had remained so. They had no soul eggs, since their original witch ancestors had been people whose eggs had "soured," as the saying went. Thus, they couldn't be threatened with the loss of these.

However, their lack of clothes when outside their cabins did humiliate them and make them feel powerless. As the first step in the interrogation, the Yawtl passed water all over their bodies. This was, in witch culture, a peculiarly insulting deed. The slaves must have enjoyed this, since they'd had to undergo the same treatment whenever Feersh's brood wished to punish them. They had difficulty suppressing their smiles.

The slaves were then told to pummel the witch's children. They hesitated until Hoozisst said they'd be thrown out the window if they didn't obey. They must not beat them so severely, though, that they couldn't answer questions clearly. At first somewhat diffident, the slaves became enthusiastic after a while. The Yawtl called them off when he thought the three had had enough softening.

"Now," he said, "the hard part starts. I have in mind burning wooden splints under the fingernails first. If that doesn't work, I'll put burning wooden splints up your genitals. After that, I'll start getting tough."

The sons began weeping and sobbing and moaning that they did not know where the eggs were. Their mother did know, but she would never take them into her confidence about them. Jowanarr said nothing, nor had she cried out when being beaten.

Jeydee spoke out of a mouth which had lost half its teeth. "Mother, tell them! We cannot take this!"

Feersh stood in a corner, her hands tied behind her. She, too, was naked and no doubt very conscious of her ugly scrawny body and breasts, which sagged almost to her navel. The long narrow face with its bulging cheekbones and hairy upper lip was set as if it were a wax mask. The blind eyes stared straight ahead.

Sloosh said, "It is a waste of time to give pain to these creatures. You might enjoy this, Yawtl, but I don't. I'm very sensitive to the pain of others. I can permit torture, if there is a rational reason for it, even if I too suffer, though not of course to the same degree as the tortured.

"But my main objection is the uselessness of this. The witch isn't going to tell us anything which will keep her children from being hurt. She doesn't really care about them. She's spoiled them, kept them from maturing, not from love but because they'd be weak and easier to handle. Her eldest daughter has been raised somewhat more strictly because she will someday be the chief, and so she has a stronger character. However, Feersh isn't going to give in if you torture Jowanarr. In fact, she might even enjoy it.

"So, I suggest you tackle Feersh herself. Not with pain or threats. She's too tough for those. She—"

For the first time, the witch spoke. "What is the plant-man saying?"

Hoozisst raised his thick tangled eyebrows as if he thought they might be making progress. He translated for her.

She said, "What he says is true. You could kill me, and I still wouldn't cry out, let alone tell you what you want to know. However, I wouldn't hesitate at all telling you where the eggs are hidden if I believed you'd not kill me. If I could think of some way to guarantee that we'd be freed once I told you, I'd do it."

Kiyt cried out, "Mother! Why didn't you say this before? Why let us be degraded and beaten?"

The witch smiled, revealing very yellow teeth. "I've been too soft with you. I thought that perhaps the ordeal might strengthen your character."

His face twisted with anger, Kiyt spat blood at her. Then he stepped back as if he feared that she might strike him.

Feersh either didn't know that he was the one

spitting or she was ignoring him. She said, "Vegetable-thing, can't we make a deal? One which you can enforce? I don't trust these savages."

"Vegetable-thing!" Sloosh said. "You don't arrange such matters by starting with an insult!"

Hoozisst translated for Feersh.

She said, "I apologize—for the first time in my life. Actually, it wasn't an insult. I am a flesh-thing, and you are what I said. But since it offends you . . . Now, what about my proposal?"

The Archkerri closed his eyes. Except for the coughing of a slave and the muted groaning of the two sons, there was silence. Finally, he opened his eyes. "It's a reasonable suggestion. I think we should accept."

"No!" Hoozisst shouted. "What about my revenge? Would you cheat me of that? We can have what is owing me and the eggs also!"

"Ah, but if revenge is in order," Sloosh said, "what about Vana's and Deyv's? You stole their eggs, and it was only with difficulty that I could keep them from torturing and then killing you. The reason I could is that they needed you to help get the eggs back. The same logic applies here."

Hoozisst was too angry to talk for a while. Then he said, "But I was under duress! I had to steal the eggs or I wouldn't have gotten the Emerald of Anticipation! Also, she would have killed me if I hadn't done what she wanted!"

"She didn't tell you to rob me of my crystal," Sloosh said. "She didn't want that. Yet, you took it. Besides, all you had to do was promise her you'd steal the eggs and then run away. She could never have found you."

"What? And be forever separated from my tribe?"

" 'Forever' is not exact. It would have lasted only until you died. However, you do have a point there. Though it's not much."

The Yawtl, scowling, stomped around for a moment, taking time to knock Kiyt down with his fist. He started toward the witch, but Sloosh said, "No, Hoozisst."

"I smell a trick," the Yawtl said. "We'll give her our promise, and then we'll find out she'll tell us but we still won't have the eggs."

"A good point," Sloosh said. "Tell Feersh that we don't just want the location of the eggs. We must be able to get our hands on them. It's possible that she's set traps around them."

Feersh listened to the translation. She said, "You tell the plant-man that I agree to those terms. But first we must be unbound. I give my word that we won't attack you if you don't attack us."

"A witch's word!" Hoozisst said harshly.

"As good as a Yawtl's," she said.

"Which would mean no good at all," Vana said.

Hoozisst raised his fist and said, "Aargh!"

Aejip rose to her feet and snarled. The Yawtl lowered his fist and backed away.

"I wasn't going to hit you. I wouldn't be that stupid. But I'm furious!"

"It doesn't take eyes to see that," the witch said. "Now, tell the plant-man that I'll cooperate to the fullest, that I'll withhold nothing, so that you may get your eggs and his crystal back."

Deyv said, "You must also tell us why you wanted them."

"I'll be very happy to do that. In fact, if you hadn't attacked us, if you'd only gotten as far as the place beneath the *tharakorm*, I'd have told you why. I never dreamed that you'd have a plant-man in your group. One of the reasons I threw the Yawtl overboard was that he'd disobeyed me. I hadn't told him to steal an Archkerri's crystal. I had no use for one.

"But I never suspected that the plant-man would follow the Yawtl. If I had, I'd not have been so negligent. I'd have had sentinels. I knew that the cable-vines wouldn't give an alarm if a plant-man touched them. But who would have thought that one of those creatures would *care* if his crystal was stolen?"

Feersh also asked that she and her children be robed at once. It wasn't proper for them to appear before their slaves without clothing, except when these were in bed with them or bathing them, of course.

Sloosh said that that was all right with him. Hoozisst objected to any agreement. He still believed that the witch was somehow tricking them. The others over-ruled him.

Feersh, now clad in a robe covered with many strange figures and a few of The Dark Beast and wearing a tall blue cylindrical hat, said that she was ready to give them their information. But she wanted them to reaffirm that they would do nothing to her once they got it.

"That doesn't need repeating," Sloosh said.

Hoozisst groaned and said, "She must have a good reason for making sure of that! I tell you, she's playing us for fools!"

"I can't do anything that the goddesses haven't already done," she said.

She paused, licked dry lips, then spoke. "Very well. Your eggs and crystal are embedded inside one of the fungus growths at the base of a tree in the forest that rings the sandy plain around the place where the *tharakorm* were moored. In fact, from what you tell me, you camped by that tree."

23

FOR a little while, no one spoke. Feersh smiled broadly as if it was all she could do to keep from laughing.

Then Sloosh moved toward her. As if that broke the spell, Hoozisst leaped at her with both hands half-closed. The plant-man had expected this, which was why he had stepped over to the witch. Sloosh's great hand closed on the Yawtl's shoulder, and Sloosh lifted him up.

Hoozisst, feet kicking, his face bent with both anger and pain, screamed, "Let me down! I'll kill her!"

"I'll release you when you promise to keep your promise," Sloosh said.

"But she tricked us! I told you she would!"

"That's a good point, but it's our fault. Mostly mine, since I should've been intelligent enough to make sure she didn't trick us. However, we must ascertain that she is indeed telling the truth. If she isn't, the agreement is no good."

The Yawtl looked at Sloosh. His anger was gone, though the pain in his shoulder was still there.

"Let me down. I won't touch her."

His feet on the floor, Hoozisst rubbed his shoulder. He said, "I think you could *squeeze* the truth out of her. Very well, how do we find out if she's telling the truth? She doesn't have a soul egg."

"Any soul egg will do."

Vana and Deyv said, "What?"

Hoozisst said, "You're crazy! Only her own egg would be in phase with her mind! Everybody knows that!"

"This is one of those many cases among you flesh-sapients where what 'everybody knows' is only what everybody says. When I lived with the People of the Striped House I made an experiment. I talked two people into exchanging eggs temporarily, though they were very reluctant to do so. And I found that any egg would do as a lie detector."

Deyv felt that the statement was close to blasphemy. But, knowing by now that Sloosh wouldn't lie, he said nothing.

Hoozisst yanked an egg-cord off a slave, breaking it and felling the slave to his knees. He strode to the witch and thrust it into her hand. "Hold that in your fingers so we may see what the egg shows!" he shouted. "Hold it against your flabby breast, you bitch!"

Feersh went gray under the dark-brown skin. She spoke steadily enough, however. "I only half-lied. It's true that the eggs and crystal are not on the *tharakorm*.

They are not, though, in the fungus around the tree. I placed them in a cave high on a mountainside. The mountain is on the other side of the river you took to get to the forest."

"Put the egg against your breast!"

She did so, and she repeated what she'd said. The egg turned blue shot with writhing starlike figures.

"So!" the Yawtl said. "You thought we'd go to that tree, and by then you would've escaped us. You would be safe someplace where you could laugh at us."

"She may have meant to cheat us," Sloosh said. "That is the way of witches. But I doubt it. She had another reason for not telling us the truth. Witch, what is it?"

Hoozisst translated.

Feersh said, "It's a long story. The main reason I sent this thief out to get the eggs is that I had to have people of a certain character to do something for me. Only *they* might be able to complete my mission. Hoozisst was my tool, a good one, but I wasn't about to reward the greedy creature with the Emerald of Anticipation. He says he's wearing it now, so he has been paid off. He shouldn't bear a grudge. If he'd been in my place, he would have done the same. Wouldn't you, Yawtl?"

Hoozisst bared his sharp teeth, but he nodded. "I was a little hasty in wanting to get rid of you," he said. "I forgot that you'd also promised to show me how the stone works."

"Which I'll do. Anyway, all this business has to do with The Shemibob."

Sloosh buzzed amazement through his beak. "She *still* lives?"

Hoozisst translated this.

"As far as I know. The last one to see her alive, to be able to tell about it, that is, was a slave of hers. She is the only one who's ever escaped from The Shining House of Countless Chambers."

She paused, undoubtedly for dramatic effect.

"I was that slave!"

Sloosh was delighted. "There is so much you can tell me about The Shemibob. We Archkerri haven't been able to get any data about her from our vegetable kin for a long time. The Jeweled Wasteland has been steadily, if slowly, growing, and where it is, there are no plants. Eventually, as you must know, The Wasteland will cover all the land mass."

"We can get those details later," Deyv said impatiently before Hoozisst could translate. "Tell your story as it concerns those whose eggs were stolen."

"Those details, as you call them, are a vital part of my story. When I was a very young woman, I went into the dreaded land of The Shemibob, which some also call, with good reason, The Bright Abomination. My mother had tried to kill me because she found out that I was planning to kill her. I had grown tired of waiting for her to die. So I fled just in time, and I was that most contemptible and pitiable of creatures, a witch with no ancient artifacts. So I decided to steal into The Wasteland and rob The Shemibob of some. I had heard that she had a great treasure of them. That's not surprising, since she had a long time to collect them and had many to begin with."

"How long?" Vana asked.

"Your language doesn't have the words for it."

"Tell her, Hoozisst, that I've taught you three of the terms," Sloosh said. "Your minds know them, even if they can't grasp their meaning."

Feersh said, "The Archkerri's words are not the same as mine. But The Shemibob has lived on Earth almost ten thousand sleep-times multiplied by a thousand plus ten thousand. How old she was when she came here from a distant star, I don't know."

"Almost as old," Sloosh said.

"Old enough to get a few wrinkles," Feersh said. She smiled, but Deyv didn't know if she meant to be funny.

"Only a very young, foolhardy, and ignorant girl would have done what I did," Feersh said. "I would've been better off if I'd hidden in the jungle around my mother's House and watched for a chance to get back in it and kill her. But I was ambitious. I thought that if I could rob The Shemibob, I would then be the most powerful witch in the world. So I dared to enter the land of The Shemibob. And The Shemibob caught me, though she did say I'd gotten deeper into her land than anyone else.

"I was her slave for a long time. It wasn't a hard life, once I got used to her terrifying appearance. Unlike the other slaves, I was very curious, and I tried to learn everything I could from her. She liked to talk with me. Sometimes I thought that the only reason she lured people into her land was so she'd have somebody to talk to. While I was there I prowled around a lot, keeping my eyes open, and picked out those possessions I wanted to take with me. But there were so many that I had to select just a few. I couldn't have carried one-thirtieth of what I desired and what could be removed. Many of the possessions were surrounded by safeguards which I dared not pass.

"She once told me that she was not inherently long-lived. One of her treasures was the secret of longevity. But she did not have that hidden somewhere in The Pulsing Castle. It was not in a concealed chamber set all around with traps. She carried the secret in her mind.

"I asked her why she didn't give it to her slaves. Then she wouldn't have to depend upon catching would-be robbers to keep up her supply of slaves. She smiled—a most ghastly smile—and she said that if she'd done that long ago, the slaves might have become as wise as she and then would either have killed her or run away with her artifacts.

"Also, there would be no use in telling the slaves now, even if she changed her mind about keeping the secret to herself. What good would it do? Within a comparatively short time, Earth would be torn apart by the power of stars too near. And then all stars and star dust, everything, would fall together and become an unimaginably enormous ball of fire. This would explode and then—"

"Sloosh has told us about that," Deyv said.

"Yes? Anyway, I wasn't as terrified or as surprised as she seemed to think I would be. We witches have our own knowledge. Though, to tell the truth, it wasn't so much knowledge as speculation which depended upon doom-tales we'd heard from the savages. Especially the Yawtl.

"And why should I care? I'd be dead long before the last sleep-times of Earth came. But then The Shemibob said that perhaps there might be a way of avoiding the cataclysm. The density of the ever-increasing amount of matter twists space itself. And this could result in gateways to another world. Or perhaps many other worlds.

"I didn't understand this completely. I had to take her word for it. But she didn't seem to be lying just to pass the time."

"Tell her that we Archkerri have similar theories about that," Sloosh said.

"You Archkerri have theories about everything," Feersh said. "Some of them are bound to be right. I asked her if she knew of any doors to these other worlds where perhaps the universe was not contracting but was young, expanding. She said that there could be one in her land, out in the crystals. It was a strange fearful phenomenon, the reason why The Wasteland is sometimes called The Bright Abomination.

"But if the phenomenon was what she thought it was, it wasn't as yet a route to another world. She had tried to enter it but had failed. Perhaps, in time, it would be penetrable. Then again, perhaps it would never be. And even if it should be, it might only be to another world like ours, one that is dying."

Hoozisst said, "A likely tale! What I think is that The Shemibob made up the whole thing. She did that so people would hear about it and come to her land hoping to get through this door to that other world. Then she'd have more slaves."

"How could anybody outside The Wasteland hear about it?" Feersh said. "I was the only one ever to escape from it."

"No, you weren't," Sloosh buzzed. "There were others."

"See?" the Yawtl said. "She lets a slave get away now and then so that they can spread lying stories to entice others to her. Undoubtedly, she allowed you to escape."

Feersh looked angry. "Really? With some of her treasures?"

The Yawtl shrugged. "She has plenty to spare—according to you."

"The story of her great trove of ancient devices is true. So why shouldn't the other story be true?"

"A true story makes you willing to believe the next story, which is a big lie."

"Enough of this," Sloosh said. "You still haven't told us why you wanted the soul eggs. Aside from the fact they had to be the eggs of people who had a certain character."

"The Shemibob knows what it is that makes a person near-immortal. If she could be captured and then tortured, she would reveal the secret. Ordinary means might not make her talk, but she has things which could force the truth from any being.

"And once one was near-immortal, one could find a way to get to another world. Then one could live forever, barring accident, murder, or suicide. When the new world became old and was about to die, one could again escape through a gateway. And so on."

"By *one*, you mean *you*," Hoozisst said.

She glared. "I'm willing to share. Anyway, I'm too old to venture into her land again. Even if I were young enough, I couldn't do it by myself. I should have tried it while I was still able, but I didn't think of it then. I was busy with many things, though mostly trying to survive. Then I captured three *tharakorm* after I decided that my House was too vulnerable. I got slaves, and I had my children so that one could inherit.

"And then I thought about how death was approaching, and I conceived the idea of how I could keep from dying and perhaps live as long as The Shemibob. So I set a Yawtl to stealing certain eggs. He was to lead their owners here. If they were smart and tough enough to get this far—that far, rather—then they might be able to do what I wanted.

"When I captured them, I treated them well. I told them that they must get to The Wasteland and then they must somehow get The Shemibob's secrets. They didn't go alone; they were usually in groups of five or six. If they succeeded, then I would return their eggs. And I would let them go with me through the gateway."

"That was nice of you," Hoozisst said, sneering. "What was to keep them from staying there, once they were near-immortal? Oh, I see . . . their eggs!"

The Archkerri said, "But why didn't you moor your *tharakorm* near The Wasteland? You could then have gotten your candidates there, and they wouldn't have had to travel so far. The Shemibob's land is near the other end of the land mass. From the mooring place to there is a very long way and full of many dangers."

After Hoozisst translated, Feersh said, "Do you think I'm stupid? I did just that in the beginning. But the people I sent in failed. So I unmoored and sailed across The Wasteland and out over the end of the land and across the ocean, which can be traversed within five sleep-times with a good wind, to the other end of the land. Then I moored at different widely spaced places, and I started the whole process over. I used different thieves, of course, most of which were Yawtl. They are a cunning species, though not of high intelligence."

"Intelligent enough to outsmart you, hag!" Hoozisst said.

"You could never have done it, if you hadn't had the dumb luck to steal a plant-man's crystal. The Yawtl make good thieves, but they are too greedy to be trusted. Anyway, I would move on from time to time to get new groups after an area had been cleared of candidates. As for the great distances to be covered, I suggested that the candidates find young *tharakorm* and float with the winds toward The Wasteland. Or that they get to the shore and sail on the ocean."

"It's a desperate scheme, and I suspect that all your candidates have failed—so far," Sloosh said. "But if you moved so much, how would they find you if they did succeed?"

"They would wait in The Wasteland until I got there."

"But by then they would have discovered that they didn't need their eggs," Sloosh said. "That is one more flaw."

Deyv said, "They would never be able to abandon their eggs forever!"

"You have much to learn yet."

"You're out of your mind," Vana said.

The witch said, "After I'd sent you on your mission, I would have put your eggs back on here. But you ruined that. However, now you know where they are. You can come back and get them after you've completed your mission."

Deyv and Vana looked at each other. Did she really believe that they were going to venture into the monster's territory? Now that they knew the location of their soul eggs?

Hoozisst was of a different mind.

"Once I have the powers of The Shemibob, I'll send people after my egg. They can risk the dangers. They won't run out on me, since I'll do as you did, hag. I'll hold their eggs until they get back. And, as an extra incentive, I'll promise them one or two of The Shemibob's former possessions."

He was indeed stupid and avaricious.

Sloosh must have read the expression on Deyv's and Vana's faces. He said, "From what I know of The Shemibob's powers, I would suspect that anyone who had access to them could *make* their own eggs."

Startled, Deyv said, "Do you really think so?"

The witch asked for a translation. It seemed to amaze her, too. "That never occurred to me! Then—oh,

Shkanshuk! Then . . . those I sent, if they succeeded, would never return to me! No, it can't be! It's unthinkable!"

"I just thought it," the Archkerri said. "But perhaps the sapients you sent out are not so sapient."

"I wouldn't want to be in your robe if you found out that one of them was now ruling The Wasteland," Vana said.

Feersh became even paler.

24

THAT they might be able to manufacture duplicate eggs hadn't changed Deyv's and Vanas minds. Second only to getting their eggs back was their desire to return to their tribes. They planned that the moment they landed, they would set back out for the cave in which their eggs were located. Having gotten them, they would head for their homeland.

Sloosh guessed this. "You owe it to your people to find a way out. You also owe it to all people, all sapients. You can give them salvation and continuity."

The two could understand saving their own tribes. But why should they bother with their enemies?

"If you could get to another world but you took only your own people, you would be guaranteeing their degeneration. They are too few for healthy breeding. In time the inbreeding would destroy them."

"What about you?" Deyv asked. "Do you intend to get your people through?"

"Of course. Really, I don't understand myself. Why should I be trying to talk you into getting humans through when they would probably do their best to destroy us Archkerri? But I am an optimist, however irrational that state is."

Vana said that it was perilous but possible to return to their tribes. It seemed impossible to overcome The Shemibob. So why not be realistic?

"You make your own reality," Sloosh said. "Within certain limits. What are the limits in this situation? We won't know until we get to The Wasteland."

When nobody else was around, Vana and Deyv discussed the possibilities.

"It's too risky," she said.

"I agree. We've taken too many risks as it is. What we encountered was bad, but at least we know what we'll face on the way back. But there—?"

"We don't have a chance, anyway. How could we do what many thousands for how many thousands of thousands of sleep-times have tried to do and failed?"

"Right."

The wind slowed down and then curved in a different direction. It was pushing them southward of The Wasteland, according to the witch. Deyv and Vana took this as an omen warning them not to tackle The Shemibob. Sloosh asked them to explain just how they'd concluded this. They couldn't do so, but they still kept their conviction.

In another sleep-time, the wind had weakened to the point where it would soon be safe to leak off the lifting gas.

"That is," Sloosh said, "if there isn't a change in the wind's force."

By then the band of light on the horizon had become even broader. Once they had landed, though, The Dark Beast would overtake them. They would have to endure at least six sleep-times of more darkness. It seemed a small price, no matter how much they longed for a bright sky.

The wind continued to fade. At last, Sloosh took a sword and punched away at a cell. He was just about to make two more tiny holes in other cells when Kiyt came running down the corridor.

"Mother says the wind is increasing!"

"May I borrow some of your expletives, Deyv?" the Archkerri said. "My language doesn't have any."

They went back up on deck. Not only was the *tharakorm* moving faster, the horizon behind them had become black.

"Do you have anything with which to repair the puncture?" Sloosh asked Feersh. Hoozisst translated.

She spread her hands out and rolled her eyes upward.

"I suppose that means no. Well, I've calculated the rate of leakage. We will be on the ground shortly after the next sleep-time. So, since the wind will be much stronger then, we must take our chances now."

Without consulting anybody about his intentions, he went below and punched many holes. Returning to the deck, he said, "If that gas is inflammable, we mustn't have any fires. Also, we must stay up here. The gas will fill the rooms belowdecks."

"I know," Feersh said after the Yawtl had relayed the message. She went to the railing and looked down with blind eyes.

Sloosh gave a buzz of exasperation, then said, "Deyv and Vana, warn the others. The witch doesn't care if we and the slaves strangle. Her children are aware of the dangers, of course."

When they got back, the Archkerri said, "The wind has swung around toward The Wasteland. Too late to do us much good, though. We'll be on the treetops in about as fast as you could run two miles. Let's hope we're as fortunate as we were the last time."

A short while later, they saw water ahead. It extended beyond the horizon, even at their altitude.

Feersh and her children tied ropes to themselves and secured the ends to a mast. The slaves hurried to do the same. The Yawtl, braving the gas, went below many times, returning with his arms full of the witch's devices.

"We're going to land on the water," Sloosh told him. "It'll pour through the holes in the bottom and the sides, and the *tharakorm* will sink. Maybe it'll first float awhile because of the gas left in the cells. But you won't be able to swim to shore with a single one of those things. You'll be lucky if you don't have to shed your weapons."

Hoozisst snarled, and he said, "We'll see about that!"

"You can't see much from the bottom of the lake. Do as you will."

Deyv and Vana had strapped the cube onto the Archkerri's back. He'd contemplated unfolding it but had decided not to. The wind would blow it across the water to the farther shore—if, that is, it was a lake. This might be the ocean for all he knew. It didn't seem likely that they had been pushed to the lower shore of the land mass. Still, his eyeball calculations could have been incorrect. There was no use taking a chance.

As they angled down, they saw some tiny white spots on the water about a mile from the beach. When they were closer, they recognized these as very large two-masted sailing ships. Deyv was impressed by their size. He'd never seen water-going craft so huge. At the same time, he felt any little optimism he'd had evaporate. The people on those ships would kill them or capture them.

The witch's two sons were weeping and sobbing and shouting that they could never swim that far to the shore. Jowanarr looked pale, but she didn't seem to be scared. Feersh, who couldn't see what was coming but had had it described to her, stood with her back to the mast. She had doffed her robe, since its heaviness would drag her down. Deyv thought that she would soon be in the same situation she was in when her mother had chased her naked and weaponless into the jungle. The difference was that she was old now. And blind. Would her children help her swim or would they abandon her? She'd given them no reason to love her.

Perhaps she was thinking the same things. If so, she wasn't letting them show on that grim face.

The Yawtl left his tall pile of treasures and swaggered up to Feersh.

"Well, hag, where are your witchery, your evil schemes, and your arrogance now? Hoozisst tricked you good, didn't he? You'll soon be sinking to the mud, and your flesh will be eaten by the fish, though it may make them sick."

Hoozisst's laugh was stopped by a hard slap from Jowanarr's palm. He staggered back, holding his cheek, his eyes slit. Then he flashed out his sword and raised it to cut the daughter down. She stared at him, her arms folded.

Hoozisst stopped. "Sure, you'd like me to kill you now so you'd be spared the agony of drowning. You're not tricking me, hag daughter of a hag. But if you should make it to the shore, you won't live long. I promise you that."

"Haven't you seen those ships?" Jowanarr asked. "Their crews will take the stuff you stole from us away from you. If you don't drown first under their weight, greedyguts."

Hoozisst whirled around, and his narrowed eyes grew large. He began swearing and stomping around while the others laughed at him. Presently, though, as the water and the vessels came closer, all on the *tharakorm* fell silent.

After a while, they saw that they'd been mistaken about the crew. It was neither human nor Yawtl. Enormous whitish things crawled around on the deck. Moreover, there were no railings, no helmsman's wheel, though the upper part of a rudder stuck above the water, no ropes to the sails. Other items were lacking, but by then those on the *tharakorm* had no time to think about these. They were only ten feet above the water's surface, then five, then they had landed.

If they hadn't been lying flat on the deck, they would have been thrown heavily, perhaps bounced out, into the lake. Otherwise, the touchdown was uneventful. The *tharakorm* rose and dipped in the heavy swells, and it began to settle. Soon, water washed over the railing. More time passed. Deyv stood up. At the moment, they didn't seem to be sinking. The wind and the current were pushing them slowly out from the shore.

The nearest sailship turned into the wind and began tacking toward them. The booms of its fore-and-aft rigged sails were moving, but Deyv didn't know anything about deep-water sailing and so couldn't know just why the changes were being made. As far as he could see, the slug-things on its deck were doing nothing except crawling around.

Some strange things were growing on or attached to the hull and the masts. They looked at first like flowers with short yellow stalks and blue petals with green centers. Their roots wrapped around the masts or clung to the sides of the hull. The flower-heads turned this way and that as if they had eyes. Those on the hull scanned the water; those on the masts moved horizontally.

He expected the vessel to come directly to the *tharakorm*. Instead, it sailed by at a distance of forty feet. When it had gone some way past, it began to turn again. Now it was headed directly toward the *tharakorm*. Was it going to ram them?

Feersh and the others had untied themselves from the masts. Her children and the slaves didn't want to take to the water. As long as they weren't sinking, they saw no reason to swim. The witch swore at them and told them that they would soon be so far from land they would never be able to swim to it. If it wasn't too late now.

It was. As Feersh drove her people with screams and insults toward the bow, the surface nearby began boiling. They halted, staring, ignoring the witch. Up shot a frighteningly enormous creature, purple-gray, finned, cavern-mouthed, with fleshy tendrils hanging from the swelling on top of its head. It went up and up while water flew up and away from it and spray formed a cloud at its base.

When it fell, it made a deafening smashing sound, and waves covered the decks of the *tharakorm* and almost washed away a woman. The slaves and Feersh's children ran screaming toward the mast behind the aft cabin, knocking Feersh over. The whirlpool formed by the monster's dive seemed about to suck in the *tharakorm*.

Suddenly, the leviathan appeared behind them, soaring up again, seeming without end. When it curved and dived, its colossal rounded head striking the water, the spray flew all over those on the *tharakorm* and was followed by even larger waves than the first time. Deyv saw one of its eyes, small compared to the body yet larger than his head. It looked cold and yellow and hungry.

Then he saw that the sailship was passing by the *tharakorm* again. It was only ten feet away. The flowers on the hull did have eyes, green with black irises. They, too, looked coldly at him before dipping to stare into the water again.

The flower-eyes on the masts were also observing the crowd on the *tharakorm*.

Some of the slugs seemed aware of the strangers. Others ignored them. They were shaped like sausages and of a pale-white translucency. Dark curving things, probably part of the skeleton, were visible below the wet slimy-looking skin. A myriad dark spots, very tiny, were just below the skin. Small seallike flippers, at least a score, lined each side of the body. The tail was slightly bifurcated. In front of the blunt head were big green eyes with black centers. They didn't seem to be part of the head; they gave the impression of being attached to it. Perhaps, Deyv thought, they were flower-eyes growing on the skin. And their roots went through the skin and flesh to the nervous system inside the skull. If it had a skull. There was no nose or air slits. The mouth held row upon row of tiny triangular teeth. He couldn't see any tongue.

The deck on which the slugs crawled was black and looked leathery. It was level and smooth except for three openings, one ten feet from the stern, one in the middle, and one ten feet back from the bow. There were no railings, and the water line was only three feet below the deck. The hull was a smooth shiny dark-green substance, perhaps bone of some kind.

As the beast passed, it left the hint of an odor, more like a wet shaggy dog than anything else.

For the third time the leviathan dived up from the surface. Though it was farther away, it was close enough to scare its watchers. The sailship-creature swerved sharply toward it, and when the leviathan rose again, it was almost under the bows. The sailship caught the monster crosswise as the fish came down. Though Deyv couldn't see what the sailship was doing, it seemed to have closed down on the fish.

With what? he thought. A little later he found out. The sailship turned, allowing him to see the upper part of a mouth stretching out over the struggling monster.

"The bow has lips!" Vana cried.

"The mouth has teeth!" Deyv cried. He was awed. He was also frightened. What if the fish hadn't been enough to eat, and the creature that looked so much like a sailship decided to have the *tharakorm* for dessert?

Like a dog with a bone in its teeth headed for a place to bury it, the sail-beast sailed toward the horizon. After a while, it turned and began sailing close-hauled against the wind.

Whitish streaks slipped over the bow and onto the fish. Other slugs went into the water from the side and swam toward it. It had ceased to struggle, and if it wasn't a carcass, it soon would be. The slugs swarmed over it, biting out big chunks. When the sailship was closer, Deyv could see that some of the slugs had apparently satisfied their hunger. Now they were carrying large pieces in their mouths and crawling back up the bow. A swarm covered the bow, forcing others to dive into the sea, from which they would shoot out and up onto the deck.

Deyv thought that the slugs must have suckers on

their bellies which enabled them to cling to the vertical walls of the bow.

Sloosh came up to Deyv and said, "We must start swimming. But if we do, either a big fish or those white things will get us. It poses an interesting dilemma, doesn't it?"

"Maybe the white things won't consider us good eating," Deyv said. "After all, we're not marine life. They may not be familiar with human beings and so might think us dangerous."

"There's only one way to find out, unfortunately," the plant-man said. "As you may have noticed, the *tharakorm* is now sinking. The cells are beginning to fill with water."

He turned toward the bow. Over his shoulder, he buzzed, "You can hang on to me while I swim."

The Yawtl screamed, "But what about the treasures of the witch? We can't leave them here! They'll be lost, lost!"

"Yes," Sloosh said. "A pity."

"Can't you expand the vessel of the ancients and put the instruments in it? We can tow it behind us!"

Deyv and Vana, despite the seriousness of the situation, laughed. Sloosh buzzed derision.

"All right, all right!" The Yawtl yelped. "So I'm crazy! If you had any sense of value, you'd be out of your mind, too!"

"Kiss them good-bye, if you wish," Vana said.

Sloosh went into the water with all of the weapons of his party in his two hands. His upper torso reared out of the water from just above the waist. Jum and Aejip leaped in and began swimming alongside the Archkerri. Deyv and Vana swam after Sloosh and, on catching up with him, clung with one hand to the straps securing the cube on his back.

Behind them the Yawtl yelled and screamed his frustration and despair. But in a short while he had joined them. Though he needed his breath for swimming, he could not stop complaining. After a while, the water slopped into his open mouth and he shut up.

Deyv felt helpless and close to panic. He could imagine open jaws with sharp swordlike teeth shooting up toward his legs. Or the giant mouth of a fish which could gulp them all down without strain. After a while he came to believe that they would drown first. The current was too strong; they were making slow progress; they'd tire out long before they reached the beach.

Those behind Sloosh were doing worse. The gap between them and the Archkerri was slowly widening. In their van was Feersh. Jowanarr was close by, occasionally calling out when her mother swam off the straight path to their goal. Kiyt and Jeydee were about twenty feet behind Jowanarr, and the slaves were strung out in a crooked V behind them.

Deyv had just turned his head to look toward the shore when he heard screaming. He looked back again. Two slaves, a man, Treeshgaquim, and a woman, Shig, were calling for help. Suddenly, the man went under as if something had seized his legs and yanked him down. Deyv hoped that it had been exhaustion, not predators, that had made him disappear so swiftly. He didn't think, however, that that was likely. Shig had resumed swimming, though she was evidently tired. Deyv tried to swim faster but failed. He'd reached his limits. Sensibly, he slowed down to save his strength. Anyway, no matter how fast he went, his speed would be a crawl to whatever was slicing through the water behind him—if anything was.

Gasping, Vana said, "That sail-beast is heading toward us now."

Sloosh looked behind him. "Deyv, untie the cube. And pull the rod."

"I was just about to do that!"

Within a minute, the ship of the ancients floated on the water. Deyv opened the door and hauled himself through it. He took the weapons from Sloosh, who hung on to the lintel so that the Yawtl and Vana could crawl over his back. The two animals followed them. Then Hoozisst and Deyv grabbed the Archkerri's hands and helped him aboard. Deyv pulled in the loudly panting Shig and shut the door quickly, since about an inch of water had already poured in. Somebody turned the lights on.

If this water was a lake, they would, theoretically, be blown to shore. If it was the ocean, they would sail along over it until they starved to death.

Sloosh, his wet leaves shining in the light, said, "Open the door, please, Deyv. We should be almost to Feersh now."

"So?"

"We need her. When we get to The Wasteland, we can use her knowledge."

"Maybe you can," Deyv said. "Vana and I won't be there." He walked away.

The plant-man opened the door and looked out. He buzzed something which Deyv didn't hear clearly because he was in the next room. But he heard the Yawtl say, "Not her children, too!"

Deyv went to the doorway, where Sloosh was pulling the witch in by her hand. Her sons and daughter were hanging on to the edge of the doorway. Water was slopping in with every down-roll of the vessel. Three slaves, a man and two women, were swimming tiredly toward them.

"Hoozisst is right," Deyv said. "They're just a burden."

"But she says she'll let herself die if we don't save them, too."

Deyv didn't think Feersh meant it. She just wanted to make sure that she had allies when the time came to double-cross Sloosh. When she asked that her slaves also be rescued, he was sure of it. In their case, however, she was making a mistake. Their loyalty couldn't be counted on. They'd shown that when they had beaten up the witch's children.

But what did he care? He wasn't going with them.

Hoozisst made some trouble then. Not about Feersh but about the treasures he'd been forced to leave on the *tharakorm*. Some had been swept off by the waves, but others were still sitting on the deck. A few more waves, and they'd be gone, too.

Sloosh said they could try to get them if they came close enough. The door couldn't be left open long, though, because he didn't want the vessel to take on too much water. When he estimated that they were near the *tharakorm*, he reopened it. After a quick look, he closed it.

"By the time you swam to the *tharakorm*," he said to the Yawtl, "we'd be too far past you for you to get back. Of course, if you want to take the chance . . . Even so, you could bring back only one item."

Hoozisst leaned out past the doorway, hanging on to it with one hand. He pulled himself back in and shut the door. Then he went up to Feersh and slammed his fist into her stomach. She fell doubled-up, clutching her belly and groaning. Jowanarr went to help her mother. Her sons looked shocked but at the same time pleased.

There was nothing to do but wait the ride out. They had only their cupped hands to bail out the water on the floor. If they opened the door to do this, more water would come in than they got out. They sat around in groups, Deyv and his group, Feersh and her family, and the slaves. When the voyagers felt sleepy, they slept. There was nothing to eat, but they didn't go thirsty.

When they had to urinate or defecate, they went upon the upper deck to a room. Only one could go at a time so that his or her weight would be compensated for by that of the others on the lower deck. The stench wasn't too bad at first. Later, it became very strong. Then they would open the door briefly and let some fresh air in. The time came when they decided not to do that except when the odor was unendurable. However, since they had nothing to eat, they ceased to have bowel movements. Three sleep-times passed, though that was about all that did. They went through a long storm, during which many would have thrown up if they'd had anything in their stomachs.

Then the wind died, and they were riding long gentle swells. At this time the Yawtl voiced what was in the minds of more than himself. But they agreed that they should stick it out a little longer. The slaves were all for this, since, if anyone was eaten, they would be the first.

Some time after this, the vessel stopped with a crash that threw those standing to the deck. The craft hit the obstacle again, much more gently, then began turning. Presently, it was bumping its length against something and rising and falling.

Deyv tried to open the door. At first, it refused to move. When Sloosh ordered everybody except Deyv to the other side so that the craft would roll upward on Deyv's side, the door opened. Deyv looked out just in time to see the hull of a sea beast rolling toward him. He slammed the door shut before the creature struck it.

Timing the swells, he opened the door again when it would be the farthest away from the hard hull. A moment later, he went to the room on the opposite side.

"We're bumping against the side of a dead sail-beast."

25

DEYV leaped from the doorway onto the hull. The creature was lying on its side parallel to a rocky beach. Its hull, though wet, was not too steep. He scrambled up on hands and feet, gripped the edge, and looked over. Whatever had constituted the deck was gone now. If it had been flesh or a leathery skin, it had decayed along with the sails and the flower-eyes and other organs subject to corruption. Only a skeleton remained, bones sticking up from the interior of the hull—if hard metallic objects could be called bones.

In three heaps along the bottom of the hull were smaller bones. These could be the skeletons of its young, the flippered sausage-things. They had died in the womb after the mother had perished.

Deyv looked along the hull. When a wave receded from the beach, it exposed most of the mouth. The lower jaw extended along and from the bottom of the bow and was set with rows of huge triangular teeth. It protruded about six feet more than the upper jaw, which was a fixed part of the bow.

Sloosh had tied one end of Deyv's rope to a chair, which he'd unfolded from the deck of the ancients' vessel. The other end of the rope he had thrown to Deyv, who worked his way along the edge of the hull. Then the Yawtl and Vana jumped out and joined him. They dragged the vessel along the dead beast until the doorway was past the jawed bow. The others came out to help. In a short time, they had the vessel up on the beach and partway into the forest. When its conical nose was secured between two trees, they looked for food. After stuffing their bellies with fruit, nuts, and berries—several of them vomiting afterward because they had eaten too much too quickly—they cleaned out the vessel. Sloosh collapsed it and had it strapped onto his back.

The plant-man went off to explore the inside of the ship-beast. It was easy to get into it from the beach, since it was lying on its side. Aejip went hunting for meat with Vana. Deyv went exploring with Jum. The only large eminence in sight was a cone-shaped mountain about fifteen hundred feet high. When he had toiled near to its top, Deyv saw that they had landed on an island. After working around three-quarters of the mountain, he became depressed. The horizon was bare of land. Either the lake was larger than any he'd ever seen or they had floated onto an island far out at sea.

He brightened when it occurred to him that it wasn't going to make any difference to him. He hadn't the slightest intention of pushing on and out. Vana and he could make a boat with a sail and return to the mainland. Neither knew how to operate a sailboat, but they could learn. If none of their group could teach them, he would watch the sail-beasts and see how they moved against the wind.

He tried not to think of them and the monster fish. Perhaps he and Vana would be lucky enough not to be swallowed along with their tiny craft. They wouldn't be as noticeable as the vessel of the ancients, which had been bumped into and tossed around a number of times, presumably by giants who'd seized it in their jaws but whose teeth had slid off the hard stuff.

Deyv decided that if he'd come this far up the mountain, he might as well go to the very top. With two hundred feet more altitude, he just might be able to see land. The path curved around and through the thick brush, which was stripped of branches along the edges. The numerous droppings showed that some large herbivores had used the trail, though so far he'd seen none.

When they'd ascended a hundred feet as the *khratikl* flies, Jum stopped. His bristling hairs and soft growl told Deyv that there was danger ahead. Quietly, he urged the dog onward. Though reluctant, Jum obeyed. The slope became abrupt close to the top, forcing them to dig into the mingled soft dirt and eroded stones to keep from slipping backward. Then the soil ceased, and the tip became a hard rock spire. There was nothing alarming on it, only a little monkey-like creature with huge red eyes and a low cooing cry.

Jum pointed his nose toward the forest to their left. Deyv went ahead of the dog into the foliage. He held the sword in one hand and his tomahawk in the other. Slowly, he brushed past the bushes and the low-growing branches of *daunash* trees. He made sure that he didn't step on any twigs.

Ahead he could see that the mountain dropped off. There was a cliff there, though he couldn't see how high it was. Out beyond its edge was something that shimmered, danced, expanded, contracted. It seemed to be about ten feet in diameter at its smallest; twenty, at its largest. Out from its center stuck a large log which had been roughly flattened on top. The other end rested on the lip of the cliff.

It was a bridge that disappeared at the other end into the shimmering.

Deyv could hear nothing, but the dog's sensitive ears had certainly detected something. Whatever the sound was, it had put fear into him. Now, seeing the shimmering, Deyv felt afraid too. And he also felt nauseated. This thing was *unnatural*.

He turned his head away to keep from vomiting. He was so dizzy that he had to sit down. Jum pressed against him, his tail between his legs. He wanted desperately to run away.

After a while Deyv became less sick. But when he looked with one eye at the shimmering, he felt his nausea return full-strength. Was this the abode of some deity or demon? If so, would he or she or it need a log bridge to get to the ground? It didn't seem likely. On the other hand, what did he know about such beings? Especially those of strange lands.

Sloosh was the one to deal with this, if anyone could. Deyv felt that it would be best to stay away from the place. He stood up but, his curiosity overcoming his dread, glanced again at the swelling shrinking brightness. Then he saw footprints in the earth at the near end of the log.

That scared him even more. Had the dweller come out into the forest?

He whirled, feeling for a terrible second that something horrible beyond imagination was standing behind him. He gasped with relief. Only the forest was behind him.

But whoever lived in that thing might be returning home at this moment. Deyv had better get away—fast. He retraced his path with an eager Jum behind him. When they reached the trail they walked swiftly down it. Deyv had to use all his self-control to keep from a headlong flight. But the rule was that you never ran in the jungle unless someone was definitely after you or you were after someone.

When he got back to camp, he was greeted by the Yawtl.

"You look as if you'd seen a ghost."

"I've seen something worse," Deyv said. He hurried onto the skeleton of the ship-beast. Sloosh wasn't there. A little while later, the Archkerri came out of the jungle burdened down by clusters of fruit.

When the plant-man heard the whole story, he said, "I won't say that you should have at least followed those tracks."

"You just said it."

"No, I said I wouldn't say it. I had to specify what it was I wouldn't say, otherwise you wouldn't know what I was referring to. Anyway, let's all go up there."

The slaves refused to go. Feersh's children dared to go only because they were afraid to be far from their mother. Besides, they didn't want to be at the mercy of the slaves. Vana quit butchering the two large rodents she'd shot and put them in the vessel for safekeeping.

As they got near the shimmering, though they couldn't see it yet, Jum dropped back. Deyv didn't call him; he didn't blame the dog. His own heart was hammering, and the hairs on the back of his neck felt as if they were bristling. When the party got within sight of the phenomenon, they felt the same sickness and dread he'd experienced. Only Sloosh had the courage to go to the near end of the log, and he looked as little as possible at the thing into which it disappeared.

"The person who made the prints is wearing boots," he announced. "I've never seen any quite like them. The heels are rather high. And the soles have some kind of marks impressed on them. I'd say their wearer weighs about one hundred and thirty pounds. And he limps on his right leg."

Deyv felt somewhat better about the possible viciousness of the tenant. He'd never heard of a god or demon who wore boots. Then he thought that that was just the problem. He'd never *heard* of one, but this was a long way from his homeland. He started to feel bad again. He felt even worse when Sloosh said they should track the person into the jungle. Deyv consoled himself with the thought that at least Sloosh hadn't said they should go across the bridge.

The footprints led them around the base of the spire, where they found a small cave. This held the remains of fires and a bundle of blankets. Far below the mouth of the cave lay the scattered bones of various animals.

Other tracks led them here and there to places where the person had buried his excrement or had been stalking animals.

They returned to the cliff. Sloosh looked at the shimmering as long as he could. When he turned away, he said, "I could be wrong, but I'll venture that that is an entrance to another universe. Feersh, do our descriptions sound like the one The Shemibob gave of her gateway?"

"Something like it," the witch said. "Only she said that hers wasn't open yet."

"Really? How would she know when it would be?"

"She didn't say."

"Did she send slaves through it to test it?"

"She tried to, but they refused. They said they'd rather die."

Deyv could understand that.

"The Shemibob also told me that she'd sent mechanical devices on wheels into it. They didn't come back, and they failed to transmit any information."

"She should have gone in herself," Sloosh said.

Easy for you to say, Deyv thought.

"It shouldn't be difficult to enter the shimmering," the Archkerri said. "It's not just a matter of closing one's eyes, though. Feersh is blind, yet she too feels nausea and dizziness. Perhaps it also emits subsonics or supersonics. The dog evidently heard it before he saw it. I'd volunteer to be blindfolded and have my ears stopped up, but I am, I must admit, too large and clumsy to crawl across that log. Compared to you bipeds, anyway. Who would like to try it?"

No one spoke up.

"I thought so. It's not that you lack courage. Any animal has that. You lack the desire to know, which raises sapients above the animals. Which makes you what, then?"

"You don't have to shame us," Deyv said. "We're ashamed as it is. At least, I am. I thought I was brave. But now I know I'm a coward. Never mind. I will be called that. I won't, I can't, face that terrible thing."

Sloosh put his war axe in the strap attached to his belt at the junction of his upper and lower torsos. He walked past the group into the forest and after a while returned with a waxy substance he'd dug out of an *avashkutl* tree. He filled his earholes with this and waited for it to dry. Then he got down on the log with his eyes closed and lowered his upper trunk until it was parallel to the log. Grasping the log with his hands, his legs dangling, he began dragging himself over the abyss. The others, unable to look long into the shimmering, glanced now and then to observe his progress.

After a few feet, Sloosh stopped. "I still feel fear. But it's not as strong. However, I am still having to fight it with all my will. I hope I can continue, especially after my scornful words to you. Crow was never on my diet."

A moment later he said, "I opened my eyes for a quick look. It's strange, but the closer I get, the less bright it is. However, it's just as nauseating."

Deyv's shame became anger.

"If he can do it, then I can!" he said loudly. "I won't be shown up by a plant-man, a vegetable-thing!"

A moment later, he wished he had said it only to himself. Now he couldn't back out.

The Archkerri was halfway over when he stopped again. He started to buzz a word, but it changed into an exclamation of amazement. A face had popped out of the shimmering.

It was so unexpected and so strange that Deyv forgot for a moment his horror and looked straight into the shimmering. It was a man's, if anyone who grew hair on his face could be called such. The hair was long and dark, falling in a bushy cascade that would have reached his waist if it had been visible. The hair on the head, also dark, was cut short. On top of it, visible only because the man was leaning over, was a small round dark cap. It fitted closely the back of his head. His skin was as pale as Vana's but with a sallow color. The eyes under the thick black brows were large and dark. His nose was big and hooked.

If Sloosh was startled, he was no more so than the owner of the face. Deyv heard a strangled shout, and then the man disappeared. A moment later, he was back again. He stared at the plant-man and at the group down the path. He said something in a strange tongue. Then he stepped out, seeming to hang on to something beyond the shimmering with one hand. The other hand held a large square dark object, which looked at first like a box. But it had strange designs on one side, and when the man gestured with it, it flopped open a little. The covers seemed to contain square leaves of some kind.

Deyv had never seen such exotic clothes. The man wore a long black blanket which had been cut so it fitted around his shoulders. Cylinders of the same material clothed his arms, and the ends of the cylinders were sewn to the blanket. Under this was a black vest, and under that another garment of white. On top of this, fitting around the neck, was a white ring, at the front of which was a narrow black cloth that hung down onto the vest.

His waist and legs were covered with a single garment to which cloth cylinders were attached so his legs could fit into them. These were stuffed into black leather boots.

The man howled his gibberish at Sloosh, shaking the black box-thing in his hand. He seemed to be trying to warn the plant-man about something. He didn't sound as if he meant to attack Sloosh.

Suddenly, water trickled out of the shimmering near its bottom. The man looked down at it, looked up at Sloosh, and shouted more unintelligible words. The trickle suddenly became a gush. It poured out over the end of the log. Then it subsided into a trickle again. Shortly thereafter, another gush came, larger than the first. This, too, subsided, only to be succeeded by an even bigger one. This soaked the man's garments up to his thighs.

The man shouted once more, pointed down at the other end of the log, then dipped his hand into the shimmering as if to indicate the near end. He let loose of whatever he was hanging on to, teetered, and put his hands together, the box still in one of them. After this, he opened his arms, turned, grabbed at something beyond the shimmering, and was gone.

Sloosh at once started moving backward. Though this method of travel was more difficult than the forward, he managed to go faster. There was something panicky in the haste of his manner. Deyv, overcoming his horror for just a minute, dashed up to help him. Vana followed him a second afterward. They grabbed hold of the skin under the tough leaves and aided him in lifting his buttocks. But he was too heavy.

"Thanks," Sloosh buzzed. "I'll make it myself! Just get out of the way!"

He got up on his hind legs, hanging on to the log with his hands, and then he lifted the front legs up. Crouching, still clutching the log, he backed onto the edge of the cliff. He raised his upper torso then and turned around. Vana and Deyv had run away as if something terrible was bounding after them.

Just as Vana and Deyv reached the others, they heard screams. They whirled. The near end of the log was just disappearing over the cliff. It struck a projection below with a crash, starting a small avalanche of stones. Later, another crash came faintly up over the cliff.

26

THE Archkerri trotted elephantinely up to them.

"He was trying to tell me that the gateway was moving," he said. "It apparently has been moving very slowly all along. That would, I think, be because the aggregation of matter in space, which makes the gateway, is also changing in density and location. The end of the log was about to slip off when I started over it!"

He buzzed the equivalent of "Whew!"

"I don't know if that hairy-faced man intended to come back over the log or if he just wanted to take one last look at this universe. Whatever the reason, it is indeed fortunate that he emerged. Otherwise, I would have dropped quite a distance. I am tough but not tough enough to survive a fall from that altitude."

"I wonder where that water came from," Deyv said.

"I've a theory about that, which I'll tell you about later. It involves a satellite of Earth and its effect upon the ocean. I'm more interested in that man. He was wearing garments which I've seen depicted in my prism, but men wore them only during a brief period early in their history. That was an unimaginable number of sleep-times ago, unimaginable to you, I mean.

"Why was he wearing them? And the hair on his face? Men haven't had facial hair for a thousand times a thousand times four hundred sleep-times. Obviously, then, the man is by no means our contemporary. If not, then what is he? It is most puzzling, very engaging."

"I think he was a demon who assumed the form of an ancient," Deyv said.

Sloosh buzzed scornful contempt.

"That's more believable than that he could be an

ancient who'd lived since man's early days," Deyv said.

For five sleep-times, the shimmering continued to spill water at regular intervals. Then it ceased. Sloosh made a rope to which he tied a heavy rock. He heaved it through the shimmering, where it remained. Then he tied the other end of the rope to a tree trunk. Two more sleep-times passed, the rope tightened, and the rock fell out of the shimmering.

"It's moving," the plant-man said. "Upward at an angle."

In the meantime, he had gone down to the base of the cliff above which the shimmering hovered. He tasted the water that had fallen from it.

"Salty. The ocean there, if it is an ocean and not a lake, contains salt. So did Earth's at one time and several times after that. Perhaps that other planet in that other universe is a young one. That doesn't mean that if we should get through another gateway, we'll find ourselves in the world to which *this* gateway is the entrance. There must be many universes, and so there can be different gateways to these."

Sloosh finally decided that the hairy-faced stranger had not originated in Earth's universe. It seemed to him highly unlikely that he had come on purpose to this island to enter the gateway. How could he know there was one here? Not only that, but a thorough search of the shore had failed to yield any craft which he might have used to get to the island.

Therefore, the man had come into this world from the neighboring one.

"But he cut down a tree here to make a log-bridge to get to the gateway," Deyv said. "He didn't make one in his world to get to ours."

"No. What must have happened is that he came through from his world when the gateway was much lower in ours than when we found it. The gateway ascended afterward, and he had to cut a log here to get back."

The Archkerri was worried that the gateway which Feersh said was in The Shemibob's land might no longer be there. It, too, must be changing location. Or it might even have disappeared.

Meanwhile, Sloosh also looked the dead sailship-beast over very carefully. For a while, he'd thought that perhaps they could right it, launch it, and sail it back to the mainland. He gave up the idea when he considered the labor it would take to do all this.

Deyv organized the slaves and Feersh's family to make boats. In a comparatively short time they had four dugouts of varying sizes, each fitted with a mast and sail. But these were swept away when an earthquake shook the island, which was followed sometime later by a tremendous sea wave. They all had to flee to higher ground to save themselves. The carcass of the sail-beast was also carried far out and, presumably, sunk. The upper part of the cliff near the shimmering broke off during the quake and fell to its base. About a fourth of the trees on the island were uprooted.

Sometime during the near-catastrophe, the shimmering pivoted a half-circle. Sloosh was the first to see this. He came huffing and puffing into the camp from the other side of the island.

"If you stand behind the shimmering, you can't see it," he buzzed. "You have to go around to the other side for it to be visible."

"So what does that mean?" Vana asked.

"What it means is that we may have passed other shimmerings and not seen them because we were on the wrong side. And the same thing may happen in the future. It is most disconcerting. Unfortunately, there is nothing we can do about it."

Deyv and Vana listened politely and then resumed making a second dugout. They had no intention of going through a gateway unless someone forced them, and then they'd have to be thrown through. Also, they had decided that this time the boats would not be a community venture. They would make their own, and if the others didn't want to, so much the worse for them.

When Deyv and Vana weren't working on the boat, hunting, eating, or sleeping, they stood on a promontory and watched the sail-beasts. From their observations they were convinced that they could sail against the wind, too.

Once, Sloosh came up to stand beside them while they watched.

"Those white slugs you see on their decks are the young of those beasts," he said. "The larvae, in fact. After a certain amount of time, the larvae change form and go into the sea. They metamorphose into small duplicates of the mother. After a while, they become adults. The male beasts fight for the females, and the winner then has to chase down the females to prove how good a sailor he is. From their union the eggs are fertilized, and these hatch out the slugs. And so on."

"How do they manage to mate?" Vana asked.

"I don't know. I do have three different speculations, though."

In his circuitous way, Sloosh was leading up to a lecture on the *tharakorm*. These, he said, were sailship-beasts of the air. Well, not really animals, since they were composed of viri, and they didn't mate. But they were, in a way, higher on the evolutionary ladder than their oceanic animal analogs.

"What has been happening in the last stages of Earth's existence is that Nature, or the Creator, or call it what you will, has burst out with many previously unknown life-forms. It has done this, I'm convinced, so that some life will be saved from the final catastrophe. Animals that had never given rise to any form of sapiency are now doing so. Take the Yawtl, for instance. He comes from a species that once was confined to quadrupedal locomotion. A very successful form in its place, but still it seemed impossible that it would ever evolve into a biped with fingers and a thumb and a brain the size of man's. Yet, here it is. Too late, unfortunately, because the Yawtl, though it

is self-conscious and intelligent, doesn't have time to
evolve a brain which can figure out a way to save
itself from the holocaust.

"But for that matter, man, who's been on Earth far
far longer than the Yawtl, doesn't seem to have the
intelligence to save himself either. Though I may be
wrong.

"Then there is the Tsimmanbul. It developed from
a highly intelligent sea-mammal. In fact, it had a
sapiency the equal of man's when man first evolved
from the ape. But it couldn't use it, at least not as
man did, because of its environment and its form,
which kept it from the land. Until recently, anyway.

"And look at the Archkerri. We evolved from a
plant form, though we have a tradition that the
ancient humans helped us do this, just as they helped
the Tsimmanbul. In any event, we are the vegetable
kingdom's leap into sentiency, its final desperate effort
to make a form which will survive the coming doom.

"There are other sapient forms of the animal kingdom, which we may or may not encounter during this
quest. There is only one sapient form of the plant
kingdom. And so far as I know, the mineral kingdom
hasn't produced a champion. But then I don't know
everything, no matter how I may appear to do so.

"And then there is the *tharakorm*, the end product
of the half-alive, half-dead kingdom. It is without self-
consciousness or a brain, as we know brains. Nevertheless, it may survive where all the other kingdoms
perish. I should modify that. The mineral kingdom
will not perish, but it will lose its present forms, all
melted into one cosmic ball of fire at the end.

"However, the *tharakorm*, which is now confined to
sailing the air, may become a sailor of space itself. It
is evolving toward that state now. For all I know,
there may be some *tharakorm* which have already
succeeded in leaving this atmosphere. They could be
voyaging through space, outward bound, their sails
spread to catch the light of the dying universe and be
pushed by it toward that space where there is no

matter whatsoever. That is, of course, if there can be such a thing as space without matter.

"But when the big bang comes, and a new universe is born, the tremendous expulsion of light will also push the *tharakorm* away from the ejected matter. No pieces will catch up with the sailship-things of outer space. Eventually, when there are abysses of space between the various pieces of matter, and stars are forming, the *tharakorm* will sail toward them. They will fall into worlds where air has formed, and they will be dissolved, and once again viri will live in unassociated forms on these worlds.

"There will be countless *tharakorm* or their equivalents falling upon countless planets. That is because, I surmise, *tharakorm* will have formed on every inhabited planet now falling toward its fiery doom. And those which come back from the far reaches of truly empty space to habitable planets will, as I've said, revert to the unassociated forms. And these will evolve into forms that are fully alive, the too-tiny-to-be-seen single-celled plants and animals that are the basis of fully alive forms, plants and animals. At one time, the ancients believed that life was formed in the warm soup seas of young planets. But that is not true. Full life evolved from half-life, the countless things that made up the *tharakorm* or similar forms.

"It's possible that this process has been going on since the first cosmic egg of flaming matter hatched. Universes are born and expand, contract and become fires, explode and expand, contract and become fires, and so on. But life in its many forms continues, passed on from one world to the next in a half-alive, half-dead state.

"Meanwhile, the increasing density of matter in every contracting universe forms strange, temporary, but not unpassable gateways to other universes. And it is these that enable those forms of life which cannot survive as the *tharakorm* do to get to young universes. Perhaps."

Deyv and Vana were awed at these visions, though they didn't really believe they were true.

Deyv said, "This is all very well, but how does it concern me? I won't live nearly as long as a *tharakorm*, and these gateways terrify me. They are not guaranteed entrances to places where the Earth won't die—for an unimaginably long time yet. Anyway, what is life to me without my own soul egg and my tribe, the people I know and love?

"No, I'm not going one step further on this crazy quest of yours. I'm going home to live out my life, as all men should do, and I'll die when my time comes, as all men should do."

"After all that you've seen?" Sloosh said, and he walked away.

"You are right, of course," Vana said. "However, what if you do get back to your native land? Only to be captured by a woman of another tribe and then have to live the rest of your life with a strange tribe? That happens now and then to your people, doesn't it?"

"Yes, but the nine tribes in my area are not complete strangers," he said. "I've met them during the Trading Season. Besides, the tribe of my wife, when I get one, will then become my own. And I will see my relatives during the Season. It's not that bad. What is bad is to be without a tribe at all."

When Deyv and Vana had finished the dugout, they took it out at once for a trial sail. Though they upset the boat a number of times, they finally became fairly skillful sailors. Meantime, the others had completed their larger craft, and they too experimented on the waters close to shore. Whenever the sail-beasts approached them, they quickly retreated to the shallows. This maneuver always worked except when one of the immature beasts chased them. Then they had to beach their boats and wait until the young predator gave up on them.

After one such incident, Vana said, "I really don't see how we're going to get to the mainland. We'd have to be very lucky to escape being noticed by them. I just don't feel like trusting to luck. I've a feeling that we've used up all that the gods gave us at our birth."

Deyv was inclined to agree with her, but he couldn't stand the idea of spending the rest of his life on the island. The slaves and Feersh's children, except Jowanarr, were seriously considering this. They'd said nothing while the boat making was going on. But now that the setting-out was due—overdue, actually—they were close to mutiny. Feersh railed at them and threatened them with torture and death. Her sons didn't laugh at her, but the slaves weren't hesitant to tell her that she was no longer the feared witch. She was just an old woman whose only weapon was her sharp venomous tongue. One slave, Shlip, dared to tell her that if she didn't shut up he'd wring her scrawny neck. Feersh turned red, so red that she looked as if she were going to have a stroke. Gasping, she swayed, then had to sit down to keep from falling.

The Yawtl enjoyed this very much. He agreed that the dissenters were probably right. Nevertheless, he wasn't going to stay. What was needed was some other method of travel. He'd have to think about it. But since this required some time, he wasn't going to leave yet either.

Sloosh had been observing the birds and winged animals. Shortly after Feersh had been put down by the slave, the Archkerri returned to the camp from the other side of the island.

"I've been watching the birds for quite a while. There are those who make this place their permanent home. And there are those who fly in from the mainland, stay awhile, then fly on out over the water. They must be going on to land across the waters. Which means that this is not the ocean but a lake." He paused, then said, "Unless they're going to another island."

"You can do what you want to do," Deyv said. "I'll wish you good fortune, though. You've been a good comrade, even if you are rather exasperating at times."

"The same to you," the plant-man said. "There have been times when I've almost thought of you as an Archkerri. If only you could think as clearly as I do . . ."

Deyv's warmth toward him was threaded with another feeling. This was not just sadness at having to leave him. It was something close to panic. Somehow the Archkerri had become a substitute for the man's soul egg. He wasn't a completely satisfactory replacement, far from it. But Sloosh had given Deyv a certain amount of security, and the Archkerri's wisdom, however distorted it was in some ways, had made Deyv feel toward him as he'd felt toward his grandmother. Several times he'd had to repress the impulse to ask Sloosh to cuddle him.

Sleep-time after sleep-time passed. Still, nobody had said, "Now is the time to set out." There were too many sail-beasts cruising around the island and too many giant fish exploding from the water.

One day Deyv was up on the promontory, watching the marine life, when Sloosh joined him and said, "I've observed that the adult sailship-beasts never attack the young ones."

Smiling, Deyv turned toward the Archkerri.

"You just gave me an idea. We'll capture a young beast that's not too large to handle. And we'll sail it back to the land."

Sloosh buzzed an exclamation, then said, "Why didn't I think of that? Because it's too aggressive an idea? Sometimes, in certain situations, personality can be more valuable than intelligence. However . . . let me consider this."

After a while he opened his eyes.

"How do you propose to control the beast?"

"I think I know how to do that. Now, here's what I have in mind."

27

AFTER much argument, a course of action was agreed upon. First, they had to make another boat, one large enough to hold all of them. Then ropes and wooden grapples would be fashioned, and a stock of smoked meat and fruits had to be laid in. If the plan went as it should, however, they'd not require most of their provisions. When all this had been done—the only serious interruption being a series of earthquakes— they caught and smoked a large pile of fish and put the catch into a fiber net.

Before the chase could be started, it was necessary to wait for the quarry. Luckily, this took only a sleep-time and a half. Along came three of the young sail-beasts, one much smaller than the other two. The voyagers launched the boat into the heavy surf without upsetting it, having practiced this until they were weary of it. Vana and Hoozisst raised the single triangular sail, then joined the paddlers.

As they approached their quarry, the beasts changed course to get away from the unfamiliar thing. Deyv, in the bow, threw out some fish and some legs of meat. Immediately, the beasts turned toward the food, which was floating on the surface, buoyed by air bladders from a sea plant. It took some maneuvering to bring the boat up alongside the youngest creature. After almost turning over once, they accomplished it. Deyv cast out some more fish, and the young beast started to turn in toward them. Vana and the Yawtl quit paddling and grabbed the ropes controlling the sail.

Deyv, praying to Soonwitl, the water god, threw his lariat. Despite the up-and-down motion of the boat and the wind blowing against it, the noose settled around the tiny projection, a sailless bowsprit, just below the junction of bow and deck. The noose was pulled tight and the rope wrapped at the other end around a stout post fixed in the thick bottom of the dugout. Jowanarr held the extreme end, ready to pay out more rope if it was needed.

Swinging sidewise, the dugout bumped into the hull of the beast. The paddles on that side were withdrawn just in time to keep them from being pinned. Deyv leaped just before the contact and landed upright on the deck of the beast. However, he had to fling himself forward to keep from falling back off the edge, since the beast was leaning to one side. He was up at once and drove the spear he'd carried in one hand into the leathery flesh of the deck.

The Yawtl came up next, the end of a rope in his hand. He quickly secured it around the spear, and Deyv caught the end of another rope tossed by Vana. There was a desperate scramble then as the others came aboard. Sloosh, of course, was last.

Deyv had wanted to untie the ropes after this phase was done. The others had said that they should wait until they were sure that the beast could be controlled. If it couldn't, they could return to the dugout. If it could be handled, then the boat could be released so that it wouldn't slow down the beast.

Deyv and Hoozisst hauled up onto the deck the very heavy net filled with smoked fish. Vana had thrown the long pole and its sawhorselike support onto the deck before she'd come aboard. Sloosh, bracing his four legs to keep his balance, carried the pole to the bow. Deyv carried the support after him, while two slaves dragged the netful behind him.

By then the flower-eyes on the masts and yardarms had turned toward the trespassers. Deyv felt self-conscious and a little apprehensive, but he didn't think that the beast could do anything about the situation. After all, it didn't have hands, and it couldn't roll over.

Deyv set the support just behind the edge of the bow and helped Sloosh tie the net to its end. The plant-man and the Yawtl handled the pole, pushing it outward until the net hung about six feet beyond the bow. Then they lowered the net until it was just above the top of the waves.

Two of the slaves had to be called to hang on to the legs of the support. Since the deck was wet, the support tended to slide to one side whenever the beast turned and so caused the deck to tip. Vana tied a rope to the end of the pole behind the straining men and the Archkerri. This was to ensure that the pole wouldn't be lost if it did slip overboard.

Deyv directing, the pole was kept pointing at where they thought the mainland should be. Their only reference was the island. Once the top of the peak was below the horizon, they would have to trust to luck. But the beast turned toward the fish hanging in front of it and headed in the right direction. Of course, it had to go off the straight line to tack against the wind, and its tempters had to take this into consideration. When it veered, they would swing the fish to be in line with its travel. When the beast had angled away too much, they swung the fish to one side. It would then change course to bring the wind at the correct angle against its sail.

"It works! It works!" Deyv cried.

"Yes," Hoozisst said, "as long as we work, work, work."

They had a long way to go. They'd have to take turns at handling the pole, and eat and work in shifts. The length of each shift would be determined by the strength of the handlers. This meant that the main burden would fall on Deyv's party. Feersh, her children, and the slaves had led too easy a life for too long. Their experiences since the *tharakorm* had lifted had toughened them somewhat, but none had the muscular strength or endurance of their captors.

Sleep-time came and passed. with much labor and short naps. By the next one, all except Sloosh were near exhaustion. Nevertheless, they couldn't slacken. From time to time they had to pull the net in and remove a few fish. These they threw ahead of them so the beast could have something to eat, to tempt it onward. They feared that if it got nothing at all, hunger would drive it to seek living fish. They prayed that it would chase the uncatchable net until they were at least in sight of land.

Halfway through the third sleep-time, the beast took off after a school of large fish with high-curving fins on their backs. For a while this led them in the direction they wanted, but then the school veered away. The beast followed it. Only by throwing out about twenty fish from the net could they entice it to get back on the right course. And there was no sign of land ahead.

By then the beast's unwanted crew was nearing the end of its energy. The stronger ones were forced to work beyond their shift and to aid the weaker from time to time.

"I think we should get back on our boat," Kiyt said. "I can't last much longer. Neither can anybody else, I'm sure."

"You'll last until I tell you to stop, you weakling!" Feersh spat. "Oh, that all of you had the guts of Jowanarr! Then I could be proud of you instead of regretting that I ever birthed such whining puny milklings! What have I ever done to deserve such a brood? My slaves are better men than you, and that includes the women!"

"Shut your ugly mouth, you old hag!" Kiyt snarled.

He ran toward the stern then, while Feersh, shrieking curses, swung her bony arms around, hoping to strike him, after which, drained by the effort, she slumped to the deck like an old dirty rag.

At that moment Sloosh buzzed distress, and his helpers shouted. Deyv spun to see the pole flying through the air over the bow. Its other end was in the jaws of a giant fish.

"It came up and snatched the net of fish!" Jeydee wailed.

If they hadn't been so utterly tired, they would have

been more vigorous in expressing their despair. As it was, they moaned or stared open-mouthed and were silent. Then they looked at each other with fatigue-red eyes. A few, past caring, went to sleep shortly afterward.

Deyv sat with his head against his knees. After a while he raised it, and in a hollow voice said, "Well, as long as the beast goes in the right direction, we'll stay on it. When it goes off, we'll take to our boat."

"That's rather evident," Sloosh said.

He didn't understand yet that human beings often spoke the obvious just to hear their own voices and also to inspire a comment on the unobvious.

Unable to ask anybody to do something that he didn't think he had strength to do, Deyv climbed the foremast. It took the last of his energy to shinny up it, or so he thought. But when he saw a thin dark line just a little higher than the horizon, he started to shout and wave an arm. The others looked up at him, wondering what had caused the brief frenzy. He clung panting to the mast, refusing to answer their queries. The black thickness might just be clouds. That was all they needed now. False hopes followed by a storm.

Too weak to stay up long, he slid back down the mast. He told Sloosh what he'd seen, then said, "Can you stand watch? We'll have to keep an eye on the beast. The moment it veers off, we'll get in the boat. We'll just have to hope that that is land."

The plant-man buzzed that he would try to stay awake. Deyv said that he knew that Sloosh could do it. He tied himself to a rope, one end of which was attached to the tiny bowsprit, and he hurtled into sleep. It seemed to him that he'd just closed his eyes when the Archkerri's huge red hand was shaking him. It was no use trying to ignore it, though he pretended that he couldn't be awakened for a short time.

Sloosh pulled him up by his hand.

"We're heading back toward the island."

The peak had long since sunk out of sight, but Deyv could see that they were going downwind. Ahead, big silvery fish leaped out of the ocean. They seemed to be going too fast for the beast to catch them, but that wasn't stopping it from chasing them.

"We'll have to get on the boat," Sloosh said. "If it's land you saw, not clouds, we might make it." He hesitated, then pointed outward. "Unless that adult beast decides to eat us."

Deyv turned around. While he'd slept, a full-grown sailship-creature had appeared. It was scudding along, all sails unfurled, heading toward them from the direction of the island. Shortly thereafter, their beast turned away from it and in the direction they wanted to go.

Time passed. The adult slowly gained on the young. Sloosh said that this was because its sail area was much larger while its body, or hull, was perhaps only twenty feet longer. "I would say, though," Sloosh continued, "that the one we're on is not *very* young. It's probably a juvenile."

They ate and slept, gaining strength, while the chase went on. They didn't know why their beast was running away from the other, but it obviously was. Otherwise, it would be pursuing fish to satisfy its hunger, which must be great by now.

The clouds, or land, on the horizon came into sight of those on the deck. They, or it, grew larger, though it was still impossible to determine its nature. Finally, the adult was only about six hundred feet behind and a hundred feet to one side of theirs. Then the young one changed course and presently was running downwind. Its passengers thought that they would now have to abandon it. They didn't like the idea, since the adult might take off after them. While they were arguing about whether or not it was wise to get into their boat, the young beast turned toward their goal.

A long time passed after this. Steadily, the large creature closed the gap. And then it was running alongside its quarry at a distance of fifty feet.

"Why is it doing this?" Vana said. "Do the adults eat the young?"

"I don't see how they could," Sloosh said, "unless their jaws can tear through the hard bone of the hull. But I've an idea. However, since the question is so close to being answered, I won't voice my conclusion. Well, perhaps I should. You could then see how close my speculation is to the reality. But if I do, I might cause a panic. On the other hand, knowing what to expect might avert or diminish the panic. What should I do?"

He closed his eyes. Immediately thereafter, they opened—and widely. The big beast had slanted in, and the side of its bow crashed against the middle of the young one's hull. Everybody standing was hurled to the deck. Seven times the collision was repeated, each time the attacker striking a place nearer the young one's bow. Then it came alongside until its front was ahead of its quarry and its bow was behind it.

Three openings appeared in the deck of the young beast. The male slave Shlip had to scramble to keep from falling in as the leathery skin beneath him started to separate along a hitherto invisible seam.

"What's going on?" Deyv cried.

"Just as I thought," Sloosh said.

Three round openings had also appeared on the deck of the chaser. Out of each rose a cylinder of the same color and seemingly of the same material as the hull. The cylinders were vertical and twice as long as Deyv and had a diameter about equal to that of his torso. Their bases were surrounded by some gray gristly stuff, the organs or muscles that had lifted them from below-deck.

Now the three cylinders moved downward, stopping at a 45-degree angle to the deck and revealing that the other ends were open. For a short while, nothing happened. And then, simultaneously, they erupted with a loud bang. Out of each shot something dark and blurred which arced over the gap between the two beasts.

Deyv, along with the others, yelled, and he fell to the deck. Only Sloosh, who'd stationed himself at the bow, remained standing. Lying on his back, Deyv couldn't see the flying objects closest to him. But the one coming down near the aft looked cone-shaped. All three struck near the openings, burst, and splattered out a sticky green fluid.

Sloosh buzzed loudly, "I would have thought you'd have followed my example after my warning."

"What warning?" Deyv screamed, but he got up and raced toward the plant-man. Vana followed him a moment later. The Yawtl was too far away to hear Sloosh, but, seeing the two take off for the bow, he ran for the stern. Jum and Aejip came bounding in to Deyv a moment later.

The recoil of the explosions had rocked the adult a little. When it had regained its former attitude and the cylinders were again steady, or as steady as they could be in the swelling sea, and as the nose of the beast started to go down, and the beast began to roll upward, the cylinders banged. Again, three cones soared out. Feersh was dragged stumbling by Jowanarr toward the bow. The others had reacted even more slowly; they seemed bewildered and uncertain which way to run. The slave named Shlip dashed toward the stern as the second salvo exploded, but he slipped in the green fluid from the first and skidded shrieking into the ocean.

Kiyt, dashing by the rearmost opening, was engulfed in a burst of blood and fluid as the impact of the cone knocked him sideways into the opening. Deyv glimpsed a foot going down into the hole, the rest of him was a red and green mess.

A female slave, Tishdom, was cut on her back and her legs by flying fragments of the shell of the cone and spattered with the sticky stuff. But she wasn't seriously hurt. Screaming, she got to the bow just as a third broadside exploded.

This time, all three cones hit the target, and a geyser of green rose from each opening and fell back. Slowly, the openings closed, the leathery sections sliding back across. Once again, the deck seemed unbroken. Though the cones that had struck the deck had heavily dented it, the dents began to fill in.

The adult veered away, its flower-eyes turning to watch the young one.

Deyv was surprised to see Jowanarr weeping. He hadn't known that she cared the least bit for her brother. Perhaps, until then, she hadn't known either.

Deyv smelled a strong almost overwhelming fishy odor. It reminded him, however, of another odor. Suddenly, he knew why the big beast had chased the smaller one and why it had shot its cones from the cylinders. He said, "Sloosh, we were caught in the mating of the sail-beasts."

"Yes. My speculations were valid. Even though I didn't know how the mating would be done, I was nearly certain that the large beast was pursuing ours for that purpose. Actually, she is not so young. She's juvenile but nubile."

"How do the males propel those cones so far? They look so big and heavy."

"I presume by compressed air."

"But why would the female run so hard? It looked as if she didn't want to be caught."

"I suspect that the females will mate only with the fastest and most skillful of the males. That weeds out the inferior males. Ah! She's turning outward now. She sees a school of large fish, and she has to satisfy another hunger. I suggest we get into our boat now."

They untied the ropes, coiled them, and then stumbled or fell into the dugout. Sloosh took over the rudder; Deyv and Vana managed the sail. Like it or not, they were once again at the mercy of the elements, sail-beasts, and giant fish. Deyv summoned energy to try to cheer them up.

"That has to be land we see."

"And if it isn't?" Jeydee whined.

Deyv shrugged. At that moment, he didn't want to die, but he didn't care much if he did. He was even indifferent to the prospect of wandering as a ghost forever if he sank without his beloved soul egg.

The tail of The Beast was slipping over the horizon behind them. The sky shone bright and white above. Around them the long green waves rose and fell. A flock of whinnying winged mammals passed over them on the way to the island. Every once in a while an adult or young female sailship-beast would appear, scudding toward or away from the boat. A few came close, the many eyes fixed coldly on them, but none attacked. And they saw some of the giant fish, though not many. What could have been low-lying clouds definitely became the peaks of mountains. Another sleep-time. Their spirits rose as far as their wretchedness and tiredness would permit.

In the middle of the next sleep-time, they beached upon soft white sand. After thanking their various deities, they plucked fruit and nuts, ate, expanded the ancient vessel, and slept in it for a long time.

Deyv had a dream. His grandmother came to him, which meant that she was dead. Live people never appeared in dreams. She said, "There is something you've been thinking, child. But the thought has been lying around in the darkness, gathering dust, and it may not see light until it is too late. So I have come to bring it out of the dark and show it to you."

Though she was a ghost, he didn't feel frightened. His grandmother would never hurt him.

"What is that thought?" he asked. He tried to reach for her, but she backed away from him.

28

DEYV said, "Vana, my grandmother told me that we're lost. We don't have the slightest idea how to get to the cave that holds our soul eggs. We'll never find them."

Vana took his story as seriously as he did. Her tribe

also talked to the dead in its dreams, though usually it was the grandfather who delivered the messages for the gods.

"Never?"

"Never. But she said that we could make our own eggs with The Shemibob's help."

"I don't know," she said. "I'm not saying that some demon took your grandmother's semblance and gave you a false message. But I would like to confer with my great-grandfather, since my grandfather is still alive. He has sometimes come to me."

Deyv said angrily, "And how will you know that the demon wasn't taking the semblance of your great-grandfather?"

"Oh, no. My demons are not yours. Yours could not appear to me. Besides, when my great-grandfather comes, he makes a secret sign. I know by that that he is indeed what he appears to be."

"Sure!" Deyv said. "But what if he'd been a demon when he first came to you, and it was then that he arranged the secret sign with you. That would mean that the demon had always been the one who talked to you. And if your great-grandfather does come, he won't know the sign. And you'll think he's the demon!"

Sloosh had to pull Vana from Deyv, whom she'd knocked to the ground. He held her up in the air while she kicked and writhed and screamed insults. Deyv got up, holding his throat.

"She's crazy! I was only being logical!"

The plant-man said, "I've observed that when a human is dealing with another, he's usually *logical* only if he's advancing his self-interests or has a desire to hurt or put down the other. Is this one of those situations?"

"Of course not!" Deyv cried. "I was just trying to point out something to her! Why'd she go mad?"

"Both of you have mixed attitudes toward the other," the Archkerri said. "I don't really have enough data about humans to analyze what motivates them. Rather, I should say, I don't know enough about you two, since individuals vary so much, to explain what your relationship is. I can tell you what it should be, but neither of you would care to listen. I mean, you'd listen, but your ears would be tuned to different vibrations from those I'd be emitting. Perhaps I should start over. What I mean—"

"I was just trying to get at the truth," Deyv said. "I had no desire to hurt her."

"Not that you are aware of. But I've observed that humans often don't know how their own psyches operate. Indeed, there seems to be more energy used in *not* knowing than in knowing. Why this is, after an unimaginable number of—"

Deyv walked away. When he was some distance from the two, he saw Sloosh let Vana down. She ran into the jungle and didn't come back until a long time after. It wasn't until after the next sleep-time that she would address him, and she did so only in matters that concerned maintenance of the camp.

Deyv was polite but stiff. So was Vana, though he couldn't figure out why she should be so, since the offense was wholly hers. But after some reflection, he saw that perhaps he had spoken too frankly. And he had to admit that if he had been she, he'd have been offended. Still, his observations *had* been logically based. When dealing with demons, you couldn't be too careful.

He shrugged. He seemed to be doing a lot of that lately, and he thought, If she wants to go back on that hopeless search, let her do it. Alone. She might want to take Aejip with her for protection and companionship, but I won't allow it. The cat is mine. I've just loaned her to Vana.

After the next sleep-time, Vana went hunting with Aejip. She returned with a young pig, a tusker, and a bagful of delicious beetle eggs. She gave these to the two slaves to prepare, then walked up to Deyv.

"I tried to summon my great-grandfather before I went to sleep," she said. "But he didn't come. So, while hunting, I did some thinking. I sat for a while under a *puh* tree and breathed in the perfume of its fruit. As you know, it helps one to think true thoughts. You *didn't* know? Well, different tribes have different wisdoms.

"Anyway, it came to me that my great-grandfather didn't visit me because he didn't think it was necessary. I could solve my problem by myself. Which I did. I decided that what you said, what your grandmother told you, was the right path. So . . . I'm going on with you."

Deyv surprised both of them by embracing her tightly. But he stepped back quickly.

She stared at him for a moment, then said, "You're happy! You would've missed me!"

"We've been together a long time, and you are a good companion, even if you're grouchy sometimes. Too touchy, I mean. But then I'd miss—"

"The dog? The cat?"

Deyv gestured. "Oh, you know."

"No. I don't."

Her shoulders stiff, she turned and walked off. Not before he'd seen the tears, though.

He felt a tightening in his chest, and he had to swallow. He hadn't meant to hurt her again. But she was, after all, a woman without an egg. She hadn't felt like one when he had squeezed her; her flesh was no different from that of a woman with a soul. And, he reminded himself, he, too, was eggless. In this situation, logic had no force.

Needing to do something, anything at all to keep from thinking about her, he went to Sloosh. The plant-man and the Yawtl were examining the Emerald of Anticipation. Deyv interrupted their discussion.

"Vana and I are going on with you."

The Yawtl burst into barking laughter. Sloosh buzzed his equivalent of mirth.

"Hoozisst was showing me how the stone operates, though so far he can use it only for simple situations. It takes a long time to get complete mastery of it. However, by coincidence, we were just asking it what the decision of you two would be. And here you come along and confirm what it showed."

The Emerald's interior was glowing with writhing designs of many colors. They looked like visual gibberish to Deyv, though apparently they did make sense. He thought it was an amusing toy but that was about all it was. Certainly, it hadn't helped Feersh much.

"According to the witch, there are a thousand times a thousand such emeralds growing in The Shining House of Countless Chambers," the Yawtl said. "And there are a thousand times that many different types of stones, each type of which has its own powers. If I could chip off one of each, I'd be the most powerful witch in the world."

"You'd need a chisel made of the metal of the ancients," Sloosh said. "Feersh stole one before she fled, which is why she was able to cut one stone off. But she was too fearful of The Shemibob to take the time to remove more."

"All that's fine," Deyv said. "Only . . . I thought that maybe you'd be pleased that we're going with you."

"What do you expect?" Hoozisst said. "That we'd jump with joy?"

"I *am* pleased," the plant-man said. "I derive a certain amount of emotional satisfaction from your company and have found you most energetic and agreeably aggressive in the dangerous situations we've encountered."

"'Emotional satisfaction'?" Deyv said sarcastically. "I thought you Archkerri were all intellect, unhampered, as you might say, by emotion."

"Nonsense. Any creature with a nervous system experiences emotions. These may be only fear or anger at the lowest level. As the systems get more complex, the number of emotions increases and so does the complexity, the interrelationships, the subtlety.

"No, it would be impossible, as far as I know, for a sapient to evolve without emotion. Sentiency involves more than just a logical brain. Besides, there are different kinds of logic. Just as there are different kinds of emotions. We Archkerri share some of your emotions but have some you lack. That's all. Except that we are able to use our intellect somewhat better than you humans do. If you weren't doomed to perish with this universe, and you may not be, you might evolve into a higher creature. By 'higher,' I mean a people who would be neither self-destructive nor other-destructive.

"Here we are, here you are, rather, you humans. In the unimaginable time you've been on Earth, you've changed your physical form very little. There was no evolutionary need for it, since you are generalized and so very fit for survival. Like the ant, cockroach, pig, and rat. You have had, however, a vastly more complex brain structure.

"Yet, though you've developed many great civilizations, you haven't been able to make yourself thoroughly cooperative or free yourself of the diseases of body and mind. It's true that you've conquered many, but new ones come to replace them. You're incapable of inventing a panacea for body and mind; you're still selfish, greedy, short-sighted, and illogical outside of a few fields of thought, and sometimes too emotional in those.

"So here you are near the end of the world, savages, beings who, given the time, would build up a great civilization again. You don't have the time, and the long, long story, the many-eons tale of humankind, will end. For what reason? I don't know. The universe, looked at logically, is, despite all its intricate order and irresistible physical principles, senseless.

"Or is it? Perhaps it's been made for emotional satisfaction, not intellectual, though the two aren't always separate. The question is: for whose?

"But if it is emotional satisfaction that is the basis of this universe, the prime reason for the existence of sentients, not immortality, then perhaps you humans are superior to us Archkerri. I shudder at the idea, but I consider it.

"What I know, or think I know, is that the existence of questions implies answers. Otherwise, we have an unbalanced equation—if there can be such a contradictory thing—and that doesn't appeal to my scientific mind. But then perhaps the universe is one cosmic unbalanced equation. It would be the only one; all lesser equations can be balanced. Perhaps it is the very lack of balance that creates space-matter.

"Do I know what I'm talking about? Perhaps. I do know that this type of thinking gives me a brain-ache. But I get emotional satisfaction from this pain."

The Yawtl had walked away during this discourse. Deyv was fascinated, but he was glad when Sloosh turned to a more mundane matter. Which now was what they'd take to get to the land of The Shemibob. After a conference which even the slaves attended, though they had no voice in the decision, the shoreline was chosen. It would be the longest way around, but they could get lost too easily in the vast jungles. Also, it was much easier walking on the beach.

"Eventually, following it, we'll get to the far end of the land," Sloosh said. "Then we can turn back into it. The Shemibob lives somewhat inland from the ocean. But we will come to a place on the beach where The Jeweled Wasteland grows. All we have to do is to enter it there. Feersh the Blind will show us—rather, tell us—where the House of The Shemibob is."

"No, I can't do that!" the witch shrilled. "I fled from her House to the opposite end. I wouldn't know the path from where we'll enter. Moreover, I'm not sure that I'd recognize now the path I took. It was many many sleep-times since I ran with brain-freezing terror at my heels. Besides, The Wasteland has been growing since then. It's not only spread outward, it's grown upward. The landmarks which I only vaguely remember are probably covered over now."

Sloosh's reply to this was, "I wonder why the stones are growing out of control?"

Thoroughly rested, they packed up and set out. By then The Beast had come around again and slid by half of the sky. Ten sleep-times passed without much incident. They saw during the eleventh a village on the beach and detoured into the jungle. On the twentieth they were warned by Deyv, who was the scout, that a House was ahead. It lay on its side, its base sticking from the jungle onto the sand. Deyv had run into the jungle and gotten close to it to spy.

"They are not human," he said. "They're even stranger-looking than you, Hoozisst."

"I'm not strange-looking," Hoozisst growled. "It's you humans who look so peculiar."

Sloosh heard Deyv's description of them.

"They're Tsimmanbul," Sloosh said. "I've met some tribes that were friendly; some that were downright hostile. We'd better go around these. No use taking chances."

The next inhabited place was a village of bamboo huts, round and with conical grass-thatched roofs, surrounded by a log stockade. Like the previous Tsimmanbul, they seemed to be engaged chiefly in fishing. This was all to the good, since it meant that the chances of encountering their hunters in the jungle were less. However, going around the fourth village, they were almost surprised by four warriors carrying a deer suspended from two poles. They dived into the bush and waited until the hunters were long gone.

The shortest of the Tsimmanbul was at least six feet six inches tall. Their skin was hairless and a dark slate-gray color with white bands running from below their armpits to halfway down their legs. In form, the bodies were human enough, though their long toes were webbed. The heads were about a third larger than those of a human of the same height, and they were beastish. Deyv thought they looked both doglike and fishlike, yet their faces were intelligent and expressive. The forehead looked as if it covered a very large brain. The mouths were very wide, curving around almost to the quite humanlike ears. These looked small but only because the huge heads dwarfed them.

They were certainly exotic-appearing. What made Deyv's neck hairs seem to bristle, though he'd seen Tsimmanbul before, were the tops of their smooth glossy gray heads. Fat and muscle bunched up on the skin, and there were openings at the peaks. These moved like lips, as if they were breathing through them. Sloosh had told him that they were air-entrances, although once they had been blowholes.

They talked with their mouths, however, in a series of modulated pipings. Sharp teeth flashed whitely in the dark faces; their gums and tongues were a fish-belly white.

"They, too, had a mighty civilization once, though it was mainly confined to the ocean," Sloosh said. "Their cities rose on pylons from the bottom or floated on the surface. At that time, they lived in peace with the humans. But, after a catastrophe, they reverted to savagery."

The Dark Beast made its circular patrol of the Earth unwearyingly. The group that walked along the ocean-shore below it was not so untiring. They stopped frequently and rested. Other times they had to flee long distances or hide to escape humans, Yawtl, Tsimman-bul, hordes of beetles or ants, and on one river a horde of poisonous serpents that poured from they knew not where to they knew not where.

Earthquakes of varying intensities shook, rocked, and threw them. The Earth opened up before and behind them, and twice almost below them.

Storms slammed down giant trees that had endured for thousands of sleep-times; rains knocked them down before they could get into the expanded vessel; lightning struck so close it knocked the Yawtl senseless. Deyv said, however, that that was no new condition for Hoozisst.

Once, a very cold wind came, the first Deyv had felt, though there was said to have been a terrible one shortly before he was born. With it came another new phenomenon, hail. The large hard ice balls bruised them after tearing through the leaves overhead and might have killed them if they hadn't taken refuge in the vessel.

There were also many times when the sandy or rocky beach ran out, and they had to climb the cliffs abutting on the waters.

Feersh's family and the two slaves became as tough as the others, though Jeydee continued to whine and complain. Finally, Deyv got so tired of it that he told them they'd have to carry the cube between them unless they quit complaining. They didn't stop, but they confined their remarks to their own language. Since Deyv didn't understand it, it didn't bother him.

Sloosh estimated that they had traveled four thousand miles along the shore. This curved so much, however, that they were still perhaps three thousand miles from the land of The Shemibob. The distance didn't utterly dishearten them. They had no keen sense of time.

In the meantime, Deyv had sought relief from his ever-increasing tension by approaching the female slave, Tishdom. To his utter humiliation and abysmal frustration, she refused him.

"No, I will talk to you and eat with you, but I won't go into the bushes with you. I'd like to, if circumstances were different, even if you are a savage. But I can't, I just can't. You don't have a soul egg."

Deyv felt like hitting her.

"What nonsense is this? You've been bedded by Feersh and her children. They don't have eggs!"

"I was their slave and had to do what they wished. I loathed every moment of it—well, almost every moment. Now I can tell them to go suck a *sheekrook*."

Deyv stomped off, angry yet feeling as if he were something unclean. Which he was.

Tishdom must have told Vana about the conversation. She came to Deyv. Instead of the jeers he'd expected, she seemed sorry for him.

"Now you know how I felt when you didn't ask me. And how I felt when Shlip rejected me. A slave!"

Sloosh, hearing of this matter, said, "I'm glad I'm not a human. But then I couldn't be. The *I* of me is unique. It is the singular body which forms the singular identity, the psyche. Flesh is the origin and shaper of that entity which you call the *soul*. Or, in my case, flesh and vegetable."

The bright sky and The Beast leisurely chased each other as if they had eternity to run. The witch and her people learned Sloosh's language.

And then, shortly after breakfast, as they were going down a jungle path to avoid a settlement, what they'd feared for so long happened.

They had no warning, no growls from the cat or dog, no evidence of the trap. The leafy ceiling seemed to fall in on them, and they were covered with a great heavy net entangled with foliage. They struggled until the leaves were picked off by a dozen grinning Tsimmanbul.

29

"AT least, they didn't kill us at once," Vana said. "Though we might regret that they didn't."

They were in a small, one-room building, the only one built of logs. The rest were the round bamboo huts that seemed prevalent throughout this country. A log stockade surrounded the village, which was on top of a high cliff. The sea boomed against its base, but nearby was a wide sandy beach which held the fishing boats. Sloosh thought they'd built the village so high to avoid the tsunamis.

All their captors except the children were painted with green and red stripes, six-pointed stars, and circles enclosing swastikas. The latter, Sloosh told his uninterested audience, were ancient symbols, so old that the earliest men had painted them on rocks and on the walls of their tents or hogans. However, the symbolism attached to them had varied greatly.

"Will the symbols enable us to escape?" the Yawtl asked sarcastically.

The Archkerri said, "Who knows? Almost anything can be a tool if it's used correctly."

The only entrance was a heavy log door with a thick log as a bar on the outside. There were four windows, all too small for any but a child to wriggle through. Two Tsimmanbul males stood guard at the door and one outside each window. Otherwise, the village seemed to be in its usual routine. The young were running around playing, the females were cooking and gossiping, males were coming in with fish, game, or fruit or were empty-handed.

The shaman sat on a bamboo stool in front of his hut. He wore a tall feathered headdress, a green and purple egg on a cord around his thick neck, a white and black checked fiber kilt, and fringed leather bands just below the knee. A thick film of rancid fat glistened over the paint and the bare skin.

On the packed earth at the shaman's feet were six half-foot-long sticks. Every now and then he'd pick these up, shake a large gourd rattle while shrilling some sort of a chant, and then he would throw the sticks into the air. Afterward, he'd study the pattern they made on the ground.

The prisoners had been in the cabin for three sleep-times. Aside from a beating by children and women when they'd been brought in, they hadn't been ill-treated. The food was good and plentiful. Their evacuations were regularly emptied from large bamboo buckets, which were washed out before being returned. And they were let out, one at a time, to exercise.

Shortly after they'd been locked up, a female had started language lessons. She stood outside the door and held up objects, giving each its name. It wasn't easy to imitate the pipings, but it could be done. Sloosh could only buzz. The teacher, however, soon was able to make a correlation between his modulated sounds and hers.

The lessons made the cat and the dog, who'd also

been shut up with them, nervous at first. After a while, they got used to it.

A good part of the time, the shaman sat casting his sticks. Other times he would leave the village on some business, no doubt sinister. When he was absent, the children would come close to the door and talk to the prisoners. The captives made more progress conversing with the youngsters than with the teacher.

A Tsimmanbul captive, whose paint showed he was of an enemy tribe, was brought in by a war party. He was put in a hut and stayed there, except for exercise, for ten sleep-times. The shaman visited him frequently, always taking in with him a fiber cage that held a giant firefly. At the end of this period, the captive was taken away. The whole village celebrated this, beating drums, blowing whistles, playing flutes, twanging tortoise-shell harps, chanting, dancing, and taking turns daubing the captive until he was a solid black color.

Then he was bound and carried out of the stockade in a palanquin. Everybody but the guards went with him. At the end of seven sleep-times, they returned. The palanquin still carried the prisoner, but he was only a skull and skeleton. The clean-picked bones were dumped out onto the ground. The shaman took the skull into his house, and the bones were burned in a huge bonfire amidst another wild celebration.

Sloosh said, "Note that there was a small hole in the breastbone and several in the top of the skull."

"What does that mean?" Vana asked.

"I don't know, but we'll find out, though I suspect we won't like it."

He paused, then said, "Still, why should they take the trouble and expense of feeding us and teaching us their language only to kill us? It doesn't seem logical. I'll admit, though, that this conclusion is based on insufficient data. Their prisoner, from what I heard of his pipings as he was carried off, spoke the same language as the others. Perhaps the victim is required to give certain responses in a ritual. That might explain why we've not been killed—as yet."

This speculation seemed to be wrong. What the Tsimmanbul wanted, at the moment, anyway, was satisfaction of their curiosity. When the captives were fluent enough to answer detailed questions, they received a barrage of them. Where did they come from? What was their tribal life like? What were they doing here so far from their homes? Was the plant-man a god, demon, or just what he seemed to be?

The idea that they thought he might be a god and yet could be so easily caught intrigued Sloosh. He asked the shaman, Fat Bull, their main inquisitor, why this was.

Fat Bull replied that catching gods and demons was the main business of his kind, the Narakannetishaw.

This was the generic name of this species, Tsimmanbul being the Yawtl's name for them. Their captors' speech didn't have consonants or vowels. The prisoners had arbitrarily assigned these sound-values to the modulation units so that they could use the Narakannetishaw names in their own speech.

Fat Bull explained that in the beginning, when their ancestors left the sea, they'd had no gods. So, feeling the need for them, they had captured them and made them their own.

"That's a myth," Sloosh said in his own language so the shaman wouldn't understand him. "Very interesting, though."

"We make raids on other villages and Houses," the shaman continued. "Be they Narakannetishaw, Yawtl, human, or Skinniwakitaw, we raid them, take their gods, and bring them here."

He pointed at his house, the largest in the village.

"And our enemies also raid us, though so far we've been more successful than they. However, we have caught a god who seems to have turned the tables on us. He's caught us. I don't mean that he's taken any of us captive, but he might as well have. We can't move him, and he insists that we sacrifice someone every thirty sleep-times. When we don't have enemies to give him, we have to use one of our own tribe. We don't like that at all."

"I don't blame you," Deyv said. "Nobody likes to be killed. But I must admit I don't really understand what you've said. How can a god force you to take sacrifices to him if he stays in one place? Which I assume isn't close to here?"

"Who can read the minds of men, let alone the minds of the gods? He has some reason, Phemropit does. Actually, we can't talk to him. So we don't really know what he wants. But it's much safer to assume that he does require sacrifices. He hasn't rejected any, so he must want them.

"We've been economical, though, killing two birds with one stone, as it were. We make the sacrifices ask the god certain things. We think that if the god does finally reply, he may come to dwell in my house. And then I, I mean we, would have great power. With this we could exterminate our enemies and from then on live in peace. We'd also be able to use their fishing space and to have more babies. In time, we'd become so numerous and powerful that no wandering tribes would dare settle down here."

"An old story," Sloosh said in Archkerri. "The once too-peaceful Tsimmanbul are now as savage as you humans."

Deyv said, "So we'll be the next sacrifices?"

The shaman smiled, a ghastly thing to see.

"Yes, unless we take some more enemies first. I'd like you to be even better in our language before you go to talk to Phemropit. You have wandered far and wide, if your story is true. You come from different tribes. Perhaps you might have the wisdom and experience which we stay-at-homes lack. You might ask him the right questions. If you do, you won't be killed by Phemropit. And you'll be set free."

He paused, then said nonchalantly, "By the way, that cube. I've spent much time in my house looking at it. What is its purpose?"

Sloosh started to buzz. Deyv said, "Shut up! Now is no time to tell the truth!"

He spoke to Fat Bull. "That is a magical weapon of immense power. Unfortunately, it is so destructive that we can't use it without destroying ourselves. If we'd set it off when we were caught in the net, we'd have slain ourselves and the netters, and the jungle would have been blown apart, and a great flame would have swept to the sea and burned your village and the people in it to ashes within a second.

"One of the things we were seeking was a shield we'd heard about. This belongs to a witch. We were going to steal the shield and use it to protect ourselves when we did unleash the weapon."

Apparently, the shaman believed the big whopper. He said, "That rod sticking out of the cube? Does pulling on that release this terrible magic?"

"If you also use a certain chant at the same time," Deyv said.

"I don't suppose you'd be willing to tell me what it is?" Fat Bull said.

"Certainly, if you release us," Deyv said. "You may have the cube as a gift in return for our freedom."

"I can torture the chant from you."

Deyv sweated even more heavily. He said, "Not this chant. It is set up so that I forget it if someone tries to force it from me. Only if I use it willingly will it stay with me."

"You're very glib," Fat Bull said. "Well, we'll see what we'll see. In the meantime, learn our speech even better. It may serve you well, perhaps save your life, maybe even free you."

The shaman rose from his squat to his over-seven-foot height. The painted beast-prognathous face poked its nose through the bars. The huge dark eyes stared into Deyv's.

"My sticks tell me that you queer strangers may be able to understand the god's language. I sincerely hope so, since I want Phemropit to come dwell in my house and tell me his secrets. Sometimes, I have bad dreams about him. Then he comes to me, walking legless, armless, and headless, and he speaks to me in his blinding manner. And he gets very angry when I can't understand him. It is not good for a god to be angry at you."

When the shaman had left, Deyv said, "I wish I knew what he was talking about."

"We'll find out sometime," the Yawtl said. "I hope that they take some more captives soon. That'll give us more time, though our death is inevitable."

Hoozisst began prowling around again, looking for a weak place in their prison. He knew he wouldn't find any, but useless action was better than just sitting.

A moment later, the ground shook and rumbled and the walls of the cabin swayed. After balancing themselves on the jellylike earth until nauseated by the motion, they threw themselves down. After a short time, the temblor ceased to affect the surface. But Deyv, his ear to the ground, could detect a very faint thunder. He got up and looked out a window. The leaves of the few trees nearby were still shaking. The Tsimmanbul were up off the dirt, piping excitedly, but ready to resume their routine.

Their guards inspected the cabin to make sure that the ends of the logs were still tightly interlocked. Satisfied, they took their stations again.

Some time later the big temblor was succeeded by two smaller ones. Nobody bothered to comment on them.

Close to bedtime there was some excitement among the Tsimmanbul. The two log gates facing the path down the cliff to the sea swung open. Several warriors rushed in, loudly piping. The shaman was summoned, and he talked for a few moments to the warriors. Then he led the entire population, except for the guards, through the gateway. Time passed. Deyv was about to go to sleep when he heard the loud chatter of the returning natives. He got up and listened while the wife of a guard told him what had happened.

Some males had come back from a hunt, and one had noticed a large fissure about twenty feet back from the cliff's edge and forty feet from the stockade. Investigation showed that the temblor had cracked the rock from side to side. Another such quake, and the mass overhanging the sea might fall off.

The shaman threw his sticks and shook his rattle. Would the gods say if it was best for the village to be moved back, far from the crack? No, the shaman said, after a dozen stick throwings. The gods say that there is no danger—yet.

Six sleep-times later, a war party brought in another captive, a Yawtl. He was stuck in the hut that had kept the previous enemy, and the giant firefly was also taken in to him. Sloosh asked Deyv to ask a guard if the captured Yawtl spoke Narakannetishaw. When the guard said that he did, Sloosh said, "Ah, I thought so." He wouldn't say why, however.

The time came when the Yawtl was painted black and carried out in the palanquin. Seven sleep-times later, he returned in it. Sloosh commented again on the hole in the breastbone and the holes in the skull.

The prisoners were not to get another stay of execution. Fat Bull told them that even if other captives were taken, they would have to face the god next.

"You know our language well enough now."

He turned and snapped his fingers. A guard brought in a large bamboo cage holding nine giant fireflies. Fat Bull removed a firefly and held it up so they could see it closely. The insect did not struggle, though it turned its multifaceted eyes this way and that.

"See this green spot on its back?" the shaman said. "Notice now how I control the flashing of its tail. I place my thumb on the green spot. I press down gently."

The insect's tail glowed with its cold light, strong enough to dispel some of the twilight of the cabin.

"Now I lift my thumb. The firefly immediately

becomes dark. It has been trained to respond to pressure. If you were to hold your thumb on that spot, the bug would emit light until its source was exhausted.

"But its power is much, and you won't be burning it out. Observe me closely now. See the length of the four pulses I make this fly emit. Four lengths of light, each a little longer than the other. With practice you'll be able to make the lengths exact. And then you'll learn how to speak our language without speaking. You will translate each word into a certain number of pulses, each word a group of so many pulses of so many lengths. Do you understand?"

"Easily," Deyv said. "The fireflies do with light what the Archkerri does with sound when he talks. All of us have had much experience with his buzzes. We won't have any trouble transferring to light pulses."

"Very good," Fat Bull said. "Bluebird-woman has been teaching you our speech, so she might as well teach you how to use the fireflies. You will become almost as fluent with the light as with the sound. And then you will have the great honor of talking to Phemropit."

"I'm not worthy of the honor," Hoozisst said.

The Tsimmanbul piped laughter. "If that is so, then we might as well kill you now. After you've had a chance to demonstrate your bravery by not crying out during the torture."

"Perhaps I was being too modest," the Yawtl said.

Grinning whitely, the shaman left the cabin.

The practice started at once. Within six sleep-times, the prisoners were just beginning to master the control of the flies. Bluebird-woman said that they should be skilled enough in another ten sleep-times.

Meanwhile, Sloosh got from a guard some information that excited him. The others found it slightly interesting. What did they care if there was a giant lake only three sleep-times' walk inland? Or that it had been formed from a crater made by a colossal meteorite?

"It fell many, many human generations ago," the Archkerri said. "The various sapients had highly advanced civilizations then, though nowhere near as high as those that moved the Earth and that made the moon and the great outer planets into small suns.

"If they had been, they would have been able to deflect or disintegrate the meteor long before it collided with Earth. This fell near here, and the explosion and earthquake that followed burned or knocked down the forests halfway across the land mass. It slew a quarter of the animal life and tumbled all the great cities. The civilizations were destroyed within a few minutes. And the few survivors became savages. They forgot their knowledge, and their descendants never recovered it. This coastline was shattered; the sea poured into the hot crater. But since then smaller cataclysms have lifted up the sea-bottom to form a new shoreline."

"All tribes have tales of this," Vana said. "Though the reasons for the cataclysm and the details vary much."

"I'm surprised that after such a long time there would even be a memory of it in the folk tales. But then the fall of the meteor was so terrible that some dim traces of the event have persisted. It had a numbing effect upon my brothers, the trees and the grass. Their own memories are vague, distorted. All plants went into shock, and many species died from this shock.

"Anyway, the god is near the edge of that ancient crater. It will be a pleasure to see the lake personally and not by report through the prism."

"A short-lived pleasure," the Yawtl said sourly.

The dreaded time arrived. The captives, excepting the two animals, were taken from the cabin and painted black. The cat and the dog, the shaman said, would be eaten after the tribespeople returned. Deyv asked permission to say farewell to Jum and Aejip. He was refused. Weeping, calling out to the animals, Deyv was carried off. Vana wept, too, but she shouted that they would come back and free them. Jum howled, and Aejip hurled herself, roaring, against the door.

Their hands tied behind them, their ankles bound, they were put into individual, brightly painted, heavily feathered palanquins. Four males lifted each of these. Amidst wild music and piping voices, they were carried through the stockade gateway. Three sleep-times later, they reached the end of their journey.

By the light of a hundred torches, they saw that they were at the top of a long gentle slope. This leveled out to a rocky beach beyond which was open water. Torch-bearing Tsimmanbul stood on the beach, and others were scattered up and down the slope. Tremendous boulders, half-buried, lined the ridge of the slope; others stuck out of the slope here and there.

Tall thick-trunked trees grew at widely separated intervals on the hill. One tree, however, about sixty yards from the top of the slope, had been entirely uprooted. It was not erosion that had done this. Something which had been buried deep under the tree had dug its way up under it and raised it from the soil, tearing out the roots and toppling the two-hundred-foot-high plant.

Sloosh, after studying the situation, said that the uprooter may have *rolled up.*

But if this were so, why hadn't the monster kept on going?

"I don't know," the plant-man said. "It does seem to have moved of its own volition, however. Yet, how could it? The god of the Tsimmanbul is stone. Could it be the mineral kingdom's bid for life?"

30

TEN warriors holding double-torches stood on each side of the god at a respectful distance. The blaze revealed Phemropit, a thing or a creature of a dark-gray shiny metal-stone. The body, if it was such, was a flattened oval, and must have weighed at least six hundred tons. It had no head, but its rounded front bore a number of depressions. Its means of locomotion, if it had any, was three endless tracks, one on each side of its body and one in the middle. The last came out of holes on the underside, the "belly."

Sloosh said, "I can't see any wheels. They must be inside the body or perhaps some other mechanism turns the tracks."

After a while, he said, "Well, maybe it's not living. Maybe it's just some sort of machine. I doubt it, though. I think that it came down with the meteorite. It should have melted while going through the atmosphere. If it somehow escaped that, then the energy released by the collision should have melted it."

"Who cares?" the Yawtl said. "In a little while we'll all be dead, past knowledge, past nonknowledge."

The captives were standing together on the top of the slope by a colossal boulder. Six guards stood behind them. Below them the whole tribe was dancing except for the drummers, harpists, and flutists. The shaman was by himself, farther down the slope, leaping, whirling, screaming, shaking his rattle.

Below him was a short post rising vertically out of the earth. Deyv noted that it was in a direct line with the front of the god, which was twenty yards below.

The dancing went on for a long while, the participants dropping out from time to time to drink an acrid brownish liquid. And then the music and the motion stopped suddenly. The dancers froze, all piping, "Phemropit!" After that, silence except for the cry of some animal in the jungle.

The shaman, crouching, stared down the slope at the stone-thing. Then he got down on his knees and bowed seven times, after which he rose and moved to one side of the post. A woman brought him a giant firefly in a cage. He removed it, and the woman ran back up the slope with the cage. Fat Bull walked close to the post and leaned over toward it, holding the firefly out.

"Great god Phemropit, lord of the fiery falling star and of the great inland sea, god of the Narakannetishaw! Speak with your tongue of light!"

His thumb pressed, and the tail of the firefly flashed in the half-dark cast by The Dark Beast above.

Deyv jumped and gasped, and many screamed. From one of the holes in the front of Phemropit a thin bright light had shot out. It spat just above the top of the post, bored into the earth above it, then disappeared.

The firefly flashed out groups of pulses of four lengths.

"Oh, great god! Here are your people again, come to worship you, to offer you more sacrifices! Take these, and this time may you be pleased to return with us to the holy House and dwell there forever and protect us from our enemies!"

Again the slim blindingly bright beam flicked out. This time it almost touched the firefly and the hand that gripped it. The shaman moved back a step, turned, and looked up the slope.

"Bring the first one!" he piped.

The captives waited in terror. They'd been told that the shaman had picked the order in which they would go, but he had not said what that was. Now the two giant males moved toward the group, halted, looked darkly at them. Deyv sweated and shook. Was this the end? After all he'd endured? If only he had his soul egg with him, he could at least stroke it and draw from it courage.

Suddenly, the two warriors grabbed Jeydee. Screaming, struggling, he was dragged down the slope. Feersh, hearing his voice, knew what had happened. She cried out to him to be brave, to show the savages that he was not afraid. He should demonstrate that the child of the dreaded witch Feersh the Blind was strong.

It was doubtful that Jeydee heard her. Even if he had, he wouldn't have acted any differently. His mother knew this, but perhaps she hoped that in his last hour he would pull from deep within him his manhood.

Jeydee continued to writhe and scream until he was tied to the post by ropes around his legs and waist. Then he stood silent and trembling while his hands were untied. The shaman handed him the big insect and said something. Deyv could hear the piping faintly, but he couldn't understand what was said. Doubtless, though, he was repeating the ritual questions to him. And promising again that if he could get the god to talk, he'd be saved.

Sloosh muttered, "Those stupid Tsimmanbul. They could talk to it if they'd teach it their language, I think. But not by standing someone directly in front of it. And they need referents, objects, to show it, so they can correlate words with these."

He shrugged, then said, "Still, maybe the thing has an intelligence which is so alien that it couldn't understand the correlation. If it indeed has a mind as we know minds."

Jeydee, very pale, held up the firefly. He pressed on the green spot, and the insect pulsed out its first message.

"Oh, god Phemropit, I want to speak with you. Your people worship you with fear and adoration. They have sent me, an enemy of the Narakannetishaw, to speak with you so that you won't be guilty of slaying one of your true worshippers. Speak to me, Phemropit. And spare me so that I may go free and so that you may talk to your people and give them your ancient stony wisdom and make them powerful. And your worshippers will grow great and spread all over the Earth and make you the god of all people: Narakannetishaw, human, Yawtl, and Skinniwakitaw. We shall conquer even The Shemibob."

The Archkerri buzzed the equivalent of a snort of disgust. "What nonsense! And I must die for their stupidity!"

The message was finished. A few seconds passed. And then the beam lanced out, piercing Jeydee's chest. He fell forward and hung from the post. Again and again, repeating exactly the group-pulses, the beam flashed. It shot through the top of the head, and blood ran down from it until it was drained.

When the beam ceased, the Tsimmanbul broke into

a frenzy of drumming, fluting, and piping. Two warriors
ran down the slope and untied the body, making sure
that they were not in the line of the beam.

The shaman piped so loudly that he could be heard
even at that distance. "Once more, the god Phemropit
has mocked us! But we will not be discouraged! We
know that the time will come when he will deign to
talk with us!"

Feersh stood crying. Jowanarr's face showed no
emotion. Tishdom and Shig, the two slaves, were
sobbing, not for their former master but for themselves.
Vana was looking around as if she'd like to make a
run for it. She wouldn't get far with her hands tied
behind her. The Yawtl seemed withdrawn, as if he was
no longer acknowledging the reality around him. Deyv
thought that was only a pose, however. The wily
Hoozisst would take advantage of any chance, no matter
how small. But he wasn't going to get any.

The two warriors brought up the body of Jeydee and
flung it down on the earth. They looked at the captives
as if to say, who's next? Fat Bull came up a few minutes
later. He piped for silence and said, "The god
Phemropit has refused to talk to us. But he has given
us meat to eat, the body of an enemy!"

There was a great cry. Jeydee's corpse was lifted up
by two huge females and carried down the other side
of the slope to the camp at its bottom. The captives
were herded at spearpoint to a log cabin near the huts.
Evidently this had been used many times to hold
prisoners while the tribe held a feast. The door was
barred, and two guards were stationed outside it. This
cabin was much smaller than the one in the village
and had no windows.

Vana said, "It looks as if we're reprieved until after
the next sleep-time."

Deyv, looking out through the space between two
logs, gasped. He said nothing until he had gone to the
wall, though. Then he whispered that they should
gather around him.

"I saw Jum and Aejip at the edge of the jungle!

They appeared for only a second, then went back in! They've escaped and followed us!"

The Yawtl said, "What of it? Even if they sneaked in while all but the guards are sleeping, and they killed the guards, how would that help us? We couldn't reach through and lift that bar in time. It's tied with a rope. By the time we got it untied, the whole camp would be roused."

"Some of us might get away," Deyv said. "I'm going to try. I won't just sit here and make it easy for them."

By then the corpse had been degutted and beheaded, and the legs cut off. Five hardwood spits were forced through the torso and the limbs, and these were placed on forked sticks over the fires. A female brought food and water for the prisoners. They ate it all, though they were glum. The celebration continued until all the brown liquor was drunk and the corpse and other food were devoured. One by one, the Tsimmanbul crawled into their makeshift huts. The guards, who'd been forbidden to drink much, sat by the door talking in low pipings. Now and then they got up to hold their torches to the entrance and look within.

"What do you make of this Phemropit?" Deyv asked Sloosh.

"Whatever else it is, it's our death," the Archkerri said. "Unless we find some way of communicating with it. Even then, it might kill us. Perhaps it can't help it."

"What do you mean?"

"I could be wrong. But I think that it uses that beam of light as we use sound. What only impinges with no bad effect upon others of its kind, as voices do to our ears, pierces beings of softer stuff. Stone or metal can take the beam; flesh can't. I think that the creature doesn't know it's killing other creatures. But then perhaps it wouldn't care if it did. I'll speculate that until it emerged from under the tree, it had never seen anything but its own metal-stone kind."

"You mean that it had lived on the meteor before it fell? That it was a native of a large rock that spun through cold airless space?"

"I wouldn't be surprised."

"It doesn't breathe air? But how could it live?"

"It might, probably must, get its food from eating rock. Or perhaps it lives off radiation, certain elements which would kill you or me but are its breath of life and its meat and bread."

There seemed little else to say about the thing. Deyv lay down on the ground in a corner. He wished he had Jum to snuggle against. During the last of The Beast's passage, the air had grown chilly. He shivered. It was then that Vana sat down by him and asked softly, "Could I lie in your arms? I'm cold."

He was so surprised that he could say nothing for a moment.

"But . . ."

"But nothing. I just want to warm myself with your body. I don't want to make love with you. I know how you feel about an eggless. I don't blame you. I feel the same way toward you. That is, I did for a long time. But lately, I've been thinking. We've gone a long, long time without the soul eggs. Yet . . . we have survived without them. They haven't been necessary, even if we do miss them now and then. Perhaps the plant-man was right when he said that we might find out we don't need them."

"We're still without souls."

"Are we? You know Sloosh is rather wise, even if he is sometimes arrogant and even ridiculous. He said that it is the body which grows the soul. No body, no soul. The eggs, he said, are mere psychological aids. They are crutches, and a healthy person doesn't need crutches. Nor can the eggs provide us with souls."

"He doesn't know everything," Deyv said. "What you're saying is wicked. It means that we've been lied to. Would our parents and grandparents and the shamans and all our ancestors have believed in soul eggs if they weren't what they said they were? They couldn't have been so mistaken."

"Sloosh says that the Earth is round. He proved that. Yet we've been told by our elders that it was flat."

"What are you getting at?"

"Just let me lie in your arms and get warm. I didn't come to you to argue. I'm tired of all the disagreements and squabbles we've had. I just want to be next to you and get warm before death makes me cold forever."

Deyv opened his arms. She lay down close to him, her breast on his, her arm thrown over his other breast, her head on his shoulder.

After a while, his shoulder became wet.

"I hope you don't mind if I weep," she said. "It is a terrible thing to die so far away from your tribe. If my egg hadn't been stolen, I'd be with my tribe, or at least with my husband's. I would've been married and would have had at least one child by now. But it's never to be."

Deyv said, "I'm weeping, too. It *is* an awful thing."

"It's not so bad holding a soulless next to you, is it?" she said. "You don't feel nauseated, do you?"

"I thought I would," he said. "But no, it isn't. You feel just like any woman with a soul. And if we were alone, I would lie with you. I think that if you had your egg, you'd make a good wife for me. Of course, I couldn't tell unless we could match the eggs."

"Do we really need them? Can't we tell what our hearts say, not some stone?"

"You mustn't talk such nonsense."

"I wish you'd both quit your nonsense," the Yawtl said. "You're keeping me awake. I would like to point out, however, that the witches don't have soul eggs, and they don't miss them one bit."

"But they're evil," Deyv said, annoyed that Hoozisst had been eavesdropping. "They don't have eggs because theirs went sour."

"Originally, yes," the Yawtl said. "The founders of the witch families had no eggs or they had mismatched eggs and so were driven from their tribes. And they found artifacts of the ancients and became powerful. They also made it their tradition not to have eggs. Why should they? They didn't need them. Besides—"

"Besides," Sloosh buzzed, "the witches are no more evil than anyone else. The tribes say they are because

they fear them and they can't understand them or
anyone who would live without the eggs. But the
witches are no more greedy for power than the tribespeople. It's just that they have the means with which
to attain more power."

"Has everyone been listening to us?" Deyv asked
angrily.

"It helps pass the time," Feersh said. "What
Hoozisst and the plant-man say is true, though. And
you two have been very stupid. You could have been
enjoying each other all during your journey. Now it's
too late." She laughed loudly.

"Shut up!" Deyv said. "You *are* evil!"

At that moment the guards began a screaming
piping. A beast snarled, and a guard fell with his back
against the log gate. Deyv leaped up and saw the
rosetted body of Aejip, her fangs buried in the
Tsimmanbul's throat. From beside the doorway came
more screaming and a deep ferocious growling.

Deyv pushed through the slaves and almost knocked
the blind woman down getting to the door. He began
untying the rope, one arm thrust through a lower
space and the other in the space above the heavy log.
Hoozisst came to aid him. Meanwhile, the cat had left
the dead guard to help Jum with the other. By then
the sleepers had been roused by the uproar. They
stumbled out of their little huts, looked around, and
saw the bodies and the animals by the torchlight.
Seizing their weapons, they ran toward the cabin.

The cat and the dog bounded off into the darkness.
Deyv had to withdraw his arms to keep them from
being speared.

The Yawtl had reached under the lowest log of the
door and pulled in the dead guard's stone tomahawk.
A little while later, he had to surrender it. The shaman
had checked on the weapons, found one missing, and
guessed at once where it was.

He raged around for a while, uttering threats at the
prisoners. They were unimpressed. He wasn't going to
torture them because they were the messengers to the

god and had to have clear minds to deliver the messages. Nor would he slay them on the spot. His god wouldn't like that.

After a while, the shaman quieted down. Before he went back to his hut, he stationed two guards on each side of the cabin. That quenched Deyv's hope that the animals might try again. They would know that they had no chance against eight alert warriors.

31

WHILE breakfasting, they wondered who would be eaten for supper. Fat Bull answered that sometime later by pointing out Tishdom. She screamed and struggled but was carried off and tied to the post. Presently, she was limp and silent, having failed also. Her body was taken back over the hill to be prepared for lunch, not supper. It was Shig, last of the slaves, who provided this item.

The shaman then indicated that Deyv was next. He stood pale, in shock, while Vana embraced him and wept.

"You won't have to question the god right now," Fat Bull said. "You have until some time before the next supper to figure out how to please Phemropit."

"This is ridiculous!" Sloosh buzzed. "You stupid Narakannetishaw could kill off the entire population of the world and still not get what you want from the god. You're going at this the wrong way. Phemropit doesn't have the slightest idea what you're trying to do. He doesn't know your language, but he is trying to communicate with you.

"What you lamebrains must do is what you did with us. That is, teach him your language."

His colleagues didn't think it was discreet to insult

the person who held their lives in his hands. But then, what difference did it make?

"He is our god," Fat Bull said. "Are you telling me that our god wouldn't be able to speak with our tongue?"

"Yes," Sloosh said. "It would be obvious to any but the lowest intelligence that he doesn't. Or perhaps I should say that it's not so much a lack of intelligence that has made you err as your pattern of thinking. To you a god can do anything, so this one must be able to speak your language. At the same time, you have refused to see that Phemropit is, for some reason, immobile. He's not moving because he doesn't want to move but because he can't."

"I'll overlook your insults, cabbage-head," the shaman said. "I can understand why you're not so friendly. But what you say about Phemropit isn't true. He's a god, and so—"

"And so he can do anything he wishes to do. Nonsense! I can prove to you that he can't move."

The shaman looked interested. He strode away and picked up his sticks and threw them seven times. Then he came back.

"Deyv must still be tied to the post. The gods so decree it."

"Very well," the Archkerri said. "Tie him to it. But first move the post a few feet to one side."

"But then the god can't see him!"

"You just said your god could do anything. Why couldn't he see Deyv? I'll guarantee that the god will be able to see him."

"And if the guarantee is no good? What then?"

"Then I'll let you tie me to the post."

The shaman burst out into shrill piping laughter.

"You'll *let* me? You have a fine sense of humor, walking cauliflower. Very well. I'll do as you suggest. I do want to tell the god what to do, for his best interests and ours. Look!"

He pointed down the slope to the right of the god. A warrior was just putting the cube on the ground.

"While I slept, my ancestor, White Flippers, came to me and said that I should tell the god that if he doesn't talk to us we'll destroy him with that."

Sloosh buzzed in his own speech so that the shaman couldn't understand him. "I've heard of bribing gods but never of threatening them. Well, theology is a strange business, but it has its own logic, I suppose."

To Fat Bull he said, "How do you propose to blow up Phemropit without also destroying yourselves?"

"Easy. We'll tie a rope to the rod and another rope to that one and as many ropes as are needed. Then we'll hide behind this hill so we'll be protected when we pull on the end of the rope."

Sloosh closed his eyes. Deyv cried out in Vana's speech that Sloosh mustn't tell Fat Bull the truth. As long as the shaman believed that the cube was what Deyv said it was, he might be tricked.

The plant-man opened his eyes. "I wasn't contemplating telling him the truth. I was just wondering why he was ignoring your statement that the cube would slay everything between here and the ocean."

The shaman said, "What are you talking about? I don't like to have you jabber away in your gibberish. Are you telling each other ways to fool me? Believe me, you won't get away with it."

"No," Sloosh said, "that's not it. We were talking about what would happen if you did trigger off the cube's devastating powers. You have forgotten that it will sear the jungle for miles around. The back of the hill wouldn't shield you."

"I think you're lying," Fat Bull said. "No magical device could be that powerful. You just want to scare us so much we'll be afraid to use it."

Deyv could see, by the light of the torch whose end was stuck in the ground, that the rope was not only being tied to the rod, it was being glued.

"You're right," he said to Fat Bull. "We were lying. You'll be quite safe if you hide behind the hill, though you might be knocked down by the blast. However, you can't threaten the god unless you can speak his tongue."

The shaman went away to do some thinking about that. After a while, he returned. He ordered that the post be moved a few feet to one side.

Deyv said, "Sloosh, I hope you know what you're talking about."

"If I'm wrong, I'll apologize."

"That's very comforting."

The digging up of the post was interrupted by an earthquake so severe that it rippled the earth and cracked open the beach. Other temblors, not so strong, followed. When it seemed that there might not be more, everybody got up off the ground, and business was resumed.

Deyv saw a pair of red eyes glowing in the bush behind a warrior with a torch. He wondered if it could be Jum's or Aejip's. At the moment, he was unbound. If he broke for the jungle, he might make it. No. There were too many armed Tsimmanbul around. They'd porcupine him with spears before he got forty feet away.

Sloosh said, "I think we could have left the post where it was. The quake has shifted the so-called god a little to its right."

The Archkerri explained what he wanted done. Deyv said, "Why do I have to be tied to the post? I won't run away."

After thinking about this strange proposal, the shaman said, "Well, it's not according to proper procedure. No, you can't be free."

Sloosh asked for a number of objects, and he picked up a flat but thick stone about two feet across. He accompanied Deyv to the post, and after some hesitation Fat Bull joined them.

"I want to know exactly what you're doing when you're doing it," he said. "And speak only my language."

The plant-man waited until Deyv was tied, then he

handed him the firefly. "As the Narakannetishaw have noted, the god emits light pulses of four differing lengths. They're in groups, obviously some sort of photonic words. What we have to do is to teach him our, that is, my language. Once he learns that, we can start to learn his."

Deyv extended the firefly in his left hand and began pressing on the insect. Sloosh had wanted to omit the ritual, but Fat Bull had insisted it be retained. At the end, the light beam shot out, but it struck the flat stone. Sloosh, standing to one side, had held it out in his hand. He withdrew it and looked at its surface. The beam had made a very small depression, warm around the rim.

"It wouldn't damage the metal-stone of its own kind," he said. "I suspect that that is shot with nickel-iron."

He pursuaded the shaman to set up another pole but one which had a slot at its top to hold the stone upright. Deyv began triggering flashes while the Archkerri held up some of the objects. Presently, the god-thing was repeating Deyv's words.

"Now," Sloosh said to the shaman, "do you see what a little intelligence may accomplish? You could have done this long ago. And you wouldn't have killed so many people so uselessly."

"They weren't so useless," Fat Bull said. "They made very good eating. Tell me, how long will it be before Phemropit will be able to understand me well?"

"At least as long as it took us to learn your speech and perhaps longer. After all, the god may have a mind which is very alien to ours. He may think in somewhat different categories, though I'm sure many of his must overlap ours."

Fat Bull said that the tribe couldn't stay out there that long. As it was, they took a chance of being attacked by their enemies every time they came here. He hurried off to make arrangements while Sloosh and Deyv continued the lessons. The shaman's people

wished to observe the lessons, and they loathed the
idea of not eating their captives. But, after Fat Bull
berated them, they packed up.

Twelve warriors and three females stayed behind as
guards. To make sure that the prisoners wouldn't
escape, the guards bound their hands and feet. Only
when the captives were exercising or teaching Phemropit
were they untied.

"Actually, I don't need you," the shaman said. "I
can give lessons to him myself. But why should I do
all the work? Besides, you might arm yourselves and
come back for revenge. I'll let you loose when the
whole tribe returns to witness the god as he starts for
our village."

"What about my sword?" Deyv said. "You promised—"

"I promised you could go free. That's all."

Fat Bull was wearing Deyv's ancient blade in a
scabbard. He'd also appropriated Sloosh's huge axe.
He was not going to give up such immensely valuable
weapons. Deyv didn't blame him; he'd have done the
same thing in the shaman's position. He was not,
however, going to leave the vicinity without trying to
get the weapons back. Probably the shaman knew this
and was counting on him to return. Then he'd be able,
with a clear conscience, to take him captive again and
have him for supper. No doubt, he was hoping to
catch all of them again.

"Does that mean we also can't have our cube back?"
Sloosh said.

Fat Bull's big dark eyes narrowed. His high forehead
and protruding face made him look part-human, part-
fish, part-pig.

"I need that to control the god."

Seven sleep-times passed. A messenger came from
the village. He said that the male appointed by Fat
Bull to guard and feed the captives' two animals had
been found dead and half-eaten in front of the cabin.
Evidently, they had somehow gotten to him.

Deyv asked the shaman if that meant that Jum and

Aejip would be killed if he called them in from the jungle. He'd seen them twice skulking around its edges.

"Not if you guarantee they won't attack us," Fat Bull said. "Actually, I don't mind much that they put an end to Whistling Eagle. He was very insolent, which is why I punished him by making him stay behind."

Deyv shouted their names until Jum came bouncing in, tail wagging, and, slavering, had swarmed all over him. The cat slunk in, not trusting the Tsimmanbul. Once she was assured that she was safe, she leaped, fawning upon Vana. Deyv's jealousy was only slightly diminished when she came to him afterward and leaned rumbling against his leg.

The lessons continued with, by now, all of Deyv's party except the blind witch and Fat Bull taking turns as teachers. Phemropit didn't tire; he apparently could store information and retrieve it as if he were a machine. He also learned, after the fourth sleep-time, that his light beam would penetrate the flesh of its teachers. He at once softened the beam so that it would only warm their skins.

Once it was time for him to learn abstractions, however, he began having trouble understanding. The concept of sex was for the moment beyond him. He didn't grasp how his interrogators ate or the reason why. He also had trouble comprehending the idea of individuation.

"It will understand these in time," Sloosh said. "But they are not in its experience, and so it just can't visualize or feel them. I refer to Phemropit as *it*, not *him*, since it has no sex."

Another series of earth shocks struck the camp. The crack in the beach widened. Some of the trees on the slope toppled over. The huts and the log cabin were tumbled. Sometime afterward a giant wave roared in from the lake, and it and those that followed washed away the earth from beneath the fallen tree. It floated away, leaving the god-thing with its rear hanging over a six-foot-high cliff.

Sloosh asked Phemropit if it could move higher up.

It replied that it could, but it didn't want to unless it was absolutely necessary. The energy required to do this would take too much of its fuel supply. As it was, the lessons, though not drawing on much of its energy, did weaken it. Sloosh didn't understand its explanation fully, but he thought that the thing would have to go into a suspended animation soon. That is, unless it could be provided with the stuff which provided its energy.

"It's been in a sort of hibernation, if I may use a biological analog," the plant-man said. "Then, some human generations ago, it decided to make an effort to force its way up from burial. It did so, but the effort took a lot of its limited fuel. I think that it *eats* rock which contains radioactive elements. I've explained what these are to you, though none of you seem to understand them."

He looked at them, then said, "If it runs out of the elements needed, it dies. In a sense, that is. It could stay *dead* for a very long time, yet would have the potential for coming alive again as long as its metal-stone body wasn't badly damaged."

Deyv said, "What happens if its energy does run out now? Won't Fat Bull consider that he doesn't have to keep his promise? He won't have much use for a dead, or at least sleeping, god."

"We won't tell him about this. But if Phemropit should cease to talk to us, we'd better run."

"Let's hope that Phemropit doesn't say anything to Fat Bull about this."

"Phemropit won't bring up the subject."

"Why don't we think about how to kill the Tsimmanbul so we can get on to the land of The Shemibob?" Hoozisst asked. "We're wasting time with this talking rock."

"Don't you have any curiosity about Phemropit?" Sloosh buzzed disgustedly. "Here's a creature unknown to Earth until now, a being of stone and metal that has a language and hence a sentient nervous system."

The Archkerri raved on, but the Yawtl only smirked.

Though he admitted that the plant-man knew far more than he did, he also thought that Sloosh was mentally off-balance and very impractical. If Hoozisst could have profited by staying on, he would have been all for it. But this business was most aggravating and frustrating.

The Archkerri didn't get to finish his lecture. The ground began rumbling and rippling, and then with a loud crack like the snap of a giant whip, the earth separated nearby. It was only a zigzag opening about three inches wide, but they didn't know what horrible sequel to expect. There was no place to run. In any event, the earth was shaking so much they couldn't even stand up.

Trees fell right and left, and one rolled toward them, its branches breaking off. It stopped short of crushing them, but the ends of some snapped-off branches lay only a few inches away. A huge boulder smashed into the tree and bounced over it, narrowly missing a Tsimmanbul.

After the temblors had faded away, everybody got up and ran toward the top of the hill. Deyv, Vana, Hoozisst, Feersh, and her daughter had their hands tied in front of them. They fell, but they managed to get up and struggle upward.

Another shock, as intense as the first one, rocked the top of the hill just as they reached it. The boulders there fell on either side of the slopes. One roared by the god, almost striking it, and stopped some feet past the shoreline.

A long time later a tsunami smashed into the hill, reaching halfway up. Wave after wave made the hill shudder, covering Phemropit, washing the ground from under him, snatching the uprooted trees away, and moving the boulders back and forth.

In the midst of this terror, only Sloosh was able to talk. Watching the ocean battle for the stone-metal creature, he said, "Too bad! Too bad! I would have found out so much about its kind!"

When the ocean finally subsided, Phemropit was not in sight.

Fortunately, though the cube had been yanked savagely many times and once struck by a boulder, it had not been carried away. The rope-chain, the other end of which was fastened to a tree at the bottom of the opposite slope, had held.

"My god is gone!" the shaman cried.

"Some god," the Yawtl said. "Here we are, safe, but the god of the sea has proven mightier than the god from outer space. I think—"

"What you think is wrong," Sloosh said. He pointed down to the riven beach.

Out of the sea rose the shiny dark-gray back of Phemropit. In a short time, its whole body was in sight, its endless tracks with their treads rotating. It came up the beach, then began climbing the hill. Though it slipped back in the soft earth three times, it kept on, and presently it was resting on the top. Its "nose" pointed slightly downward.

32

OTHER shocks followed at widely separated intervals, but these were much weaker. Three sleep-times after the big ones, a Tsimmanbul warrior ran panting into the camp and threw himself onto the ground.

After he'd recovered his wind, he piped, "Hear me, my tribespeople! The gods have turned away from us! When they shook the earth so fiercely, they cracked open the cliff on which our village was! All our people fell into the sea and were killed! All except me! I alone was spared so that I might give you the terrible news!"

Wailing and screaming, the Tsimmanbul rolled on the ground and gashed themselves with stone knives. After a while the bleeding shaman picked up a spear and ran it through the messenger, who did not defend himself. He had expected such a reward for bringing bad news.

Sloosh, the only one of the captives unbound at the time, took advantage of the mourning. He untied the others, and they grabbed weapons wherever handy. Deyv struck the shaman on the head with a tomahawk and took his sword back. Sloosh recovered his axe. When Fat Bull had recovered his senses, he sat on the ground and wailed.

"You shouldn't have messed around with Phemropit," the Yawtl said. "It has taken its revenge."

"Nonsense," Sloosh said. "It doesn't even know what's going on. It expended its little reserve energy getting out of the sea and has only enough left to communicate with us. But even that will be gone if we don't find food for it."

The Tsimmanbul rose then and formed a ring around the shaman. They began chanting in words so ancient that only the shaman knew their meaning. One by one, Fat Bull pierced them with a spear and cut their throats. When this was done, he asked Sloosh to make sure that he died. The Archkerri said that it was the least he could do. Fat Bull put the butt end of his spear at an angle into the dirt, and he fell upon it, driving it deep into his belly. The plant-man came up behind him and slashed through the fat to sever the jugular.

"Very curious," he said. "Definitely nonsurvival."

Since the Tsimmanbul were not human-appearing enough to make it cannibalism, their former captives cooked and ate them. The flesh was tender and tasty, though somewhat fishy. The skeletons were tossed into the jungle, where the insects and small predators competed for the meat still sticking to the bones.

By then Phemropit was able to tell them in what direction to go to look for its food. It was also able to describe it in its raw state and to warn them about the dangers in preparing it. From the middle of its back a small section of stone-metal sank down, and then a tall thin rod of the same substance rose from the hole.

Thinner rods which came down from a knob on top of the larger opened up. They rotated fully many times; then all but one of the small rods folded downward. The single one was left, pointing like a finger inland.

The Dark Beast had half-passed over; the open sky behind it gave plenty of illumination. In the direction in which the rod pointed was a dark area shaped like a scythe. This would line them up with their goal while they went through the jungle.

Hoozisst complained about the work and its dangers, but he went with the others. He didn't want to be left alone with the god.

"How does Phemropit detect its food?" Deyv said.

"I've explained the principles of radioactivity to you. The ore which contains his food lies some distance from here, probably on a mountainside. It will be near the shore of this lake and will be material broken off and cast out by the impact of the meteorite. Which was so large it should be called a planetoid. Which I've also described to you.

"You see, Earth itself long ago lost all its radioactivity. But the planetoid must have been of younger stuff and so still was rich in radioactive minerals. I know that because, otherwise, Phemropit's people would have run out of their food and become, if not dead, inanimate.

"Phemropit's antennae detected some of the radioactive particles emitted by this lode. As I said, the ore can't be far away, fortunately for us. Phemropit could have gone to it itself if its energy weren't so low. And when we've gotten enough to it to charge its energy bank, it will travel there on its own power."

They found the ore, a dark, large, irregularly shaped patch embedded in the red and gray of a mountainside, near the base. The radioactive ore, Sloosh explained, had been buried so deep that Phemropit couldn't detect it. But the quakes had dislodged that part of the mountain which had previously covered it. The labor of extracting the ore was long and hard. A long search of the area found a source of flint, and from this they fashioned digging tools. These broke frequently, requiring more trips for more flint. But finally the time came when they had a pile of several tons of broken ore.

They made two small wagons under Sloosh's supervision—none except him knew the principle of the wheel as a means of transportation—and they dragged them into the jungle. They had to cut a path, a weary back-breaking labor, but eventually they got the wagons to Phemropit.

It mounted the piles and took the rocks into its body through an opening in the belly. When it had "digested" a certain amount, a plate of metal-stone slid back, and the useless residue dropped out. It now had enough energy to go a few miles into the jungle. The party returned to the mountain and extracted more ore. This time, they didn't have to travel so far. Phemropit ate their offerings, dropped its stony excrement, and went on a few more miles.

A long, long time passed. And then the creature was able to dig into the mountain itself, and their work was done. Phemropit put out from its belly a structure which bore an endless track with sharp metal teeth instead of treads. The hard rock was cut apart and picked up and taken into the belly.

Another long time passed with the creature never pausing in its work. Finally, it was through. Its belly was full, and the mountain had a large hole in it. Below the hole was a great pile of residue.

Sloosh may have been beaming behind the leaves. He sounded as if he were. "There now. It wasn't so bad, was it? It certainly was worth all the time and effort."

"It had better be," the Yawtl said. "I've got calluses on my hands that will never wear off, and a pain in my back that'll stay until I die. Even so, my ghost may suffer backache throughout eternity."

Later, when they were riding on Phemropit's back, Hoozisst grudgingly admitted that the "god" had its uses. Moreover, when they came to seaside villages, they didn't have to detour. The tribespeople ran screaming into the jungle and hid until this terrifying monster and its strange riders were long gone. The passengers would get off its back and take whatever they wanted of the food or any interesting artifacts.

The Yawtl loaded its top with so many useless if pretty objects that he was forced to throw away most of them. He shouted and threatened but did as ordered. He also complained about the space that Feersh and Jowanarr took up. Sloosh, however, said that they too would have their use.

They came to a highway of the ancients which ran out from the jungle and curved parallel to the beach. Sloosh said that this meant that they were far past the great inland lake.

"The planetoid destroyed all the highways for many thousands of square miles around the crater. This highway may have been twisted and rippled, but it has straightened out."

Phemropit went on the road, and they traveled on it for many miles before they came to a junction. Jowanarr told her mother that there were signal-poles there.

Feersh said, "Stop! I can find out how far we are from the edge of The Jeweled Wasteland. If, that is, some cataclysm hasn't snapped this particular circuit."

They all got down. Jowanarr led the witch to the nearest pole. Feersh put her hands on its cool metallic substance. She stood for a long time, *listening*, as she said, with her whole body. Since she'd requested silence, the others did not talk during this time.

When she was through with this phase of her interrogation, she said, "I didn't tell you about this secret, though Jowanarr knew, of course. I have used the highways of the ancients to monitor the approach of my enemies. When you were on the highway, I knew exactly where you were and how many you were. It was when you left the road that I lost track of you."

"Most interesting," Sloosh said. "Do you know the power source of the highways?"

"No. I suspect that it comes from the heat still left in the metal core of Earth. I'm surprised that the leads from the highways to the power source haven't been broken before now by the many earthquakes. Perhaps they are very flexible. The ancients built well indeed."

Phemropit was brought up alongside the pole, and Feersh and Jowanarr got onto its back. Directed by her mother, Jowanarr felt along the rim of the pole's eye, which gave the green color. She pressed at two places, and the covering of the eye popped out. She guided Feersh's finger into the hole and onto the round metallic projection which was emitting the green light. Then she took her mother's other hand and put the finger of her left hand onto the emitter. Her finger did not touch her mother's.

The two stood there for a long time, Feersh staring sightlessly but no doubt "seeing" with the cells of her body, Jowanarr with her eyes closed, also "seeing." Then the witch withdrew her finger, and her daughter opened her eyes and took her finger away.

"The edge of The Wasteland is approximately a thousand miles away," she said. "By the highway that goes into the jungle, that is. The one along the beach would take us five hundred miles more before we'd come to The Wasteland."

Vana was more sensitive than the others to subtleties in a person's voice. She said, "Why are you doubtful about taking the shorter route?"

"There are some of the people Fat Bull called the Skinniwakitaw there. I don't know just what they are, but I got the impression that we'd be better off if we didn't encounter them."

"Could they be the things-with-a-nose-like-a-snake?" Devv asked.

"No. These beings are much much larger. I wish I knew more about them, but all I get is an impression of something massive and savage."

"Would they have anything worth stealing?" Hoozisst asked.

Feersh cackled. "No, Yawtl!"

"Then I suggest we take the longer but safer road."

Sloosh thought otherwise. He was very curious about the beings. He didn't recall ever hearing or reading anything about them.

"Of course, it may have slipped my mind."

"How could it?" Deyv asked. "You have absolute recall."

"Oh, yes. I forgot I had a perfect memory."

After the others had quit laughing, Sloosh said, "We should study this creature. It would add to our knowledge, and my colleagues would be most happy to get the data about it. I'm amazed that we haven't received reports about it via our prisms."

"You get reports about something only when you specifically ask about it," the witch said. She pointed at the pole to indicate that Jowanarr should replace the lens.

"Still . . ." Sloosh said.

They took a vote. The Archkerri was the only one who wanted to take the jungle road.

"But Feersh can find out when we're getting near these things by means of a junction light," he said. "Then we can detour around them. Remember, we'll save much time on this road."

Deyv smiled and said, "You aren't planning on slipping away to make your own investigation of it?"

"Yes. How'd you know?"

"We all knew," Hoozisst said. "And so, when the thing chased you, you'd bring it to us! No!"

They proceeded on the road by the beach. Six sleep-times passed, Phemropit making an average of ten miles after breakfast. They had to leave it to hunt until Sloosh and Deyv simultaneously had an idea. Why not let Phemropit use its cutting ray on the big herbivores? This could be done on the highway, since there were large herds eating the short grass by the road and long-necked or long-proboscised beasts eating fruit or leaves or stripping off bark and branches at the edge of the jungle. One of these would provide enough meat for three sleep-times. After which, it would become too corrupt for the humans, though not for the cat and the dog.

Vana suggested that they didn't have to stop to sleep. They could expand the vessel on top of Phemropit, tie it down, and take refuge in it. The stone-metal creature could keep on going. All he had to do was follow the road.

After that they averaged about twenty-seven miles between sleep-times.

The plant-man didn't like this method of travel. It kept him from communicating with Phemropit unless he walked backward ahead of it with the firefly in his hand. Yawtl, not known for innovative ideas, surprised everybody by suggesting they find a smooth rock with lots of mica on it.

"Sloosh can sit on the front end and hold the fly in front of Phemropit's eyeholes," he said. "And Phemropit can bounce his speech-beams off the mica and up to Sloosh."

"Excellent!" Sloosh said. "I could kiss you for that suggestion."

Hoozisst backed away, saying, "No. I never cared for cabbage."

One thing that bothered them was the absence of natives. They didn't have to worry about being ambushed on the road or attacked when they passed through a village, though this hadn't happened before anyway. What did worry them was that there were plenty of population centers, but all had been destroyed. Something had smashed the stockade walls and the huts and trampled on the inhabitants. Old bones, broken and splintered, lay among the ruins. They looked for tracks of the destroyers, but the heavy rains had wiped them out.

Their questions were answered when they came to another junction. Feersh and Jowanarr consulted a signal-pole, and when they were through they looked pale.

"We should have gone on the shorter road," the witch said. "A Skinniwakitaw has left it and come to this road. It's ahead of us by about ten miles."

"Skreesh preserve us!" the Yawtl said. "If it's that thing that's been stomping on the villages—and it must be—it could pick up Phemropit and throw it in the ocean. And us along with it."

"Luckily, we can take the road into the jungle," Sloosh said. "It would have been unfortunate indeed if there hadn't been a junction here."

Hoozisst said, "I don't know. If its ears are as big as its feet, it'll hear us. Then all it has to do is to cut through the jungle, and it's got us."

Sloosh said that it would be better to be attacked on the beach than on the jungle road. He wouldn't say why just now. He asked Feersh to "listen" again to the data coming through the signal-pole. She reported that the thing was no longer on the highway. She had no way of knowing where it was now. The highway itself, properly interrogated, could give certain details about creatures or objects on its surface and at least twelve feet above it. But the highway could give nothing about anything off the road unless it was in view of the eyes of the signals.

"You mean that when you were monitoring us, you could see us?" Sloosh said.

"Not as I could with my eyes, when I had them. No. I could feel certain impressions, which I then interpreted. Just as you do not directly see the things shown in your prism, but you interpret them."

"How big was this thing?"

"Its weight was more than the highway sensors could register."

The Yawtl made a strangling noise. "What is the upper limit?"

"A thousand or so tons, I believe."

"Is it bipedal?"

"I think so."

"Skreesh!" Hoozisst cried. He looked down the highway. "Well, at least we ought to see its head while it's a long way off. But it must have a hellishly long stride."

"And since The Beast now extends a little beyond the horizon ahead of us, we won't be able to see his silhouette until he's very close," Vana said.

Sloosh got down and used his firefly to talk to Phemropit. When he was through, he said, "I've explained the situation to it. It says that it can use its cutting ray on the thing. So why should we worry?"

"That's crazy!" Hoozisst said. "What if it comes out of the jungle and takes us on the side? Phemropit might not be able to turn fast enough to use its ray."

"A good point," Sloosh said. "However, I suggest we go ahead, anyway. Here's what we should do."

33

DEYV, Vana, and the two animals went a half-mile ahead of the others. The first carcass they found had been torn in half and most of the flesh had been savagely ripped or cut off. Not only that. The bones had been cracked and ground. There were pieces of meat and bones with meat sticking to them lying scattered over an area many yards wide. The skull looked as if teeth, each the size of an elephant's head, had broken it open and then chewed on the bone. Deyv thought that the victim had been one of those colossal hairless animals with long necks and long tails. It must have weighed at least five hundred tons. Except for the insects, the usual scavengers were missing. In fact, there was none of the normal noises of the jungle. Its tenants were either keeping quiet or had fled.

There was, however, a sound. It seemed to be about a half-mile down the road, though it was difficult to be sure. It seemed to be a heavy breathing mingled with occasional crashes, as if a mountain was being torn down.

They went on, though reluctantly, and then came across three other carcasses of the same kind as the first. These, too, were ripped apart and chewed and mangled with parts strewn on the road and along it.

They found tracks in the forest, prints at least two hundred feet long. They were deep enough that they were clear, despite their size. They looked humanoid, but the toes were armed with claws.

Nearby were big trees that had been uprooted, probably by a *kick*, and others that had been broken off, as if the thing had stepped on them.

The breathing and the sound like a mountain being torn apart were much louder now. It *was* a mountain. No. A tall hill of stone. Boulders soared up from it and fell to earth in the jungle. And then one crashed onto the grass between the forest and the highway.

Jum whimpered. Or maybe, thought Deyv, he himself was whimpering. He certainly felt as if he would like to.

Aejip, glaring, crouched close to the ground. Vana was trembling.

"I think we've gone close enough," she whispered.

"Too close."

In the darkness they could make out the hill, which was perhaps a quarter of a mile away. Or was that the monster?

Another rock, the size of Deyv, hurtled down and struck the highway itself. Jum yelped sharply. Deyv felt warm water trickling down his leg.

Suddenly, the tearing noise ceased. Now all they could hear was the enormous breathing. Was it listening?

Deyv took Vana's hand and with his other hand pointed back down the road. They ran on the grass alongside the highway to soften the sound of their steps. From behind them came a bellow, so loud that it was as if the sky had split open. They ran faster, though a second before they seemed to be racing faster than they'd ever done in their lives.

A boulder smashed into the ground a few feet ahead of them. They ran around it. In the distance, a long ways off, a light flashed off and on. Sloosh was signaling via firefly.

The long way became a short way, and they could see the plant-man and the others sitting on top of Phemropit. Deyv arrived with Vana close behind him. The cat and the dog had come in ahead by forty feet and were now sitting, panting. He threw himself down by them. He was too winded to speak for a minute. It wasn't necessary, anyway. The others could also see the gigantic dim hulk advancing toward them. The earth shook under its tread, or was it Deyv's frightened imagination? He wasn't imagining the frightful roars issuing from the thing. Nor was his nose fooling him. That rotten odor as of many long-decayed bodies, carried by the wind, was too real.

A beam shot from Phemropit, not the thin tight ray he used for piercing or communication but a fan. It shone on gigantic feet and on very thin—relatively speaking—legs. The rest of the thing couldn't be seen clearly. But it looked as if it was a skeleton from whose bones hung various organs.

That was what it was, a structure of bones thinly wrapped in muscles and bearing bags which must be the stomach, intestines, liver, heart, pancreas, spleen, and whatever other organs were necessary for its life. The wind whistled through the ribs, pelvis, and chest-bones. And the organs, bags attached to the bones, were swinging with the thing's stride.

The head was vaguely human-shaped, and it too was bone thinly sheathed in muscle naked to the air. There was no hair—at least, they couldn't see any. But then the darkness and their terror made them unable to see clearly. Where the eyes should have been were two black holes; it had to have eyes, but at this distance the holes seemed to be empty.

Phemropit began swiveling, its left track moving faster than its right, the middle track elevated. Suddenly, the thin beam lanced out, and it drilled a hole in the Brobdingnagian left foot of the monster. There was a scream that deafened Deyv, and the thing stopped. Phemropit turned to the left, the ray stabbing out, and the two feet were sliced in half horizontally.

Blood spurted out, soaking the ground around it, some gushing out almost to Phemropit's "nose."

And the thing began to topple.

Luckily, it fell backward. Otherwise, its upper body would have struck Phemropit and those sitting around it. The stone-metal creature would have been undamaged, but Sloosh and the others might have been crushed. Or they might have been spared. There was plenty of empty space within that enormous skeleton.

It struck with a crash like a dozen large trees falling at once. Some organs were torn from the bones. The lungs didn't come loose, but they ruptured. And the spinal cord was shattered just above the shoulder bones.

The thing lay on its back, staring upward.

Sloosh got down from Phemropit's back and with a firefly in his hand led it to the thing's head. If he had thought that the coup de grâce was needed, he changed his mind. The monster would never again trouble anybody, including itself.

"Most curious," the plant-man said. "I can't believe that it would occur naturally. Surely, it's descended from something that the ancients made in their laboratories. But why would they?"

He tried to cut out a section of the muscles wrapped around the finger bones. After he'd failed to make any impression with the edge of a stone tomahawk, he used his great metal axe. But he had no more success with the metal than with the flint.

"Hmmm. It's got veins and arteries, of a sort, but it's not really muscular tissue. It looks like bands of thin film of some material I'm not familiar with. It's extremely hard, yet it has to be supple. And its strength must be many times that of genuine muscle. It would have to be to move such a gigantic and heavy body."

Deyv called Sloosh's attention to the two animals. They were sniffing at the blood from the severed feet but refusing to lick it. Deyv got down to smell it, too, and he wrinkled his nose.

"It stinks of fish-oil, but it also has an odor that I can't identify."

"Unfortunately, I can't help you, since I have no sense of smell," Sloosh said.

Vana pointed out that the beetles and ants that should have been swarming over the blood and the carcass were absent.

"It's poisonous," Sloosh said. "Well, I would love to stay here and dissect this thing, but I lack the tools for that."

Nevertheless, they were too shaken to push on immediately. They walked around the carcass, staring at it. After a while they saw the muscle-film begin to melt. The stuff dripped down from the bones and formed pools of red liquid. Then the pools began to evaporate.

It took much longer for the organs to melt, but they did. Eventually, all that was left was a skeleton that looked as if it had been picked clean by scavengers. Deyv hesitated about touching even this, but he finally went into the apish skull. It was big enough to house several human families. Now that the eyes, brain, and other organs had disappeared, the insects had lost their fear. Ants, beetles, and spiders crawled around the interior of the skull. Presently, a huge scout of a bee swarm explored the skull, and then it flew off. Sometime later it came back, leading a horde of its fellows. They set to work at once covering the eyeholes and the bottom with a gelatinlike substance that quickly hardened. In time, the skull would contain enough honey to feed a whole village for many sleep-times.

The travelers decided to push on. They kept to the shoreline highway, and when they came to a junction, Feersh and Jowanarr listened to the signal-poles. The

Dark Beast and the bright skies alternated. Phemropit's riders came to an area where the skeletal monster had not been, not for some time at least, and they encountered sentients again. These gave the travelers little trouble, which caused Sloosh to congratulate himself on having insisted on getting "food" for Phemropit.

They came to a place where the grass, bushes, and trees were pale and dry with approaching death. Yet there had been no dearth of rain.

Sloosh buzzed satisfaction. "The jungle is bleached, not from disease or drought but from lack of nourishment. The jewels have put out their long roots and are sucking up the minerals. We are very close to the edge of The Wasteland!"

A short time later, they came around the bend of a bay, and they were dazzled by The Jeweled Wasteland, The Shining House of Countless Chambers, The Bright Abomination. The light from the sky reflected from an unimaginable number of faceted translucent stones. Those on the edge were as tiny as melon seeds. Others were as small as fingertips, as large as a man's head, as huge as the skull of the bony monster dead on the road behind them. They covered the ground completely. They formed great masses, hills, columns, stalagmites, weird beautiful figures that looked beastlike or had vaguely human faces. The piles formed valleys, ravines, canyons, and avenues that would sometimes run straight for a mile. Water had collected in small and large pools from a recent rain. Here and there were piles of stones which had been broken off from the main growths by severe earthquakes.

The swarming life of the jungle and the seashore stopped at the edge of The Wasteland. No birds sang, no monkeys chattered, no insects buzzed there.

Sloosh looked at the road, which ended abruptly, buried under the shining stony growths.

"I can't imagine The Shemibob letting this get out of control," he said. "I wonder why she has?"

No one had an answer. They set up camp by expanding the vessel of the ancients, and they began the work of storing up food. The hunting and fishing and the smoking of meat and fish occupied them for twelve sleep-times. During this time, some of them made short explorations into The Wasteland. They collected loose stones which Feersh said could be useful.

After the thirteenth sleep, they ate breakfast and all except Deyv and the animals got onto Phemropit's back. Deyv walked ahead a quarter of a mile as a scout. His duty was not so much to warn of living dangers, which they probably wouldn't encounter as yet, as it was to look for routes broad enough for Phemropit to pass through.

The Beast came and went twice, and they traveled toward the stronghold of The Shemibob in a circuitous manner. Only three times were they stopped by barriers. Then Phemropit knocked down the walls of glittering jewels or, if it couldn't bull its way through, it used its cutting ray. It didn't like to use the latter method, though, since this used up too much energy.

Four times they came upon oases, areas about a mile square on which the stones could not grow. These held a rich soil on which were fruit-bearing trees and nut-bearing bushes. There were some songbirds and small animals here. The latter kept the birds from getting too numerous, and their own population was kept down by a periodic disease that killed all but a tenth of them.

Feersh explained that The Shemibob had established a number of the oases throughout the area. Sometimes she liked to leave her castle and vacation here. The oases had enabled the witch to survive when she'd run away.

After resting here and adding to their provisions, the party went on. The Beast passed over ten more times. Once, Vana, whose turn it was to scout, was caught in a flash flood in a ravine and narrowly escaped drowning. Sloosh, warned by the rumbling, told Phemropit to get up onto a ledge before the full force of the water struck. Even so, the stones broke loose beneath the creature, and it rolled helplessly down the slope. Its passengers leaped to safety, but Phemropit disappeared into the stream.

When the flood had subsided, it was sitting at the bottom of the ravine, unharmed. Fortunately, it had landed upright. If it had been on its back, it would have had to be abandoned. It was too heavy to be uprighted without the necessary equipment.

They went on. An earthquake shook some stones down on them, and a monolith of green, red, and yellow stones toppled near them. Phemropit had to force his way through a barrier of fallen stones at the end of a canyon, but he burst through after several tries.

The heat during the end of the bright-sky periods became almost unendurable. The party expanded the cube, tied it to the stone-metal creature's back, and got inside. Though they had to go out now and then to check the route, they were quite comfortable most of the time.

And then they came up over the ridge of a slope. There below them was a great oasis. In its center was the glittering castle of The Shemibob.

34

A river flowed out of an opening in the surrounding cliffs of jewels. It wandered through forests and meadows and plunged into another opening at the opposite end. By the stream and through the grassy open places grazed small herds of animals. Some of these, Sloosh said, had long been extinct outside The Shemibob's domain. Feersh assured them that they were not dangerous.

"But something has happened here," she said. "You tell me the forests look as if they have been growing wild for some time. When I was here, they were well-tended parks. And you see no human beings, Tsim-manbul, or Yawtl? Where are the slaves?"

They had found a path down the cliffs that was just wide enough for Phemropit. They crossed the river by swimming, except for Phemropit, who traveled on its bottom. And now they were standing at the edge of a large meadow. A mile away was The Shemibob's stronghold. It was a huge structure made of scarlet and violet blocks, emitting a slightly pulsing light and held together by a bright yellow cement, which would last for many, many generations yet. Its towers and turrets rose high, though none went above the top of the encircling cliffs of jewels. A canal led water from the river to the moat around the castle.

Feersh had told them that they had little, or perhaps no, chance of getting far before being detected. The Shemibob, however, might allow them to come up to her door before she acted. Or she might even let them get into the castle. It depended upon her mood.

"But it seems as if things have changed since I was here," Feersh said. "Maybe she's gotten rid of her slaves. Or . . . she may not be here. Could she have died?"

After some discussion, they decided to walk on in as if they owned the place. When The Shemibob attacked, she would find that she didn't have just simple thieves to combat. Phemropit would show her that.

The creature didn't understand exactly what was going on. Even after all the time it'd had to get acclimated to its new environment, it was often puzzled. But it did have a sense of gratitude. Or perhaps it was a feeling of loneliness that made it so amenable to its rescuers' requests. In any event, it was prepared to fight for them.

"But we mustn't act hostile," Sloosh said. "Not until she definitely shows she's not friendly. That she has kept thieves as slaves doesn't mean that she will make us slaves. We're here for a number of reasons, of which theft concerns only one of us. The most important is the desire to get into another universe, if that's possible.

She should understand that and perhaps welcome our help."

Deyv didn't say anything, but he couldn't see how any of them, even the knowledgeable Archkerri, could help such an ancient and powerful being as The Shemibob.

They went across the meadow and through a grove of trees. From the grove a broad winding walk of some bouncy yellow material led to the moat. This was at least three hundred feet wide. Its clear waters revealed fish of many sizes, shapes, and colors. The drawbridge was down. After some hesitation, they crossed it. The doorway was high and wide, pointed at the top. There was no evidence of a door. Over the open entrance shimmered a curtain of some very thin transparent stuff.

Deyv put out his hand to push it aside. The fingers encountered only air, cooler than that outside.

He turned. "I can't feel the curtain."

"That's because there is none," the witch said.

Deyv shrugged and stepped inside. The others followed him, Phemropit rumbling in last. They were in an immense anteroom on whose walls hung many paintings. The floor was covered by a carpet so thick that Deyv sank up to his ankles. Beyond was a room that made the anteroom look small. He went into it and stopped, astonished and awed.

The walls went up and up and up, the ceiling in a dark which made it invisible. Below it, though, the light was bright. It came out of the walls themselves as the light did in the ancients' vessel. Row upon row of murals, rising into the darkness, were on the walls. If he wasn't so concerned about The Shemibob's whereabouts, he would have been fascinated by the paintings. They seemed to be scenes from Earth's history, from its prehistory, even. A whispered question to Feersh confirmed his idea.

"But they are the least of the wonders here," she said.

They passed across a floor of smooth green stone into which brightly colored mosaic patterns were set.

Phemropit was behind them, its treads making a loud grinding noise. The owner certainly wouldn't like her floor scratched, but leaving the creature behind was unthinkable.

The next room was even larger. Its walls were set with round glowing knobs spaced among the heads of animals, fish, birds, great insects, and sentients. These were not, as he'd first thought, carved representations. They were stuffed, and each was also covered with a thin transparent film. Feersh whispered that the film kept them from disintegrating. Some were as old as The Shemibob.

Vana commented, in a low voice, that there was no dust anywhere.

The witch said, "She has devices which draw out the dust and burn it."

At the far end of the mighty room and of the narrow green carpet leading to it was a platform. This was made of a solid block of gold. There were seven steps to its top, on which was a high-backed sofa of some soft green material. It was about fifty feet long, and the seat was five feet above the platform.

"What giant sits here?" Deyv asked.

"There is only one allowed there," Feersh said. "But she doesn't so much sit as lie."

They went from the room into a great corridor. This was lined with pedestals and chests of many kinds of hard polished wood. On these were statuettes and busts and other objects, many of gold or silver. Some pedestals lacked the ornaments, and when this was reported to the witch she looked puzzled.

"As we go through the castle," she said, "describe what you see."

They did that, though there were so many things to tell about that they grew weary of it. At last she said, "It is much as I remember it being. But things are missing here and there. And it's evident that the slaves are gone. I think they've fled, and they've taken some of the treasures with them."

"Which means," Sloosh said, "that she gave them

their freedom and allowed them to take the treasures. Or she was in no position to stop them from fleeing and also robbing her before they left. I favor the latter speculation."

"I do, too," Feersh said. "She really needed slaves for only one thing. Companionship. People to talk to. She has machines to do any work which the slaves did. But she kept them in a room from which she seldom let them out."

"Then," Sloosh said, "what happened to The Shemibob?"

They found an immense kitchen on the first floor and by it a larder containing enough food to feed Deyv's village for an uncountable number of feasts. There was also enough liquor to make his whole tribe drunk forever, it seemed. And there were enough drugs to keep it stoned for a little longer. The food was as fresh as when it was first brought in. According to the witch, it stayed fresh, no matter how long the passage of time, until it was brought out from the larder. Then it became subject to decay.

"Except for our mortality," Deyv said, "this place seems much like that which the shaman says we will go to after we die. If The Shemibob is gone, why shouldn't we just stay here and enjoy life? Of course, we'd have to get our tribes and bring them here. And, who knows? We might find The Shemibob's secret of immortality."

"But eventually the supplies would run out," Sloosh said. "In the meantime, you'd be having children, and this place would become overcrowded. Though, given your tendency to quarreling and thus to violence, over-population might not be a problem. In any event, you'd find the storehouse empty. So what would you do then? You'd have lost the ability to hunt and to grow crops by then. You'd all perish."

Deyv said, angrily, "I know that. I was only dreaming."

"That is because you are not the fear-trembling youth who set out to find a wife in an enemy tribe. You have been through many experiences, have traveled widely, have seen much that you would not have seen if the Yawtl had not stolen your soul egg. You have matured, and that far past what you would have matured if you'd remained a simple tribesman. Still, you have much to learn."

"You do, too," Deyv said.

"Happily, yes. If I knew everything, what would I have to live for?"

While at the rear part of the second floor, Deyv had a frightening experience. He entered a huge room in which the illumination was almost as dark as the light when The Beast was fully overhead. Many vague forms swam in the air. They glowed faintly, providing most of the light. They were of many colors and hues, and were shaped like tadpoles. They writhed and rotated on their horizontal axes or sometimes reared up, darting here and there.

He thought about going back to get a torch or, better, staying out of the room entirely. Vana came along then, and, emboldened by companionship, he decided to investigate. He had no sooner passed the doorway than one of the scarlet figures dashed at him, turned just before it touched him, and flicked its tail out. Deyv screamed with pain and clutched his face.

Vana ran into the room then, crying, "What's the matter?" Another figure, turquoise-colored, swam writhing to her and its head touched hers briefly. She sank down onto the floor, moaning. Deyv's agony had passed as swiftly as it had come. He leaned down to bring her up to her feet, but she said, "No. I'm fine."

"I thought you were hurt."

"Far from it," she said. "I was in ecstasy. Only, it's over now."

She rose. "Where's the turquoise thing that touched me? I'd like it to touch me again. I've never felt such exquisite sensations."

Deyv took her arm and pulled her out.

"I don't know what those things are, but they're dangerous."

After getting her reluctant promise that she wouldn't

go back into the room, he went to get the others.
Feersh at once told them what they'd encountered.

"The Shemibob has many art forms of the ancients.
This room contains one type of them. They were made
by the same people who made the soul-egg trees, the
people who were destroyed when the planetoid fell."

"What's their purpose?"

The witch shrugged. "What is art all about? These
seem to give intense pain or intense ecstasy, depending
upon which one touches you. It is also a pleasure just
to stand away from them and watch the interplay
among them. If you do this for some time, you begin
to detect certain patterns made by the relative positions
of all the things.

"The Shemibob thought that they must have a
therapeutic effect, too. But to get this you have to be
of strong stuff. She would sometimes enter the room
and station herself so that she could be touched at the
same time by one form giving pain and another giving
ecstasy. She said that she couldn't endure the opposing
sensations for long. But when she left the room she
felt that she had gained a little wisdom. Not intellectual
wisdom. Emotional.

"I didn't understand what she meant by that. And
I refused her invitation to enter the room. I was afraid
to do anything but stand outside and watch the
designs."

Sloosh made a suggestion. From then on, if they
came to a chamber which held anything outside their
experience, they should refrain from entering.

"Art can be both rewarding and dangerous. The
ancients have refined both of these features in their art
to a degree unknown before them. And after them."

Deyv and Vana went out with the animals to eat
their lunch on the drawbridge. Afterward, they decided
to go for a walk. But when they were almost halfway
across the bridge, they were stopped. Something invisible and impalpable kept them from advancing a
step beyond it.

Alarmed, they went to get the others. Sloosh tested

the barrier and got no farther than Deyv and Vana. He
then sent Deyv down into the moat. Halfway across,
he came against the unbending resistance. He swam
back and was pulled up the steep wall of the moat by
a rope. They went to the back end of the castle, and
this time the Yawtl swam in the moat. He reported
that the barrier was there also, though much closer to
the outer ditch of the moat than in front.

Vana tried another side; Deyv, the opposite. The
results were the same.

Feersh said, "The Shemibob has allowed us in but
won't let us out! If she's dead or has left this place,
we're doomed! We'll never find out how to dissolve the
barrier!"

"We're far from hopeless," Sloosh said. "We haven't
investigated more than an eighth of the rooms. I
suggest we get to work."

The fourth floor had a tremendously large laboratory.
The Archkerri said that he thought that soul eggs could
be made in it. Unfortunately, he hadn't the slightest
idea of how to do it. Only The Shemibob could show
them.

"But is it really necessary that you have the eggs?"

Deyv and Vana looked at each other. They read in
each other's face the same thought. Somehow, they had
managed to get along without the stones. And for a
long time they hadn't even missed them. Yes, strange
though it was, they didn't need them any more.

"What you say is true, Sloosh," Deyv said. "It's a
very strange feeling to know that. Both uneasy and
exhilarating. But we can't return to our tribes until we
have our eggs. There is no getting out of that."

The Archkerri's huge hand, partly sheathed in leaves,
made a circular gesture.

"We are your tribe!"

The Yawtl laughed, and he danced a jig while
grinning maliciously. "Some tribe!"

"Well, what I mean," the plant-man said, "is that
you have a temporary tribe. However unhomogeneous
this group, its members do get along with each other.

And we've been most efficient. When we get out of here, you can look for a human tribe that doesn't require eggs. If you can't find any, then you can become witches and raise your own tribe. You'll have plenty of ancient devices to give you great power."

"No," Deyv said. "We'd die if we thought we had no chance of returning to our people."

"Do you really think you two could retrace that journey all the way? You'd get lost. You'd get killed. I'm sorry to say that, but facts are facts."

"Facts can be reshaped," Deyv said.

"Yes, in a manner of speaking. But . . ."

He paused. From down the vast hall had come a strange and loud noise. A hissing like a chorus of a thousand snakes.

Feersh put her hand upon her heart.

"The Shemibob!"

35

FEERSH's descriptions had prepared Deyv for the real being. Also, he had encountered so many monsters that he had become, though not blasé, hardened to shock at the sight of them. Nevertheless, he was awed when the owner of the castle appeared in the enormous doorway.

She seemed at first view to be half-snake, half-human. Her body was that of a python's and at least forty feet long. Her skin, however, was scaleless, smooth as Deyv's. It had a silvery quality, as if impregnated with metal, with dark spindle-shaped markings on the back and sides. The body was raised from the floor in a most unsnakelike manner by twenty pairs of short thick humanoid legs. These were black up to the thighs and silvery to the body. The feet were also human, though they were very broad and three-toed. The catlike nails were painted crimson.

Her forepart curved upward where the legs ceased, giving her the effect of a snake-centaur. She had shoulders and quite womanlike arms and hands, but these were four-fingered. The two large cone-shaped breasts showed that she was, despite the ophidian body, a mammal. Or perhaps she wasn't, in the strictest sense of the term. Feersh had said that she gave, instead of milk, blood. She did bear live young; she was no egg-layer. The hairless reddish delta of her sex was located just below the point at which her body became vertical.

Her head was twice the size of Deyv's, similar to a human's but more triangular than the face of any member of *Homo sapiens* could be. The cheekbones were very prominent. The chin was very pointed but had a deep cleft. Her lips were very everted and very red. The open mouth showed pointed teeth, a fox's. The tongue increased the snakish look, being slightly bifurcated. The nose was short but hawkish. Her eyes were very large in relation to the head and completely leaf-green. The forehead was broad and high, so large that it seemed that the relatively tiny face had been attached to it as an afterthought.

She lacked head-hair, having instead very long and thick silvery quills banded in the middle with black. Feersh had said that the young were born bald and a good thing, too. Otherwise, the quills would have made birth even more painful for the mother.

The Shemibob looked angry, and though she spoke in the witch's language, which Feersh had not yet allowed her fellow travelers to learn, her intonations were obviously furious. Deyv's fear of her was somewhat tempered by his amazement that The Shemibob could recognize the witch after all this time.

Feersh replied, at the same time pointing to her companions. She seemed to be telling The Shemibob that they didn't understand the speech.

The snake-centaur at once opened a huge hand and revealed a mouth-buzzer. Obviously, she had been prepared to talk to the Archkerri, too, which meant that she had been observing them for some time. No doubt this was through the devices, disguised as objets d'art, which, Feersh had said, were in every room.

The Shemibob put the buzzer in her mouth.

"I was roused from my sleep by an alarm," she said in the language of Sloosh. "I decided to let you roam about while I studied you. But I couldn't abide any longer that monster's destruction of my carpets and its chipping off pieces of my floors and stairs. What is that strange thing?"

Feersh explained about Phemropit. The Shemibob lost her anger at once. She said, "I had thought there was nothing new in this world. It is pleasant to be wrong, in this case, anyway. Now Feersh, tell me what happened to you after I allowed you to escape. And tell me also why you and these beings were foolish enough to enter my palace."

That took a long time. For a while, the intruders stood up, since they were afraid to sit down in The Shemibob's presence without permission. In the middle of the witch's tale, the snake-centaur said that they could rest if they wished. All except Sloosh and The Shemibob pulled up chairs, which had been furnished for the slaves, and seated themselves. The Shemibob walked back and forth in front of them and twice took a paper tube enclosing some sweet-smelling drug from a table and smoked it. Now and then she would interrupt the witch to question one of the others. Deyv began to feel more at ease. She wasn't, at least, going to destroy them, nor had she intimated that they would become her slaves.

When she'd heard the story out, she paused to light up another tube.

"So, each of you has made this incredible journey for different reasons. As for the poor devils you sent here to steal my treasures, Feersh, none got here. Well, Deyv of the Red Egg of the Upside-Down House and Vana of the Green Eyes of the Yellow-Haired Tribe and Hoozisst of the ever-thieving Yawtl, I can make you new eggs. And I can teach you how to use them in ways none of your kind has ever thought of. Or, if thought of, dared to realize. But what good would they be?

"As for you, Sloosh of the Vegetable Tribe, I could answer many of your questions. And I could make you a new prism. And I could allow you to work in my laboratory. But what good would that do?

"You, Yawtl, could have so many treasures that you would never have to steal again. Not that that would keep you from your thievery. But what good would they do you?

"You, witch, could have new eyes and new devices and could see the effects of your new powers. But what benefit would they be to you?

"And you, Jowanarr, you wouldn't have to wait for your mother to die to become an exceedingly powerful witch and start your own family. But what use would that be?"

She puffed out a cloud of sweet-smelling purple smoke, and she laughed. It was a disturbing sound, a peculiar flapping with an overtone of arrogance. It also sounded sinister.

But all that may be my imagination, Deyv thought.

"I could just make you slaves to me. I need someone to wait upon me, but by Thrinkelshum! I need someone to talk to more! I won't enslave you, though. I don't have to. I will accept you as guests who are, however, not my equals. Not that that will last long."

"I detect an ominous note," Sloosh said.

"Well you may," she said. "The fact is that you're prisoners here. *But so am I.*"

"Ah, the invisible barrier! Then it's not of your doing?"

"No. However, I have only one excuse for being trapped by it. I let my slaves go before it closed entirely. Or, I should say, before it expanded. So they went, not without some fighting among themselves for various treasures. But I stayed. If I perished, it would be for a good cause."

The Archkerri asked her what she meant by that.

"The barrier is not of my making. It is the gateway to another universe. Or so I believe. But once it was a tight blazing phenomenon beyond the cliffs in that direction. And—"

"So that is why we didn't see it," Sloosh said. "It has moved. And if I understand you, it has expanded. And in doing so became attenuated. It no longer exhibits its brightness or radiates whatever it is that causes so much horror and nausea in its viewers."

"You're almost one hundred percent correct," The Shemibob said, staring with her leaf-green eyes at him. "You're very perceptive. Except that you aren't perceptive enough to know that I do not like being interrupted. I'm being amiable just now. There are limits to that state, though."

"I beg your pardon," Sloosh said.

"It is not always easy to obtain. But I grant it. What you may not know, Archkerri, since you've not had my experience, is that gateways are one-way. You may—"

"Again, I beg your pardon," Sloosh said. "I believe that some gateways may be one-way. But we had an experience which we did not reveal at once, since it didn't seem germane to our story at the time."

He told her about the shimmering off the cliff on the island and the man who'd popped in and out of it.

"So, you see, not all such phenomena are one-way."

"Then I was wrong. It feels good to be wrong twice in a short time after such a long time of always being right. I thought I had the mathematics of the gates figured out. I've spent a thousand *weevrish* working on it. So—anyway, it's true that the gateway expanded. But it still has a heart, a center, a focus, which shines as horribly as the whole thing did once. That is deep within the castle. I'll show it to you when it is time for you to see it.

"Meanwhile, know, my leaved friend, that our time here is short. That is, it's short to me, though it may seem long to your short-lived colleagues. And even to you. This gateway is one-way, which means that we are getting no water or air from outside it. My machines have been making air and sending excess heat into the gateway, and soon they will have to start manufacturing water. Eventually, the raw materials of these will run out. Then we die of oxygen-starvation!"

"Most interesting and definitely relevant," Sloosh said. "However, this gateway exhibits some features that are startling. What it is, really, is a two-way gateway within certain limits and one-way only in its center, as you call it. I would've thought that when the gateway expanded, it would have swallowed up all that which it now covers. Thus—"

"It just doesn't work that way," The Shemibob said grimly. "At the moment I'm not concerned about why it acts thus. I'm only concerned about how I can use it."

"Most commendable. Still—"

She rolled her eyes with disgust or incomprehension or both. She said, "First, I must meet this Phemropit-thing."

They left the room and went down the corridor toward the staircase. On the way Sloosh informed her that Phemropit was not really its name. That had been the Tsimmanbuls' invention. The creature had no individual name for itself. It called itself "I," indicating a certain sense of individuation.

"Then how did it know when it was being addressed or summoned?" The Shemibob asked. "How could it refer to another of its kind when that one was not in sight?"

"Out of sight, out of mind," Sloosh said. "In its environment, it never referred to anyone who wasn't directly in line with its microwave or light-beam detectors. I don't understand its culture, though it has tried many times to explain it to me. But you must realize that the planetoid on which it lived was rather small, perhaps not more than four hundred miles in diameter. This, with the airlessness and the extreme cold of space and the absence of surface illumination, made for a peculiar society. Peculiar to us, that is."

"Begging your pardon for the interruption," Deyv

buzzed, hoping she wouldn't be angry, "but it does have a name. It knows when we are addressing it as Phemropit. And it calls us by our names."

He swallowed, then continued, "I've always heard of you as The Shemibob. Am I being insolent if I dare ask what your name is?"

She stared down at him and laughed. "I am The Shemibob because I am the only one on Earth. I have a personal name, but I have not used it since I landed here nor do I permit lesser beings to address me with it. Does that satisfy you, little human male?"

"Certainly. Only—"

"Only what?"

"One more question, if I may. Why have you allowed the jewels to grow out of control? Eventually, they will spread everywhere, and all life on land will be destroyed."

She laughed and said, "Do you think I am a gardener who prunes my jewels as if they were plants or pulls them up as if they were weeds? That would be a strange sight!"

She gave another of her flapping laughs. "Actually, I could check their growth. That is, I could before I became prisoner in my own castle. But when I was able to do so, I saw no reason why I should. Long before the slow-growing stones cover this land with their glitter, this Earth shall be destroyed. Why, then, should I bother?"

"Thank you, O Shemibob."

They found the creature on the second floor in a large room. It was facing a great sphere of cut quartz that was pulsing light of different lengths. Sloosh had told it that these were random and for aesthetic purposes only, but it had not given up trying to decipher them.

"That is why I sometimes wonder if it's truly intelligent," Sloosh said. "But I suppose that its mind just works differently from ours."

"From mine, maybe," Hoozisst muttered. "The plantman's mind is as alien as Phemropit's."

The Archkerri stood in front of the creature, barring its view of the sphere, and flashed him a message with the firefly. As Phemropit turned around to face the others, The Shemibob laughed.

"I'll give you a better thing to pulse light with than that insect."

Introductions were made, after which The Shemibob, quickly learning how to operate the firefly, asked Phemropit many questions. When she was done, she said, "I may have a use for this thing. Let's go down now and see the heart of the gateway."

They went into what seemed to be a room smaller than most. It turned out to be a lift. It dropped swiftly into the depths, six open doorways and hallways beyond them flashing past. It slowed down and stopped gently at the seventh doorway. The Shemibob led them down a well-lit hall, turned a corner, and did not stop until she was halfway down the next corridor.

About twenty feet beyond, half in the wall, half sticking out, was the dreaded brightness. Again, Deyv felt his knees weaken and his stomach turn.

"Familiarity with it has only slightly thinned my horror," The Shemibob said. "But I have made myself get near enough to it to experiment. Watch, if you can."

She took one of a score of long wooden poles leaning against the far wall. Deyv watched her out of a corner of one eye, his hand shading it, which could darken the brightness. He wanted to run away, but his experience with the other phenomenon had shown him that he could endure the sight of it, if he didn't look at it too long. Turning his head away now and then eased his nausea somewhat.

The Shemibob went up to the blazing expanding-contracting thing, her eyes fully upon it. She stuck the pole into it and then moved up to it, her face only a few inches away. Deyv thought that she must be brave indeed. But then she was The Shemibob.

The pole had gone almost completely into the brightness.

She said, "Now I'm probing around in it. I can feel what seems to be walls. They're hard. At least, they stop the end of the pole abruptly. It seems to be a tunnel of some sort, because I can feel the floor and the ceiling.

"Notice that the bright disc is at an angle in the wall here. You can't see that part which disappears into it. But I can thrust the pole past the edge of the wall. It goes into that other world beyond the wall. The far side of the tunnel, if it is one, is there. I get the impression that there is shallow water on the floor of the tunnel. But I have no way of determining that. The gateway conducts nothing at all. No vibrations, no solids, nothing."

She pulled back on the pole. Only that part which had not penetrated the brightness remained. The rest was within the gateway.

Sloosh said, "Does that mean that anyone who tried to go through would be severed?"

"Only if he tried to back out," she said. "I've used animals in various tests. Those which I put entirely in stay alive. I've tied ropes to them, and I've felt them tugging at the ropes. When I release the ropes, the ropes are dragged in all the way. Those animals that I've partially put in and then tried to pull back were severed in half."

"Very strange," Sloosh said. "But facts are facts, even if we don't know what or why they are. What's kept you from going through yourself?"

"I've used longer poles. The tunnel begins to narrow about ten feet in. Is that just a temporary narrowing or does it expand again? As it is, the tunnel is not wide enough for me to turn around in. Does it dead-end? Is it near the surface of that other Earth or is it deep? What is the temperature in the tunnel? Is the air in it breathable? And so on."

The Archkerri closed his eyes a moment. When he opened them, he said, "Do you have some system of communication at a distance? If you do, someone could go through, and he could tell you what it's like there."

"Yes, I have means for talking at a distance. And I've put a machine through which could report to me. But as I said, neither light nor vibration nor a flow of *shenrem* comes through."

"Ah, yes," Sloosh said. "Stupid of me to ask that. But I had to."

"Probing with a pole works because I can estimate how far the obstructions are that stop the pole."

"What's a *shenrem*?" Deyv asked.

"Invisible-to-the-naked-eye energy particles that can be made to flow in different directions along a conductor. They can be modulated to indicate certain things, such as degree of temperature, or to show pictures. I'll explain it to you some time."

Sloosh said, "The focus is big enough to allow Phemropit to enter. And it could cut away the narrow part of the tunnel. But I doubt it would volunteer."

"Ask it."

The plant-man did so. He then said, "Phemropit doesn't see any reason why it should. I don't blame it. What good would it do, anyway, unless we followed it in?"

"I have to make up my mind sometime," The Shemibob said. "When the air gives out, I can either be asphyxiated here or enter the gateway. There is no choice, of course, not to an intelligent person."

They returned to the first floor. Deyv felt depressed, and from the expressions and the silence of the others, they did, too. Despite what The Shemibob had said, he felt that he would rather choke to death than go through that abomination.

Six sleep-times passed. During this time, Deyv learned more of the owner's past life. She had come from a world which revolved around a star so far away that his mind could not imagine the distance. Her star was about to go nova, and her people, though they had great powers, could not move their planet far enough away to escape the all-ravening fury of the exploding star. So she had left with many of her kind in a spaceship. By the time she had come to Earth, only she was alive. The others had died while looking for a habitable world—from accidents, hostile beasts, and sentients; from suicide; from radiation.

Deyv felt even gloomier. Life was so fragile. Even the great Shemibobs were vulnerable. And when she finally died, though she'd lived out many, many generations of humans, she would be just as dead as they. That didn't console him any.

He was lying on a bed and thinking these dark thoughts when Vana came through the doorway. He sat up.

"What's wrong?"

She lay down by him.

"Our time is limited," she said softly. "We'll soon be dead. We've wasted too much time because we couldn't stand the idea of making love to an eggless. But that doesn't mean anything now. I've been waiting for you to come to me and tell me what I just told you. You didn't, so I killed my pride, and I've come to you."

Deyv took her in his arms, saying, "I've thought of this. But I was afraid you'd reject me."

"Is this rejection?" she said, and she began kissing him.

A moment later, they rolled apart, their hearts beating hard, staring at each other, gray beneath their pigment.

"What in Thriknil is *that*?" Deyv asked.

That was a loud rumbling noise, a crashing of many heavy objects, a shaking of the bed, and screams from down the hall.

Jum and Aejip bounded into the room, the dog howling, the cat screeching.

"It's an earthquake!" Vana cried.

"It can't be," Deyv shouted. "Things outside the barrier can't affect the castle!"

The Yawtl, his eyes wide, ran into the room.

"Come with me!" he screamed. "The Shemibob says we have to go through the gateway!"

Deyv shot out of bed.

"Why?"

"She says the barrier is contracting! It'll crush the castle and everybody in it!"

36

THOUGH frightened, Deyv stayed cool enough to put on his breechclout, fasten his sword belt, and grab his tomahawk. Vana ran out of the room, presumably to get her kilt and weapons. Deyv went out into the corridor and almost collided with the Yawtl, who had dashed out of his room. His eyes were wild, and he was naked. But he wore the Emerald, and he clutched his spear, sword, and tomahawk.

He shouted something to Deyv. His voice was overridden, however, by the rumbling, groaning, and crashing. Down the hall a cloud of dust spewed around the corner as a wall gave way. A gigantic block of stone toppled and blocked the corridor halfway.

Sloosh, the witch, and her daughter came running, Jowanarr pulling Feersh by one hand. A moment later, Vana dashed from her room, holding her possessions. The cat was close behind her.

"Down to the gateway!" Sloosh buzzed loudly in Deyv's ear.

Deyv didn't need the order, but he was reluctant to go. It seemed—almost—better to stay and be smashed under the ceiling than to face that horror.

Sloosh, who was holding the cube under one arm, and the axe in one hand, buzzed something else. It was drowned out as the wall at the far end of the corridor roared downward and inward.

They all ran then. When they got to the elevator, they found The Shemibob, carrying a large leather bag, and Phemropit waiting for them inside it.

"Hurry! Hurry!" she screamed. "If the shaft falls in, we're trapped!"

They needed no urging. The moment the last one came in, The Shemibob said the code word. The lift dropped, much faster than the last time. It stopped with such force that it brought most of them to their knees. They tumbled out without climbing over any-body—the doorway was very large—and they raced down the hall. Phemropit was going its full speed, which still left it fifty feet behind the others.

When they got to the burning wavering expanding-contracting gateway, The Shemibob hesitated only a second. With a scream that was intended to help her overcome her fear, she disappeared through the brightness.

Sloosh, his leaves shaking, followed her.

The humans and the Yawtl were frozen. While they were trying to pump up their courage, and not sure they could do it, the stone-metal creature rolled on through. It had never said anything about the effect of the gateway on it. Perhaps it did not share its companions' terror and nausea. Whatever its reaction, it went on as if it lacked any emotion whatsoever.

Down the hall behind them something crashed. Ahead and underfoot was a quaking. It was then that Deyv realized that the entire castle might be squeezed, ground into powder, and sucked through the gateway. If they were to keep ahead of the many tons of ground material, they had to get through at once. He also noticed that the air was getting very hot. The machine that sent excess heat through the gateway could no longer cope with the burden. The friction of com-pression would soon make the air so hot that they'd burn up in it. And the great heat would undoubtedly fry them.

Vana shouted, "Deyv! Hoozisst! Help me get Aejip through! She won't go by herself!"

That was far easier ordered than carried out. The cat was crouched, teeth bared, claws out, snarling, almost out of her mind with fear. When Vana approached her, holding her hand out, trying to speak soothingly, she had to leap back to avoid the cat's fangs.

More blocks tore loose from the cement that had held them firm for countless generations of humankind. The stone floor was buckling, and a blast of hot air ripped the sweat from their skins. Dust blew in, choking them, making their eyes smart.

Hoozisst screamed even louder than The Shemibob had. His arm over his eyes, he leaped through the shining.

Deyv cursed him for being a coward. Now only he and Vana were left to handle the cat. He stopped and picked up Jum's struggling, howling 165 pounds and hurled the dog through the gateway. Then he picked up his tomahawk from the floor, where he'd dropped it, and he ran at the cat.

Aejip reared up, claws flashing out at him. Deyv struck her hard alongside the head with the flat of his weapon. He suffered deep gashes along his left arm, but the cat dropped, stunned. Another blow, lighter than the first, knocked her out completely. He hoisted the limp body up by the front. Vana grabbed the rear legs.

Deyv said, "One, two, three," and at the third swing, they tossed Aejip through.

A huge block of stone crashed twenty feet away. Deyv picked up his tomahawk and leaped through the abomination. He was so scared of being smashed that he felt no terror or sickness. He landed in a place lit up by a ray from Phemropit. Before he could recover, he was knocked sprawling by Vana.

When he got up, he began slapping Aejip on the face to make her recover her wits. This was not a remedy recommended to anyone, sane or insane, but he was past caring about consequences. After a few hard blows with the palm of his hand, the cat opened her green eyes. Deyv backed away. She rose unsteadily to her paws. Instead of attacking him, she crouched as if she were withdrawing into herself, occupied with mysterious feline thoughts.

Deyv looked around. They were in a tunnel cut through solid gray-red rock. The floor was covered with a foot of water, some severed wooden poles were float-

ing on its surface, and it was rising perceptibly. Ahead
was the narrowing, not wide enough for the giant
members of the group. The Shemibob and Sloosh,
though they'd entered first, were now behind Phemropit. Evidently, they'd climbed back over Phemropit,
squeezing between it and the ceiling.

Phemropit was now shooting its most powerful ray,
cutting along the walls. When it sliced off a section, it
swiveled slightly to one side and cut off another section. The slices fell down, forming a growing barrier.
How was Phemropit to get over that? There was no
way that the others could pick up and toss the pieces
over behind it.

It was hot in the tunnel. This was due not just to
the hot air coming in from the squeezed castle. The
stone being cut by the creature was also giving off heat.

Phemropit rumbled ahead, its nose pointing up as
it climbed up the pile of thin rock sheets. Its ray shot
out, and as it moved on and up, the ceiling scraping its
back, it removed more stone from above. It backed up,
and then it charged ahead, its ray cutting through the
rubble. It was in its native element now, mining, en-
larging a shaft. It needed no instructions.

Dust poured through the gateway. Deyv turned to
look behind him, expecting to be hit with terror and
nausea again. But this side of the gateway was dark.
If it hadn't been expanding and contracting, he might
have thought it was just a round discoloration on the
wall.

Vana had her arms around Aejip's neck and was
talking to her in a low voice. Jum looked as dazed as
the cat, but he was standing up beside the wall. Deyv
went forward. He yelled to make himself heard above
the roar coming through the gateway.

"We can't stay here long! Either the heat or the dust
will get us soon!"

"Obviously," the Archkerri said.

He was doing the only thing that he could be doing.
Standing, waiting for Phemropit to complete its work,
conserving his energy. The Shemibob turned the upper

half of her body around and gave Deyv a smile she must have thought encouraging. The sharp white teeth, however, made her look as if she'd like to bite someone.

Deyv shouted, "I could get by and go ahead. I could see what's ahead of us."

The Shemibob screamed, "No! Phemropit would have to stop cutting. We can't spare a second!"

She held in her hand a cylinder which could project pulses of light. This artifact was to be used to communicate with Phemropit. She'd given others to the whole party, but all had forgotten to bring theirs along. Sloosh had neglected also to bring his cage of fireflies. The Shemibob was the only one who could signal Phemropit.

The heat and deafening noise increased. Those behind the stone-metal thing crowded closer behind it. The dust was so thick that they could scarcely see a foot around them. All began coughing, Sloosh's huge mouth under the leaves making noises like a lion with a sore throat.

Suddenly, Phemropit backed up. Its companions had to retreat hurriedly to keep from being run over. The air from behind Deyv felt as if it were giving him a first-degree burn. The dust poured over him like the spray from a waterfall. The only one he could see, Jum, looked like a gray statue.

Then a great half-leaved hand reached out, groping, felt his face, lowered, traced his neck, shoulder, and arm. It closed around his hand and pulled him forward. Deyv turned and felt behind him, and he had Vana's hand.

In a loud voice interrupted by racking coughs, he asked her where Aejip was.

"She's with me!" Vana shouted, and she went into a frenzy of coughing.

They moved rapidly after that, The Shemibob with her hand on Phemropit's rear, Sloosh behind her, all in a chain held together by touch. Deyv hoped they would come to no more narrowings, but he didn't have much confidence. He had never felt such a sense of

inevitable doom, not even when he had been tied to
the post to question Phemropit.

They were moving swiftly forward now, but the heat
and the dust were not lessening. The ground-up castle
was shooting through the gateway; little pieces of stone
spattered on Deyv's back. Now and then he jumped
with pain as a larger piece struck him. Then the tunnel
began to curve. Though the heat and dust were still
strong, the fragments ceased to stab him.

Who had made this tunnel? Or was it natural? He'd
questioned The Shemibob about the coincidence of a
tunnel being just in the right place for entry. If the
gateway had been a little to one side either way, there
would have been only solid rock beyond it.

She had replied that she couldn't calculate the
mathematics of interuniversal physics. She didn't have
the data needed for that. But she speculated that gateways, for some reason, tended to locate in "weak" spots.
By this she meant that there were places in both
universes where air or water existed on each side of the
"walls" of the contiguous universes. It was here that the
gateways were attracted.

But she could be wrong.

"It's a good thing that the entrances don't exist above
the atmosphere," she'd said. "Otherwise, the side of the
gateway that impinges on a planet with air might suck
this air out into the cold empty space of the other
world.

"This might eventually happen. There's no telling
when the ever-increasing density of matter might shift
the gateways to such a location. In which case life on
Earth will die even more quickly than I've thought."

Deyv had thought that she was less comforting than
Sloosh, and that took some doing.

Suddenly, the dust cloud thinned, and the heat
cooled somewhat. Phemropit emitted a fan-shaped ray
of light. The Shemibob turned a rheostat on her device,
and its light added to that of the stone-metal creature.
They were in an immense cavern. Stalagmites and

stalactites glittered with many colors and hues. The ceiling shone as if speckled with mica. The air, however, was dead and heavy.

They went ahead over the irregular floor, changing direction once to avoid an abyss. The water on the floor was still about six inches deep. They splashed it on themselves to wash off the dust, and they drank deeply to quench a thirst they'd been too occupied to notice until then.

Deyv saw the top of a skull projecting from the water. It was the remains of one of the animals sent through by The Shemibob.

Feeling weak, Deyv sat down on a cool lump of rock.

Vana said, "You're bleeding badly."

She called Sloosh, who had nothing to offer except advice that Deyv direct his cells to speed up the healing process. The Shemibob, overhearing them, opened her huge bag and pulled out a large jar of ointment. She smeared the purple stuff over the gashes, and the bleeding stopped a minute afterward.

"Here. Eat this," she said, handing him a small cube wrapped in a thin silvery tissue. It had an unfamiliar but very delicious taste. He devoured it, and he felt better in a short time. She passed out cubes to the others, whose strength returned quickly.

"I packed things which I thought we might need in case of a hasty flight," she said. "I'd intended to tell you to do the same, but I decided to put it off until after sleep-time. I hope that teaches me a lesson."

They went on until they came to the far wall of the cavern. Though they went up and down its length, they could find no exit of any sort. There was a very small crevice through which water was trickling. It was this that was slowly flooding the hollow.

The noise, dust, and heat were now pushing from the mouth of the tunnel. Faint clouds of dust like the outriders of a ghost horde advanced toward them.

The snake-centaur took a small device out of her bag and placed it against the wall near the trickle. Its round face glowed with strange figures. She studied them for a minute, then moved the device along the wall in both directions and at different levels.

When she returned to the trickle, she said, "There's only five feet of rock between us and water at this point. I don't know how far under water we are. It makes no difference in what we have to do."

She described her plan, and they agreed that it was the best one. Though it was desperate, it might—it had to—succeed. Sloosh expanded the vessel and opened its door. The Shemibob glued the tip of its nose to Phemropit's rear with a piece of cloth from the bag.

"The cloth won't tear, but I don't know whether or not the glue will hold. Once it sets, it could hold two boards together though a thousand men pulled on each one. But we won't know what forces will be brought to bear on it. When the water comes gushing in, it may sweep up Phemropit and smash it against the rear of the cave. Or turn it upside down. Or . . . well, we shall see."

She explained to the creature what it was to do. It answered that it fully understood. But if the plan didn't work, it wanted everybody to understand that its experiences with them had been most educational and gratifying. Though of a weird quality.

By then it was evident that they had no more time to talk. Clouds of dust enveloped them. A river of packed dust was flowing from the tunnel. Its heat spread out, making them sweat from more than fear.

Vana, however, the most sentimental of the crew, ran in front of Phemropit with the light-device. She said a so-long to it and then patted it on its nose. It couldn't feel her hand, of course, but it may have felt some emotion. Then Vana ran back through the dust, coughing, and Deyv pulled her inside. The room was crowded now, The Shemibob's body filling a quarter of it. Sloosh shut the door. The lights were already on; the air system was working.

They didn't speak, though they gave little gasps or muted cries or, from Sloosh, occasional short buzz-ejaculations. Outside, Phemropit was moving horizontally from side to side to cut a wide but thin hole through the rock. This took some time because of the thickness of the wall. It would also be an increased drain on its energy supply.

They knew it had finished that stage of the work when they felt the vessel moving backward. The water would be spraying out in a powerful sheet. Its force wouldn't, or shouldn't, be enough to move Phemropit backward, however. It was backing toward a rise in the floor. Once its angle was changed, it would start cutting above the slit first made. Then it would move forward so that its nose would dip down. This would be done very slowly. The rock wall had to be thoroughly cut through vertically until that slit met the horizontal.

After a long time, the vessel moved back again, then forward. Slowly, it turned as Phemropit turned, its beam slicing through the rock above, making another horizontal slit. And after what was by no means an eternity, though it had some of its aspects, the vessel went through another series of maneuvers.

"Phemropit will have to be far enough back to avoid being struck when the cut-out section is propelled inward," The Shemibob said. "It said it comprehended that. Even so, the water may hurl the section back far enough to hit Phemropit. Or slide over it and strike our vessel. Then we'll see if the glue is strong enough."

The vessel suddenly shot backward. Its passengers were shot with bruising force against the far wall. For some time, there was no motion after that. Since the hull was soundproof, they couldn't hear the roar outside. But they could imagine that and the rapidly rising water also. Phemropit had to wait until the cavern was completely flooded before it would be able to advance through the hole. As it was, its treads were probably moving forward at their fastest speed just to keep from being pushed backward.

More of the delicious cubes were passed around. Another near-eternity, in an emotional sense, crawled by. Then they felt the vessel move forward. The floor

went up and down, roughly at times. By slight tenden-
cies of their bodies to lean this way or that, they knew
that they were changing direction horizontally. Sometimes, vertically.

"I think," Sloosh said, "that the wall of the cavern
was probably part of a mountain. How deep it was,
there's no telling. But if it rises above the water to
make an island, and the island has beaches, we might
make it. Provided, of course, that Phemropit doesn't go
in the wrong direction. And that there are inclines up
which it can go. If they're too steep . . . well, this
candy is a new experience to me. What is its chemical
makeup, O Shemibob?"

Deyv groaned. Where Phemropit went, they had to
go. How could it determine which way to go, inland or
out to sea?

After a while it became evident that they were
generally traveling up. Now and then Phemropit was
forced to go down or even to backtrack. Once, they
didn't move for a long time. Their animated locomotive
was sitting, considering some obstacle. Deyv could
imagine it, its light ray piercing through the darkness
of the depth. Or was there light above from the bright
sky? Or had Phemropit just given up?

Then they resumed, and they yelled and grabbed each
other as the vessel rolled slowly to one side. It righted
after a while, but Deyv wondered what would happen
if it had turned completely over. Nothing, he concluded, except that they'd be sitting on the ceiling.
What if Phemropit was on the edge of a steep cliff
and it gave way beneath the creature? It and its trailer
would drop into the abyss. And there might be no way
to get back out of it.

They came to a slope up which Phemropit slowly
went, slipped back some distance, went back up again,
slipped, tried again, slid back, then all of a sudden
traveled steadily upward. Shortly after this, the passengers felt as if they were on the surface of the water.
Surely, it had to be waves that were bobbing the floor
up and down?

Then they were moving forward on a very gentle slope. Then all motion stopped. They waited, tense, sweating, wondering if they were indeed on a beach.

"This is the blind spot, the weak place, in my plan," The Shemibob said. "I had nc time to think of a signal Phemropit could give. I'm not sure that any could've been arranged. How will we know when we're safe? If we open the door, and we're fooled by our sensations, not to mention our hopes, we'll be inundated. Drowned."

The vessel began turning in a short radius. It went around and around.

"What in Khokhundru is it doing?" Hoozisst said. "Has it gone crazy? It's like a dog chasing its own tail."

Sloosh and The Shemibob looked at each other. The latter smiled and her flapping laughter rang out.

"It's signaling us! It's turning the vessel on its horizontal axis. It's trying to tell us to come on out!"

"I don't know," the Yawtl said. "If you're wrong . . ."

For an answer, Sloosh opened the door. Light and air flooded in. Whooping, shedding tears, they tumbled out onto warm and comforting sand. Beyond the beach was a jungle and beyond that the cone of a tall mountain.

Deyv looked at the sky of a new world.

He groaned. Tears of frustration and anger flowed; his hands clenched.

Above was the crowded sky of blazing stars, broken here and there by dark shapes. On the horizon, coming toward him, was the snout of The Dark Beast.

Vana said, "We're back in *our* world!"

"THE last time I looked, there were four gateways on or in or above Earth," The Shemibob said.

They were by the vessel, which had been dragged to the edge of the jungle and wedged between two trees. They had slept and hunted and eaten and now were gathered to discuss the situation. They were not cheerful.

Above them, drifting across the brightness, were the great undecipherable characters.

When the first of them appeared, Sloosh had said, "Well, at least we know we're on the equator."

"One of the gateways was around my castle," The Shemibob said. "Another must have been the one you saw on that island. The third is, like this one, on the equator. And the fourth is this one. What that means is that this gateway is only the other side of that around my castle. So the other one on the equator may not be an entrance to another universe but an exit from a gateway located halfway across Earth.

"Which means that the other equatorial phenomenon may be on the other side of the one you saw above the island. There is, of course, only one way to find out. Go there and enter it."

She paused and smiled. "That is, if it's accessible or hasn't disappeared entirely."

Deyv didn't see that there was anything to smile about.

The Shemibob reached into her bag and pulled out a sphere half the size of Deyv's head. It seemed to be of cut quartz, a twin of the one Feersh had had in her *tharakorm.* Jowanarr said something to her mother in witch language, leading Deyv to believe that it was a duplicate.

310

The snake-centaur put her hands around the globe and closed her eyes. In a short time, the sphere began to glow, the light at first a spark in its center, then spreading out until it pulsed a milky light. Then four red sparks floated through the whiteness.

After a while one of the sparks became larger than the others.

The Shemibob opened her eyes and looked at the globe.

"The big glow is the gateway nearest us," she said, "the one below us."

A red line crept out from the largest spark, ending finally at another. She placed the globe in the palm of her right hand and stared at it. Presently, the spark at the end of the red line began to move, swinging as if it were a stone tied to a cord. When it ceased oscillating, it was in a different part of the sphere.

The Shemibob raised the globe to eye-level and sighted along the red line. For a few seconds the spark at its end expanded, becoming three times the size of the one at the other end.

She sighed and lowered the globe. The sparks and then the milky light faded. After she'd put the globe back into the bag, she said, "I'm famished. Give me a big piece of meat and a large pile of those crested roots, Deyv. This psychoelectrical manipulation drains me of energy."

He hastened to obey her. Before she began eating, she said, "We won't have any trouble locating the fourth gateway, though we might have difficulty getting to it. All we have to do is to follow the red line."

The Yawtl said, "What other treasures do you have in that bag of yours, O Shemibob?"

"You will see them as the occasion arises to use them, O Master Thief. But quit thinking about stealing them. You don't know how to use them, and so they would be valueless to you."

Later, Sloosh took Deyv and Vana aside.

"We won't need that sphere to get the general location of the gateway. It's in the same line as that on which the sky figures go. Also, if you wish to go home, all you have to do is to stay beneath the figures and travel as they do. They are, I believe, exactly on the equator."

"Thanks for the information," Deyv said. "But I'd already figured that out."

"And you're determined to accompany us only as far as the gateway? Then you'd go on toward your home area?"

"Maybe," Vana said. "Perhaps our tribes are located between here and the gateway."

Sloosh buzzed a sound equivalent to a shake of his head.

"Then you two will settle down with your people and perhaps have a long and possibly good life, by your lights. But your descendants will perish in a horrible manner. I don't mean those many generations from now. I've revised my estimate of how long life can last here. The quakes are increasing in frequency and intensity to a degree unpredicted by the scientists of my people. At any time a gateway may form which will suck the air from Earth. Or it may emit a disintegrating heat from a nearby star or possibly from the surface or heart of the star.

"I can think of other possibilities. One of these gateways that leads from one place to another on Earth might form in the bottom of the ocean. In that case, the water could pour out and drown all on land. Then—"

"That's enough!" Deyv said. "You're putting too much responsibility on us. And too much preguilt. By that I mean we'll be guilty before we've even committed the deed."

"In this situation, it's *not* doing the deed that will cause the guilt."

"Whatever," Vana said. "Anyway, we're going to try to talk our tribes into taking us back without our eggs. We can prove that they're not necessary. Of course, they might refuse to believe us even if we demonstrate that it's true that eggs aren't needed. We're living proof of that. But our people are steadfast in their beliefs, and they might drive us out or even kill us."

"I have to admire your courage, though I deplore your stupidity," the plant-man said. "If you hadn't lost your eggs and had stayed with your tribe, would you believe someone in your situation?"

Deyv and Vana looked at each other, and they said, "No."

"So there you are!" Sloosh walked off to The Shemibob and began talking to her.

Deyv said, "I wonder what he's up to now?"

Presently, the two came to Deyv and Vana. The Archkerri's expression, if any, was hidden under his leaves. The snake-centaur was grinning.

"Sloosh has convinced me that there's no need any longer to keep these from you," she said.

She opened her bag, reached in, and withdrew her hand. Opening it, she revealed two soul eggs attached to leather cords.

Deyv cried, "It's mine!"

Vana shrieked.

"Not the originals, of course," The Shemibob said. "Sloosh talked me into charting the electric potentials of your skins and your brain waves while you slept. Hoozisst's also. From these it was comparatively simple to reconstruct the eggs. But Sloosh wanted me to withhold them until it became evident that you were sticking to your determination to return to your tribes. Of course, Hoozisst couldn't get his until you got yours. Sloosh just told me that there is no reasoning with you, that I might as well give them to you now.

"You must realize that he hasn't been hiding them from you for any reason other than your best interests. He has a good heart, even if it is on a different beat from yours."

Deyv and Vana felt too happy to reproach the plant-man. They put the cords around their necks and closed a hand around the stones. Deyv's began to pulse with a red light which shone brightly. Vana's glowed greenly.

"Now," Sloosh said, "you two can see if they match in phase and if you're true mates or not."

Deyv's happiness boiled away, and a small panic rushed into its place.

"We don't need to find that out!" he said. "We already know we're well matched!"

"Yes," Vana said, her voice shaking. "We know that. So why bother?"

The Shemibob was smiling, but whether it was with delight at the unexpectedness of the gift or amusement at their reaction, Deyv couldn't tell.

"You two sound very much as if you're afraid to take the test. What would happen if your stones showed that you were mismatched? Would you then refuse to obey what your mind and heart tell you is true?"

Sloosh said, "I very much fear that they would. Despite their wide travel and many experiences, they haven't learned much."

"Why couldn't you have waited?" Deyv cried.

"What do you mean?" Sloosh asked. "I expected you to be angry because we'd not given you the eggs as soon as they were made. But I certainly didn't expect this."

"They're afraid of being separated," The Shemibob said. "The eggs might tell them that they aren't to be lifelong mates. But there's another, perhaps deeper fear. That is, that perhaps the eggs aren't infallible. Perhaps they don't tell the truth, perhaps they and their ancestors have been believing a lie. In which case, they know that they, and their ancestors, and their tribespeople have been fools. On the other hand, a part of them would like that.

"Of course, they could settle the question at once by trying to phase the eggs. But they're afraid to know the truth. Which is understandable. They don't want to lose each other. Or doesn't your vegetable-heart grasp this?"

"It's half-protein," Sloosh said. "But I comprehend you. What I would like to suggest—"

Vana said, "Deyv, I don't like to stand here and be talked about as if I'm a character in a tale or someone on the other side of the mountain. Let's do it and get it over with."

Deyv swallowed and said, "Very well. But not here. I want privacy."

They walked into the jungle, Vana's hand in his. It was filmed with sweat. Or was that his? It was both. Her skin felt cold, too.

He looked back through a break in the foliage. The Shemibob was dipping into the bag again. She was handing something to the plant-man. His prism! Of course, if she'd made eggs for them, she would have made a crystal for Sloosh. But that couldn't be given until after the eggs had gone to the humans.

Jum and Aejip came through the brush after them. Deyv told them to go back. It was necessary to be as little distracted as possible during the phasing.

They came to a great tree on the other side of which was a big flat-topped rock. They straddled it, facing each other. They slowly extended the stones until they touched. Each was held by a finger on top and bottom so that they could clearly see the reactions. With the other hand each touched the other's lips. Deyv felt a tingling in his lips and the finger, and he saw tiny green threads begin to form in the center of his egg. These were duplicated by threads of the same diameter and configuration in Vana's, except that they were red in hers.

The threads, still extending, began to twist in on themselves. They curved around and met other threads and slid alongside them, then twined around them. Deyv felt great joy. It was evident that they would be in complete phase or at least as much as any stones ever were.

Still, they had to finish the test. Sometimes, though rarely, the threads did not go further than a certain stage. Then it was up to the shamans and the grandmothers to determine if the match was good enough to permit marriage.

Now the threads formed a design called, in Deyv's tongue, *shvashavetl*. This was the name of a four-winged insect related to the butterfly. Seen from above, the insect looked much like the matching design, a long slim straight body with two oval wings on each side and, at the head, two out-curving antennae.

But the stones were not yet done.

Deyv and Vana waited, their fingers trembling but not losing contact with each other or making the eggs separate.

Suddenly, and startlingly, though it was expected, the tingling became a burning. And the designs in the stones seemed to explode, to become red and green tadpole shapes darting in a frenzy in many different directions.

Both snatched the eggs back and withdrew their fingers. Tiny lightning leaped between the fingers and lips, crackling. The figures shooting around inside the eggs flashed brightly and were gone. The eggs resumed their normal green and red colors.

Weeping but smiling, the two leaned over and embraced.

On the way back to camp, Vana said, dreamily, "Deyv, what would you have done if we'd been mismatched?"

He hugged her.

"I might've thrown my egg away. No, I suppose I wouldn't have. I need mine to be accepted by my tribe. I don't know, to tell the truth. I'm glad I don't know. But what would you have done?"

"The same, I suppose. Whatever that might have been."

They walked a few paces more. She stopped abruptly, looking alarmed.

"I just had a terrible thought! What if The Shemibob made the eggs so that they would phase regardless of our characters? That'd be a fine trick to play on us!"

"You're as bad as Sloosh," he said. "Why would she do that?"

"Because she didn't want us to be outcasts forever. Still, why should she go to all that trouble? She seems to like us, as we like Jum and Aejip, though not as deeply, of course. So maybe she did it out of affection. Or maybe out of a perverse sense of humor."

"We don't know that she did it."

They summoned up the courage to ask her.

She smiled for a while, then broke into a loud flapping laughter. When she'd recovered, she said, "You two are more suspicious than the Yawtl! Let me ask you, what difference would it make if I had given you two eggs guaranteed to phase even if your souls were not entirely congenial? Your tribes would be fooled, and so would you, and what harm could that be? It might even be that the eggs themselves would be the means of making you well matched just because you think they couldn't be wrong."

Vana spoke with some anger, more than she wanted to reveal but far less than what she would have liked to let loose.

"Well, what is the truth?"

"You'll never know!"

The Shemibob exploded into laughter again. Sloosh, who'd been standing nearby, buzzed his equivalent of great amusement. Deyv and Vana, furious, feeling like fools, walked off. After they'd cooled off, however, they agreed that the eggs, whether false or genuine, served their purpose. So why should they continue to be angry at The Shemibob? After all, she'd done them an invaluable service. If she enjoyed the joke or enjoyed their reaction to what might not be a joke, it was slight repayment. Nevertheless, they couldn't keep from wondering about it from time to time.

They asked Sloosh if he knew the truth. He replied that he knew no more than The Shemibob and could give only the same answers.

"But I must warn you that the eggs have more than one disadvantage. You have to pay for anything good.

Or for anything bad, for that matter. Aside from their
initial charge, the eggs derive their energy from you.
They tap the electricity, the bio-power, of your cells.
This is very slight to begin with, and it takes time for
the eggs to accumulate it. You know that you can't use
the eggs too much. Otherwise, they won't operate.
Even so, what energy they do use is gotten only by
hastening your metabolism. Which means that you
have to eat more. Which also means that you age
somewhat faster. An egg-bearer's natural lifespan is
shortened by an eleventh or a tenth. If you'd kept on
being eggless, you might've been the longest-lived of
your tribe.

"I suggest that you quit wearing them until you're
getting close to your homeland. And after that, whenever you're out of sight of your people, put it in a bag."

"What about your prism?" Vana asked.

"I'm wearing it all the time now because I'm charg-
ing it. When it's ready to be used, I'll put it aside.
Unless I have a need at that time to use it."

"We should tell our people about this," Deyv said.

"They won't believe it. They're too fixed in their
ways."

38

THE Dark Beast had gone over four times when
they came to a highway of the ancients. After traveling
on it for two sleep-times, they came to a junction. This
time, the eyes on top of the poles did not flash. They
looked dead, and after Feersh and her daughter had
tested them, the witch said they had indeed died.

"So," Sloosh said, "the connection to the power
source or the circuit itself has been broken. It's no
wonder. The quakes have been getting worse. After
being subjected to so many minor strains, so many

cataclysms, even the wonderful work of those wise people has succumbed."

"The end of our days is approaching," Hoozisst said.

As if to emphasize that, the ground began shaking. They fell to the road and hung on while it rose and fell, swayed and twisted. Trees along the wayside leaned or toppled. Finally, the temblors ceased. They got up and resumed their walk without a word. Phemropit rumbled along behind them. Even it had quit commenting about the quakes.

The Beast cast its shadow many, many times. Vana's belly began to grow big. Phemropit inquired about this phenomenon and was staggered by the explanation.

"We know nothing of such fantastic things," it said. "From the beginning, we just *were*. We do have a tradition that we were made by some being quite unlike us. But that is something that is quite unlikely to be true. All of us were there at the beginning, that is, when we first became conscious. We had fully developed minds, but they were empty. We ate by what you call instinct, but we didn't have a language. That we had to invent, and there was quite a lot of disagreement on which system of signals to use.

"Of course, we couldn't argue much, since we were using different systems—about ten were prevalent then, I believe—and so we often didn't know what the other was saying. This worked out eventually, however. We are a rational people.

"One of us said that we had to have had a maker. We just couldn't have formed out of the matter of our world. Others said they couldn't see why not. But by the time our world fell on this one, the school that favored the maker theory had triumphed."

By then, Phemropit said, accidents and some disputes had cut their numbers down a little. It didn't matter. If their world hadn't been destroyed by the fall, it would have become too small to feed everybody.

"Eventually, our world would have been a pile of excrement and a nucleus of the rock which makes our food. We'd have been stacked on top of each other,

trying to fight through those below while the bottom
layer ate up what was left."

"Maybe not," The Shemibob said. "You may have
eaten so much of your world that it wouldn't have had
enough mass to attract you. You'd have floated away
from your world, floated forever through space. Or until
you were drawn to a large mass, another planetoid or
planet or star. Or, finally, by the rush of all matter
toward a common center."

Sloosh took his prism and held it up against the
trunk of a giant tree. Deyv watched from under his
shoulder. It was fascinating for a while to watch the
many strange designs forming within the crystal. He
got tired of that eventually and wandered off. But when
the plant-man came back to camp, Deyv asked him
what he'd heard from the vegetable kingdom.

"My people have moved now," he said. "They, too,
are seeking a gateway. In fact, the very one we're looking for. But they're taking their time. We'll get there
long before they do."

"Why have they suddenly gotten off their leafy
butts?" Deyv asked.

"Because they've realized that they don't have much
time left. By that, I mean *their* time. It would seem a
long time to you. Anyway, I told them that I'd be
pleased to join them. I mentioned I might be bringing
along some rather interesting sentients."

Deyv was surprised. "You mean you were talking to
them? I didn't see you doing anything but viewing the
designs."

"I was sending electrical analogs of my thoughts, the
upper layer of them, that is, through controlled pulses
from my skin."

Deyv thought that this was wonderful until Sloosh
told him that he, too, could do it. It would take him
a long time to learn how, though.

The Yawtl, hearing of this, asked Sloosh if he'd
teach him. The plant-man said he'd be glad to.
Hoozisst had also gotten the witch to show him how
to operate his Emerald of Anticipation. He had been

refused when he'd asked The Shemibob to instruct him in the mysteries of the quartz sphere. Later, however, she had relented.

Sloosh said to Deyv, "I would think you'd want to know all these things."

"I would if I thought it'd do me any good," Deyv said. "But Vana and I'll be leaving you, and we won't be taking the devices with us. So why bother?"

"Maybe The Shemibob and I will give you gifts."

"Why should you do that?" Deyv asked, his eagerness showing.

"Why indeed?"

Deyv meant to take up the subject again soon. After the next sleep-time, he became so interested in another matter that he forgot about it. He mentioned to Sloosh that The Shemibob had never said anything about the giant figures that floated over the equator. Had the Archkerri asked her about them?

"Of course," Sloosh said. "Do you still believe that I'm lacking in that curiosity which distinguishes the sentients from the nonsentients?"

By which he implied that if Deyv was actually sentient he was on the borderline between the have-minds and the have-not-minds. Deyv ignored that, and he asked, "What does she know about them?"

"Nothing. She knows of their existence, but she knows no more of their origin or what they mean—if anything—than I do."

The plant-man continued, "However, we may have some answers to our questions soon. We're approaching the area from which they emanate."

The Archkerri was always surprising Deyv.

"How can that be? They're coming from behind us."

"No. They're coming from a place ahead of us. The figures you have been seeing originated there. But they've traveled around the planet and are now coming home."

"They're not birds?"

"I wouldn't care to say what they are or are not until I have examined them."

The Shemibob produced from her bag a plate on which she could write with a slender rod. When she wanted to erase the writing, she merely pressed a little button on the side of the plate. She and Sloosh, while riding on Phemropit's back or in camp, were often discussing the characters she drew on the plate. From what Deyv overheard, they were trying to make sense out of the flying figures. They didn't seem to be having any success.

Bright sky and Dark Beast chased each other around and around. Vana swelled. The snake-centaur applied a crystal to Vana's belly and announced that she would bear a boy. This pleased neither of the prospective parents. It was more fun guessing.

In the meantime, the two marred their otherwise cordial intercourse by a long-lasting dispute. Who would go with whom to whose tribe?

"Vana wants me to be adopted by her people, and I, naturally, prefer that she come to mine," Deyv told Sloosh. "Don't you think that it's better for everybody concerned if the husband brings his wife to his House?"

"Don't involve me in these intricate and irrational human matters," Sloosh said. "However, I can't resist a problem. It seems to me that there are three ways to solve this.

"One, you two can go into the jungle and see who catches the other. The loser goes off willy-nilly to the tribe of the other. That's the way you usually settle these matters, isn't it?

"Two, you get your two tribes to become one people, merge. Though I suppose that'd cause other problems, as the solving of one problem usually does. There'd be the question of which language would be used. But if they agreed to use a Trade Language, then that'd be solved.

"Three, you could throw a stick up in the air, and if the end you pick strikes first, then she goes with you. Or vice versa. Personally, I think number two's the best."

Deyv told Vana of his conversation. She thought

that number three was the best and by far the quickest.

"You're not a good loser," Deyv said. Hastily, seeing her anger, he added, "Neither am I. Forget it."

The Shemibob applied her crystal to Vana's belly again. After reading the designs in it, she said, "The baby will come in exactly the time it will take for three more circuits of The Dark Beast and one sleep-time."

Deyv forgot his resentment toward Vana and started toward her to embrace her. At that moment, a severe quake struck. He waited until it and succeeding, though lesser, temblors had passed. He took her in his arms and said that it would be the happiest moment of his life when the baby was born.

"That makes me happy, knowing that," Vana said. "Now, if only—"

"If only what?"

She didn't reply, but both knew.

The Dark Beast completed two more circuits. It was in the sky a third time, almost upon the travelers, when Sloosh said that they were about a hundred miles from the source of the flying figures. All they had to do was journey fifty more miles on the highway and then turn right for fifty more. Hopefully, they'd come to a junction where a highway would go in the desired direction. If not, then they'd have to cross the heavily forested mountainous area.

They were near a steep mountain on their left when Sloosh announced this. On their right was a hilly area. Sloosh paused, then said, "Deyv, Vana, will you be leaving us? Or will you go with us to the source?"

"If you're returning to this highway, we might as well go with you," Deyv said. "It won't hurt to waste more time, we've been gone so long now. Besides, I'd feel safer with Phemropit and the rest of you with us. It won't be easy for just the two of us to take care of a baby without protection."

"I agree with you," Vana said. "But you might have asked what I thought before you spoke."

"Woman," Deyv said, "we're in trouble. The ways of your tribe are just too different from my tribe's.

Among my people, certain things are women's and others are men's. But in cases like these, it is up to the man to make the decision."

Vana opened her mouth to reply. She may even have uttered a word. If she did, it was lost in the sudden rumble, followed by a great noise as if the world had cracked. In fact, that was what had happened, though locally. One of the bellowing rifts opened up directly below the road on which they had paused for a moment. The highway dropped for a foot, then the hanging section began to stretch. At the same time, it swayed from side to side. They felt as if they were on a suspension bridge over an abyss, a bridge pushed by a high wind. It rocked back and forth and sagged as they scrambled, screaming, for the edges of the sudden cliffs.

Phemropit, which had been on the outer lane, did not move for a moment. It probably was not immediately aware of the situation. But its sensors told it that it was in danger of falling off, and its tracks began turning. Too late. Its enormous weight bent the rubbery material to one side, and it slid off. Its tracks still turning, it disappeared into the gap.

Deyv was vaguely aware of this but only because he happened to look behind him for a second. He was busy trying to keep Vana and himself from sliding off. They were, fortunately, in the middle of the highway when the quake struck. They had been hurled onto their faces when the rift opened, but they struggled up onto their hands and knees and crawled toward the ground. It was not solid; it was bouncing like the breast of a running woman. But whatever small refuge it offered, it was better than dropping into the chasm.

To their right was a roar that drowned out the ground-rumble. The side of the mountain was sliding toward them, the soil, the trees, the huge boulders.

He shouted at Vana to hurry, but she couldn't have heard him. It would have made no difference. She was going as fast as she could.

Jum leaped past them, his mouth open as if he were howling. Something touched Deyv's ankle. Sloosh, he supposed. The Shemibob was almost to the edge of the abyss. He didn't know where Aejip, the Yawtl, the witch, and her daughter were. At the moment, he wasn't the least concerned about them. All he wanted was to get himself and his mate to safety. If they went down, three lives would be lost. The baby's might be destroyed anyway, since Vana had been propelled forward hard upon her belly.

They were ten feet away from the edge when The Shemibob ran back onto the hanging part to help them. Her forty legs moved swiftly; her front part was stretched out so far that she used her arms as legs. When she got to them, she cried something, it didn't matter what, and she grabbed Vana. Then, rising with her in her arms, she turned, almost fell over to one side, righted herself, and sped away with her burden.

Deyv crawled sobbing after her. She put the woman down on the ground, and she came back for him. Instead of trying to pick him up, she held out a hand. He seized it, felt a grip as mighty as the plant-man's, and was lifted up and over her head, her back arcing backward. He thought his arm had been jerked out of its socket. He fell screaming with pain, almost striking Vana. The impact knocked him half-senseless, and for a while he didn't know who he was or what was happening around him.

He was aware, though, when The Shemibob hoisted him up under one arm and Vana under the other and began running toward the jungle, away from the mountain. Something huge and dark rolled by them. A boulder. Then it stopped, and he was being carried past it.

By then, so he was told later, the temblors had ceased. But the avalanche pouring down the mountainside was shivering the ground. Despite this, the snake-centaur managed to stay on her feet—a good thing she had so many of them—and to get them to the edge of the jungle. Trees lay across each other or leaned at different angles. Here and there were some small boulders that had rolled or leaped across the highway and crashed into the bushes or the trees. The Shemibob deposited them behind a rock and then turned to see what had happened to the others.

Deyv had gotten most of his wits back, but he wished he hadn't. His right shoulder and his left leg hurt very much. He groaned, then asked, "Why did she have to throw me?"

Vana said in a dull voice, "Because she had to. You would've been hit by a flying boulder. As it was, the impact almost bounced her off into the hole."

"Aejip and Sloosh?"

"The Archkerri was almost hurled off when that boulder shot away like a stone from a sling," The Shemibob said. "But he wasn't, and he's somewhere near us. The others are safe, too. Except, I regret to say, Phemropit. Jowanarr is also down in the chasm. She almost made it, but the side of the highway dipped too far. And she fell."

She peered through the dust that was beginning to settle around them. By then, the avalanche had spent its fury. Deyv heard a faint wail, and he asked, "Who's crying?"

The Shemibob said, "Feersh. She's wandering around stumbling over rocks and tree branches, and if she doesn't stop, she'll fall into the chasm, too."

Vana asked, "How could she have survived?"

"I don't know," The Shemibob said. "Her daughter must have pointed her in the right direction. Certainly, the Yawtl wouldn't help her."

She reared up even further, and she shouted, "Hoozisst, you thief! Bring that bag to me!"

She muttered, "I left the bag by the edge. Would you believe it, that greedyguts walked across the highway while it was still swinging, and he came back with my bag. He was going to run off with it!"

Presently the Yawtl, grinning slyly, came to her and handed her the bag.

"I was saving it for you, O Shemibob."

"Sure you were," she said, smiling savagely. "So why didn't you look for me?"

"I was just going to put it in a safe place."

"Which is where it is now. Do you really think you could get away with it? Go bring that poor blind woman here before she steps over the edge."

"I'd rather lead her onto thin air," Hoozisst said. "I owe her a death."

"Get her!" The Shemibob said sternly.

Apparently, Hoozisst wasted no time in telling Feersh that her daughter was dead. She came to them wailing even more loudly, though whether because she felt grief for Jowanarr or for her worsened plight, no one knew.

Presently Sloosh, followed by the two animals, came to the boulder. He said, "It was fortunate that I'd not had the cube unstrapped from my back. I was just about to ask that it be taken off when the quake struck."

Jum, knowing that his master was in pain, whined while licking his face. Aejip lay down by Vana but rose a moment later and moved away. Sloosh said, "What's the matter, Vana?"

"The Shemibob was wrong," she said, her face grim with pain. "My time has come sooner than she predicted."

39

WHILE Sloosh straightened Deyv's leg and then set it with two long splints of wood, The Shemibob helped Vana. The baby came swiftly, impelled by the shock of the earthquake and his mother's narrow escape from death. He was rather small but healthy, and after The Shemibob had cleaned him and wrapped him in a cloth from her bag, she put him in Vana's arms.

Sloosh unfolded the vessel so that mother and child would have a warm, comfortable, and safe place to rest. Vana herself carried the baby into it, but she reeled with weakness. Deyv gave his breechclout to The Shemibob, who washed it and, after it had dried, used it to diaper the baby.

The Yawtl went out to peel bark off an *utrighmakl* tree to make bark-fiber cloths. It wasn't his wont to do service for others, but he must have thought that he might get back into the good graces of The Shemibob by being useful. The work also took him away from her. "Out of sight, out of mind" was an ancient proverb but still applicable.

Both Deyv and Vana ate and drank much and spent time directing their healing substances, Vana to her torn tissues and Deyv to his broken bone and swollen muscles. Vana also began nursing the baby.

Other temblors of a lesser energy came, and the vessel was lifted a dozen times into the air an inch or so, but the shocks were of little consequence. Hoozisst, in the midst of working the bark, found time to make a crutch for Deyv. It was shortly after this that Deyv and Vana were called from the vessel. He hobbled on the crutch; she carried the baby against her breast.

What Sloosh had summoned them to see was a pool of some silvery stuff that had filled the fissures. It was, Sloosh said, a liquid metal, no doubt made by the ancients. It must have been in a huge container or containers which had been long-buried by accumulating dust or washdowns from the mountains. Or perhaps by a cataclysm. In any event, the containers had ruptured, and now the liquid was seeping out.

Sloosh didn't have to point out the strange qualities of the liquid metal. In the fissure into which Phemropit had fallen the stuff was flowing over its edges. And there on its surface bobbed boulders, large and small. And Phemropit and dead Jowanarr.

"Stay upwind of it," the Archkerri said.

He indicated a large bird that was also floating on the shiny gray surface.

"It flew over and then dropped as if shot. The metal, if it is metal, gives off poisonous vapors."

Though standing twenty feet away, Deyv could smell a bitter odor. It caught at his throat and made his eyes water.

The Shemibob brought out a rope from her bag, a thin gossamery material through which the light shone. She attached a stone to one end of the rope with a sticky stuff.

"To give it weight," she explained.

Then, holding her breath, she ran near the edge of the fissure. She cast the rope out with such accuracy that the stone landed on Phemropit near its snout and stuck to its surface. Immediately, she backed away, the rope running through her hands. When she stopped, Sloosh got in front of her, his great hands closing around the rope. They pulled together, and the stone-metal creature turned its nose toward the edge. At The Shemibob's command, the Yawtl left his bark pounding to help pull. All three, tugging hard, slowly drew Phemropit along the side of the fissure.

By then the silvery liquid metal had drained off Phemropit's detector and ray holes. It flashed that it was aware of what they were doing. The Shemibob used her light-device to tell it that when it was over the highway, it must use its tracks to help itself off. The creature replied that it had already thought of that.

Though the rubbery material of the highway had sagged, it had started to contract in order to shorten itself. Most of it was floating on the silvery liquid, but a section was still curved underneath. This arc was near the other side of the fissure, downwind. Those hauling Phemropit could not go to that side to pull the creature over the part under the surface. They had to strain to drag it over the end of the "bridge" nearest them until its weight forced the highway down.

The Shemibob called out that Vana should lead Feersh to the rope so that both might add their muscle. Vana gave the baby to Deyv to hold. He sat on top of a small boulder with the child and watched the pro-

ceedings. Presently, the creature's front end passed over
the highway. Its haulers rested for a moment and then
resumed their labors. It seemed that despite their most
strenuous efforts, they weren't going to be able to drag
it far enough for its foremost treads to catch. Then
The Shemibob signaled that it should start turning its
treads. Hopefully, these would give it some slight
propulsion forward.

The idea worked. Inch by inch, it moved forward,
the section began to sink, and then the treads caught.
They were going so fast, however, that Phemropit almost drove itself over the road and back into the great
crack. This ended about forty-five feet beyond the
highway and narrowed considerably. Phemropit would
have gone in nose-first, "head" down. Though it may
have floated back up, its end would have been sticking
up, its body wedged between the highway and the walls
of the fissure. The situation would have been hopeless.

Phemropit caught itself just in time and backed up,
The Shemibob flashing just how far it should travel.
After that, it turned its tracks, the left moving more
slowly than the right. It swiveled until it was parallel
to the highway, and it traveled up on the highway,
which bent under the massive weight, and was then on
solid ground.

Everybody cheered in his or her manner except the
baby. He began crying loudly. Vana hurried back to
him, since it was his feeding time.

The Shemibob led Phemropit to a nearby river,
where it plunged in to cleanse off the traces of silvery
metal. These killed some fish downstream. Phemropit
almost got stuck in the mud of the bank coming out,
but it finally ground its way onto harder earth.

The Shemibob waited until the rope dried off before
she poured a liquid from a small bottle onto the stone
attached to it and to Phemropit. In a short time, the
glue dissolved, and she rolled up the rope and put it
back in the bag. Deyv noticed that Hoozisst watched
this procedure very intently.

They decided to move the vessel down the valley in

case another quake should open other fissures and spill out more of the poisonous liquid. Several sleep-times later, they resumed their journey. By then Deyv's leg had almost knit and his shoulder had almost healed. Everybody was happy, or as happy as their natures and the situation permitted. It would have been a terrible loss if Phemropit could no longer have given them its protection. They felt fairly secure with it; it could scare or drive off almost any enemy or predator. Riding on it enabled them to get a rest when they were tired of walking. Though it went more slowly than their normal gait, it compensated for this by traveling during sleep-time. All it had to do was to follow the highway while they snored in the vessel on its back.

Deyv and Vana were well aware that this good life would cease sometime. They would have to go on by themselves, burdened by the baby. The prospect was appalling. But they were determined to get back to their homeland.

Thrush, the child, was healthy. He was, however, somewhat strange-looking at first to his parents. Neither had ever seen such a hybrid before. He had his mother's kinky hair, but it was black instead of yellow. His eyes, once they'd lost their natal blue, were neither Deyv's brown nor Vana's green but hazel: brown with specks of green. His skin was lighter than his father's but darker than his mother's.

Sloosh commented that Thrush was probably a beautiful baby, from a human viewpoint. He wouldn't know. This led him into a short discourse on the races of *Homo sapiens*. According to him, humanity in its early days had been divided into a number of races, though it wasn't always easy to distinguish one from the other. Then mankind became homogeneous, so interbred that it formed one race. In time, because of changing conditions, new races were created, few of which duplicated previous ones. Then there was one race again. Then, a differentiation into three or four. Then, homogeneity again. And so on.

"This child should grow up to be big, healthy,

vigorous, and perhaps intelligent, by human standards. It is time that entirely new genes were brought into your tribes. Even with the custom of occasionally taking new spouses from other tribes, the intermarriage is still confined to a small number."

Deyv and Vana were warmed by his predictions. But, as usual, he had to spoil his compliments.

"However, it is doubtful that the child will survive the journey, since his parents probably won't either. Once you set out without us . . ."

They arrived at last at the point where they must turn to the right if they were to go to the source of the flying figures. They didn't leave the highway for rough country, though. Not yet, anyway. There was a junction with a road running to the left and one in the desired direction. The latter took them about fifty miles before it abruptly ended. Beyond it were foothills and past these a range of mighty mountains.

Here not only was there no road, there was no vegetation. Not a single plant grew on the bare rocks, from which the soil had been washed off long ago.

"Another wasteland," Sloosh said. "And not even with the redeeming beauty of The Shemibob's land. Still, it does have a certain majesty. A grim forbidding one, though."

Deyv wondered aloud what had killed the trees and the bushes.

"This is what we Archkerri call The Dead Place," Sloosh said. "We know nothing of it because there is no vegetation to report on it."

The Shemibob said that she was equally ignorant. "Knowing and not knowing are light and its shadow, two states entirely different yet as closely related as brother and sister. If you conquer one, you automatically conquer the other. Let's set out for the conquest."

She might also have said that conquering either abstraction always involved overcoming the physical. In this situation, it was the mountains. As they'd done before the breaching of The Jeweled Wasteland, they had to store up enough food to last them. At least, they hoped it would be enough. Thirst would be no problem, since it rained heavily here. But water would be. The flash floods that raced down the ravines and the valleys and the passes would be more deadly than those in The House of Countless Chambers. And, as far as they knew, the land had no oases.

The Dark Beast had passed over five times before they had what they considered enough provisions. The baby grew larger. In the meantime, the parents had come no closer to deciding whose tribe they would live with. It wasn't a matter that soured their every moment, but it did darken slightly every thought when they were together.

Just before they left camp, the Yawtl proposed that Feersh be left behind.

"She's no good to us. She's only a burden, a mouth that eats our food and gives us nothing in return. If we don't take her, we'll have just that much more food. Now, I'm not inhumane. We could put her out of her misery so she won't starve to death or be eaten up by some beast."

The witch opened her mouth as if to protest, then closed it. Her dignified expression said that she would let the others defend her—if they so wished.

"Let the lesser beings speak first," The Shemibob said.

Since Sloosh didn't consider himself to be in that class, he kept silent. Deyy and Vana looked at each other. Though they exchanged no words, they were thinking the same thoughts. Were they as much on trial as the witch? Would their decision make them higher in the estimation of The Shemibob? Or lower? Or were they perhaps being too sensitive?

Whatever the truth about them, the Yawtl was also on trial. He didn't know that, not being capable of perceiving such subtleties. As cunning as he was, he lacked certain faculties which humans had. Some humans, anyway.

Vana said, "The witch has been very useful even if she is blind. For instance, though she isn't capable of hunting, she has been preparing the food we've brought her. She can cook, and she smokes the meat and fish. And she has offered to take care of the baby so that I can hunt and rest. This she has done, though she wasn't used to doing such things when she was the mistress and had many slaves to do her bidding."

"Nor has she whined and complained even though her lot has been worse than any of ours," Deyv said. "Whereas Hoozisst, though he is strong and capable and has his sight, is always complaining about this and that."

The Yawtl, snarling, said, "I won't forget this!"

"It's nice that you have a good memory," The Shemibob said. "And it's too bad that you are so vindictive. You knew, as did Deyv and Vana, how useful she's been despite her handicap. And you must also have realized—or did you?—that she has a strong and adaptable character. Here she is, a once all-powerful lord of her immediate environment. One who didn't even have to walk through her *tharakorm* if she didn't want to but could be carried by her slaves. Yet, since her life has changed, being reduced to a level lower than that of her slaves, she has done her best to cope with the changes. From what I've seen of humans, many in her situation would have succumbed, simply died or become parasites. She hasn't done either. She's done her best to survive, to be useful, and her best is quite adequate."

"So what?" Hoozisst said. "She may be admirable, as far as character goes, though I won't admit that. But it's what she can do for us that counts. I say she's a hindrance, a nuisance, a heavy liability."

Deyv said, "If you were severely wounded and couldn't be of any use for a long time and, in fact, it cost us time and labor, even danger, keeping you alive, would you wish us to abandon you or kill you?"

"But you'd know that once I got well I would be a great asset," the Yawtl said.

Sloosh must have thought that the lesser beings had spoken enough. He said, "You hate Feersh because she once controlled you and you dared not rebel against her. She also robbed you of your soul egg, which you now have, and she tried to kill you. But if you'd been in her place, you would have done the same. So why, in this respect, are you any different?

"The difference is that if you'd been blind and deprived of your high position as master, you would not have adapted so well. If you're such a complainer in your present position, so vindictive, what would you have been like in her place?"

"We're not talking about possibilities," the Yawtl said. "We're talking about facts!"

"Some things are not realities," the Archkerri said. "They appear to be facts because the individual thinks they ought to be. To him, they *must* be. But let me ask you this. Don't you have any feeling, any ability to put yourself in Feersh's skin, which would enable you to identify yourself with her?"

"That bitch!" Hoozisst said.

Sloosh threw his hands up and said, "O Shemibob, you speak to him."

"It would be useless," The Shemibob said. "I believe, though, that the humans have spoken up for her, though only from a utilitarian viewpoint. However, they do have some potential for empathy. Though empathy can be a dangerous thing, leading to a false attitude toward reality.

"Still, the basic question here is one of usefulness. So, ignoring the other aspects of the question, I say that Feersh has been, is, and may continue to be of service to us. I therefore say that she will go on with us."

Deyv and Vana had expected that the witch's fate would be put to a vote. Apparently, The Shemibob hadn't considered this. But she had at least asked their opinion. Moreover, she had in some unspoken manner, they felt sure, judged them. They couldn't be sure, but they believed that they had come out better than the Yawtl.

Still, they could understand quite well Hoozisst's stand.

Vana, however, stated it well, Deyv thought, when she said, "Our baby is contributing nothing, and he is a definitely heavy liability. Why didn't Hoozisst demand that Thrush be left behind?"

40 ᐧᗌ

THE pall cast by The Dark Beast was not quite at its heaviest when Phemropit and its riders came around the shoulder of the mountain. Below them was a valley. Two valleys, actually, for there was a smaller one in the center of the large one. Out of the inkiness of the former rose The House of the Flying Figures. It was a vague bulk, an intimation of vastness from which soared a dimly lit column or tower. Its upper part was brighter, nimbused by the horizon light flowing through a notch in the mountain range opposite.

They were silent for a while, staring through the darkness, trying to put a shape to the structure below the column. The wind had died; not a sound was to be heard. Ever since they had crossed the boundary of The Dead Place, the only noise had been that which they had made or, sometimes, the wind's sobbing or shrilling through peculiar rock formations or the thunder and lightning of storms and the splash of rain. Other than themselves, they'd not seen a living creature—no plants, no insects, no birds, no beasts. Even the stones looked lifeless compared to those outside this land. Somehow, they gave the impression that something had been drained, or sucked, from their stony essence.

Yet, a sick thing had to be still living. They often came across a small rock, or a large boulder, or a stratum in a mountainside that appeared to be infected. From irregularly shaped patches on these slowly oozed a foul-smelling liquid, cloudy, irresistibly analogous to

pus. They had scraped at the dripping patches, thinking
that they must be lichen of some sort and thus The
Dead Place was not entirely dead. But they got only
particles of stone which were, for some reason, darker
than the main body of the rock.

Now, after a long journey made circuitous because
there were so many steeps up which Phemropit could
not climb, so many passes to find, they were almost to
their goal.

Vana shivered and broke the terrible silence. "I wish
we'd stayed on the highway toward home, Deyv."

He did, too, but he only said, "This is the coldest
place I've ever been."

The Shemibob flowed down off Phemropit's back
and signaled that it should start the descent. After a
while the going became so steep that the others also
got off. They stayed behind Phemropit so that if it
started sliding, they wouldn't be crushed by it. By
sleep-time, however, they had reached the floor of the
valley without mishap.

Just as they did, they were startled by a great noise,
a booming metallic note like that which the giant
bronze gong in The Shemibob's castle gave when struck
by a hammer. Its echoes rang around the valley. They
shivered and clutched their hearts.

When all was silent again, except for their heavy
breathing and the pulse of blood in their ears, Sloosh
spoke. His buzzing seemed almost sacrilegious; there
was something in the place that might resent it. Or so
it seemed to Deyv at the moment. A thing, he was
convinced, *brooded* here and did not want interruption.

Sloosh said, "I wonder if that could be an alarm of
some sort? Perhaps there are detectors here, and when
we entered their field, they set off this warning signal."

"Warning whom?" Deyv whispered.

The baby began crying then. Vana tried to hush him
up, but he would not quit until she had given him her
breast. Deyv started to ask if they should bed down or
push on. Another vast note rang through the valley,
and its echoes raced around the mountains. The baby

quit feeding to scream. Why it had not been frightened when the first note sounded, no one knew. Perhaps it had been too scared to voice its fear. Or perhaps it had been only half-awakened.

The echoes died; Thrush continued to yell. Vana petted him and said soothing words and finally got him to drink again. Shortly after the silence came again, it was shattered by another metallic roar.

The Shemibob said, "I counted twenty-one seconds between the sounds."

The Yawtl said, "So what?" But when the fourth bellow was followed by the fifth, he said, "You're right."

There was, by unanimous agreement, no use in going toward The House while the terrible noise continued. They expanded the cube and all but the plant-man and the snake-centaur got inside and closed the door. These two said they would stand guard until they could stand the noise no longer. Those inside could hear nothing with the door shut, so they managed after a long while to get to sleep. Deyv did awake a number of times, startled by that brazen thunder. But he had only dreamed it.

He was awakened after a too-short sleep when the door was opened. Sloosh stuck his head in and said, "The noise has stopped."

Deyv asked, "Are you sure?"

Sloosh said, "What?"

He was deaf, and so was The Shemibob. But their loss of hearing was only temporary, and it had not been complete. They had been able to detect all vibrations, though they'd been very feeble at the end.

"But if they'd gone on much longer, we'd have had a permanent injury," The Shemibob said. "I counted one thousand and fifty strokes with twenty-one seconds between each."

There was no use asking the meaning of this. Perhaps there was none. They wouldn't know until they got to The House, and probably not even then. All Deyv was sure of was that he was very uneasy in this place, where it was either too silent or too noisy.

The baby was fussy and didn't want his milk. Vana said that she'd been so upset that her milk had probably soured. The Shemibob took a bottle from her bag and from it produced a tiny pill. She told Vana that she should get the baby to swallow it. He would then calm down, probably sleep much, but the drug wouldn't harm him. After some hesitation, Vana took the pill. Thrush spit it out several times before accepting it. Vana then asked if she could have one. The Shemibob refused, saying that Vana wasn't an infant, though she sometimes acted like one. This made Vana so angry that she lost her tiredness and regained her courage.

The vessel was folded up and tied onto Sloosh's back. They ate a little—no one felt hungry—and they started across the dark hushed valley. Phemropit's fanlight lit their way; the only sound was the striking of its treads against the loose rocks. The House loomed larger and larger, and after a while they had descended into the small valley and were beside it. Phemropit stopped. Before them was a window three times as tall as Deyv and ten times as wide. The walls disappeared on both sides of the window into the darkness.

The Shemibob took a cylinder from her bag. Its end shot out a bright light through the transparent material of the window. They pressed close to it to look within. But all they could see was a floor many inches thick with dust.

The window was smooth and cool, and so was The House around it. The material of which both were made was very hard. After some discussion they agreed that they might as well test the material. If they made so much noise that they attracted the tenant of The House—if there was one—they were not necessarily making a mistake. He or she or it—Deyv hated the ominous sound of that it—probably knew they were here. If it didn't, it would find out sooner or later, so why not sooner?

Deyv thought of several reasons why, but he knew they wouldn't dissuade The Shemibob and Sloosh.

Sloosh hammered on the window and the wall with the great metal axe. He made neither dent nor scratch.

The Shemibob said, "We can look for a door or we can try Phemropit's cutting ray. It might be more polite, and politic, if we try a door."

They agreed that that would be best. First, though, Vana insisted that the vessel be expanded and attached to Phemropit's back. She would put the baby in it and thus be unhampered by him if fast action was needed. The baby would be safer there, too.

They did that, and then they started around The House. This took a very long time, during which they counted one thousand and fifty windows before they got to the one from which they'd started. Sloosh had made a small cairn of rocks to mark this.

"The same number of windows as the number of strokes," Deyv said.

Sloosh's reply to this was inevitable. "Must you always point out the obvious?"

Deyv forbore to mention that they'd found no doors. Or, at least, anything that looked like one.

None of the windows showed anything but darkness and dust. If there were walls beyond, they were too far for The Shemibob's or Phemropit's lights to penetrate.

They went into the vessel to eat. It seemed very cozy there, warm and well lighted, a place to stay for a long time. The baby had awakened and was making small whimperings. Vana nursed him while they talked about what to do next. The Yawtl and the humans, except for Feersh, were all for giving up and getting out of this dreary spooky land at once. The witch was logical about the situation, saying that there was no sense in coming this far just to give up.

The three dissenters looked at each other, their thoughts evident. Logic might get them killed; emotion was rational in this situation.

"This House has been here for a long time," The Shemibob said. "It was here when I came to Earth. Sloosh, do you know when it was built?"

"No. But I do know when it emerged from the

ground. At least, I presume it did. That would be when The Dead Place first came into existence."

"Why didn't you say something about this before?"

"You didn't ask me, and I never thought the time was relevant for bringing the subject up. Now it is."

The Shemibob was more than irritated. Deyv had to grin. So, it wasn't only lowly humans who found the Archkerri maddening.

"Well, when was it?" The Shemibob asked. Under her silvery skin was a bright pink glow.

"You understand that the plants from which I get my data have no sense of time," he said complacently. "It's up to the operator of the prism to work out the chronology from the nature of the data and from various referents and comparisons. Also, for the plants to record something, they have to be where they can *see* and *hear* it. In this case, they didn't record when The House was built. Therefore, they were not present when it was.

"They first recorded its existence at the beginning of the civilization preceding the last two. This was when The House rose along with a part of a sea-bottom. I assume that all three civilizations knew of it, but their records have been lost. Even the traditions about it vanished among the humans and other sentients.

"Actually, the plants didn't directly record The House. They recorded the existence of The Dead Place. They must also have recorded the speech of the civilized peoples when these spoke about The House and The Dead Place in the presence of plants. But that does us Archkerri no good, since we don't know how to interpret any of the languages used.

"The origin of The House and its purpose are mysteries. It's possible that the three civilizations managed to decode the flying figures. But I wouldn't know what they read—if anything. In any event, it's obvious that they never managed to get into The House."

"If the ancients, with all their wisdom and powers, couldn't read the message of the flying figures, then we surely won't be able to," the Yawtl said. "And if they couldn't get into The House, how can we? Also, O Shemibob, you surely have had a chance to study the figures during your long, long life? If you don't know what the figures mean after all that time, how—?"

"Little thief," she said, "there may be a key to the code in The House. If we can't get into The House, then perhaps we can see something through a window which will enlighten us. In any event, we will act as if we will be successful."

"What about you, Archkerri?" Deyv asked. "I know you take your time getting around to investigating certain things. But you've known for a long, long time about this place. Why—?"

"At least fifty expeditions came here. None ever returned."

The Yawtl cried, "Then what are we doing here? Let's get out! Now!"

"And you didn't tell us that either!" Vana said disgustedly.

"There's always a first time," Sloosh said.

The Shemibob told Phemropit to use its cutting ray on the window. The tight beam lanced out and stayed on one spot for a minute. Phemropit turned it off then, saying that it didn't want to use any more energy when doing so was useless. It was right. The window was still whole and unmarred.

"I just had a strange thought," Vana said. She was shivering. "Think of when this building was on the bottom of the ocean, in the black and terrible cold of the waters. Did that great gong ever boom out then? Did its vibrations sound along the mud, disturbing only the weird forms that scuttled there? And how many times?"

"They knew just as much about it as we do," Deyv said. "But they probably had the good sense not to go near it."

The Yawtl urged that they leave immediately. It was obvious that they couldn't get inside, and he was happy about that. Perhaps whatever had eaten up the nosey

Archkerri was sleeping now. But who knew when it might wake up? Especially now, when they were making such an uproar.

The Shemibob said, "Look!"

She pointed upward. They turned to see, against the light in the notch, the first of the flying figures in the sky. After it, in single file, came others, and then the leader was lost in the darkness. Phemropit, at The Shemibob's request, backed up until it came to a slope. It went down this until it was at an angle from which its fan-light fell upon the top of the column. Dimly seen, the first of the figures, a giant ♯, dipped down, shrinking swiftly, and was swallowed. Those behind it also went into the opening. This couldn't be seen by the watchers, but the top of the black column had to be open.

"Unless," Sloosh said, "the figures just evaporate there."

"Hardly likely," The Shemibob said. "But then this is not a likely phenomenon."

"If they can get in, we can," the plant-man said.

"When did we start to grow wings?" the Yawtl growled.

His comment was not far off the mark. The walls went straight up for two hundred feet and then curved out to make a wide overhang. The roof was a squat pyramid, an estimated one hundred feet high. From its tip the column rose for perhaps four hundred feet. It seemed to be about fifty feet in diameter.

"There wouldn't be an opening in it, anyway," Sloosh said. "The rain and dust would get in."

They talked for a long time but could think of no way to enter. Nevertheless, the Archkerri and The Shemibob did not want to give up. Not yet. After checking the supplies, they estimated that there was enough for the return journey plus seven more sleep-times.

The others didn't like the idea of staying in the dismal and frightening place a second longer than necessary. Phemropit's opinion wasn't asked for. It would go along with the majority; one place was as good as another. But then it hadn't heard the mighty clanging.

Thunder growled from the direction in which The Dark Beast came. After a while a strong wind arose, and lightning flashed. The wind became a hurricane. Rain, half-frozen, struck them. They went around The House to the side where the wind would be weaker. They huddled inside the vessel and waited for the storm to pass. Finally, they went to sleep, and when they awoke and opened the door, they found that the elements were still raging.

Moreover, the small valley in which The House stood was in three feet of water. Heavy cataracts were pouring over the edge of the large valley.

The Shemibob got out and struggled against the wind to the front of Phemropit. There she signaled that it should take them out of the small valley. If the water there was getting deeper, Phemropit should go up onto the mountain slope. She came back dripping wet, her porcupinelike hair bending like riverbank reeds after a flood had subsided. She stationed herself by the door, opening it now and then to check on Phemropit's progress. It took a long time to get out of the small valley; the water rose almost as fast as Phemropit did up the slope.

The floor of the big valley was by then three feet under the surface of the boiling flood. Before Phemropit reached the foot of the nearest mountain, it and the vessel it bore were underwater. It slogged on ahead, and presently the tilt of the floor showed that it was on a steep incline. After waiting to make sure they were high enough, The Shemibob opened the door. Phemropit's fan-light revealed a broad and wide ledge of rock a few feet ahead. She got out and directed the creature to go under the ledge. Here they were safe from the direct blast of the howling wind, but the rain pouring down the mountainside curtained the ledge. They were under a waterfall which made invisible anything beyond it.

Another sleep-time came. They ate sparingly, since they couldn't know how long they'd be stuck there. Suddenly, the wind began to die, and the rain stopped. When the cataract had finally thinned to a number of trickles, they looked down the mountain. The clouds were losing their grim blackness, and some of the bright sky behind The Beast was silhouetting the peaks to the left. They still couldn't see well, so they went back into the vessel. In another sleep-time, though, the clouds were gone, and enough of The Beast had passed for them to see the situation.

Far off, the upper part of the roof of The House reared out of the water.

"There's no place for the water to drain out," Sloosh said. "It'll have to evaporate. Meanwhile—"

"We can go in the vessel to The House and get on the roof," The Shemibob said. "Maybe there are windows on it."

The Yawtl and the humans sighed, but they made no useless protests. The Shemibob unglued the vessel from Phemropit's back after it had gone down to the waterline. She took out ten more coils of the very thin and light but very strong rope and glued their ends together. After connecting one end to Phemropit and one to the nose of the vessel, she gave the creature detailed instructions. The door was closed, and the passengers settled down for a long ride.

Now and then the door was opened so they could be sure they were going in the right direction. It was also necessary to make sure that there was enough rope to keep them on the surface. When Phemropit got to the floor of the small valley, there was only about a foot extra. But that was enough.

The creature, following its instructions correctly, stopped when it was alongside The House. Leaving Feersh with the baby and the animals, they climbed up the steeply sloping roof. Halfway between the edge of the roof and the column were windows as large as those at ground level.

They braced themselves around one and looked

within it. Below, illuminated dimly by The Shemibob's device, was a gigantic room. The walls were bare. The floor was covered with dust, and here and there, on pedestals, were what they at first thought were rough columns of rock.

The Shemibob said, "No. They were once statues of granite."

Nobody said anything.

She said, "Don't you realize what that means? Look at them. You can still make out the general shapes. Some were statues of human beings. Others were of bipeds of some kind, and some were of quadrupeds. That one there"—she fixed her light on it—"was a bird. You can see that those projections were once wings."

Sloosh started to buzz but changed his mind.

The Shemibob spoke with a note of exasperation. "Those were statues carved from granite. But they are *eroded*. Yet there have been no winds in there. The air, I'm sure, doesn't even move. Or, if it does, very slowly. And I'll wager that there has been no change of temperature or humidity in there since The House was built.

"But the hard granite has decayed and has eroded as if it had been subject to eons of exposure to sun, wind, sand, and extremes of heat and cold.

"Now can you see how *old* this House is?"

They were awe-struck.

The Shemibob had brought along another device from her bag. She unfolded it into a thing which looked like an egg that had been cut in half and the cut part sealed over with a silvery screen. A tripod folded from the artifact. She put the three legs down against the window with the round end of the egg pointing downward. The discs on the ends of the legs stuck to the transparent material.

She turned a little dial on the side. On the flat end of the device a picture appeared. She adjusted the dial, and the objects in the center of the room became large and bright.

There was a huge block of dark material, the same

unchanging stuff of which The House was made. Twelve steps up it led to a large chair, also of the same material. It had a high back and arms covered with designs. Deyv could not see them clearly because of the angle and also because the arms of the being in the chair partly covered them.

The man sat stiffly, upright, unmoving, staring straight ahead.

Deyv had a creepy feeling that the man was looking into eternity. Perhaps into infinity.

He wore a cap of scarlet edged with white fur. Its long tasseled top lay behind his head against the back of the chair. Under it was a broad round face, red-nosed, red-cheeked, red-lipped. The thick eyebrows were white, as was the long hair flowing from under the cap.

A long and thick white beard fell over a large round paunch to the belt-line. His jacket was scarlet, edged with white fur. His belt was wide and black. His pants were scarlet. His calf-length boots were scarlet with white fur around the tops. On the third finger of his left hand was a simple gold ring.

"It certainly looks lifelike," Sloosh said. "It must be made of the same material as The House, though."

"I am not sure that it's just a statue," The Shemibob said.

Deyv felt like leaving at once. If he'd been alone, he might have. However, if that had been the case, he wouldn't have thought that it might be other than a figure made by the ancients.

"Why do you say that?" Sloosh asked.

"There's no dust on it. Also . . ."

She swung the device so that they could see the floor in front of the block. There were footprints in the dust. They led away from and to the block.

"Let's get away from here!" the Yawtl said.

Nobody replied, but Deyv wondered if the others felt their skin prickling coldly, too.

The Shemibob moved the device so that they could see on its screen the thin slab towering behind the block. This bore a gigantic yellow arrow attached at one end to a knob in the center of the slab. In a circle around the arrow were very small characters evenly spaced. These startled Deyv and added to his unease. They were the same figures as those that flew through the sky. They were in the same order if the character at the top was to be the first and those that followed were read toward the right.

A little to the left and below the top character was a knob. The point of the arrow rested against the knob.

"Aha!" The Shemibob said loudly.

A moment later, Sloosh said, "I know what you mean."

Deyv asked what they were talking about.

"The hand and the figures constitute a *thrigz*," Sloosh said. "Your language doesn't have a word for it. It's a machine to tell the passage of time."

"Be still," the snake-centaur said. "I'm counting."

After a long while, she looked up from the screen.

"One thousand and fifty characters," she said. "Exactly the number of those that have appeared over the Earth since I've been here and probably long, long before that. Exactly the number of strokes we heard. These, I presume, came from the time-teller."

"And the hand has stopped," Sloosh said. "Does that mean that time itself . . . no, that couldn't be."

"Earth's time is done," she said. "Practically done, anyway. What is a few hundred or even a few thousand more circlings of The Beast to the passage of time this instrument has registered?"

"Then," Sloosh said, "when the hand has passed from one figure to the next, twenty-one million years have passed?"

"Approximately."

"And this machine strikes each such passage?"

"I suppose so."

"But why? What is all this about?"

"That is the type of question which the humans sometimes have asked you. And you have told them that the questions are unanswerable. Therefore, foolish."

Sloosh said, "I am justly reprimanded. My apologies."

"We heard the final telling of the time. The flying figures have come home to roost forever."

"Until the new universe is formed," Sloosh said.

Deyv did not understand this. The Shemibob, however, looked as if she comprehended it too well.

"The flying figures," the Yawtl said. "They must have come from someplace in the column. But you'll never be able to open it and see what mechanism makes them, sends them out around the world, pulls them back, shrinks them so they can enter the column. Even if you could, you still wouldn't be able to learn what they mean."

He seemed pleased by this. The Shemibob and the Archkerri might be higher beings, but they too could be mystified. In the presence of this eons-old enigma, they were as helpless as he.

The Shemibob said, "Some of the figures are letters which humans used in their writing from the beginning. That X, that T, that H, and that O, and others have always been used here. They are simple, naturally formed figures, so natural that they've been used on other worlds, including my native planet.

"But many of the characters are unfamiliar to me. And I believe they were unfamiliar to the great civilizations which saw them floating above in the sky when the Earth rotated more swiftly on its axis. They probably had more success than I've had in interpreting the message. It must be a message, a spelling out of Earth's doom and, perhaps, the means for escaping the doom."

Sloosh said, "Perhaps. It would have been better if, instead of letters of some alphabet, the sender of the message had used moving pictures. These could have been understood by anyone."

"That does seem the logical thing to do," she said. "Perhaps the figures were designed as directions to The House. Anybody could follow them to it. In which case, we should be able to see something that will enlighten us."

From somewhere in Deyv's mind a thought seeped out like water that had forced its way up through rock.

"Now I know what you meant when you said that the figures won't go out again until a new universe is formed!" he said. "But . . . if the House and its occupant are waiting until then, wouldn't they—perhaps— have come from an older universe to this one? I mean, couldn't they have survived the death of the universe that existed before ours? They passed unscathed through the fall of all matter and the formation of the giant fireball and its explosion and the formation of this universe? The House is made of something which will outlast the deaths of many worlds!"

Sloosh patted Deyv's shoulder. "Very good. You are learning."

"What nonsense," Hoozisst said. "Why would anyone stay in The House while the Earth was a good place to live in? Surely, that man, if he is a man and not just a statue, would leave The House to enjoy life. What sense is there in sitting frozen on that chair and only rousing, and that not often, to look out the window?"

"We don't know that he does stay in The House," The Shemibob said. "Of course, that would imply a longevity that makes even mine look as short as a mayfly's existence."

The Yawtl snickered.

"Besides, there is no guarantee that The House would be drawn to a planet," Sloosh said. "It might float through space until it falls with all other matter toward a common point."

"Perhaps," The Shemibob said, "it makes no difference to the tenant."

"The point is," Hoozisst said, "is there anything there that will tell us what the flying figures mean?"

The Shemibob sighed and said, "No."

"Then we've wasted our time and put ourselves in danger for nothing."

"You're too practical, too unimaginative," Sloosh said. "This universe wasn't created for the likes of you."

The Yawtl lifted one lip to show some sharp teeth, but he said nothing.

Deyv looked from the screen into the sombre depths below the window. Was the statue really a human being who woke up now and then after an unimaginably long nap? Who then walked through a hall and into a room that held a window and looked through it to see how the world had changed? And then he walked back to the throne and became a statue again?

What woke him up and what put him to sleep again, that is, turned him back into a stuff that nothing could destroy?

Deyv shook his head, and he shivered.

Sloosh said, "I wonder why the hand on the *thrigz* is yellow and the figures are blue?"

The Shemibob gave her flapping laugh. "What is the color of time?"

Sloosh buzzed laughter. "I don't know. What is the angle of a thought?"

"Or the temperature of love?"

"Or the rate of acceleration of instinct?"

"Is a dead ray of light gray or blue?"

They burst out laughing again. This was cut off by a cry from the Yawtl. "His finger moved!"

Startled, all looked at the screen.

After a while, Deyv said, "I think I see it move, too." He wanted desperately to get down off the roof and into the vessel.

The Shemibob said, "No, it didn't. You imagined it. So did Hoozisst."

"It's like watching a corpse and thinking you see its chest rise and fall," Vana said. She didn't sound too certain, however.

They kept on looking at the finger with the gold band. There wasn't a sound. It seemed as if the whole world had died.

Finally, The Shemibob said, "We have less time than I thought. We should go now."

Deyv did not recall ever having heard words that made him as happy.

41 🌿

SEVENTY times The Dark Beast had crossed the glaring skies.

Thrush was walking now and babbling, on the edge of mastering many words and forming short sentences.

Vana had just announced that she was again pregnant. Neither she nor Deyv had given in on the dispute about which tribe they would live with.

Phemropit said that it would soon need more "food." They must look for another source of the ore from which it got its energy. The Shemibob had promised that they would keep an eye out for it. But she confided to the rest that there was not much chance they would find the ore.

This made Deyv sad. Though he found it impossible to love the creature, he did have a certain fondness for it. Moreover, he and the others depended heavily upon it for transportation, meat, and protection. When it expired, they would have a much less comfortable and safe life.

Shortly after this, the Yawtl said that they were getting close to his native village.

"What do you propose to do?" The Shemibob asked. "Take your egg and the Emerald to your home and be a shaman there? Or go on with us to look for the gateway? It would be best if you did both. You might be able to talk your people into coming with us. Then, if we get through the gateway, you and your people will have a new world to settle down in. You might also find new and valuable things to steal."

"If!" Hoozisst said. "I am not one to put much faith in if's. Besides, this gateway probably leads only to some other on this planet. I'd find myself in a worse situation and might never get home."

"Then you will die and your tribe with you."

Deyv thought that if the Yawtl's village was nearby, then so was the place where Feersh had moored her *tharakorm*. And near that was the cave in which she'd hidden his and Vana's eggs. He asked Hoozisst if he would lead them to it.

"What can you give me for this service?" Hoozisst asked.

"Nothing," Deyv said angrily. He hesitated, then said, "Nothing except not cutting your throat. After all, Yawtl, you owe me. If it wasn't for you, I'd not be in this mess."

"Thank him, then," Sloosh said. "If it wasn't for him, you'd not have had all these educational experiences. You'd be a simple savage squatting in the mud, incapable even of dreaming about the wonderful things you've seen. Not to mention having known me."

"I owe you," Hoozisst said, his eyes narrowed. "But it's not what you think."

Later, Deyv told Vana of his conversation.

"But we can find the cave by ourselves."

"Do you really think it's necessary? We have these." She lifted up her soul egg.

"I'm not sure they're true ones. You know what The Shemibob said when I asked her if she'd fixed them so they'd show a phase-in even if we were mismatched."

For some reason, Vana burst into tears and ran away. Deyv figured out why she'd done that a few minutes afterward. He was sorry that he'd hurt her. But the truth had to be faced. Anyway, he wasn't certain that The Shemibob was just teasing him. Look at how stubborn Vana was about his going to her tribe.

Another thing worried Deyv. That was that the baby had no soul egg. Both he and Vana had looked for a soul-egg tree during their journey. Of course, they'd found none, since these were either well protected by their owners within the villages or by the Houses or hidden in the forest. Anyway, even if one had been found, it might not have had a matching egg for Thrush. What if, when they got back to their tribe, whichever it was, no match could be found?

Thrush would be killed. It wasn't so bad to lose a baby before you came to love it. At least, that was what Deyv had been told. But to see a spear thrust into the baby now—that vision was unendurable.

He told Sloosh about this.

"You *are* a savage! Could you do this?"

"What else could I do? I wouldn't like it, I'd be grief-stricken. But that is the ancient way of my people."

"Sometimes," Sloosh said, "I don't know why I bother trying to talk you into going through the gateway."

They ate heavily of a sow that Aejip killed. The Yawtl surprised everybody by insisting on cooking it. He explained that he was in a good mood because his journey was soon to be ended. He wanted to do some service for the others as a slight repayment for what they'd done for him.

Deyv awoke with someone yelling in his ear. He had a bad headache, and his mouth felt as if it had been filled with sand which Aejip had used to bury her excrement. Then Vana was shaking him and shouting that he should wake up.

"Feersh has been killed! Her throat's been cut! And The Shemibob's bag has been stolen!"

Deyv tried to sit up, but his elbow kept slipping. "What? Who?"

"The Yawtl!" Vana said. Her face looked drawn and pale, and her eyelids were heavy. "He did it! He did it! Thank Tirshkel, Thrush is safe!"

Deyv staggered up to find the room in the vessel in an uproar. It took him some time to determine exactly what had happened. Only Vana at first was aware of it. She'd eaten less than the others because she'd had a stomach upset. The drug that the Yawtl had put in the meat had affected her less. She'd awakened first and despite a sluggish feeling had gotten up to check on the baby. He was still sleeping, having eaten some of the drugged meat.

Then Vana had seen Feersh, lying on her back, her mouth open, a bloody slice ringing her neck. So deep had been the incision that the bone of the windpipe showed.

Sometime during the journey, the Yawtl had found in the jungle a plant containing a drug. He'd prepared it in the pork, in what form no one knew. He must have put aside a piece for himself of undoped meat. Everybody recalled seeing him eat; they would have thought it strange if he hadn't.

After all except himself had fallen asleep, he'd killed the witch. And then he'd taken off with the bag and all its treasures except for The Shemibob's flashlight and Emerald of Anticipation. She had kept them by her while she slept.

Why hadn't he just cut everybody's throat? That would have been logical. It would have kept them from pursuing him. Also, he could have dragged their bodies out, though it would have been perhaps too much for him to haul the great weight of the Archkerri and The Shemibob. Then he could also have taken the priceless vessel.

No. That would have been too much for him to transport at the same time as the bag. He could have hidden it, though, and come after it later.

Sloosh's opinion was that Hoozisst had spared them for two reasons. One, though he was often sarcastic about them, he really liked them. Except for the witch, whom he hated because she'd cheated him and tried to murder him. Two, the Yawtl probably wanted to give them a run for the treasure.

"We ran him down once, and that hurt his pride. He's giving us another chance, rather giving himself one, to elude us this time. He'll not only have the bag of treasures but the satisfaction of beating us."

"But," Deyv said, "he knows that you can see his psychic tracks. He can't lose you."

"He can if I get tired and give up. Or if I don't chase him at all."

"He won't be able to return to his village," Vana said, "until you've given up on him."

"Until *we*'ve given up," The Shemibob said. "Which may be never."

They buried the witch, loaded up, and set out. Sometime later, Deyv had a consternating thought. What if the Yawtl went to the cave and took their eggs? It would be just like him; he'd have a good laugh envisioning their faces when they found them gone. He told Vana of this, and she started worrying, too.

Just before sleep-time, there were several mild tremors of the earth. The Shemibob consulted her Emerald and said that a severe shock could be expected soon.

"Maybe," Deyv said. "By the way, your Emerald didn't do any good predicting when Hoozisst would steal your bag."

"It can operate only on the information I give it," she said, looking down at him from under long-lashed silvery eyelids. "It did say that the Yawtl would try to steal the bag—"

"I didn't need the Emerald to know that."

"Don't interrupt me, lesser one. I didn't need it either. Nor did I have to have it tell me that he would be getting ready to steal the bag when he departed from his usual behavior pattern. That departure was his offering to cook our supper. Unfortunately, I was so involved in a philosophical discussion with Sloosh that I failed to take note of his deviation."

"Ah!" Deyv said, grinning. "Then even the greater ones can make errors."

"Don't get smart with me," she said, but she smiled. "As for the Emerald, you mistake its nature. It's not a magical device. It's scientific, and it is only as useful as its operator makes it. It's chiefly valuable for analyzing a large amount of data, which even my mind can't handle. Not so swiftly, anyway."

Not long after lunch, they were shaken by a series of quakes. They would have been thrown to the ground if they hadn't happened to be riding Phemropit. At this place, the highway ran through a narrow valley, and avalanches from both slopes almost reached them. One boulder rolled to within a foot of the stone-metal creature.

They went on, and shortly before suppertime, they came to a very narrow part of the valley. Before them was a pile of rocks, trees, and mud, hurled down by the temblors they'd experienced earlier.

"The quake was even more severe here," Sloosh said. He walked up to the edge of the great tangle and pointed into it.

"Hoozisst's trail ends there."

It took much digging by them and some bulldozing by Phemropit to uncover the Yawtl. He was lying face down under four feet of mud, his arms crossed on his chest. Bone stuck out from one crushed leg, and the right side of his jaw was shattered.

Though they dug here and there for the bag, they failed to find it.

"It's no use," The Shemibob said. "We could work here for a long, long time and still not find it. And yet . . . I could be standing right above it now."

She finally decided that they would have to go on without the bag.

"Hoozisst didn't mean to do us a service, but he did. If we hadn't been slowed up by having to recover from the effects of the drug and to bury the witch, we would have been here. And we'd have been killed, too. It wasn't such a bad trade, my treasures for our lives."

After covering the Yawtl again, they pushed on over the rubble. This extended for about a mile, and then they were back on the highway. Phemropit rayed a deer, which was a quarter of a mile ahead of them, and they dined. It began to rain heavily then, so they went into the vessel. While they slept, Phemropit rolled ahead on the highway.

Deyv was awakened by Vana.

"What's the matter?" he mumbled.

"Phemropit has stopped."

They opened the door and looked out cautiously. Seeing nothing alarming, they got down and went in front of the creature. The Shemibob signaled, "What is wrong?"

"I'm almost out of food. If I keep moving I'll use it all up. I must now do what you call going to sleep. Unless you can find more ore for me."

"I'll be frank with you," The Shemibob said. "There is very little chance that we can locate the ore."

"Then I'll have to shut down. That is too bad. I have enjoyed being on this strange world and knowing you. I've also learned much. If it hadn't been for you and the others, I would have been very lonely. As it is, I've learned new concepts, things which I would never have known if I'd been on my world. So, thank you and good-bye."

"Wait!" she signaled. "I'm sure the others would like to make their farewells."

That didn't take long. One by one they flashed a few words. And then Phemropit's light-hole became dark.

Vana wept and patted the hard nose. Deyv had not felt much sorrow, just regret that their mighty transporter and protector was no longer available. Vana's tears, however, evoked some sorrow from him.

They put the folded vessel on Sloosh's back and seated the baby by it. Deyv didn't look back until he was a quarter of a mile down the road. The huge dark creature was motionless, waiting. No one would come to help it, though. It would sit there until some cataclysm dislodged it or buried it. Now and then it would rouse from its "sleep," stirred by some mechanism which Deyv did not understand, and it would "look" for salvation from some passer-by. It would never get it.

Vana, who'd also turned to look, said, "We've lost three of our party in a very short time. Do you think that omens ill for all of us?"

"I was trying not to think about that," he said.

Ten sleep-times later, they came to a junction. Sloosh called them to a halt.

"This is where we part. That is, if you insist on looking for your soul eggs. That road will take you into the area of Hoozisst's village and the cave. But you may never find the cave. As for The Shemibob and me, we'll keep on. Now that she no longer has her detector-sphere, we will have a hard time finding the gateway. But we'll succeed."

Deyv felt desolate and lonely. He would miss the two very much, not only for their protection but for their companionship and their knowledge. Also, he and Vana would have to take turns carrying the baby. And they'd no longer have the vessel to take refuge in.

Vana's face showed that she was thinking the same thoughts.

"If the Yawtl had stolen our eggs, there'd be no doubt about what we'd do," she said slowly. "But—"

"That's true," Deyv said. "So . . ."

They looked at each other, and Deyv said, "We'll go with you!"

The Shemibob, fingering her Emerald, said, "I thought so. This stone predicted that you would. But I really didn't have to consult it."

Deyv didn't like I-told-you-so's, even from one of the higher beings. He was too happy about the decision to resent The Shemibob very long, however. The only shadow in his joy was the thought that this was only putting off the inevitable. When they got near their homeland, they'd have to make up their minds again. No, they wouldn't. There couldn't be any doubt that they would have to say good-bye then.

Or was there?

42

"THERE it is," The Shemibob said. "The gateway." Sloosh did not comment that that was an obvious remark. He never said that to her, though he was quick enough to say it when a human uttered one.

They were in a thick part of the jungle, halfway up a high hill. Here, perhaps a hundred feet above and close to a thick branch of a giant tree, was the swelling, shrinking, dazzling bright and dread-making circle. They had located it after much questioning of many tribes in a wide area. These would not have given answers to the two humans if they'd been alone. These would have, instead, killed them. But the Archkerri and The Shemibob frightened them. The tribes thought they were either gods or démons, and they usually ran when they saw the two. Then the strangers would just stay in the village or House until the tribespeople decided that perhaps the two terrible beings were not intent on destroying their homes. Seeing that the three humans associated on familiar terms with these creatures also helped reassure them.

One or two of the braver would venture timidly near them. The Shemibob and Sloosh would make signs of peace, and eventually most of the tribe would straggle in. The snake-centaur would draw a picture of the gateway in the mud and would try, through sign language, to make them understand what she was seeking. For a long time, the tribespeople didn't comprehend her.

But the twelfth folk they came to spoke a tongue related to Vana's. Though it was only half-intelligible to her, she could still get enough of a message across. These directed them to a tribe which had once lived near the gateway. The tribe had come to the Place of the Trading Season, where, through the Trade Language, its members told of the shining horror. To this tribe went the five travelers, where they learned enough of the trade tongue to ask their questions and be answered.

Their informants were not aware of the exact location of the gateway. They could give a general direction and a vague estimate of the distance to it. Having learned this, Sloosh used his prism to communicate with the plants. After a long, long time, from breakfast almost till supper, the Archkerri got the location. This was not exact, but as they traveled Sloosh kept using the prism. The closer they got, the better their information became. Two sleep-times before they got there, he had pinpointed it.

Vana, after one glance upward, had kept her eyes on the ground. Her belly was huge now. The baby would come in a little over twelve and a half circuits of The Dark Beast.

"Now that we've found it," she said, "what do you two intend to do?"

Sloosh said, "When my people get here, I'll go through the gateway with them. Of course, some won't want to stop their particular researches and so won't come now. Or perhaps not at all."

"I will stay here to help him build a bridge to the gateway," The Shemibob said.

"Then we'll stay awhile and rest up," Deyv said.

The Shemibob smiled knowingly. "You might as well delay the inevitable. It couldn't hurt."

Deyv didn't reply. He helped Vana untie the cube and take it down from Sloosh's back. The Archkerri picked it up and went down to the foot of the hill. A swamp surrounded the hill, a foul place stinking from many sources, choked with plants of many kinds, buzzing with bugs, croaking with froggish monsters, dangerous with poisonous things, insectile, reptilian, and mammalian. Sloosh would have preferred to expand the cube at a higher place, but the only flat ground was by the water.

The three humans went with him. Vana wanted to put the baby in the vessel for a nap, where it would be undisturbed by the insects. Sloosh pulled the rod. The craft unfolded slowly. Too slowly, according to Sloosh.

"It's a good thing the journey's ended. The power supply is about exhausted."

He looked at the vessel. "Too bad, though. The Shemibob and I have been tracing its circuits. We think we know what controls start its propelling power. We're afraid, however, to activate it. There's no telling what might happen. Still—"

"I want to be a long way off if you decide to experiment," Deyv said.

After making sure the baby was comfortable, Deyv called Aejip and Jum. He told Vana that he was going hunting, and he waded through the green-coated water and black mud toward higher ground. Much later he was far from the home base, still unsuccessful in getting game. He was stalking a large bird with bronze-colored feathers, a white-edged fantail, and a red bag hanging from its neck when he heard voices. He froze, along with the two animals.

The speakers came nearer, talking softly, but they were near enough so that he could determine that their language was unfamiliar. Or was it? Didn't it sound somewhat like Vana's?

Unable to suppress his curiosity, he snaked through the foliage. Aejip and Jum followed him. He stopped when he saw a trail before him. Going away from him were two men, tall, skins a little darker than his wife's but with kinky hair like hers, though brown instead of yellow. They wore bark-cloth kilts and carried the standard weapons of jungle dwellers everywhere: blowguns, flint or chert tomahawks, knives, and spears. Their legs were painted black to just above the knees, and their spines were colored with red.

They stopped to talk about something before they came to a bend. They turned toward him a moment. Their eyes were slanted. No. Not really slanted. That impression was caused by a fold of flesh in the inner side of their eyelids. Their noses were blobs, quite unlike his beautiful long curving nose. Their lips were very thin and a blue band was painted below the lower one. The nipples were encircled with red. Radiating from each side of these were two seven-pointed stars.

One carried over his shoulder the same kind of bird Deyv had been hoping to kill.

He decided that they were returning home from the hunt. He waited until they had gone around the bend before following them. It was necessary to know where the enemy lived and how many there were. Also, how well defended they were and the degree of their aggressiveness. He didn't have to show himself to find out the latter two features. His long experience had given him some ability to discern these just by watching people in their daily routine.

The trail led to a lower ground, where there was a small swamp. The men ahead waded through it as if they knew that it wasn't dangerous. Deyv saw a gliding animal, its hundred ribs spread out to make the thin air act like thick water. It swooped over the heads of the two men, but they paid it no visible attention. The creature curved upward near Deyv and landed on a branch of a tree. Seeing Deyv, it turned its triangular head downward and made a clattering sound. Though its body was snakelike, it had sleek bluish fur and greenish eyelids. Deyv ignored it, since the men must know what was dangerous.

His animals growled very softly and sidled by, their eyes intent on it until it was well past.

Deyv, equally softly, said, "Calm down, Jum, Aejip. It doesn't mean ill to you."

Presently, the two men came to a hill and climbed up its steep slope. This was naked of trees, having been cleared long ago. It had also been planted with some tall pod-bearing vegetable which didn't require terracing. The trail led up the hill and onto a small plateau in the center of which was a stockaded village.

Deyv couldn't follow beyond the swamp, but he climbed a very tall tree whose top was level with that of the hill. Beyond the wall of thick logs he could see the roofs of some conical huts on the far side.

Unable to see more than a few of the villagers, he started to climb down. He stopped when a giant rodent emerged from the swamp and began to eat the plants on its edge. It was furred in black except for its ears, which were red. Its body was thick with fat, and it looked as if it would be two feet higher than he if it was to stand up on its two legs.

Unnoticed for some time, it devoured plants, blue stalks and white heads and green pods. Then a boy on a high observation tower of wood began yelling. In a short time the men, followed by women and children, raced down the trail. Deyv didn't know if the entire population was there, but he counted two hundred and twenty. He felt an irrelevant sense of pride that he could now do this. Sloosh had taught him well.

The beast had stopped eating when the first wave of warriors poured down the hill. It regarded the yelling, spear-brandishing figures for a moment before turning to amble off through the swamp. About thirty men waded after it, some throwing their spears. Most of these missed; those that hit bounced off. Several blow-gun darts struck and also failed to stick.

Deyv looked through the now open gate. Directly in his line of sight was a man-sized idol, a thing with a fierce scowling face, two long tusks sticking upward from the lower jaw, four arms, and an enormous belly. The face was human enough, but the upper part of the head was shaped into something birdlike, a creature with half-opened wings and a tremendous beak.

On the other side of the hill was a tree even taller than the one on which he stood. He climbed down and worked his way around through the swamp, Jum and Aejip following. They waited at its base while he climbed this, though they didn't like standing in water up to their shoulders. When he got near to the top, Deyv found that he could see the whole village. It was arranged like most such places, with a shaman's house in the center. There were, however, large wooden tanks containing water. He supposed that these were reserves to be used if an enemy besieged them. There were also many roofed bins containing the pods.

In one corner was a soul-egg tree.

This explained why the tribe had located in such an inconvenient place. Rather than live in an advantageous site and make sure that their precious tree was well hidden, they'd chosen to erect houses and a stockade around it.

By then the hunters and plant gatherers and fruit gatherers were coming in. He made another count, getting two hundred and fifty.

The cooking began. The shaman came out of his house bearing a wooden table at each end of which were affixed small reproductions of the idol. He set the table down before the god. After a dance the villagers swarmed around it, throwing pieces of cooked meat and fruit on the table. The shaman danced again around the table, apparently blessing the food or making an offering of it to the god. A hare was brought out of a cage. The shaman cut its throat and carried it by its legs over the food, its blood dripping over it.

After this, the shaman ate a piece of the bloodied meat, and the villagers, in a single file, came around the table. The adult males ate the meat, and the women and children the fruit. After that they departed for their own huts and supper.

Deyv left. He got lost once but found his way after some searching and after a long while was back at the vessel. The others were relieved to see him; they'd been afraid that something bad had happened. He told them his story while he ate.

"I doubt they'll come around here," Sloosh said. "They must know about the gateway, but they'd be afraid of it. This place is probably taboo."

After breakfast, they set to work to build the bridge to the gateway. Deyv climbed up to the branch by the abomination and let down the rope of The Shemibob to haul up bamboo logs. As long as he kept his back to the shimmering, he could work. But when he accidentally glimpsed it, he had to stop until his fear and nausea passed.

They didn't have many flint tools with which to cut the bamboo. However, Deyv's sword and the Yawtl's, which they'd taken from his body, and Sloosh's axe could hack wood all day without the edges becoming dulled. Eventually, they had a structure from the ground to the branch above that near the gateway. This enclosed a lift. A pulley arrangement on roughly carved wheels and spindles allowed them to haul themselves up, though only one at a time.

The Shemibob did most of the work building the bridge out to the gateway. She was better able to withstand the effects than the others.

"A good solid engineering tool," Sloosh said. "Now, if only an earthquake doesn't shake it down."

He and the snake-centaur went up with poles and probed the shimmering. They lost some poles, though they were aware that they could not withdraw them the tiniest bit without their being severed.

When they came back down, The Shemibob said, "There's a solid floor about fifteen feet below the gateway. It's probably earth or sand. We could push the poles in an inch or so after they met resistance. We don't know, of course, how far the floor extends in any direction."

"Also, of course," Sloosh said, "we can't know how hot or cold it is there. It might be on top of a mountain from which it'll be impossible to climb down. Or it might be a very small island far away from a large land mass and without any wood with which to build a boat. Or it might be snow on top of an ice pack. If it's a very young planet, the air might be poisonous. Then—"

"Shut up!" Deyv said.

"Why are you so fearful?" the plant-man asked. "You're not going there." He paused, then said, "Or is it possible that you do have some faint desire to get out of this doomed world?"

"None at all," Deyv said. He wasn't sure that he wasn't lying, though.

During sleep-time, Deyv's grandmother came to him out of the dark mists of his dream.

Deyv said, "It is pleasant to see you again, Grandmother. You haven't visited me for a long time."

"It's not for pleasure that I come to you," she said.

"The dead have no pleasure. I have come to help you with your problem. You want to take Vana to your tribe as your wife, and she wants to take you to hers as her husband. You are both very stubborn. Neither will give in. You won't even accept the sensible suggestion of the plant-man that you throw a pointed stick up in the air and let its fall decide which path to take.

"So I have come to tell you what you must do. The dead have no pleasure, but they do have wisdom. You must obey me."

"I will do what you say, Grandmother," Deyv said. "Only . . . I hope that you remember that I am of your flesh and blood, of your tribe, and that you favor me."

"Vana has borne a child which is of my flesh, and she will soon bear another. I can't favor you over her. Here is what you must do to satisfy yourself and her. Also, to save your people and hers."

He woke Vana after his grandmother had floated backward into the mists. He insisted they they go into another room of the vessel, where their talking would not disturb anybody. There he told her of his dream.

"So, you see that she has found the solution. We will tell our tribes that there is a way out from the death that grows closer with each circuit of The Dark Beast. We will tell them that our two tribes must become one. That way, we have no troublesome dispute, and we save our people and our children for generations to come. We will lead them here and pass through to a better world."

"You're crazy!" Vana said. "They would never listen to us!"

Sloosh, hearing about this during breakfast, had a similar reaction. After thinking about it for some time, though, he said that perhaps the idea wasn't so bad after all.

"You two alone cannot convince your peoples. But if you were to be accompanied by The Shemibob and myself, you might do it. We would give you the authority you'll need. They'll be awed by us, and whereas your testimony that the world will soon be unsafe for life would mean nothing, ours will."

"Why should you do that? It'll be a long, hard, and dangerous journey."

"I have nothing else to do except wait for my people. In fact, I don't even have to do that. They're capable of going through the gateway without my aid. However, I do plan on trying to get the locals to go through it, too."

"I still don't understand," Vana said. "Why are you so intent on saving humans? They're a danger to you here. And if they go to that other world, they will be dangerous there. They might even try to exterminate the Archkerri."

"True. I'm acting on something you don't understand because you're a tribal creature. I have a much broader and more humane attitude. Humans are sentients. Therefore, however inferior they may be to us Archkerri, they are still our brothers. I will try to save even the Yawtl people if I get a chance.

"Also, let's say that I'm paying a debt. It was the humans who made us vegetable-sentients. It was done when humans had a great civilization and were, in many ways, as wise and humane as we. If it hadn't been for them, we would never have existed. So . . . I'm acting out of gratitude. Can you understand that?"

"No," Deyv said. "But I'm glad that you feel that way."

"I will teach you and your kind how to feel as I do."

43

THE first step in the journey was not the packing. Sloosh said he must find the location of their two tribes. From the information collected from his plant-people, he would make a simple map. This would be in mud, since he had no papyrus. But the Archkerri only had to look at it once to have it fixed in his mind.

The process would take at least five sleep-times and possibly extend to eight. He went to work at once. In the meantime, Deyv, The Shemibob, and the two animals left to spy on the local tribe. The Beast was again covering the sky, making conditions more favorable for them to escape detection. They got rather close to the village during the sleep-time, halfway up the hill before a sharp-eyed sentinel saw them. His alarm brought the warriors racing from the gate. By then the two had gotten safely into the swamp.

Deyv, The Shemibob, and the animals returned much later. This time, they witnessed a raid on the pod-plants by seven adults and six young of the giant red-eared rodents. The awakened warriors charged the invaders, but on this occasion the beasts fought them. Two of the creatures were killed with spear thrusts through the eyes, and the others lumbered off. The price for the tribe's victory was high: four men killed, six mauled badly.

A severe quake struck as the casualties were being carried back up the hill. Deyv didn't see what happened after that. He was too busy running through the water to escape a falling tree. The mud and the water heaved up under him, throwing him headlong several times. He did escape the falling giant narrowly. The Shemibob picked him up and carried him for some distance before setting him down. The two animals, half-drowned and thoroughly frightened, found them a little later.

The party got back to camp to find things in a mess. Trees had been uprooted or tilted here, too. The bamboo lift and bridge had been shaken apart. A mud slide had buried the front part of the vessel, though it had not quite reached the door.

After Deyv had made sure that Vana and the baby were all right, he was taken aside by Sloosh.

"I'm afraid I have bad news for you. I can't find either of your tribes."

Deyv had had enough shocks for the time being. He didn't understand what the plant-man was talking about.

"You mean your plants have failed you? Did the quake shake them up?"

"No," Sloosh said. He sounded angry. Deyv knew then that Sloosh didn't like what he had to report. It took much to upset him.

"What I mean is that your people and Vana's have, for some reason, left their area. Not only that. The other tribes there have also gone."

Deyv felt sick. He asked slowly, hesitatingly, "Are you sure?"

"You understand that getting data from the plants is not an easy business. It takes time, patience, and much skill in requesting and interpreting. The mindless plants can only report what they've recorded. But I *am* fairly sure. I covered a large area, which is why I took even longer than I'd expected.

"As to why they deserted, I can't say. The quakes, however, have been even stronger there than in any area we've traveled in. Perhaps that is why they left. They wanted to go to a more stable place. They won't find any. Not for long, anyway."

"Could you track them down?"

"Not unless I knew their general area. You see, the plants record visual and aural data only. But they don't *see* with eyes or *hear* with ears. Nor would any data which could identify the individuals of the tribes mean anything to the plants. That data would be mixed in with everything else recorded. I'd have to have at least the general area in which the tribes were before I could start my questioning. Then I'd have to sort out the nonrelevant data. All this would take much time and work. As it is, the task is almost hopeless.

"In addition, the quakes are disturbing my informants. They're subject to a lot of what I call noise. It's analogous to static, though it's not at all the same.

Transmission of data has been getting more difficult. It's going to be worse. That's because the quakes will increase in frequency and severity. The matter in space is becoming more dense. As the density increases, the effect puts more stress on this planet. The Shemibob told me that there are twenty dead stars which are within—I told you what a light-year is?"

Deyv nodded and said, "Yes. A light-year is the time it takes light to travel in—"

"It was a rhetorical question. I know I told you. Anyway, these are within half a light-year of Earth. They are forerunners of The Dark Beast, and behind them, only a light-year away, are ten. And behind them, only two light-years away, is a horde. And behind them is the main bulk of The Dark Beast."

The leaved face and the beak, restricted to a buzz, were not perhaps as capable of modulation of expression as the human face and voice. But Sloosh was certainly communicating his agitation. Deyv reverberated to it. He felt that doom was falling swiftly upon him. It was invisible, but its near presence was heavy.

"Consider this," Sloosh said. "It was good that you delayed your journey. Otherwise, you two would have gotten to your homeland only to find your people gone. You wouldn't have had the slightest idea how to track them down. If you'd returned here, you might have been too late. The gateway might have been gone or have winked out. Or it might have shifted so much that it would have been unreachable."

Deyv sank to his knees and began howling. His tribe, his parents, forever lost!

After he'd given his tears to the wetness of the earth, so many that he had no more—at the moment—he lay face down, silent. Then Sloosh's huge half-leaved hand lifted him up onto his feet.

"Vana is still quivering from the quake. She was very concerned about her baby and also the life within her belly. I wouldn't say anything about this until she's recovered."

Deyv rubbed the tears from his eyes and said, "I'd

have gone to her now and told her. But I'll wait, do as you say. You're very perceptive, Sloosh. Almost human."

"I suppose you think that's a compliment. So I'll accept it as such. Still . . ."

Deyv had hoped to delay telling Vana until she'd had a good sleep. He was unable to conceal his sorrow, though he didn't say anything about it and tried to act as if nothing unusual had happened. It was no use. Vana knew immediately that he was very upset about something. He denied it, but she attacked him with many questions and finally told him that he was lying to her. She didn't like it; they were married, his concerns were hers and vice versa. If he didn't tell the truth, he was a *shrinkell*, a small dung-eating beast which emitted an offensive odor.

Deyv told her what troubled him. She turned pale and began to cry out and staggered off to get a knife to gash her flesh. He followed her to take the knife away from her.

"You'll frighten the baby," he said. "Go off somewhere until you are over your grief."

Her tears had started him weeping also. Thrush, hearing his mother, began to howl. Deyv went into the vessel to soothe him while Vana went up the hill and crouched behind a tree. After a while, she came back with red but now dry eyes.

"What do we do now?"

"Sloosh says that we could try to get adopted by the tribe near here. He has more in mind than our well-being, though. He hopes to get them to go through the gateway. But he says that they aren't numerous enough to provide the minimum needed to avoid the bad effects of inbreeding. He wants to find other tribes and get them to go through, too."

"It would be nice to have a tribe," she said, "even if they have strange ways and a strange god. But they're more likely to kill us than to take us in."

"I have an idea that might work. If it does, they'll be happy to adopt us."

In the meantime, they had to rebuild the lift and

the bridge. Deyv found time to scout around the area when he wasn't building or hunting. He located two more tribes, each about ten miles from the hill-people in opposite directions. Both lived alongside a river, a tributary of which fed the swamp. They were of the same race as the swamp dwellers and spoke dialects of the same language. They also suffered from the depredations of the red-eared rodents.

Failing to learn enough of the swamp dwellers' tongue by eavesdropping, he decided to kidnap an informant. He and The Shemibob hung around the hill at a discreet distance until a woman carrying a big basket of nuts came along. He shot her with a dart whose point was coated with an anesthetic. The Shemibob picked her up; Deyv took the basket, which had spilled only half its contents.

Vana tried to reassure the woman that she would not be harmed. It did no good. She was terrified by Sloosh and the snake-centaur, whom she was convinced were beasts or demons, or what she called dream monsters. Vana, by far the most linguistically competent, quickly learned the tribe's language. After a while she was able to soothe the woman's fears somewhat. When she allowed the woman to take care of Thrush, she gained more of her confidence.

Be'nyar said that her tribe called itself the Chaufi'ng, that is, The People. The idol was not a god but a representation of the founding ancestor of her tribe, Tsi'kzheep. She had no concept of gods. To her there were only elemental forces, some good, some evil, some indifferent. The world had been created by a bird, the Ngingzhkroob. Rather, the bird had laid a primal egg from which most living things had been hatched, including Tsi'kzheep.

And when would they let her go?

Soon, Vana promised. She also told the woman that the world would soon be destroyed. But the tribes nearby could go through the gateway to a young world and so be saved.

Be'nyar trembled and said that the shimmering thing

was an evil force. It was taboo—as Sloosh had guessed—and her people would never enter its mouth. They'd be committing suicide, be eaten up in the force's belly.

Vana told Be'nyar that that wasn't true. She had gone through just such a shimmering and had not been harmed. Be'nyar listened to her story of the transit politely—she had to—but it was evident that she thought Vana was lying.

Deyv, listening to the dialog, learned that the Chaufi'ng believed that as long as the statue of Tsi'kzheep was in their possession and intact, they would be able to defend themselves successfully against their enemies and prosperity would be theirs.

He told Vana to tell the woman that Tsi'kzheep hadn't been doing very well against the red-ears.

Be'nyar replied indignantly that Tsi'kzheep could get rid of them instantly if he cared to. But he had been offended by something the tribe had done. It wasn't known yet just what that was, but the shaman was trying to find out.

Deyv decided to try speaking her language. It was the only way he'd ever become fluent in it.

"If we kill the red-ears, will your people then regard us as friends?"

He had to repeat himself slowly for her to understand him.

She said, "I don't know. Perhaps Tsi'kzheep would be insulted. Then again he might not be. You'd have to ask the shaman."

Further questioning revealed that the Trading Season would start after the next circuit of The Dark Beast was over. There were six tribes which met at the trading place. It was the Chaufi'ng's turn to host the meeting. There was no trade pidgin all could speak. Instead, a sign language was used.

Deyv groaned. Another language to learn! But it had to be done if he was to carry out his suddenly conceived plan.

He called the others aside and told them what his idea was.

The Shemibob said, "It might work. One should not fight the superstitions of a people but use them to get what one wants. Usually that's done out of an evil or selfish motive. In this case, it'll be for good."

The following sleep-time Vana awoke them with the beginning of birth pangs. To enforce the feeling that they did not intend to harm Be'nyar, she was allowed to assist in the delivery. A beautiful girl was born. Everybody was happy but Thrush. Shortly after the infant had been cleaned, her parents took her up the hill and gave her her secret name. Her public name was Keem.

Deyv went out with The Shemibob, Sloosh, and Jum to hunt down the lair of the red-ears. He took with him Be'nyar's soul egg to make sure that she wouldn't try to run away while the four were gone. It wasn't likely that she'd try anything, since Aejip was keeping an eye on her. However, Deyv believed in taking no chances with her.

They came back without finding any red-ears. The next trip, they saw one gnawing through the trunk of a small tree. It picked up the log after stripping off the branches and carried it a quarter of a mile to a giant tangle of tree trunks. Since the area around it was stripped except for the stumps, its followers had no place to conceal themselves. They stayed far behind the beast, and if it saw them, it was paying them no attention.

The tangle turned out to be both food and a home for the beasts. Its triangular entrances were formed of logs which opened into triangular tunnels. These were both at ground level and halfway up. The hunters counted twenty of the red-ears after a long observation. From time to time, some left and others came in. The latter not only bore logs in their mouths but also carried nuts, fruits, and pods in a skin fold on their bellies.

The woman Be'nyar had said the beasts were totem animals and could not be attacked except when they intruded upon the personal territory of Tsi'kzheep, which was the hill on which the tribe lived, and the swamp immediately around it. However, since the red-ear was not the totem of Deyv's party, they could slay the beast without fear of reprisal from the Chaufi'ng. Just how they could do that, the woman did not know. The red-ear's only vulnerable spots were the eyes and the anus. The creature seldom lifted its protecting tail when in combat.

It had, however, not encountered sentients with such brute strength as The Shemibob and the Archkerri.

Deyv ran up to the nearest beast, which had been placidly chewing on chunks of wood ripped from a log. It dropped its food, reared up on its hind legs, roared, dropped down to all fours, and charged. Deyv turned and sped away. Though the animal was huge and clumsy-looking, it was, according to The Shemibob's calls, gaining on him. Deyv decided to put more distance the next time between him and a red-ear before the chase began.

He ran between the two giants, who had been standing motionless, their huge clubs lifted. As hoped, the red-ear was intent only on Deyv. Its eyesight didn't seem too good, and it might have mistaken the two for stumps or rocks. Whatever it thought about them, it paid them no attention. As it came between the two, they brought down their bludgeons simultaneously, striking it on top of its head. It went down without a sound, lay quivering for a few seconds, then, growling, started to get up. The clubs broke its spine just behind the head.

Deyv got his wind back before going out to lure another. Another victim fell, while those around the tangle moved uneasily, growling or whimpering. A third died. But the fourth time what Deyv hoped would not happen did. Two beasts thundered after him at the same time. He didn't have to shout at his coworkers to move out. They were ready, each striking a red-ear. These fell to the ground but got up very quickly. Apparently, it took two clubs striking together to make a great impression on those thick skulls.

Sloosh and the snake-centaur brought their clubs down on their targets, once, twice, thrice. Blood poured out from the open mouths of the red-ears. A fourth stroke by each clubber snapped the spines.

When the sixth red-ear started after him, Deyv ran a few steps, then wheeled. A poisoned dart sped from his blowgun into its gaping mouth and embedded itself in its tongue. The point was coated with six layers, five more than he'd have used for a man. Even so, the beast had only slowed down a little by the time it came between its executioners. There was, however, no need to hit more than once. It couldn't get up, and presently it died in convulsions.

The seventh died in the same manner.

On the eighth run, *three* red-ears lumbered after him. The Shemibob sent Jum out to distract them. Jum had obeyed orders to stay back, though he had whined with eagerness. Now he raced up to one animal and caused it to rear up on its hind legs. But another grabbed him and tore him apart.

Deyv did not know what was happening until he heard Jum's yelp. He glanced over his shoulder. Though he had little breath to spare, he yelled with horror. There was nothing he could do. The dog was dead, and the lead beast was too close. It perished from poison and the clubs. The others were close behind it; both tumbled on the earth, one going head over paws. Deyv had to run to Sloosh's rescue. His intended victim had apparently suffered only a glancing blow. Deyv snatched up his spear, which had been left sticking upright in the earth, and he drove it through the eye into the brain.

Then he burst into grief. Jum was a member of the family, his furry brother.

Nevertheless, the bloody work had to continue. After it was over he buried Jum deeply, and he sent up a prayer that his spirit would be waiting for his master in the world which the shaman had promised was waiting for both of them.

"I am sorry indeed," Sloosh said. "But he did save

you, and perhaps all of us. We couldn't have handled three at once. At least, I don't think so."

It was necessary to go into the tangle itself and seek out any red-ears that were hiding there. They lit torches and went into the dark stinking place. Now was when they most needed Jum, who could have smelled out any lurker ahead of them. However, they found only some small cubs, which they quickly dispatched.

They made two fiber nets and hauled the heads in them. Long before they got to the camp, they heard the keening of a woman in mourning. Deyv ran, thinking that this was indeed an evil day. One of the babies had to be dead. He arrived panting and covered with swamp mud. Vana was sitting outside the vessel, holding Thrush in her arms, rocking back and forth. His face was twisted, as if the agony of dying had been incised, and his left arm was swollen and greenish.

Nearby was Aejip, also dead, her mouth still gripping a tiny green snake with a scarlet head, the fangs locked deep into its flesh. Her eyes were open and glazed; her nose was expanded to twice its normal size from the venom.

Vana screamed, "I didn't even see the snake until it had struck! Thrush had picked it up and was bringing it to me to look at! Aejip grabbed it from his hand, but it was too late! It bit Thrush, and he died almost immediately!"

The woman captive said, "It must have come out of the water."

After they had buried the baby and Aejip and mourned for the prescribed time and in the prescribed manner, though this did not ease them of all their grief, they returned to their routine activities. But Vana kept saying, "The woman Be'nyar was right. This is an evil place. We shouldn't have come here."

"Any place is bad where bad things happen," he said. "And bad things can happen anywhere. Come, woman, let us get to work. We must get Keem to a world where perhaps there are not so many bad things."

He didn't believe that. But at least that other world might not be falling apart.

44

"THE next time we unfold the vessel," Sloosh said, "we should perhaps leave it that way. It expanded even more slowly than the last time. There may be enough power left for a dozen more times, I don't know. But I don't want to take the chance."

A round plate on the control room panel had been glowing red for some time. Sloosh said that this must be a warning that the fuel was about to give out. Not that he needed that indication.

They packed up, and all moved out. Coming near the hill, they heard a mighty hubbub, the chatter of the tribes gathered for the Trading Season, the music provided by their hosts, the bleats and squawks and chirpings of goats and birds brought in for the event. An odor of cooking drifted down the slope toward them. Deyv felt nostalgia for the Seasons when he had attended such occasions. Tears ran down his cheeks as he thought of his people. He would never see them again.

Vana, too, was weeping.

From behind the trees they saw that the pod-plants had been reaped. Where they had grown were the lean-tos of the visitors, with women preparing food, children running around playing, and men sitting around gossiping or bargaining.

"It seems a shame to disturb such a harmonious scene," Sloosh said. "Imagine that! Six different groups of humans in one place, and they're not fighting!"

"The stockade logs were disarranged by the last quake," The Shemibob said. "They're still setting up some."

As if this remark had caused another temblor, and Deyv wasn't sure that it hadn't, the ground began to shake. Those on the hill fell silent; the beat of drums and the shrilling of noseflutes stopped. The animals and birds ceased their racket, causing Deyv to wonder why they had not been hushed before this. Animals were supposed to be very sensitive to the quakes, detecting them long before they became evident to humans. But then Jum and Aejip, who'd long behaved strangely when a temblor was coming, had lately been as surprised as their master. He hadn't thought anything of that until just now. Maybe they were getting used to the shakes.

This one was a minor quivering of the earth for a few seconds. After a few minutes, the crowd resumed their noisy activity, and the animals and birds took up their own uproar.

"Here comes the second shock," Sloosh said, referring to the anticipated reception their appearance would get.

Dragging a net full of red-ear heads, Sloosh stepped out from behind a tree and waded through the water. The Shemibob came next, also hauling a net and Deyv on her back. He'd decided at the last moment he'd ride her. He was to act as intermediary, and despite his reluctance to mount a higher being, he could gain more authority if he appeared to be controlling the snake-centaur.

Vana came last, carrying the baby in one arm, a spear in the other hand prodding the captive ahead of her.

They were sighted almost immediately. Shrieks and yells went up, and there was a frenzied scramble to get back up the hill. By the time the strangers had reached the foot of the hill, it was deserted. The gate swung shut on the last of the stampeding refugees. Faces appeared over the stockage, and the observation tower swarmed with frightened men.

The intruders reached the plateau on which the village stood. Sloosh opened his net and hauled out the heads. A concerted cry of wonder rose from the onlookers. The plant-man began to hurl the heads over the gate.

Waving his spear, Deyv shouted, "Here are the gifts we bring you! You will be attacked by the red-ears no more! Your plants and your warriors are safe from them! We have slain them for you to show our friendship!"

Having finished dispensing his load, Sloosh emptied The Shemibob's net onto the ground.

"Come out and get these!" Deyv shouted. "Each tribe can have its own trophies! You may put them up on poles to remind you how the mighty Deyv and his friends, The Shemibob and the Archkerri—and his mighty wife," he added, knowing that Vana would be displeased if she were left out, "slew the monstrous red-ears easily. Just as easily as they could slay six tribes in a very short time."

"Don't overdo it," The Shemibob said softly.

"But we come as friends, not to kill! We come to lead you to a place where earthquakes will not tear your land apart and destroy you! We have come to save you!"

Vana urged the captive forward.

"Here is the woman Be'nyar!" Deyv said. "We took her from you so that we could learn your language and your customs! In fact, all your secrets! As you can see, she is unharmed! Come out and get her!"

The shaman of the Chaufi'ng, Diknirdik, was standing on a platform inside the wall near the gate. With him were the shamans of the other tribes. He was a tall broad-shouldered fellow of middle age, wearing a double-coned hat fringed with feathers. Small red feathers were glued to his upper lip; the rest of his face was painted with thin vertical stripes of white, black, and green. He lacked four upper teeth.

He turned and said something to his colleagues. They talked fiercely for a moment before he gave his attention to the invaders again.

"Go away!" he bellowed. "We appreciate your gift of the red-ear heads! We thank you for them, and we will honor you by sacrifices to our ancestors! We'll tell them that you are our friends, and thus they won't harm you!

"But we have no need of your further presence! We are afraid that the demons with you will scare the children!"

Deyv laughed and said, "Not to mention scaring your brave warriors!"

The Shemibob said, "Don't insult them without a good purpose! They need to be soothed, not angered. But you must still keep them awed of us."

"I know that," Deyv muttered. "I have some intelligence."

"Then use it!"

"Very well," he bellowed. "We will go back down to the bottom of the hill. There we'll set up camp until you decide to come out and be friendly. Believe me, so far you haven't acted as friends! Watch us! When we get there we'll demonstrate a little bit of our magic!"

When Sloosh pulled the rod of the cube and it unfolded, a loud cry of amazement and fear came from the village. The plant-man said, "I hope we don't have to collapse it again. I wouldn't guarantee that it'd do it completely."

"It's too bad I don't have my bag," The Shemibob said. "However, if I can't handle them with my wits alone, I deserve to be killed."

"They are ignorant and superstitious," Sloosh said. "But they have the same intelligence as their civilized ancestors. Don't underrate them."

"My apologies. I've been so used to dominating the lesser beings that I forget they're really not so inferior if I don't have my devices."

"They certainly outnumber us," Deyv said.

"But we've got them buffaloed," Vana said. She looked up the hill. Be'nyar was still standing outside the closed gate, and she was crying to be let in. The shamans were in another huddle.

"So far," Sloosh said, "we have them buffaloed. Well,

let's partake of the delicious-smelling food which they so kindly left for us."

They ate and then relieved themselves in the swamp water nearby. This was used by the tribe for this purpose, which did not keep them from taking their drinking and boiling water from the same place. Vana and Deyv went farther out to fill their fired-clay vessels for their own drinking. Long ago, Sloosh had explained the connection between disease and lack of sanitation.

Vana nursed the baby. The others walked around for a while, talking, and then all went into the vessel to sleep. Before retiring, though, they watched the village for a while. Be'nyar was still at the gate, but she had stopped beseeching entrance. Now she was huddled on her knees, her head bowed.

They'd decided against setting a watch. If they pretended to be indifferent to the tribes' actions, they would impress them. Such nonchalance would make them think that the strangers were so powerful that they didn't care at all what measures the villagers took.

After they were inside the vessel and the door was closed, Sloosh said, "We may be taking the wrong approach. All we know of the temper of these people is what Be'nyar has told us. She may have been lying. Or she may have given us insufficient information because we failed to ask the right questions."

"What difference would it make?" The Shemibob said. "They can do nothing while we're locked in the vessel. Setting up a guard won't alter the situation. I'm going to sleep while they stew about this."

She retired to another room. Sleeping with them would make them her peers, according to her way of thinking. Deyv didn't understand why. He'd questioned her about it, though with some trepidation, and she had said that the fact he didn't understand it made clear the difference between them.

Sloosh also bedded down in another chamber. He didn't mind sharing the same quarters, but they did. Though it was impossible for him to snore, he "talked" in his sleep, and the resultant buzzing often woke them up.

Deyv dreamed that his grandmother came to him.

"This is the last time we'll meet, beloved grandson. Spirits can't cross from one world to another."

Behind her, vague in the shadow of a dark woods, were two figures. Jum and Aejip.

"Don't leave me!" Deyv cried out.

"I must. Farewell, baby. You go to become a man. You don't need me any more."

She backed into the dark grayness and disappeared. For a time, the eyes of the beasts glowed brightly, though there was little light to be reflected. Then, like dying candles, they guttered out, and he awoke sobbing.

Once more he dreamed. A great gong, like that hidden in The House of the Flying Figures, was beating somewhere over the horizon. He woke up sweating and trembling, and it was a long time before he could sink back into sleep.

In the third dream he was squatting before a hut and fingering his soul egg. Suddenly, someone tapped him on the shoulder. He looked up. The man in the red suit on the chair in the House of Flying Figures was standing by him. His broad fat face was jollied with a smile, but the eyes were a fierce hard blue. He held in one hand a hammer of metal and a bunch of metal nails. His other hand was behind his back.

"Here. Take these. Go and build a square house. And do not squander your time."

They all awoke about the same time. Deyv opened the door cautiously. He looked around it. No one was waiting to spear him. To make sure, he crept around to the other side. No lurkers there. The woman Be'nyar had been let into the stockade. A few men were watching from the walls. Returning to the door, he called in that it was safe to come out. They breakfasted on fruits and nuts, since the meat left by the campers had turned rotten and was covered by flies, ants, and beetles.

Sloosh said, "If nothing else, hunger will drive them out from the village. Besides, they must be very crowded in there."

"We don't want them to get so desperate that they attack us," The Shemibob said.

Vana picked up the baby, and they walked up to the gate. Deyv cried out, "Tell your shamans to come out to talk to us!"

One of the watchmen disappeared. After a long wait, during which Deyv could hear a high-pitched squabble, which meant that the shamans were not conversing in the sign language, the sentinel came back.

"Diknirdik will come out if you will promise by your ancestors not to harm him."

"We're not here to do evil!" Deyv shouted. "We have come to save you from it!"

Sloosh said, "Telling them that might make them even more suspicious. Beware the man who promises salvation."

Presently, Diknirdik's head and shoulders rose above the wall. He spoke loudly enough, but his voice trembled.

"Greetings, strangers! Why do you wish to speak to me?"

"Come out, and we'll tell you why!"

The shaman's eyes rolled; his hands gripped the pointed ends of the logs tightly. He was in a bad situation. If he left the village, he might be torn apart by the monsters or borne off to some unimaginable but doubtless horrible fate. If he didn't come out, he would be showing cowardice and would lose face.

Deyv said, "We released Be'nyar to show our good faith."

"She is of no importance," Diknirdik said.

"Very well then," Deyv said. "I'll come in alone and talk to you. This shouting is wearing my throat out. And my neck hurts from looking up."

Vana said, "You shouldn't! Once they have you in their power—"

"That's all right," The Shemibob said. "If he dares that, then they'll think he's not the least bit worried about them."

The shaman said, "No, you stay out there. The gate will be opened a little, and we can talk to each other from each side of it."

There was, however, a long delay. Finally, the sound of a massive wooden bar being pulled came to Deyv. Slowly, the gate swung open. When there was a gap of two feet, the shaman appeared in it. Deyv could see the shamans from the other tribes behind him and many men with spears and blowguns. Beyond them was the head of the statue of Tsi'kzheep, and ranged in line on both sides of it were the wooden heads of the great founders of the other tribes. Be'nyar had said that these were brought along to the host village during the Trading Season.

A stench of unwashed bodies and unburied excrement floated through the gap. The Shemibob was right. Conditions were so bad in the overcrowded place that sheer desperation would soon drive them out.

The Shemibob came up behind Deyv. Diknirdik backed quickly, saying, "Tell her to get away!"

The snake-centaur laughed, causing the shaman to jump. She retired while Deyv asked, "Is it all right for the woman and the baby to stand with me? They can't hurt you!"

Stung by the sarcasm, the shaman bit his lip, but he said, "Yes. Why do you need her, though?"

"She speaks your language better than I do. She can tell me the right word if I forget it."

When Vana stood by Deyv, the shaman looked thoughtful. Was he planning on grabbing all three of them? Deyv doubted it, but if he'd been in the shaman's place, he might have tried it. No, he wouldn't have. He'd have been as scared as he.

Deyv said, "Listen," and he went into his prepared speech. He told them about the inevitable destruction of their planet and explained how the gateway might be a means of escape. During this there were many gasps and cries of wonder and sometimes of dubiety from those behind the gate. He still had to shout to make himself understood above the voices of the interpreters, mostly the shamans, who were translating to the non-Chaufi'ng.

When he'd finished, he drank from the gourd handed him by Vana. Then he said, "You must have many questions. I'll answer those which are relevant. I am tired of standing, however. Bring stools for me and my woman."

This was done speedily. The stools were handed through by a warrior, Diknirdik being above such menial work. Deyv decided that it would be carrying arrogance too far if he didn't say thanks. Besides, that might make his listeners more at ease.

"That is a very interesting tale," the shaman said, "though I understand little of it. I won't say that you are lying, since I don't want to offend you. But this thing about The Shimmering Demon is hard to believe. We know that it is not an entrance to another world, unless you call the stomach of the demon another world, and it may well be. It is not, however, a world where we would care to be.

"Could it be that you've been sent by the demon to lure us into its mouth?"

"Would we go into the shimmering if it was the mouth of a demon?"

"You would if you were its friends and it used you to get people to eat."

Sloosh buzzed, "The shaman is very logical within his own framework of thought."

Deyv said, "We've come here because we want to save at least some human beings. We don't want mankind to die out. That is our only reason. My woman and I would like to join your tribe, be of your people, since our own tribes are gone."

Diknirdik swallowed and said, "There is another reason why we can't go with you. The hill where the demon lives is forbidden ground."

"Then break the taboo!" Deyv said. "It was based on the wrong assumption, on your ignorance. There is no demon there!"

The shaman looked around as if he were drawing courage from those near him.

"Oh, we couldn't do that. It would anger our ancestors. They would haunt us forever; they would do bad things to us in this life and the next. Be'nyar disobeyed their will, so we had to punish her. She was killed while you were in your—uh, thing. And her body was eaten by the dogs."

45

DEYV awoke once and went outside for a look around. The contrast between the silence in the vessel and the din outside was startling. The villagers were certainly not sleeping. Drums beat, flutes shrilled, and chanting in six tongues soared upward and fell down the hill. Smoke from a large fire rose from the center of the stockade. The gate was closed; the only observer was a man on top of the bamboo tower. He must have seen Deyv step out of the vessel. He would, however, have difficulty making himself heard above the uproar.

"I hope your ancestors tell you the right thing to do," Deyv muttered. He went inside, closing the door after him, and he lay down. After some tossing and turning, he slipped into a dreamless sleep.

Some time afterward, he felt the floor lift and fall. He was safe, however, unless the earth opened wide enough to swallow the craft. He closed his eyes but quickly opened them. There had been only one movement. What kind of a temblor was that?

By then The Shemibob was out of her room.

"Did you feel it?"

"Yes."

He got up and swung the door out a few inches. A yell from many throats greeted him. A spear shot over his shoulder and thudded against the wall behind him.

He caught a look at a dozen fierce faces near him and beyond them a horde digging a deep wide hole in the side of the hill. He shut the door and turned wide-eyed toward The Shemibob.

"I think they're going to bury us!"

By then the others were awake. The baby began crying. Deyv told Vana to take her where she wouldn't be disturbed.

"Not until I know what's going on!"

He told her what he'd seen.

She said, "I'll be back as soon as I've fed and changed Keem."

The Shemibob picked up the spear. "They mean business. They must have worked themselves into a frenzy to attack us, though."

Sloosh buzzed the equivalent of the human snort.

"Ancestors? Their ancestors are themselves telling themselves what they want to hear! It's my opinion that they also drugged themselves, all of them, so they could get their courage up."

"It doesn't matter *why* now," the snake-centaur said. "It's *what* they're doing that counts. Also, what we do."

There seemed to be only two choices. They could stay inside and be buried. Eventually, since the power supply was low, the air-making machine would quit, and they'd be asphyxiated. Or they could storm out, hoping to scare the people into taking refuge in the stockade again.

"I think we'd be dead before they had a chance to get frightened," Deyv said.

The plant-man said that there was only one way to test that speculation.

"We have to do something quick," Deyv said. "That hole looked like it's about half-done. All six tribes must be working on it. It's mud, easy to dig."

"Ah, well," Sloosh said. "This is what I deserve for trying to save the unsavable."

There was silence for a while. Sloosh was leaning up against a wall, his eyes shut. The Shemibob stood on her forty feet, swaying slightly, silvery eyelids half-closed, her fingers steepled. Deyv was sitting with his back against the wall, a physical simile of the situation they were in.

What to do? What to do?

He could put himself into a sleep and try to summon his grandmother again. However, she had said she would come no more, and she might be angry if he summoned her. If he was to get a good idea, he would have to do it by himself. The Shemibob and the Archkerri, the higher beings, were as empty of fruitful thought as he.

Vana entered, holding the baby to her breast. Evidently, she had been unable to wait until after Keem was fed. Deyv told her just what they could do. He did not try to make it seem that they had much chance to get out alive. He wouldn't have fooled her if he had.

"Oh, if only you still had your bag of treasures, your powers," she said to The Shemibob.

"That's it!" Deyv shouted as he sprang up from the floor. "Power! Power!"

The Shemibob blinked and said, "What do you mean? What power? I don't have any."

"*You* don't!" he cried. "But the *vessel* does!"

She and Sloosh looked at each other. The plant-man said, "We don't know how to operate it. We could kill ourselves. But we'll die anyway."

"Better that than to choke to death or be run through with spears," The Shemibob said. "We'll at least be trying."

"There might be enough fuel left to get us a short way into the air and a longer way horizontally. It might be enough to give us a chance to outdistance them. Or they might be so scared they'll not dare chase us. But the impact when we come down . . . most desperate, most desperate."

"Come with me," The Shemibob said. "We'll see if we can make even more sense of the circuits. We don't have much time."

The two hurried out. They would be careful to stay

in the central portion so that their weight on the upper level wouldn't roll the craft over. Vana came to Deyv and said, "Hold us."

He embraced her. The baby started crying again. Deyv stepped back and said, "She's afraid I'll take her from you. I wish that was all she had to fear."

Time passed. Deyv went up the stairs in the middle and sat down on the corridor floor. He could see The Shemibob and Sloosh working in the control room. Presently, she looked up and saw him.

"We're almost ready," she called out.

The chairs had not been unfolded, since neither of the two could sit on them. The panel had been moved down at a 45-degree angle to the floor. Lights twinkled on them. On the panel were a large dial and a slim stick.

Suddenly, the floor began to tilt upward.

Deyv cried out.

Sloosh buzzed, "No! We haven't started it! The tribesman are starting to carry us to the hole!"

Vana's voice came to him from below. "What is it?"

Deyv could see the section of wall in front of the two operators become silvery. Then it cleared, and he was looking at the slope of the hill and the village on it.

"We've got it!" The Shemibob said.

The back end began to tilt. Shortly, the floor was level.

Sloosh turned and said, "You and Vana get into a room and put your backs against the rear wall. We don't know if we can control the acceleration!"

Deyv hastened to obey. As soon as they were settled, The Shemibob's voice came faintly through the door. "They're carrying us to the hole! Hang on!"

Deyv didn't know what to expect, a mighty roar, a surge that would throw them into the wall, or what.

They fell hard, and then they felt a bumping.

The people had dropped the vessel. It was moving slowly up the hill.

He could imagine those outside, screaming, running every which way to get away from the suddenly animated vessel. Perhaps they thought that the magicians inside had made it come alive and now it would be chasing them to eat them. They would also be regretting very much that they had not accepted the offer of friendship.

The front end rose high, then flopped down. It bumped a little more. It stopped.

The Shemibob's face was in the doorway. She looked serious but undisturbed.

"It just doesn't have enough energy left to get us off the ground. We're inside the village walls now. We went through the entrance. You two get out and bar the gate."

She withdrew. Deyv and Vana opened the door and stepped out. Vana followed him a moment after, having placed the baby on the floor first. She was screaming as if she were trying to vomit her lungs.

Together, they ran to the gateway. The tribes were standing in the swamp near the trees and looking up at them. Their voices, shrill and quavery, floated up faintly.

Though it was a task for six men, Deyv and Vana managed to shoot the massive wooden bar. He stepped back, panting but grinning. He didn't know why he was so exultant, since their situation had improved only a little. Those who'd been inside were now outside, and those who'd been outside were inside. Nevertheless, they had an extension of life. It might not last for long. But it had given them a chance to stretch their lives out a little longer.

They returned to the vessel, noting on the way that it had knocked over the statues of the ancestors and the tables in front of them. The nose of the vessel was almost touching the opposite wall. Sloosh and The Shemibob were outside now, pushing it away from the wall. Before Deyv got to them, they had turned the vessel around to face the gate. From within the opened door came the baby's crying.

Vana hastened inside to take care of her. Deyv asked, "Why didn't you steer it into the swamp?"

"Because my cabbage-head friend suggested that we could still get the tribes to follow us through the gateway."

"Why is it that when someone thinks of something that another should have thought of, the first person is subjected to insults by the second?" Sloosh asked.

The Shemibob laughed and said, "His idea puts us in more jeopardy. But it might work."

She told Deyv what it was. They got busy then, carrying the wooden statues into the vessel. It was he who suggested that they could strengthen the plan by picking off the eggs from the soul-egg tree. The Shemibob replied that that would take more time, which they might not have.

Deyv climbed the ladder to the walk behind the wall and looked the situation over. By then most of the people had come out from the swamp and were massed along the bottom of the hill. The six shamans were sitting in a circle, with the Chaufi'ng apparently doing most of the talking. At least, his hands were flying more and faster than the others'.

Many of the people were staggering or lying on their backs. Sloosh had been right when he'd said that they'd drugged themselves to gain courage.

Deyv climbed back down and reported.

"I think we've got enough time."

The Shemibob sent Vana to watch the tribes. Then the three worked swiftly, knocking off the ripe soul eggs with a pole or breaking off the others with clubs. When they had piled all the eggs in a back room on the lowest level, they sat down to rest awhile.

Presently, Vana called out that the warriors were gathering at the foot of the path. Deyv ran to help her observe. He had been with her for only a moment when the men, waving their spears, yelling, hopping, whirling, came slowly up toward them. He helped her get down with the baby, and they sped back to the vessel.

"They're going to attack."

"Are the shamans leading them?" Sloosh said.

"No. They're watching from the bottom."

"I thought not."

They got into the craft. The Shemibob and Sloosh went up into the pilot room. Deyv wanted to go with them, but she said that he might tip the vessel over. As it was, the two controllers had to be very careful about shifting their weight.

"There has to be some way this vessel maintained its stability, but we've not been able to locate the controls. You stay below with Vana."

The vessel moved again across the earth of the enclosure, tipped down, and began bumping along. Deyv hoped that it had enough energy to carry them far past the tribespeople. If the power failed while they were still on the hill or only a little ways past it, they'd be in a bad way again.

They were, he could tell, going down the slope. Then the floor became level, though there was some bobbings, due to their disturbance of the water. A little time passed, far too little, he thought. And there was a cessation of movement.

Sloosh came down first.

"We got about a mile. Get rid of all the eggs now and all the statues later. Except Tsi'kzheep. I'll carry it."

The vessel was floating in water about two feet deep. They threw out the eggs, which sank into the mud. The vessel was pushed toward a bed of tall reeds, and the statues were removed and hidden within these. Sloosh pulled the rod, hoping that there was enough energy to collapse the vessel for the final time. This was half-realized.

"Well, at least it'll be easier to conceal," Sloosh said. He picked it up and waded to the muddy shore and disappeared in the jungle. When he came back he said, "Help me wipe out my tracks."

After this was done they headed for the hill of the gateway. Now and then they could hear voices of their pursuers faintly.

"I hope they don't get faint hearts when they get

near the gateway," he said. "But they must be very angry because we took their ancestors and their eggs."

The Shemibob said that they could always make more statues and wait until new eggs had grown.

"Let's hope they're so furious and drugged they won't think of that," the plant-man said. "Anyway, Be'nyar said that her tribe believed that it would be safe and prosperous only as long as Tsi'kzheep was in existence. That suggests that they wouldn't think of replacing it."

Once they were some distance away from the place where they'd dropped the eggs and the statues, they did their best to leave tracks, torn leaves, and broken branches behind them. The baby began crying again. Vana started to hush her up. The Shemibob said that she should be allowed to bawl. The pursuers might hear her and so know that they were on the right trail.

By the time they reached their goal, they were all, except for the baby, very tired. They rested awhile at the bottom. Before they'd gotten their wind back, they heard voices among the trees in the swamp.

"They didn't follow us," Deyv said. "They must've taken a shortcut. They figured that we'd be coming here."

The Archkerri said that that was good. If the tribes had taken the same path, they might have stumbled over the statues. They rose and toiled up the slope to the tree above and by which the swelling dwindling abomination shone. One by one they pulled themselves up on the lift, Keem excepted. Vana held her. After throwing their weapons through the shimmering, they sat down on the great branch, keeping their faces away from the gateway.

"I hope all this was worth it," Deyv said. "If we go through, and then we find that we're back on Earth again—"

Sloosh said, "I have a theory about that. Not that it will make you feel any easier about our ending up on this world. I think that it's possible that most of the gateways admit to a younger world. Just as heat won't radiate from one body to a hotter body, so the gateways won't let objects through from one world to an older world or one just as old. Admittedly, the analogy could be false, I have no evidence to support it. But—"

"How then do you provide for those gateways that only admit objects from one place on this planet to another?" The Shemibob asked.

"Those are local aberrations. By 'aberrations,' I mean that they are anomalies only from our viewpoints. They're just as natural as anything else. But the sentient tends to think in terms of anything as either malignant or beneficial, that is, how it affects him. The malignant is, therefore, unnatural. Philosophically, I don't admit such terms. But as a living being who's concerned about survival, though not to the extent of these humans, I sometimes lapse into egoism."

"You still haven't given an explanation of the local routes."

"I'll think of something. Just now I'm too busy with *them.*"

He pointed at the first of the pursuers to emerge from the cover of the trees.

Others followed. When the stragglers caught up, there were an estimated five hundred and twenty gathered at the foot of the hill. These included the young children.

"The mothers wanted to be in at the death so fiercely they even brought along their infants," Sloosh said. "They are very angry about the sacrilege. Good. I didn't like to think that the babies would be abandoned to starve to death."

"You forget that they would have gone back after them if they decided to go through the gateway," Deyv said.

"I doubt it. By then they would have recovered from the effects of the drug."

While the rest stayed knee-deep in the greenish water, the six shamans slowly advanced up the hill. They were singing a ritual chant designed to placate The Shimmering Demon. They begged its pardon for treading upon the forbidden ground, but they had to save their ancestors from the terrible blasphemy which the monstrous strangers had caused. They would atone for it by casting the offenders into the demon's mouth.

Deyv had to smile at that.

46

HE waited until they were within easy speaking distance. He rose and called, "Hold!"

The shamans stopped, holding their left hands to shade their eyes so they could see him but not the brightness. They were crouching as if they expected some demonic whip to lash down upon their backs.

Deyv lifted the statue of Tsi'kzheep, found it too heavy, and gave it to Sloosh.

"See your ancestor!" he called. "The founding father of the Chaufi'ng! I have cast the ancestors of the other tribes into the gateway to the other world! They are waiting for you to join them so that your people may live forever and worship them forever! If they had stayed here, they would have perished along with their descendants! But we have talked to them and they have seen our wisdom! They agreed to go through the entrance to a better place, and they are getting impatient because you are not there to solace them with sacrifices and prayers! They are becoming angry because you would leave them there while you stay here because of cowardice and let them fade away, unnourished by the blood you once gave them to eat and by your dreams, in which they would come to you and advise you on what you should do to keep the tribe healthy and prosperous and great in war!"

The Shemibob said softly, "That is fine rhetoric, Deyv, but don't get carried away. A few strong words are better than many weak ones."

"I think I'm doing fine," he said with some sharpness.

He gestured at the statue of Tsi'kzheep.

"All but one of your ancestors have gone to that other world and with them the soul eggs of the Chaufi'ng! Chaufi'ng, if you will have the eggs for the babies to be born, you will have to go after them!"

"Don't dwell on that point too long," The Shemibob said. "The soul-egg trees of the other tribes are untouched. Stress the ancestors."

"You told me *I* was to talk to them. Don't interrupt —please!"

It was a frightening yet heady experience to tell The Shemibob to keep quiet. But, though she wasn't in a situation where she could reprimand him, she would probably do so later. If there was a later.

He indicated the statue again.

"Now Tsi'kzheep goes to join the others! And he has told us that he wants you to follow him!"

Sloosh walked out onto the bridge, his eyes closed but his ears open to Deyv's soft instructions. When he heard Deyv tell him to stop, he halted a few feet from the shimmering.

"Now," Deyv said, "lift it up, slowly. Stop! You've got it centered. Now, pitch it straight forward!"

The shamans and the people at the bottom of the hill cried out in horror as the figure disappeared.

Vana said, "If they do go through, they're going to be very angry. There won't be any eggs, which will infuriate the Chaufi'ng, and the other tribes won't have their ancestors. Moreover, if Sloosh is right, there won't be any soul-egg trees either."

"I know that," Deyv said. Then, seized by impulse, he said, "Give me your egg."

"Why?"

He was afraid if he told her, she'd refuse.

"Never mind! Give it to me!"

While she removed the cord from her neck, he took his off. He dangled the eggs high so that all could see them, but he had to wait until the tribes had ceased their uproar before he spoke.

"The ancestors told me many things before they

went on their journey! One was that we really don't need our eggs! They had their use in this world, but they're not needed in the next!"

Vana cried, "No, oh, no! Don't!"

"You know they're not necessary," Deyv said fiercely to Vana. "We've both known that for a long time but didn't want to admit it to ourselves. We have to throw them away! Then the tribes won't be so angry when they find that there are no soul-egg trees there."

Then he shouted, "Look! I leave these here!"

He cast the eggs out into the air, and they fell to the base of the tree. Despite his brave words, he felt a pang of loss.

"A very good idea," The Shemibob said. She removed her Emerald and, after Deyv had called everybody's attention to the act, she dropped it onto the ground.

"Now, Archkerri, your prism!"

"But it might be useful there! I may be able to speak to the plants there! It's true that they might not have the capability that the plants have here, but I won't know until—!"

"It's necessary, Archkerri! Do it!"

After Sloosh had reluctantly thrown the prism, Deyv cried, "See! The Shemibob and the Archkerri have discarded their magical devices, too! Your ancestors required this as a token of their friendship and good faith!"

"I hope they don't look into the logic of that," Sloosh buzzed.

"They won't," the snake-centaur said. "They're too upset to think straight."

Deyv flung his hands straight up.

"Now! I go to follow your ancestors to a better world!"

He turned with his eyes shut. Following Vana's instructions, which she gave quaveringly, he advanced to the edge of the bridge, stopped, and bent his knees. Though he wanted desperately to turn and walk away, he leaped.

47

HE fell into a bright light, was aware of trees around him and long grass below him, and he landed. His knees bent, he fell, rolled, and was up on his feet. They hurt but not so much that he couldn't walk.

Beyond were the statue and their weapons. Sloosh had cast them as far as he could so the jumpers wouldn't land on them.

He was near the edge of a cliff. If the gateway had been ten feet further to one side, it would have admitted him to a fatal drop to the rocks at the base. Beyond that was a belt of trees and a beach of white sand and a blue sea that sent its rollers thundering onto the land.

In the other direction was a forest populated mostly by tall trees unlike any he'd ever seen. They were conical, and instead of leaves the branches had a heavy needlelike growth.

The sky was blue. Near its zenith was a yellow blaze that was impossible to look at long. It was that that gave the light and the heat.

If what Sloosh and The Shemibob had said a young Earth would look like was correct, he was on a young Earth.

He'd been counting while observing. At one thousand, he stood beneath the gateway and forced himself to look almost directly at it. But it was a dark spot in the air, a strange but undreadful phenomenon, like the gateway in the tunnel. Then Vana shot through, and he jumped to avoid being hit but ready to aid her if she was hurt. She rolled and, like him, came up on her feet.

"Are you all right?"

"Yes. Are you?"

The Shemibob, holding the screaming baby, came through next. Her forty feet flattened out under the impact, and her legs bent far under her weight. But she was unhurt. She handed Keem to Vana, saying, "Here. She knows the difference between my nipple and yours."

Sloosh shot through and landed squarely but still fell forward. He got up complaining that he must have sprained his upper spine.

"We Archkerri are unusually subject to backaches, anyway."

Though he was to move around slowly and carefully for some time, he was not by any means totally incapacitated.

Tsi'kzheep was set up where the next to come through, if there were any, could see it at once. It had been decided that the statue should be kept as a focal point, a rallying and sustaining symbol, for the tribes. Though it wasn't the direct ancestor of any but the Chaufi'ng, it was the brother of the five other founders. They would tell the tribes that Tsi'kzheep had sent the others ahead to look for a home for their children. In the meantime, it would shepherd the six tribes. The Chaufi'ng dialect would become the common speech of all. And Deyv would be the chief of all.

The people were going to be shocked by the idea that a nonshaman would lead them. And the shamans were going to make trouble; there'd be a power struggle. This, however, was only one of many problems in the merging of the six groups into one.

Deyv wanted to go exploring at once. Instead, he had to pitch in to help make a great pile of grass. Otherwise, there would be many hurt or even killed. They pulled the long grass and threw it down beneath the gateway and then cut off branches to make a barrier along the sides of the mass. Once these were placed, they formed a simple but effective windbreak.

The yellow glaring light in the sky, the sun, crossed the heavens. Deyv saw his first sunset, a frightening but beautiful sight. They ate some nuts and berries they'd collected around a fire. The sound of the surf came faintly to them, interspersed by calls of night birds and, twice, a coughing roar. The air became chilly, causing them to regret the loss of the vessel. They took turns feeding the fire while the others slept.

The sun rose, draped in many colors. Deyv went hunting and returned when the sky-light had just dropped down from the zenith. He carried the back leg of a large animal.

"The rest was too much for me or even you, Sloosh, to carry. And it's too far away for us to go get it. It would be eaten by then by some beasts that look like wolves. I'd have liked to bring back the head, but it would've been too much. It has six knobs on top of its head and two long curving tusks sticking down from the upper jaw. Yet it eats plants. I saw some beasts which resembled some we know and some which are very different."

Vana started to cut up the leg while Deyv made forked uprights and trimmed down a thick branch to make a spit. The Shemibob came running then and told them to go with her to the edge of the cliff.

Below, walking on the beach, were a dozen bipeds.

"Hairy, bent-necked, slanting foreheads, heavy brows, outthrust jaws, chins not well developed," Sloosh said. "They are precursors of the fully human or something like the fully human. Poor devils! If our tribespeople do come through, those half-humans are doomed."

"Their kind would be doomed anyway when a higher type evolved," The Shemibob said.

"I wonder," Sloosh said, "if something similar happened when our Earth was young. That is, did full humans come through a gateway from an older and perishing universe? And did they wipe out their lesser ancestors? Or perhaps I should say, cousins?

"I speculate this because there is nothing in the memory of the plants about intermediates in the evolution of the prehuman to human. Full man appeared suddenly, and he ousted the preman. Through violence, of course."

"If that is a fact instead of theory," The Shemibob said, "then humankind is far older than we thought."

The bipeds stopped now and then to dig up shellfish in the shallows. They also did not refuse to eat a large dead fish that floated in.

When they'd disappeared around the bend of the beach, the watchers went back to their meal. The sun sank; the stars came out. Then black clouds came up, bearing thunder and lightning. Soon a cold rain fell, forcing them to take cover under the trees. They spent a miserable sleepless night and had difficulty starting the fire in the morning.

Though he was tired, Deyv had to hunt again. It was close to dusk before he returned with a half-grown piglike beast.

"There just isn't enough cover for me to get near enough to use the blowgun."

"It's time we made a new weapon," The Shemibob said. "This will be a simple but effective one, and it will have a far greater range than your blowgun or your spear. When we find a wood that is springy enough, I'll show you how to fashion part of it. It will be able to propel a short slim spear with great force. But it takes much practice to learn how to use it well."

Morning came again, bringing with it discouragement.

"How long do we wait here?" Deyv asked The Shemibob.

"We'll set up a camp, make lean-tos, and wait for thirty days. If they haven't come through by then, we look for a better place. We should go south, since I suspect we're in an area that gets snow and ice. You wouldn't like them."

Both humans were downcast and worried. Would their daughters have to bear children by their sons? Eventually, according to Sloosh, their descendants would be inbred and would degenerate. The human species would die. The minimum number needed to perpetuate a healthy race was five hundred.

Another day passed. Before they went to sleep in the

little hut they'd built, Deyv said, "This waiting is making me nervous."

"You always were impatient," Vana said. She kissed him. "At least, we'll have each other and our children. And The Shemibob and Sloosh will be with us, and our children and our grandchildren and perhaps their children. The Shemibob and Sloosh will be a big comfort. They're very wise and will teach us many things that would take us many generations to learn."

Deyv wasn't consoled. It was a long time before he could get to sleep. Suddenly, shockingly, he was being shaken by the shoulder.

"Get up! Get up!" Vana was saying.

"It can't be time for me to stand guard yet," he said sourly.

"No, no! They're starting to come through! Can't you hear them?"

He got up quickly. Sloosh was throwing more wood on the fire so that the big blaze would render the area more visible. Men were crawling out from the pile of grass. One by one, at a count of twenty seconds between, men were falling through, yelling or screaming.

The first of the men to carry a struggling, shrilling child dropped through.

The shaman of the Chaufi'ng staggered toward Deyv. He looked dazed.

"The sky was bright when we decided to enter the demon's mouth," he said.

He looked upward. "That is a strange Dark Beast."

"There is no Dark Beast here," Deyv said. "And when the light comes, you will see such a sight as you never dreamed of."

The shaman spoke slurringly, and his eyes looked strange. Deyv didn't know whether the tribes had taken drugs again to nerve themselves for the leap or whether they were suffering from shock. Entering this world was like being born. The psyche reeled under this strange birth and thus the body was stricken. All the leapers-forth would be in a trauma.

Tomorrow—a word Deyv had learned from The

Shemibob—tomorrow there would be trouble when the six tribes discovered that their ancestors were not there. But they would be in shock, and they would follow those who were in full possession of their faculties.

Deyv and Vana and Sloosh and The Shemibob were so much more experienced. They had gone through many shocks. They had, in a sense, been born many times. They would be adults leading little children.

Sloosh came to Deyv from the bonfire.

He said, "You are smiling; you look as if you are about to start dancing. Why?"

"We were there, and now we're here! We live! Our children will live! Joy!"

ABOUT THE AUTHOR

Philip José Farmer was born in Terre Haute, Indiana, and has lived most of his life in Peoria, Illinois. He holds a B.A. in creative writing from Bradley University. In 1953 he won the Hugo Award as most promising new science-fiction author. He is most noted for his novel *The Lovers* and the *Riverworld* series.

DEL REY

The brightest Science Fiction stars in the galaxy!

THE BEST OF ROBERT BLOCH Lester del Rey, editor	25757	1.95
THE BEST OF FREDRIC BROWN Robert Bloch, editor	25700	1.95
THE BEST OF JOHN W. CAMPBELL Lester del Rey, editor	24960	1.95
THE BEST OF L. SPRAGUE DE CAMP Introduction by Poul Anderson	25474	1.95
THE BEST OF EDMUND HAMILTON Leigh Brackett, editor	25900	1.95
THE BEST OF C. M. KORNBLUTH Frederik Pohl, editor	25461	1.95
THE BEST OF HENRY KUTTNER Introduction by Ray Bradbury	24415	1.95
THE BEST OF MURRAY LEINSTER Introduction by J. J. Pierce	25800	1.95
THE BEST OF C. L. MOORE Introduction by Lester del Rey	24752	1.95
THE BEST OF CORDWAINER SMITH J. J. Pierce, editor	27202	2.25
THE BEST OF STANLEY G. WEINBAUM Introduction by Isaac Asimov	23890	1.65
THE BEST OF JACK WILLIAMSON Introduction by Frederik Pohl	27335	1.95

LG-4

ANNE McCAFFREY

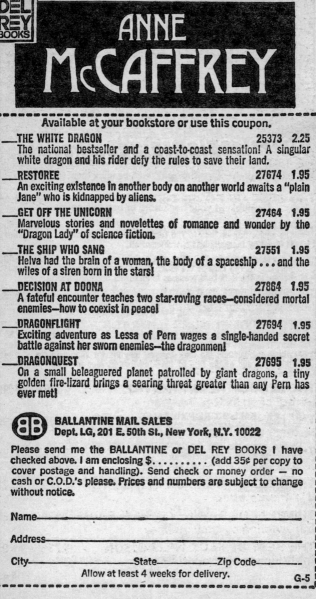

Available at your bookstore or use this coupon.

___**THE WHITE DRAGON**   25373   2.25
The national bestseller and a coast-to-coast sensation! A singular white dragon and his rider defy the rules to save their land.

___**RESTOREE**   27674   1.95
An exciting existence in another body on another world awaits a "plain Jane" who is kidnapped by aliens.

___**GET OFF THE UNICORN**   27464   1.95
Marvelous stories and novelettes of romance and wonder by the "Dragon Lady" of science fiction.

___**THE SHIP WHO SANG**   27551   1.95
Helva had the brain of a woman, the body of a spaceship . . . and the wiles of a siren born in the stars!

___**DECISION AT DOONA**   27864   1.95
A fateful encounter teaches two star-roving races—considered mortal enemies—how to coexist in peace!

___**DRAGONFLIGHT**   27694   1.95
Exciting adventure as Lessa of Pern wages a single-handed secret battle against her sworn enemies—the dragonmen!

___**DRAGONQUEST**   27695   1.95
On a small beleaguered planet patrolled by giant dragons, a tiny golden fire-lizard brings a searing threat greater than any Pern has ever met!

BB   **BALLANTINE MAIL SALES**
Dept. LG, 201 E. 50th St., New York, N.Y. 10022

Please send me the BALLANTINE or DEL REY BOOKS I have checked above. I am enclosing $. . . . . (add 35¢ per copy to cover postage and handling). Send check or money order — no cash or C.O.D.'s please. Prices and numbers are subject to change without notice.

Name_____

Address_____

City_____State_____Zip Code_____

Allow at least 4 weeks for delivery.

G-5

J.R.R. TOLKIEN'S
Epic Fantasy Classic
The Lord of the Rings

One Ring to rule them all,
One Ring to find them,
One Ring to bring them all,
And in the darkness bind them.....

Twisting the skills he learned from the Elven-smiths, the Dark Lord created a Ring of awesome, malevolent power, a Ring to control all the other Rings of Power, bending them to the will of whoever controlled the One. And then, the One Ring was lost.

Available at your bookstore or use this coupon.

—**THE HOBBIT, J.R.R. Tolkien** 27257 2.50
The enchanting prelude to **The Lord of the Rings,** in which the One Ring is found by the unlikliest character of all.

—**THE FELLOWSHIP OF THE RING, J.R.R. Tolkien** 27258 2.50
Part One of **The Lord of the Rings:** the quest to destroy the evil Ring is begun, as the Dark Lord prepares to make war upon Middlearth.

—**THE TWO TOWERS, J.R.R. Tolkien** 27259 2.50
Part Two: the armies gather for the battle which will decide the destiny of Middlearth, while the Ring Bearer moves ever closer to the fulfillment of his quest.

—**THE RETURN OF THE KING, J.R.R. Tolkien** 27260 2.50
Part Three: the concluding volume tells of the opposing strategies of the wizard Gandalf and the Dark Lord as they vie for victory in the War of the Ring, and of the fate of the Ring Bearer. Also includes appendices and index.

—**J.R.R. TOLKIEN FOUR VOLUME BOXED SET** 27493 10.00

BB **BALLANTINE MAIL SALES**
Dept. NE, 201 E. 50th St., New York, N.Y. 10022

Please send me the BALLANTINE or DEL REY BOOKS I have checked above. I am enclosing $.......... (add 35¢ per copy to cover postage and handling). Send check or money order — no cash or C.O.D.'s please. Prices and numbers are subject to change without notice.

Name_____

Address_____

City_____State_____Zip Code_____
Allow at least 4 weeks for delivery.
NE-6